Catriona McPherson

The Turning Tide

HODDER

First published in Great Britain in 2019 by Hodder & Stoughton
An Hachette UK company

This paperback edition published in 2020

1

A CIP catalogue record for this title is available from the British Library

B format ISBN 9781473682405
eBook ISBN 9781473682399

Typeset in Plantin Light by Palimpsest Book Production Ltd,
Falkirk, Stirlingshire

Printed and bound in Great Britain by Clays Ltd, Elcograf S.p.A.

Hodder & Stoughton policy is to use papers that are natural, renewable
and recyclable products and made from wood grown in sustainable forests.
The logging and manufacturing processes are expected to conform
to the environmental regulations of the country of origin.

Hodder & Stoughton Ltd
Carmelite House
50 Victoria Embankment
London EC4Y 0DZ

www.hodder.co.uk

This is for Alex and André
and Pip and CJ

Prologue

'I don't know, Alec,' I said. 'It's hardly the Riviera.'

We were standing at the top of a small beach on a sunny afternoon in July and it was undoubtedly pleasant, but I felt no particular tug towards shedding my cardigan jersey, nor even my hat, for a fresh breeze was whipping at the wavelets and sending little scraps of dry seaweed scudding over the sand. Or was it shingle? It was either the coarsest variety of the one or the finest variety of the other. Alec had shrugged out of his tweed coat, removed his cufflinks and rolled his shirtsleeves to the elbow. He stood with hands on hips, taking ostentatiously deep breaths of the fresh air. I could not have said why I found that annoying but, as I rummaged for a cigarette and match, I knew my action was not innocent.

'Delightful,' Alec said. 'Who doesn't love an island?'

'*I* love an island,' I said. 'Capri, Mallorca, even the Isle of Wight, at a push, in a sheltered spot, but I can't see this taking off. In all honesty.'

'It could hardly be more sheltered,' Alec said. 'Three westerly beaches, facing upriver.' He swept an arm around the prospect before us as though I might have missed it.

The Forth is quite two miles wide at its mouth and forms a broad enough expanse of water to make a picturesque view framed by the Lothian coast to our left and the Fife coast to our right. 'It's delightful,' Alec went on. 'And a hop, skip and jump from town. You're being the most awful bore, Dandy.'

'Bore?' I cried, stung. He had never accused me of it before.

1

'Well, killjoy then. I applaud their enterprise and wish them well. In fact, if they were looking for investors, I could be persuaded.'

'I wish them well too,' I said. 'Naturally. And I applaud their optimism, but I shan't be ringing my broker.' Alec made as though to argue further and I went on: 'Besides, we're doing what we can to remove the obstacles. The venture won't succeed if things are really as bad as they suggested.'

Alec did not reply for a moment. He turned away from the beach and swept the gentle green hillocks that made up the inland portion of this little island with a shrewd gaze. 'Where did they say she was holed up?' he asked. 'Did you follow the topographical section of the lecture?'

'Duck House,' I replied. 'On the north-east tip. That-a-way, in other words. Shall we?'

Alec looked at his wristwatch and then back at the tide. 'Better get on with it, if you're sure you want to. We don't want to get cut off.'

'We wouldn't get cut off,' I said. 'They're keeping an eye on us from the mainland. If we don't start onto the causeway in good time, someone will put out in a dinghy to fetch us. And yes I do want to. No one has suggested she's a danger. Just an oddity.'

Still though, neither of us was exactly rushing to meet her. I ground out the stub of my cigarette, buried it in a hole I gouged out of the sand – which seemed more and more like shingle as I felt it grate against my boot heel – then squared my shoulders.

As matters transpired, we were saved the effort of navigating the island and tracking down the Duck House and its inhabitant. She had heard us, or seen us, or by coincidence happened upon us. However it came about, here she was, bursting out of the gorse like a pheasant to come staggering down onto the beach.

We knew she was living alone and we knew that the island's

amenities were basic, so we had expected a measure of dishevelment. But either she had worsened since anyone had last seen her or we had been grievously misled. This woman was utterly wild. Her hair, loose to her waist, was matted and knotted and stuck with twigs, and her face was streaked with earth and with smears of whatever she had last been eating. Her feet were bare and black with dirt and her skirts were ragged. Above her skirts she was quite naked. I saw Alec drop his gaze to spare her the distress I was sure she did not feel. For she made no attempt to hide herself. She came tearing towards us, talking in a sort of shrieking mutter.

'Go,' she said. 'Go! Save your souls, in the name of Mercury.'

'Mercury?' Alec said, looking up again in spite of himself.

'Do not cross the river,' she said, coming close enough for me to smell her sour breath. She gazed up into my face. She should not have been looking up at me, for she was taller than me by a good four inches, but for some strange reason she was curled over on herself like a crone, so she was forced to twist her head to one side to meet my eye. As she did she rocked her chin in a yearning, beseeching rhythm, although whether the movement was meant to communicate something to Alec and me or was simply an attempt to soothe herself I could not say. If it *was* her way of driving off her demons it was evidently not working; she was talking faster and faster and not just her head but her whole body was rocking now.

'Don't drink the blood-red cinnabar,' she said, spittle flying from her mouth with every hiss. 'He who drinks of slaked lime and angers Mercury will be crushed like oyster shells and lost in the warren. Barren and blighted. Bringing forth the spawn. Before Mercury and all the serpents. Save yourselves. Save yourselves. Go, go!'

I am not ashamed to admit it. We went.

3

I

The first time we, meaning Gilver and Osborne, were asked to look into the case of the Cramond Ferry, we declined.

It was May of 1936, and life at Gilverton was offering plenty in the way of interest and activity. My elder son, Donald, had married Miss Mallory Dunnoch of Wester Ross the previous midsummer and they had come back from their peculiar Norwegian honeymoon full of plans to restock the timber at Donald's estate and do all sorts of strange things to the farm cottages to increase what Mallory called 'insulation', a scheme that sounded unhealthy in the extreme. I shuddered to think what sickly state the farmworkers' children would be in by spring once their cottage walls were baffled with wadding under new plaster and their windows re-glazed to banish all draughts. I mentioned fresh air as often as I dared and then left them to it.

When my husband Hugh caught the infection however and started striding about our own cottage rows, tape measure in hand, I rumbled as stiff a warning as I could rumble. Then, when I saw him eyeing up the windows of Gilverton House itself, with a view to encasing us all in glass like so many fairy-tale princesses, I put my foot down.

'No,' I said. 'I'm surprised at you, Hugh. What would Nanny Palmer say? What would my mother say? Or yours? What would *you* of five years ago say, when you were making such a fuss about a few radiators? What the dickens has happened to you?'

'What does Osborne think of the notion?' Hugh said

slyly, which I took as indication that Alec Osborne, my fellow detective and our neighbour here in Perthshire, had been beguiled by the Norwegian nonsense and that Hugh knew it.

'It's all very well over there,' I continued. 'With all that crisp air and frost waiting when one ventures out, I daresay huddling like a rabbit in a burrow between times does no harm. But here, in our damp drizzle, no chance to fill the lungs with Nordic what-have-you, we need all the air we can get, day and night.'

'I think there might be a flaw in your logic,' Hugh said. 'If the air is so below par, shouldn't we try as hard as we can to banish it?'

'They jump into icy water too, Mallory tells me,' I said. 'And beat themselves with branches. Are you suggesting we add that to the daily round?'

Then, one day in November, all thought of building works and renovation schemes suddenly receded, although the replanting on high ground sailed on. Donald came over after breakfast and hung around my sitting room, spilling tapers into the hearth and disarranging letters on my desk.

'Are you quite well?' I said.

'Fine,' Donald said. He went over to the window and tied the curtain ropes into some kind of Scout's knot.

'Is Mallory well?' I said.

'Mallory is fine,' Donald said with an excess of heartiness.

I exchanged a look with Alec, who was there, as is his wont, going through our correspondence.

'I think I'll take a turn, Dandy,' Alec said. 'I've got a bit of a head this morning. Come on, girl.'

Bunty, my Dalmatian, leapt up and raced Alec to the French window, nosing ahead of him and then plunging out onto the lawns as though escaping a month's incarceration.

'Well?' I said, when they were gone.

'Mallory's going to have a baby,' said Donald. 'And she misses her mother so. She's sick and sad and she's scared to ask you to step in in case you tell her to buck up.'

'In case I *what*?' I said. 'Is this the reputation I have? Good grief, Donald.' I was on my feet already and ringing for my head housemaid Becky. 'How is your cook looking after her? Has she ordered ginger? Can Mallory manage arrowroot? I'll set Mrs Tilling on it. Good *God*, Donald. How long have you been shilly-shallying about telling me? What a goose you are!'

'I felt bashful,' he said.

'Bashful? Why?'

'*Why*?' He blushed to the tips of his ears. 'Why do you think?'

'Oh for heaven's sake,' I said. 'Babies happen, my dear Donald. It's no mystery. Everyone has been managing to welcome babies into families without dying of embarrassment since Cain and Abel. Where do you think *you* came from?'

'Mother!' His face was purple now, and to be fair to him I might have put it more delicately. I felt a slight warmth in my own cheeks as he strenuously did not look anywhere near the area of my person where he had come from.

'Don't worry, darling,' I said. 'I shall look after her. Mrs Tilling and me between us. Congratulations.' I gave him a quick hug. 'Well done.'

'Well done?' he said, a new flush suffusing him. 'Well *done*?'

Poor thing. But it was good practice for dealing with Mrs Tilling, our cook, who has known him his whole life and takes a great interest in all babies. Not to mention Grant, my maid, whose special area of interest is mystical rather than medical but who is equally encroaching in her way.

Besides, Mallory really was spectacularly unwell throughout her pregnancy. She was not, in fact, having a baby; she was having two and as she grew, like something from a German fairy tale – her stomach of course, but also her arms and legs and fingers and toes and at last her very eyelids swelling – we all of us became inured to conversations around the dinner table that would have seen our parents take the vapours.

'I was reading an article about beetroot juice,' Hugh said one evening. 'As a diuretic. I've sent over a basket to see if they can get any pressure off Mallory's bladder.'

'Mallory?' said the acquaintance who was dining with us. 'A pig?'

Hugh is not prone to fits of the giggles; it is one of the reasons I set such store by Alec as a companion of my days. But his lips twitched then. We let the chap go on thinking Mallory was a prize breeding-sow and tried a little harder to maintain a decency or two.

By the time of the first letter from Cramond, the expectant couple had fled their own place and come back to us at Gilverton, the better to organise shifts of companions. Mallory was spending her days upon a couch, banked up with roughly seventeen strategic pillows, and her nights wandering the passageways, courting sleep and failing.

'Do we want to look into a mad ferryman?' Alec said one morning, as we sat to either side of the fireplace ripping through the letters as smartly as we could before he started work on the replies and I went to rub Mallory's feet and advise her on engaging a monthly nurse.

'Wouldn't they be better with a doctor?' I said.

'Reading between the lines, it's being kept hush-hush. Oh!' I looked up. 'Not a ferryman. A ferry*woman*. That's more interesting, isn't it?'

'A ferrywoman is certainly more remarkable than a ferryman, generally speaking,' I said. 'But I'm no more interested in curing her of madness. Even if I could.'

'I think they think, or at least hope that is, that it's not actually madness in the meaning of the act.'

8

'You're not making much sense, darling,' I said. 'Pass it over.'

The letter, when he had shied it into my lap and I had taken a moment to read it through, did not make much more. 'You will have heard of the Cramond ferry,' it began with more confidence than was warranted. 'You may have taken it on trips from Fife to Edinburgh. Even if you prefer the train or the inland road, you will have heard of our dear Vesper Kemp, for twenty years the toast of Cramond and with every reason to anticipate many more years of "reign" at the oars, until the current situation arose. Recently, you see, our dear Vesper has begun exhibiting signs of distress we are at a loss to explain. We are naturally loath to broadcast our concerns and do not wish to take recourse to medicine (having found that, when it comes to ladies with nervous trouble, the cure is frequently more severe than the complaint). We would welcome the gentle attentions of a confidential expert such as yourself. Matters are becoming difficult to manage. Yours sincerely.'

'I can't make out the signature,' I said. 'Could you?'

'No,' said Alec, 'and there's no one obvious that might be this "we", is there? I can't imagine the parents of a ferrywoman could turn a phrase like "gentle attentions of a confidential expert". Shall we, Dandy?'

'Ordinarily,' I said. 'But I don't much want to be far from home this next while.'

'Hardly far,' Alec said.

'And stranded,' I added. 'The whole point seems to be that the ferry's not running.'

'Very well,' Alec said. 'I shall send our standard regrets.'

I mentioned it to Hugh over lunch. I was slightly trying to distract Donald, who had taken to looking up every couple of minutes as if he could see through the ceiling above him and the floorboards above that to where Mallory was reclining, hoping to divine her current state by some kind of telepathy.

9

'I heard as much,' Hugh said. 'Well, it's overdue.' I arranged my features into a look of interest and encouragement and after another mouthful of lamb, he went on. 'Edinburgh's very own Grace Darling. Less thrilling by far, but still. She was the only child of the Cramond ferryman and when he went off to the war she took up her oars and carried on in his stead. When he failed to return, poor chap, she dug her heels in. It caused something of an upset, as I recall.'

'How do you mean?' I said, although truth be told I could guess exactly what she dug her heels into and the kind of upset it caused.

'Hundreds, nay thousands, of chaps coming home with injured legs and healthy arms who could easily have rowed a little coble over the mouth of a river, but Miss Kemp denied them all.'

'How unseemly,' I said. 'At least Dr Inglis had the grace to die when she got back from her field hospital. What an upstart the girl must be.'

Hugh, finally, sensed the reception his tale was getting and harrumphed lavishly.

'Dr Inglis is a case in point,' he said. 'She overtaxed herself and died. And now this Miss Kemp has, likewise, overtaxed herself and become unreliable. If women would stick to—'

'Father,' Donald said. Hugh, surprised to find himself interrupted by his son, stopped talking. 'I bet if you asked Mallory whether she'd rather do what she's about to do or a spot of rowing, she'd leap at the chance to be a ferrywoman.'

I hid my smiles by taking a sip of water before speaking again. 'And Dr Inglis survived a POW camp as well as the battlefield hospital, Hugh. She died of cancer. She would have died of cancer at home in Edinburgh at her embroidery, I daresay.'

'The fact remains,' Hugh said, 'it's no kind of ferry service at all if the ferryman won't put out unless the weather is to his liking. I don't,' he added holding up a hand to my objections, 'I don't mean storms fit to cause a shipwreck, but George at the club tells me she moored her boat and refused to row seven times in the month of April alone. Which is a scandal. With so many men looking for work? It's a disgrace.'

I agreed with him and was glad that Alec had refused the commission. Then, just at that moment, Mallory's maid – who went somewhat unconventionally by the name of Julia, rather than 'Preston' – put her head around the door with a worried look. Donald shot to his feet, Hugh tutted, I hurried out of the room, and the question of Vesper Kemp, the Cramond ferrywoman, was forgotten.

2

The second letter, a veritable *cri de coeur* this time, arrived in early June, neck and neck with the babies, and I have only the sketchiest memory of reading it at all.

'More from Cramond,' Alec said. He was walking round my sitting room, bouncing at the knees as though upon a rope bridge, the better to soothe the squawking scrap of humanity he held in the crook of one arm as he manipulated the morning's letters with his free hand.

'Cramond?' I said. I was rocking from one foot to the other, swinging my arms as though scything, except that I held not a scythe but a wailing grandchild. I could not recall ever being left alone in a room with one of my own babies, *sans* nanny, *sans* nursery nurse, *sans* even useful housemaid who had graduated from a childhood beset with younger siblings, but my grandchildren were obtruding into my life much more than either of my sons had ever done. This was because Mallory had sacked her monthly nurse before her nanny arrived and lasted only one night at Benachally before Donald packed her and both babies into his motorcar and brought them back to Gilverton. Julia, the maid, had stayed put but was no help at all. I privately wondered if she had been taking lessons in insubordination from Grant.

'But why, dear?' I said, when I had been alerted to the invasion and had gone to find Mallory in Donald's old bedroom, where she sat surrounded by baskets and bundles. 'She came very highly recommended from the agency and Nanny is still in Alnwick until Tuesday.'

'She was a brute,' Mallory said. 'She swaddled them so tightly their little faces changed colour. When I unwound them for their baths they were covered in creases.'

'Swaddling has to be pretty firm to be any good,' I said. 'If you let them lie on a towel and kick their legs for a bit after bath time, the creases usually fade.'

Mallory gave me a troubled look. 'And she had some very strange notions about me too,' she said. She gave a significant glance in Donald's direction. He started to life and shuffled off mumbling something about scaring up some tea. I looked after him fondly. He adores Mrs Tilling and she him; it would be a while before we saw him again.

'What sort of strange notions?' I said.

'Well,' Mallory said. 'I know *she* was the monthly nurse and *I* merely the mother but . . . look at me.' I looked but, not knowing to what aspect of herself she was drawing my attention, I could not grasp at an answer. 'She was adamant,' Mallory went on, 'that I should bind myself and drink strong coffee and that she would take sole charge of their feeding.'

I blinked at her. I was terribly fond of Mallory and I know times change but if my monthly nurse had ever offered to suckle my babies all by herself and spare me the indignity I should have jumped at it.

'Well, good for you,' I said diplomatically.

'But, after she left, I gave it a go and it's awful!' Mallory said. 'It *hurts*, Dandy. And I'm exhausted. So we came here. Don said your good Mrs Tilling had all his old bottles.'

'But they've been used for orphan lambs for the last twenty years!' I said. 'Do you know where the nurse has gone? We could entice her back with a rise in wages. I could put my foot down about the swaddling, if you're sure about her over-zealousness.'

'They had lines round their necks!' Mallory said. 'And I don't mind about the lambs. If the tops were boiled, where's the harm?'

13

It did not come to that, thankfully. Once Mallory was settled in a warm bed, with Mrs Tilling, Grant, Becky and me all twittering round her (although Julia was nowhere to be seen), she gave the enterprise another try and found it just about bearable. Hugh wrote to the new nanny at Alnwick, pleading with her to set off sooner than she had planned and offering inducements, while the rest of us hunkered down to see the adventure through to its conclusion.

Bunty, daffy as most Dalmatians usually are, took a dim view of the change in her circumstances. She sniffed the new arrivals once and removed herself to the kitchen away from the din. Alec, in contrast and to my surprise, delighted at the babies and pitched in.

We needed him. Mallory's position was that whenever the twins were not actually taking nourishment they should be far from her, to allow her to rest before the next bout. Resting had more picture magazines and chocolates about it than I might have expected but they kept her serene and the rest of us were just about coping. Hugh was not troubled by any of it, naturally; he retired to his library with his dogs, and if either of the twins set to and really tried to shatter glass with their squeals, he and the pack of hounds simply went for a walk. As for Teddy, he had taken off for London within hours, as who could blame him.

'Oh, do be quiet,' I said, staring down into the tiny, cross, sweaty face as my impersonation of a scything farmhand entered its eleventh minute. I was watching the clock because at the quarter-hour we were going to swap them over and see if perhaps the change would settle them. My grand-daughter, Lavinia Dahlia Cherry Gilver (the poor mite), took a deeper breath than ever and managed to reach an even higher pitch of yelling.

Alec was having more luck with my grandson, Edward Hugh Lachlan Gilver, who was now snuffling and wuthering instead of shrieking. Alec lifted him up and clasped him to his shoulder, giving his well-padded little bottom a series of rhythmic pats in time with the knee bounces.

'You should put a cloth over your coat,' I said.

'Pfft,' said Alec. 'We're past that. Anyway, Cramond, as I was saying. Do you remember the ferrywoman?'

'Vaguely,' I said. Those mornings of sitting in peace to open letters seemed like the misty days of a distant past now.

'Well, it's worse,' Alec said. He held the letter up behind Edward's downy head and began reading. '"It was bad enough when she refused to cross in fine weather but instead forced passengers to wait for clouds and rain".'

'What?' I said. 'When Hugh said she was making trouble about the weather I assumed it was bad weather that was the problem. Perhaps whoever wrote the letter made a mistake. Missed out a few crucial words.'

'Perhaps,' Alec said. 'But shush, Dandy. Let me finish.'

I raised an eyebrow. Of all the people in the room I was the last one who needed shushing. Edward had started up again in earnest and Lavinia was sobbing as though her heart would break. I put the knuckle of my little finger in her mouth to let her suck it, a habit I despise but one which I have been forced to succumb to. She spat it out, the minx.

'It goes on,' Alec said, '"but now she refuses to row across the river at all. She fills the dog cart with passengers and drives all the way up one side of the river to the crossing at the Cramond Brig then all the way down the other side, a terribly inconvenient journey of some four miles instead of five minutes in her natty little boat. She makes no charge but there have been grumbles from people missing appointments or being late for meals. We are seriously concerned. We are, to speak plainly, at our wits' end. That is why we renew our petition to you today. We can offer very pleasant accommodation in either a private home or a charming inn and we are willing to pay a bonus on top of your fee. For confidentiality and sympathetic attention from your most unusual

15

firm, we are willing to pay handsomely. I await . . ." etc.'

'Are you tempted?' I said. 'I must admit to being intrigued. If it's *not* a mistake of the letter writer, if Miss Kemp really stopped sailing in good weather and has now stopped completely and stopped charging for her carting services too, I do admit to being intrigued by the puzzle.'

'Stuff!' said Alec. 'You're thinking of a pleasant private home with no infants in it.'

'Or even a charming inn,' I admitted. 'But I can't abandon my post at a time like this. You could go.'

'I could,' said Alec, 'but don't you think the unusual feature of our "most unusual" detective firm that makes us perfect for this case is probably you, darling Dan?'

'Hmmm,' I said. 'Who's it from anyway, Alec? Who *is* this "we" with the range of accommodations and the deep pockets?'

Alec had folded the letter but he shook it out again. 'It's more than one person,' he said, which told us precisely nothing the pronoun had not already revealed. 'I shall send them, whoever they are, our continuing regrets. I'll try to make them even more regretful.'

3

When the third letter came, we leapt on it. It was now July, Lavinia and Edward were growing more bonny every day, the Alnwick nanny – Nanny Plantagenet, which beggared belief but she said it in such a severe tone and with such a warning look in her eye that none of us, not even Teddy, essayed a quip – was installed at Benachally and peace had descended upon Gilverton again.

'Donald's besotted,' Teddy said at breakfast one morning. 'Were you like that with us, Pa?'

Hugh was behind *The Times* and said nothing.

'Was he, Ma?'

'Take a wild flying guess,' I said. 'And don't call me Ma.'

'I thought not,' said Teddy. 'If I ever get landed and it takes me the same way, do give me a clump on the side of the head and tell me to can it, won't you?'

'Landed?' I said. 'Good grief, Teddy. I thought your slang would get better once you came down and stopped racketing about with that bunch of dilettantes. But it's getting worse. "Can it"? When I think what your education cost us, I could weep.'

'Mother dear,' Teddy said. 'Should I ever enter matrimony and be blessed with children I charge you with ensuring my devotion to them causes no nausea. Better?'

'Much,' I said. 'But I refuse the commission. I think it's sweet that Donald adores them and they are certainly adorable.'

'You're going soft in your—' Teddy began, but he did not

17

finish. I was delighted with my grandchildren and yet the fact of being a grandmother was unsettling in ways I had not expected. 'What's adorable about them?' he said instead. 'They're hardly conversationalists. They leak from every possible leaking point. They're noisy. They stink to high heaven off and on. And they look like medicine balls.'

I had to bite my cheeks at that. When I described them as 'bonny' I was being kind. Nanny Plantagenet apparently viewed the inhabitants of her nursery the way a dedicated competitive gardener views the contents of his cold frame: that is, if one is not going to grow a whopper then why bother growing anything at all. She had them on sugared rusks far too early, in my – admittedly shaky – opinion, and had begun putting cocoa powder and Ovaltine in their bedtime bottles almost as soon as she arrived. One result of this regime was that they slept for endless hours every night, stupefied by rich food like Roman emperors, and that fact alone meant that no one, from Mallory herself to the lowliest nursery maid taking a turn on the night shift, had a bad word to say. They were as fat as little pink piglets by mid-July, bursting out of their first sets of garments and, at bath time, quite jaw-dropping. Even Teddy had come to marvel once.

'Stone the crows,' he had said. 'Are they supposed to have rolls and rolls of blubber? Do all babies look like that under the ruffles?'

'Get out if you can't be civil,' Donald said. 'They are perfect, aren't they Mother?'

'They're very healthy and sweet.'

'Edward looks like . . . what's he called . . . the round god who's always laughing. The one with his tummy resting on his knees.'

'The Buddha?' I said. 'Nonsense.'

'How dare you!' said Donald.

Unfortunately, just at that moment Edward tucked both his feet under him, waved his arms and poked his tongue out of one corner of his mouth. The resemblance was un-deniable. Donald's brow lowered but Mallory laughed.

'My beautiful little Buddha!' she said. 'And what about Lavinia? Who does she remind you of, Ted?'

But Teddy, wisely in my opinion, declined to answer. Lavinia looked like Edward after a good feed. From her pouch-like cheeks to her little fat feet, she resembled a bunch of pink balloons in varying sizes. Besides, Nanny P was muttering in the background, clearly displeased that not only Mummy but also Granny, Daddy and an uncle, of all things, were cluttering up her day nursery along with two baths and the accompanying kettles and towels. I dropped a kiss on each damp head and left. Teddy followed me out.

'That's made my mind up,' he said. 'I'm not going to be at home for the jamboree.'

'What jamboree is this?' I said, pulling on my gloves as we made our way downstairs to where my motorcar was waiting.

'Mallory's picnic,' Teddy said. 'Hasn't she told you? "Asked" you rather?'

'Mallory doesn't need to ask me before she goes on a picnic.'

'She's not,' said Teddy. 'Going on one, I mean. She's hosting one. Apparently her mother did it at Applecross and her sister took over. So Mall's trying to get it off the ground here.'

I was still barely listening. I did not live in my daughter-in-law's pocket nor she in mine.

'Did you hear me, Ma?' said Teddy. 'Mallory is bringing three charabancs full of mothers and babies from the East End of Glasgow to have a weekend's camping and picnicking. It was supposed to be at Benachally but Donald reckoned the low meadow at Gilverton is better suited and the lavator-ies are closer.'

I did not know which bit of this extraordinary report to splutter over first. 'Don't say "weekend",' was what I went for eventually. 'Friday to Monday, darling, please. Your poor father already thinks you're some kind of revolutionary, because of the hair and what have you.'

'Thursday to Tuesday,' Teddy said.

I sank back into the comfortable seat of my Morris Cowley and let the horror wash over me. Three busloads of East End women and children, camping on Hugh's precious wildflower meadow, making use of the stable-block lavatories and, no doubt, ransacking the house itself once the weather failed, as the weather always does whenever Scottish picnics are attempted.

'So I'm going,' said Teddy.

'Going where?' I said, wondering if I could join him.

'Oh, I'll be able to get an invitation to shoot something somewhere,' he said, quashing my hopes.

When we arrived back at Gilverton, I went straight to Hugh in his business room to share the enormity. But Hugh was taken up with even graver matters. He was sitting at his desk, as ever, surrounded by papers and plans, dogs at his feet and ledgers at his elbow. This arrangement usually sees him at his happiest but there was a slump to his shoulders this afternoon.

'Dreadful news,' he said. 'Young Peter Haslett is dead.'

'No!' I said, gasping. 'Oh poor Simone and Angus! What happened?'

'He was off on some tear,' said Hugh. 'Sailing, as far as I can gather. And he leaned over and toppled in. Drowned.'

'Poor boy. Oh, Hugh, he wasn't even thirty!'

'Twenty-four,' Hugh confirmed. I closed the door behind me and came to sit in the chair opposite his desk, the one I think of as the steward's chair from all the long hours Hugh's steward spends in it, plotting and scheming with his compadre. For it is really as much a partnership these days as the partnership between Alec and me. They might have started off as servant and master but they are just two countrymen now.

In just the same way, the Hasletts of Fife, who were mild acquaintances at the outset of my marriage had become, over the long years, dear friends, as close to Hugh and me as our distant and seldom-seen siblings. We had seen their children born and watched them grow. We had seen their estates struggle and watched them sink. We had been through an unspeakable war together and were now girding ourselves in case of another one.

'But Peter's been sailing since he was a tot,' I said. 'What happened?'

'Took the boat out on his own after a party,' said Hugh. 'There was no one else on board to fling a lifebelt after him.'

'Oh *poor* Simone!' I said. 'What a stupid waste. We're all so worried that they might have to fight and then to lose a fine boy in a silly way like that!'

Hugh merely shook his head. We did not agree on the likelihood of another war. Hugh thought it inevitable, while I found it unthinkable. Neither did we agree on what it would mean if it came. Hugh was able, or so it appeared at least, to view the prospect of waving his boys off to battle with equanimity and pride, while I would cheerfully have smuggled them both to a desert island to keep them out of it.

'There are worse things than a daughter-in-law of a socialist bent,' I said and Hugh looked up at last.

'Teddy?' he said. 'Who has he met? Truly a socialist?'

'Donald, I meant. Mallory is set on turning Gilverton into a workers' paradise. Gilverton, mind. Not Benachally.'

'Oh, the picnic,' said Hugh. 'Hardly socialism, Dandy. More like *noblesse oblige*. I thought it a splendid idea, but I wonder now about the wisdom of having so many small children playing by a river. Perhaps we could set up some games and pony rides on higher ground. Or perhaps we should plan for it all to be inside from the off. The forecast is dire.'

'You knew about it?' I said.

'Mallory is a fine girl,' said Hugh. 'Times are changing.'

I was thunderstruck. I wandered off towards my sitting room in a daze. I am not a brute and have a heart as warm as any other. The pictures of the poor people without work in the cities had caused me many a pang during the newsreels and had I not just said I would take my own sons to an island and hide them there if I was forced to? I could hardly disparage the men who marched and chanted, begging for work to feed their own children.

Still, when I got to my sanctuary and found Alec installed I was glad to start thinking of cases and commissions, rather than troubled times and the sacrifices they threatened to extract from me.

'Another one!' Alec said. 'A third one!'

'A third what?' I said, throwing myself into a chair. 'Where's Bunty? Have you rung for tea?'

'You sound cross,' said Alec. 'No idea where Bunty is; the door was open so I assume she's off rabbiting. And yes – Becky says there's a honey cake. Third letter from Cramond. Another summons from our mysterious correspondents. And you'd think after me answering twice "To whom it may concern" and "Dear Sirs", they'd print their names, but they haven't. Shall I read it to you?'

'Please do,' I said, then I prevented him by continuing: 'Has it ever struck you as odd that we haul poachers up in front of the magistrate if we catch them and yet I let my dog chase rabbits even though I feed her twice a day?'

'I don't stick the law on poachers,' Alec said. 'Nor does Hugh. Not for rabbits and coarse fish. Are you all right?'

'Fine,' I said. 'Unsettled, that's all. A friend's son died.'

'Well, listen to this letter,' said Alec, 'and take your mind off it. "Things are desperate here," it says, but then it said that last time didn't it? "Poor Vesper has gone to live on the island and perhaps that is best until we can resolve the shocking matters that are happening here in our peaceful little community. There was a tragic accident. A poor young man fell out of the ferry, which he should not have been in, which Vesper should have been in charge of, and he has died, at the age of twenty-four. It is heartbreaking, but it was, without question, an accident. Vesper, however, insists that she killed him. She has said it to me, to our good Miss Lumley and to dear Miss Speir. So far none of her confidantes is mischievous enough to pay attention or, God forbid, pass her fevered imaginings on to the authorities. But it is only a matter of time. If she keeps telling people she killed him, sooner or later someone is going to believe her. If it got back to the boy's family, for instance, no one could expect them to be able to resist having a villain to blame for the tragedy. Mrs Gilver and Mr Osborne, I beseech you. Please come to Cramond in all haste and help us.'

'Peter Haslett,' I said.

'Who?' said Alec. 'Haslett? The Newburgh Hasletts?'

'It was their son who died,' I said. 'Hugh just told me.'

Alec gave a low whistle. 'What do you want to do?'

'I want to go to Cramond in all haste and help,' I said. 'I want to hear what this nameless friend of Speir and Lumley has to say about it all and I want to find out what happened to Peter. I still don't care all that much about a ferrywoman with nervous trouble but I was at his christening, Alec. I want to know why he died.'

'Has Hugh been talking to you about Germany again?' Alec said.

I nodded in acknowledgement of the thing he had not put into words. He knew why I was so desperately concerned with the death of a young man before his time. 'He didn't actually need to,' I said. 'It doesn't need to be mentioned anymore. It's there all the time. Like a . . . like the hiss of a gas leak.'

'Let's see if we can blow it away,' said Alec, 'with some fresh sea air.'

4

Of course, we had to find out who our client was before we sallied forth, even to Cramond. Alec sent another letter asking outright for the name of our correspondent, the identity of the 'we' he had been bandying around, and some idea of where we should present ourselves.

The reply came by telegram, from the Reverend Mr Gerald Hogg, of Cramond Kirk. He bid us arrive at the manse in time for luncheon on the following day where we would meet the others he spoke for, and he promised us a billet with any of them; either there at the manse, with 'dear Miss Speir' at Cramond House or with 'good Miss Lumley' at the Turning Tide.

When we arrived, however, it was to find Rev Hogg in a state of some flusterment. Departing Gilverton had been easy enough, except for the question of leaving Grant behind. She thumped around in bitter silence as she packed my things and no amount of pointing out that she was now near the top of the hierarchy in the matter of the Great Picnic could console her.

'It's only Cramond, Grant,' I said. 'Hardly thrilling. And I expect it'll be a short trip. Miss Kemp needs a doctor. Our job seems to be to point that out to Mr Hogg. We'll only be gone a day. And I might well be staying in a hotel. I don't need a maid.'

'I quite like a hotel too,' Grant said. 'And you mightn't. You said you might be at Cramond House. Don't let this Miss Lumley's maid do any washing for you, please. If it

24

turns out you're there long enough to need laundry work, let me know and I'll come over.' I said nothing. Grant's belief that she alone can take care of my possessions is too stout to brook argument.

The journey across the Forth was as pleasant as it could be. The sea was calm and the boat was quiet. I paid more attention to the ferryman and his mate than I would usually, given our current mission, but they were the usual sort: which is to say, they were taciturn men in boiler suits with no romance about them anywhere. I had half a mind to ask if they knew Vesper Kemp, if they counted her as one of their number, even if they could guess what ailed her. But the words of Rev Hogg's letters came back to me. He wanted this matter taken care of quietly and regaling local ferrymen with the problem was likely to work against that aim.

When we were on dry land again and trundling along the shore road towards the Dalmeny estates, I took the chance to share with Alec what Hugh had shared with me the previous evening when I asked him. He was a fount, on this as on so many topics.

'There has always been a footpath through the estate to a passenger ferry,' I said. 'I'm less sure about carts and carriages, or indeed motorcars. We might get stopped and have a stick shaken at us, but I know the Roseberys a little, and we won't be run off. Then, when we get to the mouth of the river, we'll have to take Miss Kemp's last favoured route. Up one side and down the other.'

'You don't suppose these Roseberys would have thought it worth scaring her off in some way, do you?' Alec said, looking around himself. The road wended through thin wood-land, brambly and ferned, with glimpses of hayfields flashing between the tree trunks on our right and glimpses of shell-bedecked beaches flashing between them on our left.

'Why would they?' I said.

'If there was no ferry, there would be no walkers tramping

25

through their grounds,' said Alec. 'If I could stop people tramping through *my* grounds, I'd have to consider it.'

Alec had taken to Scottish life with some gusto but he still, after all these years, mourns the English trespass law that saw walking enthusiasts, birdwatchers, naturalists and pests of every type strictly kept to a very few marked footpaths at his childhood home, and allowed landowners to drive them off every other inch of forest, meadow and mountain. In Scotland, by contrast, the populace is free to trample over any ground they feel moved to trample over. It works well enough, most of Scotland not being worth guarding. No one, even in the sturdiest boots, can do much damage to a sheep-infested hill top or a moorland covered in bracken.

'I don't think they'd take the trouble,' I said. 'Look.' We were passing the great house as I spoke and it was far enough from the shore path to be untroubled by the tramp of feet there. It sat massive and serene behind its lawns, like a slumbering lioness, looking down over the shore and the river with impassive reserve.

'What about this place?' Alec said minutes later as we skirted another house, this a more ancient building by far – a castle by any reckoning – that sat at the water's edge as though to guard its neighbours from the ravages of Fifers.

'It's not a house,' I said. 'Hugh tells me it holds the Roseberys' library.'

'It's close to the path,' Alec said. 'Easily close enough for passers-by to be an annoyance.'

'But anyone who banishes the library to a damp castle half a mile away surely isn't much of a reader,' I said and Alec laughed as we passed on.

'I'll never get used to this country,' he said. 'Not if I live to be ninety. But I take your word for it.'

Presently, we arrived at Coble Cottage, the ferryman's dwelling. It was built of grey stone with crow-stepped gables and sat on a promontory formed as the River Almond emptied into the breadth of the Forth estuary. Alec craned out of the side window as we passed. 'Nice little place,' he said. 'Pity it's sitting empty. I do hope we can resolve all this, Dandy.' At my glare he hurried on. 'I don't begrudge the girl her job or her cottage but if she's not *doing* her job or *living* in her cottage there are plenty of deserving individuals who would be willing. That's all.'

'I hope we can resolve it too,' I said. 'Either by finding out that the strange Miss Kemp really did have a hand in poor Peter Haslett's death, in which case she will go to jail and a new ferryman will be found, or by confirming that she is not mixed up in his death at all and should stop her histrionics. Once I've finished boxing her ears for her silliness she might go back to rowing a ferry or she might not.'

We were now tracing the west bank of the Almond upstream and, before long, the chimneys and rooftops of the hotel at the Cramond Brig were in view. We wedged the motorcar between the walls of a hump-backed bridge, bounced over it and started down the other side. Then, oddly, we got a little lost. There was a mill and another mill, which are reassuring when one is trying to hug a riverside, but after that we found ourselves meandering away from it past a post office, a school and myriad cottages before, after much longer than either of us had expected, I spied a church and the gates to a manse and we swung in, ready to meet our client.

But not at all ready to meet with his flusterment. Nor the pursed lips and grim looks of the two ladies who had joined the reception committee. I took a guess at the problem.

'I do apologise for being a few minutes late,' I said. 'We took a bit of a tour of the vicinity, if you can believe it. One would think driving up one side of a river, then over a bridge and down again would be a hard journey to fail at. But fail we did.'

'No, no, you didn't,' said Rev Hogg. He had introduced us to the ladies with an easy courtesy but his colour was high and his hand shook as he ushered us through from his drawing room into his dining room, where luncheon was laid out. It was a cheerful apartment, not at all what the words 'manse dining room' would draw to mind. Long windows were open to a garden bursting with flowers and the meal on the table, although cold, was plentiful and fresh-looking. Alec dug into a plate of cold roasted pork with his usual gusto. I gave Rev Hogg an interested look, waiting for the explanation.

'There *is* no road,' he said. 'Two estates, you see. Cammo upriver and, umm . . .' Here he broke off and cleared his throat. Then he fixed his sherry glass with a stern look and shut his mouth.

'Cammo upriver and me,' said the grander of the two ladies, who had been introduced as Miss Speir. She looked to be in her sixties and, while she was dressed in modern enough clothes as not to be peculiar, she yet had something of her Edwardian heyday still about her in her high, ruffled collar, her broad waistband and the frizzed hair across her forehead. 'But it's nothing to do with my estate, Jerry,' she said. 'It's the mills and it's over with now anyway.'

'The mills?' I said.

'Four mills,' Miss Lumley said. She was not the equal of Rev Hogg and Miss Speir, judging by her appearance, for she had dyed hair, rather too many baubles and bangles for luncheon time and a hemline short enough to be startling, for a woman her age. Despite lacking social cachet, however, she was perfectly at home and willing to take the floor. 'Between the Cramond Brig and the sea,' she explained. 'And they fought like cats over the water all the years they ran. Well, the one furthest upriver and the one furthest downriver were always fine but the two in the middle were at war for quite three hundred years. Peggie's Mill and

Fair-a-Far they're called. They took to building weirs to help their own wheels.'

Alec tutted as though in genuine disapproval. I tried to cast my mind back to the many discussions of water works I had been party to, whether canals, locks, reservoirs or dams, and could just about recall the dire consequences of slowing a millstream with an extra weir.

'Then they exacted revenge for the weirs, by withholding passage over their land.'

'How unneighbourly,' I said.

'Catch the upstream miller letting a Fair-a-Far cart trundle by loaded with ironwork wrought by the theft of his water!' Miss Lumley cried. 'And catch the downstream miller letting a Peggie's cart go straight to the sea to put a load of illicitly milled paper directly onto a boat! So there was never any to and fro, to establish right of passage, back in the mists of history when roadways were born.'

'But these days?' I said. 'Surely these days? If the mills are no more?'

'And thankfully that is the case,' said Miss Lumley. 'Cramond is a pleasure ground, Mrs Gilver. The sludge and mess of four mills have no place here.'

'But age-long habits are hard to break,' Rev Hogg said. 'Whether they be for good or for ill. We here at Cramond are a cosy band of old friends, but the animosity between the up mills and the down mills is too deeply entrenched to be easily done away with. If anything, it's spread further. Each man for himself. No fellow feeling anywhere. It's most distressing. I could preach a sermon on it but none of them are churchgoers.'

I tutted in sympathy. Then, feeling that we had exhausted the conversational fruit of the history of Cramond's roads, I put a bright smile on my face and waited for someone to start in on the topic at hand.

'Yes, well well,' Rev Hogg said, interpreting the bright smile. 'Now then. As I was just explaining to the ladies while we awaited your arrival, Mrs Gilver, Mr Osborne, it's about our dear Vesper.'

'And when you say she's "your" Vesper?' I said. 'Is she a ward? Is she related to you? Any of you?'

'Certainly not!' Miss Speir said, with some vehemence, as though to be related to a ferrywoman would be a stain on her family name. As I suppose it would be.

'Not officially,' Miss Lumley said. 'But she's been known to us all her life and, when her father went off to the war and she was left alone, we took an interest, didn't we, Mr Hogg? I'm at the Turning Tide Hotel, Mrs Gilver, right on the front, and I see into her cottage from my top windows, so I got in the habit of keeping an eye on her.'

I nodded. Miss Lumley, then, was the proprietress of the local pub. That explained the hair dye, the baubles and the offer of rooms there.

'And of course she's one of my flock,' Rev Hogg added. 'Her mother died when Vesper was quite a small child and her poor father didn't come home, as I think you know. She is most assuredly "our" Vesper.'

'Unusual name,' Alec said, coming up for air. His plate was clean and he was eyeing the serving dishes, clearly getting his second wind.

'Yes,' Rev Hogg said, with a grimace. 'If I had been minister here I might have led her parents away from such a notion, but I was not. I arrived in the parish when Vesper was a tot in Sunday school.'

'It's a family name,' said Miss Lumley. 'And it's better than Frieda. I'd swap.'

Miss Speir gave a tight smile, either because her own name was worse still or because the bumptiousness of Miss Lumley pained her, no matter what Rev Hogg had to say about old habits and settled friendships.

'It must be a sorrow to you all to see her so . . . troubled,' I said.

'Ill,' said Miss Speir. 'Unwell. She is in need of medical attention.'

'I agree,' said Miss Lumley. 'I had an aunt who was taken the same way after a confinement. It took her months of rest before she was herself again but she got there in the end.'

'And so our commission is to persuade her to be seen by a doctor?' I said. 'Surely you who know her and have known her since she was a child would be better placed to take that on.'

'Oh dear, dear, dear,' said Rev Hogg. He had put his knife and fork down and he was not so much wiping his hands with his napkin, as kneading it in them, working it into a tight ball. Miss Speir and Miss Lumley both sat forward, as if ready to catch whatever I might be about to pitch at them.

'We don't agree that persuasion is necessary,' said Miss Speir. 'We think, although our place in Vesper's life is un-official . . .'

'And although she is thirty-five years old and so hardly a child,' Miss Lumley added.

'And although it grieves us both— all,' Miss Speir added.

'Oh dear, dear, dear,' said Rev Hogg again. 'It certainly grieves *me*. The very thought of it grieves me deeply.'

'So you think,' Alec said, 'that Miss Kemp's troubles are severe enough that you might have her committed?'

The Misses Lumley and Speir bowed their heads in acknowledgement of their grief and agreement. Rev Hogg, however, was having none of it.

'I shall hold out against it until the bitter end,' he said. 'I did not write to you three times, Mrs Gilver, Mr Osborne, to enlist your help in such an unfeeling scheme. I would do almost anything rather than see our dear Vesper in some godforsaken – and I mean godforsaken; I make no apology for the term – in some godforsaken lunatic asylum.'

'Not a lunatic asylum, Jerry,' said Miss Speir. 'A quiet, pleasant nursing home, where she might—'

31

'Worse!' Rev Hogg thundered. His napkin was once again taking the brunt of his consternation. I thought I heard the stitching on the hem give under the pressure of him twisting it. 'Insidious! A serpent in long grass is so much more deadly than a serpent on the sand. I will never consent to our dear Vesper being incarcerated in such a place. I will fight it. I *am* fighting it. Mrs Gilver, Mr Osborne, you are here to investigate and confirm my strong conviction that Vesper is not ill, but is troubled by something we can all – together, as a battalion, as her family more or less – discover and then deal with.'

He sat back at the end of this remarkable speech and finally let his napkin go, dropping it onto his hardly touched luncheon plate.

There was a longish silence, as might be well imagined. Rev Hogg himself broke it.

'Excuse me,' he said, stumbling to his feet and pushing his chair back. 'I won't be a minute. I must just . . .' And, on unsteady feet, he left the room.

We all listened to his footsteps crossing the floor of the hall and then fading as he entered a different room and closed the door.

Miss Lumley drew a breath, but before she could speak, Miss Speir chipped in, rather hurriedly.

'Let me explain,' she said. Her disinclination was clear, but even clearer was her desire to prevent us getting Miss Lumley's version. 'It's Mrs Hogg.'

I looked after the good reverend. 'Has he gone to fetch her?'

'She's not in the house!' Miss Lumley said, ending in a squawk. 'Good grief, she's not roaming around in the house!'

Miss Speir gave her a quelling look and resumed the narrative. 'I presume Jerry has gone to compose himself,' she said. 'As Miss Lumley says, Mrs Hogg doesn't live here. She has been resident in a place . . . one forgets the name . . .

getting on for twenty years now. It's probably perfectly pleasant.'

'*We've* never been,' Miss Lumley said, darkly. '*He's* there every Saturday.'

'Oh dear,' I said, echoing poor Rev Hogg without meaning to. 'And so he didn't tell you about his campaign to get us down here?'

'Not a dickybird,' said Miss Lumley, with a great deal of asperity. She might have as much sympathy for the man as did Miss Speir but she was hiding it well. 'The first we heard at all was when we saw how many places had been set for lunch this very day!'

'So you've had a wasted trip, I'm afraid,' Miss Speir said. 'If you want to set off home immediately, we shall make your apologies.'

'I wouldn't dream of it,' I said. 'We are made of stern stuff, Mr Osborne and I, after all these years. I'm afraid our sensibilities are much too blunt to be touched by Rev Hogg's outburst.'

'And besides,' Alec said, 'Mr Hogg is our client. Or prospective client, at least. And, since Miss Kemp is an adult, unmarried and without immediate family, he has quite as much right to address her plight as . . . anyone else.'

He spoke mildly but his point was clear. It was certainly clear to the two ladies, each of whom bristled like a hen in a dust bath.

'We are all intimately concerned,' said Miss Lumley. 'We are trying, after the dark days, to put Cramond back to rights.'

'Dark days?' said Alec. 'I don't think I know the story. As you might be able to tell, I'm not a local chap.'

'My dear Miss Lumley meant the war and great depression,' said Miss Speir. 'The crash and the slough of despond following it. We are trying to lift our beloved village out of it, you see. And that little— And our poor Vesper is making it much harder.'

I waited to see if her exasperation would bubble over into something more than hints. When it did not, I gave her a nudge.

'What is it you're doing?'

'*What?*' said Miss Lumley.

'For the village.'

'Putting it on the—' said Miss Speir, stopping herself just before she finished.

'Map?' said Alec. 'How?'

The two women fixed one another with desperate glares.

'We haven't had time to decide how much we should let—' said Miss Speir.

'Slip?' said Alec.

Miss Lumley started to life and spoke soothingly. 'Nothing so mysterious,' she said, with a laugh that did not quite ring true. 'Just that we want the island to be a holiday spot. There are cottages and an old whinstone quarry and it's ever so nice. So secluded and yet so handy.'

'Yes!' said Miss Speir with far too much relief. 'Delightful.'

'But,' Miss Lumley added, bitterly, 'while Vesper's got herself parked there having twice daily doo-dahs it's not much of a draw. Not to mention the fact that there's no ferry!'

'Although,' said Alec, 'when someone claims to have killed a man, who'd get on her boat anyway?'

The dust bath was even more lavish this time.

'How about this?' I said, pouring oil. 'Miss Kemp is in retirement on Cramond Island, as you say? Well, how's the tide this afternoon? Could Mr Osborne and I take a walk over there and introduce ourselves? We might not be able to make a snap decision but we could get a better view of matters once we've met her, couldn't we?'

'Yes, you take a stroll across the causeway,' said Miss Lumley. 'I'll watch the tide for you. We have boats and boatmen a-plenty if it catches you unawares.'

'You agree that it's worth a try?' I said.

'Oh very much so!' said Miss Lumley. 'I think you'll easily be able to make a decision, once you've seen her.' I knew she was upset by the whole mess and I knew she must be ruffled by the recent exchange with Rev Hogg too, but I was still surprised by her tone. At the bottom of all this was the misfortune of a dear friend. How could she speak of it with such relish? How could prospective triumph in a disagreement outweigh all finer feelings so completely? I had to exert some effort to keep my distaste from showing.

Alec's mind was running along the same lines as we trudged towards the island an hour later. 'Did you wonder, Dan,' he said, 'why they're at loggerheads over her? The girl herself almost seems to have been forgotten in the midst of the quarrel.'

'I certainly think Mr Hogg was naïve to imagine he could engage us on the quiet and then just have the other two fall into line when we arrived,' I said. 'I can't remember a more excruciating scene in all our years of detecting.'

As we trudged back to the mainland again after that even more excruciating scene, with poor Vesper in her rags, raving about Mercury, Alec spoke again. But his mind and mine were not running in tandem this time.

'We're taking the case,' he said. 'Or, if you won't, I am.'

'What?' I said. 'Why? We're not doctors.'

'She's not ill,' said Alec. 'Or at least not *just* ill. She's terrified. And it's our job to find out why.'

5

First, though, we had decisions to make about our accommodations. We swithered, to use that wonderful Scottish word, all the way back over the causeway, weighing up the respective merits of a business transaction with Miss Lumley the publican against the extra comforts to be found in a country house.

In the end the matter was taken out of our hands. We stopped in at the pub first, since it was closer to the shore, and found the bar rather more lively than might have been expected for the middle of a weekday afternoon. A great many men seemed to be gathered there, and they were not the worthies who frequent all bars at all times from opening to last orders, nor were they farmworkers or fishermen. For one thing it was too early for working men to have downed tools and for another the bar was a step up from the sort of place where working boots and soiled clothes are welcome. It was as neat as a pin, with much burnished wood and glittering brass, and the hand of its lady proprietress could be seen in the many tatted mats and crocheted cushion covers dotted around.

The men – ten or eleven when I took a closer look – were neither ramblers, nor birdwatchers, nor fathers of families on their holidays, nor old enough to be retired, nor young enough to be students on their long vac, nor grand enough to be gentlemen of leisure. They were dressed similarly, in coats and ties, and yet each had a little something about him: one wore a feather in his hat; another had waistcoat buttons of jet that glittered and winked in the lamplight; one wore spats, to my astonishment. And all of them had a writing pad or sheaf of loose papers. As a man close to the door lifted his pint pot to his lips, I saw ink on his fingers. I was clawing my way to an explanation for them all when I felt Alec grip me hard by the elbow and pull me backwards out of the door into the street again.

'Press,' he said when the door had swung shut on the scene.

'Ah!' I said. 'You think so? Reporters?'

'Don't you? Here to scoop what there is to scoop about poor Peter Haslett.'

'I don't think that,' I said. 'Those reports have been written, Alec. Hugh read about it in the paper yesterday. The inquiry has been held and the Fiscal has ruled it an accident. There's nothing more to say.'

'That's worrying,' Alec said. He looked around and moved closer, lowering his voice. 'What if it's Vesper who's the story? What if news of her confession is beginning to spread already?'

I nodded. 'We certainly don't want to add fodder to the tale,' I said. 'There's another pub that might put us up just round the corner. No doubt we'd have to pay, but it won't be a great expense.' I thought the better of it though as we turned and began to climb towards the Cramond Inn. The street was deserted as far as I could tell, but it was only a few feet wide with cottages clustered cheek by jowl on either side. And each of these cottages had open windows, and each of these open windows had a veil of net hiding the room beyond. Behind the veil, there was no way to tell if a room was empty or if a host of villagers was watching us and listening. As soon as I had the thought it became real to me. I could feel their eyes upon me and hear their careful quiet breathing. I even thought I could see shifting shapes behind the netting.

I looked up the steep street towards the manse gates.

Cramond House lay that way, beyond the gaze of hidden villagers and beyond the reach of the most determined news-paperman. On the other hand, I thought, turning down to face the way we had come, to be installed in a public house was to be in the thick of village life, ear to the ground for any news.

Alec was nudging me. 'What's this?' he said. 'We are being borne down upon, Dandy.'

I looked where he was nodding and saw Miss Speir and Miss Lumley coming down the hill, walking in the middle of the street like a pair of cowboys on a picture show, Miss Speir striding in her sensible shoes and Miss Lumley tippity-tapping along on her foolish ones, her many ornaments jingling at every step.

'We saw you heading back,' Miss Speir called. 'Through Jerry's spyglass.'

'Good for you, staying ahead of the tide,' Miss Lumley shouted.

A pained look plucked at Miss Speir's face, as though she had not just been shouting in the street too. 'It's always a concern,' she added, as the two of them drew near, 'with newcomers to Cramond.'

'It must be a middling inconvenience to Cramond locals,' Alec said.

'I have a seagull,' said Miss Speir. It was an utterance that conveyed no information to me, beyond a brief wild vision of a coastal carrier pigeon, but Alec looked impressed.

Miss Lumley had now done more than draw near; she had drawn close enough to speak in a whisper. 'We saw your encounter with Vesper too,' she said. 'On the beach.'

'Good,' I replied. 'It would have been hard to summarise if you hadn't.'

'Shall we discuss it inside?' Alec said.

'Inside *there*?' Miss Lumley said, with a glance over her shoulder. 'That's not my place.' She actually brushed past me and stood foursquare in the doorway of the Cramond Inn. 'That's a pub, not a hotel,' she said.

They were both village inns as far as I could tell and, if anything, this looked a little plusher than the Turning Tide. 'Although really and truly,' Miss Lumley went on, 'I've nowhere to put you anyway. I wish Mr Hogg had given us some notice. I could have reserved the best rooms – with washbasins and a sea view – but I can't actually turf people out.'

'We popped our heads in as we passed,' I said. 'And trade does seem to be quite lively.'

'Oh you did?' said Miss Speir. She sounded displeased but I was at a loss to account for her displeasure. Was she shocked that I had entered a public house? But she knew I was a working woman and she herself was walking down the street with the landlady. Was she offended that we considered the inn when the other option was her house? But she had hardly been welcoming over luncheon. 'Well, not to worry,' she went on. 'Jerry and I decided that you'd be far better as my guests while you're among us. I was just coming to tell you.' She gave me a stiff smile and I returned it.

'Thank you,' I said. 'I know it was sprung on you. We accept gratefully.'

'I'll just slip up to the manse and get the car,' Alec said. 'Then I can take you home, Miss Speir, and you can show us the way.'

'Oh,' said Miss Speir. Miss Lumley had quietly sidled past us and was now disappearing around the corner, back to her hotel with its views and basins. 'We took your motorcar to my house once we decided. My maid is unpacking for you both as we speak. Besides, I'm used to this hill. I walk up and down at least once a day to take the sea air, and over the causeway and back too as often as not. There's no need to be concerned about me.'

That was not what was concerning me. And I was sure

39

that was not what was causing the storm playing out on Alec's brow. He said nothing, but merely lifted his hat in a gesture of chivalry and offered his arm for the climb up the steep incline of the village street. I fell in behind them. If the inn was fully booked then there really was nothing for it but to bunk at Cramond House, but to take Alec's motorcar and drive it there, then to snaffle our bags and hand them over to the servant, all of that was very odd. Add it to Miss Lumley barricading a pub doorway and I began to wonder what exactly we had missed that had brought all those men to the village and why exactly we were being so strenuously prevented from finding out about it from anyone.

The gates to Cramond House were closer than I had thought, and we did not even have to climb as far as the kirk again before we turned in at a drive with Alec's motorcar just visible, parked on a sweep at the end of a long avenue. The house itself was the usual jumble of schemes and extravagances, with an ancient middle, a newer wing thrown out on the west side, from where we approached, and a splendid Palladian frontage added on the east side, complete with crested pediment, soaring steps and balusters, all facing a field full of ponies. I had my own private view of Gilverton, of course, formed over the course of many a draughty winter and stuffy summer, but I agreed with Hugh that it was pleasing to the eye in its own way, being absolutely of itself, nothing added by way of ballrooms or billiards rooms and nothing taken away by purse strings or conflagrations, since its foundation stone was laid. Here at Cramond, the fortunes and follies of the inhabitants had produced something rather less restful.

As I looked away from it, moreover, I saw that even this scrapbook of architectural fashions was not the whole story, for just across a straggling rose garden lay the remains of an ancient tower, fourteenth century at a guess, its glassless windows looking blindly out and its roof choked with ivy. And yet it was not quite deserted.

'Miss Speir,' I said, 'I don't want to alarm you but I think there's someone in that old tower over there. I just saw someone pass a window hole.'

'Builders,' Miss Speir said. 'I'm getting sick of waiting for it to fall down and so I've told the local builder and stone merchant that he can help himself to whatever looks useful. He's putting up a riverside villa, which he reckons to sell as a bolt hole for some bright young thing. Perhaps an artist or what have you.'

'But shouldn't you . . .' Alec began. He was staring fixedly at the tower now, having stopped halfway up the soaring steps to the grand doorway of the house. 'I mean, isn't it worth preserving? An ancient tower like that?'

'Not ancient,' said Miss Speir. 'Fifteenth century and ten-a-penny in these parts. It's got no claim to a place in history, Mr Osborne. Nothing ever happened there and as for architecture: whatever carvings and engravings there ever were are long gone now. It's just a collection of stones. It'll look better as a few pretty villas than a ruin.'

I could not help smiling. If every Scottish family took that practical view there would be far fewer tall tales about Queen Mary stitching tapestries and Prince Charlie watering horses and the handful of towers and castles with genuine histories would be able to shine through.

My attention was drawn away from the tower again anyway, as the front door above us opened and a maidservant of great age, although still erect and sturdy, came out on the doorstep to welcome us.

'Tea's laid, Miss Speir,' she said. 'And the minister's here.'

'Is he?' said Miss Speir. Once again, I thought she sounded aggrieved and once again I was stumped as to the source of her grievance. 'Well, well. Mrs Gilver, Christine here will show you to your room. Mr Osborne, if you follow and then carry on and turn left, your room is at the end of the passage with a view over my rose garden. I'll tell Jerry you'll be with us in five minutes or so, shall I?' She shooed us away towards a grand staircase with such a series of flurried gestures that I was reminded of a shepherd attempting to get a collie, only half-trained, to run out and gather a huddle of flighty ewes. Alec and I shared a look as we followed 'Christine' but said nothing.

I undertook a swift reordering of my opinions as I entered what was to be my bedroom for the length of my stay at Cramond. Surely the hotel, if it charged for the privilege, could not have expected anyone to sleep in such a dingy chamber, the wallpaper faded to the colour of weak tea, the curtains thin and dusty and the carpet down to the weft in the middle and nibbled by moths at the edge. The bed was lumpy, the looking-glass spotted and the washstand with its jug and bowl hinted that any attempt to secure a daily bath would not go smoothly. I unpinned my hat, rinsed my hands in cold water and let myself out into the passageway again just as Alec came around the corner.

'How's yours?' he said.

'Grim. Yours?'

'Bleak. And no beer on tap downstairs.'

The tea to be had downstairs was nothing to gladden the heart either. It was lukewarm, weak although Indian – which should always be strong – and was served with squares of cold sodden toast scraped over with paste of unknown origin.

Miss Speir and Rev Hogg sat stiffly on either side of an empty fireplace. I surmised that the discussion had after we had left for the island had been a difficult one.

'Now then,' Alec said, once he had washed down the nasty toast with a good gulp of disappointing tea. 'There is one thing we need to be very clear about from the outset.'

Miss Speir raised her eyebrows and pulled back her chin – inadequate at the best of times – until it disappeared completely. I supposed she was startled at being addressed that way in her own drawing room and I foresaw having to be scrupulous about letting her know we were working on a case, not holidaying at her meagre expense.

'Clarity is ever our friend,' said Rev Hogg, an unusual stance for a minister I thought; a little fudging, or at least a measure of gentle shading, being so often necessary to reconcile the church with the outer world.

'I don't suppose,' Alec said, 'that there is the slightest chance Miss Kemp really did kill Mr Haslett? Is there?'

'None whatsoever,' Miss Speir said stoutly. She even banged her cup down into its saucer as though for punctuation.

'Indeed not,' said Rev Hogg.

'In the legal sense,' Miss Speir added. 'Of course, morally, it is not hard to mount an argument that lays it at her door.'

'Come, come now!' said Rev Hogg.

'If she had been in her coble, pole in hand, where she belonged,' said Miss Speir, 'then necessarily young Mr Haslett could not have taken the coble out on the river alone, could not have got into difficulties, and could not have fallen in and drowned.'

'But there's no doubt that's what happened?' I said. 'He was alone?'

'He was alone,' said Rev Hogg. 'At least . . . if anyone was with him, then that person has not admitted it.'

I cocked my head onto one side.

'Jerry!' said Miss Speir, who had shifted in her seat like a horse with colic as she saw me considering. 'Why are you making mischief? He was alone.'

'I made a philosophical point, not a legal one,' Rev Hogg said.

'I understand,' I said and was rewarded with a smile. 'If he was alone when he died there is no one to bear witness to his being alone when he died. Quite so.'

'The boat ran aground empty,' said Miss Speir, 'and his body was found. He was alone.' I could see that the minister's small, scholarly point was causing her great consternation. 'Besides,' she added, 'Vesper was on the island. There are two witnesses to Vesper being already on the island while the coble was still moored at the steps, remaining on the island when it put out onto the river, and still being on the island when it drifted into open water and the alarm was raised.'

'That seems conclusive,' I said. 'Who are these two witnesses?'

'But surely you won't need to go bothering them?' said Miss Speir. Her chin had disappeared again.

'Bothering whom?' said Alec.

'Friends of his,' said Rev Hogg. 'Or classmates anyway. They're all at the college together. The two of them are on the island running an experiment and Peter Haslett came to visit them.'

'An experiment?' I said. It was five years since I had cringed and thrilled to see Mr Boris Karloff as the creature in that unspeakable picture show but still the very notion of a scientist working away at his strange obsessions made me shudder.

'Yes, they're students at the School of Agriculture at Edinburgh. They're doing a potato trial.'

'Ah,' I said, feeling the dreadful spectre of a secret laboratory start to fade. 'On Cramond Island?'

'No slugs,' said Rev Hogg. 'No mice.'

'Ah,' I said again. 'I see. Very handy.'

'Miss Kemp must surely be rather a disruptive element,' Alec said. I certainly hoped so. Remembering Vesper's nakedness and the wildness of her talk – serpents and cinnabar! My ears were still ringing with it – I hoped these two lads, whoever they were, found her annoying rather than alluring.

'They are managing to keep out of her way,' said Rev Hogg. 'She's taken up residence in the Duck House – a greatly inferior little place compared with Coble Cottage;

44

practically a bothy – and when she's not holed up there she roams the beaches. The potatoes are in plots by the old steading.'

I still rather thought I would take a shirt over next time and try to persuade Vesper to don it.

'I'm glad to hear the poor boy's death is nothing we need to dwell on,' I said, 'but just before we move off it, do you happen to know how he came to drown?'

'I'm not sure I understand the question,' said Miss Speir. 'He took the coble out on his own and fell in.'

'Why didn't he swim to shore?' Alec said. 'Presumably he could swim?'

'I don't know,' said Rev Hogg. 'Do you remember hearing anything on the topic, Miss Speir?'

'Even if he could swim,' Miss Speir said, 'swimming in a pool in a bathing suit and bare legs is very different from finding oneself suddenly submerged in cold water wearing tweeds and brogues.' It was a fair point.

'Is it deep though?' I said. 'Where the ferry crosses? Would he actually have been out of his depth?'

'He must have been,' said Miss Speir. 'It would take a particularly foolish young man to drown in water he could stand up in.' It seemed rather heartless, but once again it was fair comment, looked at dispassionately.

'Perhaps he hit his head,' Alec said. 'On the edge of the boat or a rock.'

'Look!' said Miss Speir. Rev Hogg shifted uncomfortably and a pained grimace contorted his features. He knew what she was going to say and he had been hoping she would not. 'The young man was in his cups, if you must drag it all out into the cold light of day. He went off on his own after drinking with his friends, took the coble out in a moment of the over-confidence that wine can bestow, lost control of the pole in a moment of the clumsiness wine can bestow and fell into the water, where yet again the effects of having drunk

45

far too much prevented him from swimming to shore.' She sat back and glared at us. I did feel rather brutal.

The tide would not be in our favour again until the early hours of the morning but Alec and I agreed we did not want to waste the rest of the day without another attempt at communication with the benighted Miss Kemp. And so after tea we made our way back down to the river mouth, to mention Miss Speir's name at the boat club.

'It's an awfully long row,' I said, as we turned off the steep hill onto a set of steps serving as a shortcut to the shoreside.

'We're not rowing!' Alec said. 'Good grief, Dandy. I'm forty in case you'd forgotten.'

'But there's not a breath of wind,' I said.

At that Alec stopped dead and stared at me as though I were an imbecile. We were already attracting attention from the doorways and drying greens of the cottages that opened off this stairway and a couple of women paused in the act of unpegging the day's wash from the line and waited to see what we were up to.

'We're not sailing,' said Alec. 'Miss Speir just told us we can borrow her Seagull. Weren't you listening?'

'What's a Seagull?' I said, prodding him until he started moving again. I did not mention carrier pigeons.

'A two-stroke,' Alec said.

'A what?'

'Honestly, Dandy. How you can know the names of fifteen different kinds of hat brim and yet not know what a two-stroke is!' Alec shook his head but gave in at last. 'An outboard motor.'

'There aren't fifteen different kinds of hat brim,' I said. 'And I don't approve of outboard motors. They've ruined lakes and rivers. Nasty, noisy, smelly things.'

'Well, one of them is going to ruin Cramond this evening,'

46

Alec said, 'delivering us to the island and back in time for supper.'

The boat club was just coming to life as the various clerks and schoolmasters who were its mainstay arrived home from work, ready for play, and a pleasant young man pointed out a natty little red affair, complete with oily carbuncle weighing it down at the back. We descended the steps and took possession.

'Wait just a moment,' I said. Alec had taken off his coat and rolled a sleeve, ready to tackle the rope that started the thing. 'There's the ferry.' A few yards off from Miss Speir's neat craft, a larger and somehow scruffier boat was tied up at a set of wooden steps, at the head of which hung a bell.

'So it is,' Alec said. 'What of it?'

'One would think,' I said slowly, staring at the boat as it bobbed and eddied, 'that they'd moor it on the other bank after what happened with Peter Haslett.'

'That would be rather sentimental,' Alec said. 'If there's no one in the cottage, the boat would be stranded. Look, if we're going we better go, Dan.'

'I wonder where it was the night he died.'

'*Was* it night?' Alec said.

'He'd been drinking.' I ignored the fond smile this display of rectitude earned me. I should have known better. Teddy, in his Oxford days, did not wait, checking the yardarm; perhaps scientists from the agriculture school were no better. 'But whatever time of day it was,' I went on, 'it's hard to see how he could have been drinking with his pals on the island and then taken the boat unless it was moored over this side. If it was over at the cottage where it belonged, the walk over the causeway, up one side of the river to the Brig and back down again would have sobered him up.'

'Why is it bothering you?'

'I don't know, but it is and I've learned not to ignore such things.'

Alec's only reply was the rip and roar of the little engine springing to life as he tugged on the rope. I knew that it was a matter of some consequence to a gentleman that any engine should start at his first touch, but I hid my smile as a look of serenity bordering on smugness spread over Alec's face. He lodged his pipe – unlit – in his teeth and sat down at the tiller to take us walloping over the water.

It was marvellous. I am generous enough to admit it. Oddly, the noise was less annoying inside the craft, and the nasty, oily smell was unfurling behind us to spoil things for the few walkers taking the air. It did not trouble Alec and me at all.

Of course, given the Seagull, there was no chance of a stealthy approach and I foresaw having to search the entirety of the island for Miss Kemp if the engine noise frightened her. As it turned out though she was drawn to it. We were just pulling the boat up the shingle when she came out of the gorse bushes again as she had last time. She was still not wearing anything above her skirts but she was, unlike earlier, armed with a large stick. I should have called it a club if that did not sound so alarming.

'Miss Kemp,' I said, in ringing tones. I wondered if she would simply rush forward and wield that club of hers but she stopped and dropped it. My spirits sank a little. I am not a fool and I know I have not been girlish for a good many years, but still an air of effective command is not a talent I ever pined for.

When Vesper spoke though, I discovered it was not my peremptory address that had disarmed her.

'Oh,' she said in a very small voice. 'You're not them.'

'Not whom, dear?' I said. I strode forward and, although she took a step away from me, she did not run. 'Now look what I've brought you. A nice light comfortable shift to wear.'

She did not pick up her stick again, which was a relief, but she did take a few stumbling steps backwards away from us. 'Who are you?' she said.

'My name is Mrs Gilver and this is Mr Osborne,' I said. 'Let's just pop it on, shall we?'

'Who sent you? Who are you working for?'

'It goes over your head without any trouble,' I said. 'Mr Hogg asked us to come.'

'Mr Hogg?' She straightened further and took half a shuffling step towards us.

'Yes,' I said. 'We had luncheon with him and with two ladies who are terribly worried about you.' But she was retreating again. And, as she moved, she bent over until she was in the crab-like semi-crouch we had seen before.

'No!' she said pointing at the shift. 'Snake house!'

'What?'

'Serpents will coil around me under cover,' she said. 'I must keep the light on my skin to drive them away.'

I turned to Alec with a look I hoped he could decipher. I meant it to say: *Right then, friend. You said she's not mad. You think up what to try next.* Unfortunately Alec either did not understand or – what is more likely – found it convenient to pretend as much.

'You're right, Dandy,' he said, in any case. 'I'll melt away a few minutes and let you deal with Miss Kemp. Halloo when you need me.'

With that, he turned smartly on his heel, spraying shingle out around him, and fairly trotted up the beach into the gorse.

'Snakes, Miss Kemp?' I said, once he had gone.

She stared back at me blankly.

'There are no snakes in Scotland,' I told her.

'Coiling around me, on my skin.'

I did wonder then whether there might be a grass snake or two here on the island where foxes and badgers couldn't get at them. I supposed it was not too ludicrous to think if there were a nest of harmless grass snakes one of them might well snuggle up to an unexpected warm body suddenly come to live among them.

'I think – I really do,' I said, 'that a nice long shift, like this one here, tucked into your waistband and tied at the neck and cuffs, would rather be a guard against snakes than an invitation to them.' I held it out to her and smiled.

She stood and looked defiantly back at me for another moment or two. The breeze had picked up and she was magnificent, if scandalous, standing there with her long skirts against her legs in front and billowing out behind, and her tangle of hair now lifting and streaming free. Her arms were corded and brown to the elbow. Her neck, shoulders and stomach were, naturally, snowy white, but they also showed the outlines, under the skin, of as fine a collection of muscles as ever graced an anatomist's model or indeed a bantamweight boxer.

Because I was looking so attentively at her I saw the change. Suddenly, she appeared to slump, a puppet with her strings cut, and instead of the look of defiance on her face – chin up and eyes flashing – she frowned and her mouth dropped open.

'What am I saying?' Her voice was taut with anguish. 'Snakes? What am I thinking?'

I held the shift out further and she took it from me and shrugged into it, letting it fall down over the top of her skirt like a pinafore.

'There,' I said. 'That's better. And – I don't mean to interfere – but do you have a hairbrush? I never had a daughter but I had a sister and I can remember how to make a plait. Shall we tidy you up a bit?'

'Who are you?' she said. 'You're not from *our* church.'

'I'm not from any church.' I meant it to reassure her.

'But then who *are* you?' she said. She was beginning to tremble again and she was scuttling backwards too. 'I can't go back. I'm safe here.'

I didn't approach her any more closely, thinking it best to treat her as I would a nervous colt. I simply stood my ground and kept smiling. After a minute or two, like that colt – poised between fear and curiosity – she spoke up again.

'What do you want?'

'I'd like to ask you some questions. To take the answers back to Mr Hogg and reassure him.'

'I'm eating,' she said. 'There are raspberries and there's sorrel and dandelion leaves.'

'And potatoes,' I said, wondering if the undergraduates would be able to tell what predator was scuppering their 'trials' if Vesper crept forth in the night in search of harvest.

She frowned at me. 'And eggs,' she said. 'And fish.'

'Can you catch fish?' I said. 'Golly, clever you. I've been taught to cast more times than I can remember. Every summer for years on end and all I ever caught was a clump of seaweed. And once, the branch of a tree behind me.'

'I guddle,' she said. 'I can guddle a fine fish.'

We had begun walking up the beach, companionably side by side, towards where Alec was waiting. He fell into step with us as we left the shingle behind and began on a path of packed dirt that led uphill in a north-easterly direction. It seemed that Miss Kemp was taking us to her home; this Duck House we had heard of.

'Well, I'm sure Mr Hogg will be very happy to hear it,' I said. 'But can we bring you some tea perhaps? Some milk and bread. Or perhaps not bread if you don't have a good larder to keep it in, but oatcakes perhaps?'

'I have tea,' she said. 'I'm fine for tea and I drink it black.'

'Excellent,' I said, although shuddering. 'And so, Miss Kemp, can I take some answers too? To soothe the good Mr Hogg's worried mind?'

She was not walking with such a sure tread now, or so it seemed. But Alec was in front of her and I was behind her and the gorse on either side was tremendously sturdy, as is the way of gorse. It was hard to see how she could bolt even if she wanted to.

'The thing is,' I went on, 'no one seems to understand why you left your cottage and came to live here instead.'

Vesper mumbled something unintelligible. Alec craned round trying to make out her words and I sped up until I was practically on her heels.

'What's that?' I said.

'He's dead and I am better away from people. You should go too. Before I do something to harm you.'

It did not sound like a threat. Her sorrow at the prospect was clear.

'I'm glad to hear you say it so plainly,' I said. 'Because that means I can speak just as plainly back. Peter Haslett drowned because he took the coble out. Now, you might think you are to blame because, had you been there at the time, he could not have done so. But he was a grown man if not the wisest one, and he should have known better. Would have known better if he had not been drinking.'

Miss Kemp said nothing.

'But if you were here – and we are led to believe you were – then you did not kill him.'

'I wasn't here,' she said. 'I was up the river. Snakes upon me.' I did not know if her reference to snakes was some kind of epithet I had never heard before, or perhaps a return of the notion that had so recently been troubling her and disrupting her wardrobe, or even – unlikely as it seemed – a sincere recounting of the events of that fateful day.

'Snakes upon you?' I said. Alec stopped walking and turned round to face her. He had heard a note in her voice that I had missed. But now I saw, with dismay, that she was shaking and her eyes were rolling in their sockets. She was clawing at the shift too. I did not give much for its chances of surviving the day.

'Ate his head!' she said, rapping the words out through clenched teeth.

Alec caught my eye over her shoulder.

52

'What are you saying, dear?' I asked calmly.

'Ate his head.' She spoke with greater deliberation but still through tightly closed jaws so that the words hissed and whistled.

'You didn't . . .' I could not bring myself to repeat the dreadful words '. . . harm young Mr Haslett's head,' I said. 'His body – his whole body – was taken home to his family and buried there. Now, what makes you say such a thing?'

'Snakes upon all of us,' Vesper said. 'She ate him and I ate him. Ate his head. I ate his head. The snakes and me. I ate his head. I did. I did. Run away now. In the name of Mercury. You need to get away from me!'

I was rooted to the spot on that little packed-dirt path but perhaps Alec was shifting his weight, ready to move. Whether he was or not, when Vesper suddenly flew at him and shoved him aside he fell heavily into the gorse and she was gone with a last whisk of her skirts before either of us could stop her. She stripped off the cotton shift as she went and it fluttered to the ground.

6

'Ouch,' Alec said, as I hauled him out of the gorse bush. He rubbed his rear with both hands and winced.

'She's a strong girl,' I offered, hoping to soothe his bruised feelings. 'And I know you are far too fair-minded to condemn her for a shove, but after speaking to her again, Alec, surely you're ready to agree that the poor thing is out of her wits.'

'I don't know, Dandy. Even if she is, I'd like to know what drove her there. And who. But I'm still not sure. I think she's frightened and she's terribly upset but . . .'

'Well, if a girl claiming to have bitten off someone's head, thinking there are snakes crawling over her and rushing about shoving people into gorse bushes doesn't convince you, I don't know what ever will,' I said. 'I say she's off her rocker and needs a doctor as a matter of some urgency.'

'Shall we follow her?' Alec said. 'See that she's all right?' At my look, he gave in. 'You're right. Let's leave it for tonight. I want to get some dinner while the pub is serving. I shudder to think what Miss Speir's cook is planning to lay on for us if that tea's anything to go by.'

'Isn't that rather rude?' I said. 'We are her guests.'

But Alec was not listening. 'When you and she walked up the beach she seemed to have calmed down. And she'd put her shirt on.'

'Yes,' I said, as we retraced our steps towards the boat. 'It happened quite suddenly. She . . . woke up, is the only way I can describe it. She suddenly came to her senses and said "What am I talking about?" as though she'd awoken from a spell.'

'And what *was* she talking about?' Alec said. 'Oop!' He had seen what the tide had done since we dragged the boat onto dry land and he broke into an ungainly run, slipping and sliding down to where it was beginning to float.

'Snakes,' I said, catching him up. 'The reason she was dishabille, if you please, was that a shirt is an invitation to snakes to coil around her body. Truly, Alec, she is out of her mind.'

'I'd have thought all those long heavy skirts are more of a draw to a self-respecting snake,' Alec said. He had stepped into the boat and now he handed me in after him. '*Are* there snakes?'

'Let's ask at the pub,' I said. 'Then if Miss Speir cuts up rough about our missing dinner we can say we were working and the eating was incidental.'

With that, Alec pulled at the starter rope again and the outboard engine roared into throaty life. He let it drop and I averted my eyes from the way it lay coiled on the bottom boards, the vibration of the motor making it tremble so that it seemed alive.

I did not want to alarm Alec on the very serious subject of his dinner but I remembered all those newspapermen, or whoever they were, who had been ensconced at the Turning Tide at luncheon time and were the reason we had been thrown onto Miss Speir's dubious hospitality. However, when we rose up the stone steps to the quayside, having moored our craft, and sauntered over, it was to find the lounge bar empty but for a courting couple, sitting close together on a banquette under the window and gazing into one another's eyes. The dining room, which could be glimpsed through an open door, was even emptier than that; its tables were set and its fire lit but not a soul could be seen there.

'I'll nip through to the public,' Alec said. 'See if there's anyone there who'd welcome company.'

'You do that,' I said and then I followed him. If Alec thought

I was going to sit all alone averting my eyes from the simpering lovebirds while he detected, he could think again. Besides, the public bar of the Turning Tide was no den of iniquity. To be sure, it had no upholstered seats nor rugs on the floor, and the air was redolent with pipe tobacco and the sweet stench of beer but the few working men in caps and boots were such as I would not hesitate to pass the time of day with if I met any of them on the high road.

My entrance into their sanctum caused a little stir. The barman stopped polishing glass tankards and waved his cloth at me as though trying to stop me, like a train. 'We've got a lounge bar, Miss,' he said. 'And a parlour, Madam,' he added as I came out of the shadow of the doorway and he got a better look.

'Oh don't mind me,' I said. 'I'll quite happily perch on a stool as long as you have a bottle of brandy.' At the barman's look of surprise, I added: 'I've had a bit of a shock, you see. Well, a fright.'

'Oh?' said the barman. 'I'm sorry to hear that, madam. What befell you?'

He was a comfortable sort of fellow, expansive around the middle and florid above the collar, and his expression spoke of just the sort of hospitable nature needed to spend hours each day serving food and drink, but there was also just a hint of sharpness in his eye; the sharpness a good barman needs to keep order on a Saturday night, when the talk turns to politics and horseflesh. He was no fool.

'I daresay you were right, Alec,' I said. Alec gave a helpful grunt. He did not know what tale I was spinning but he knew well enough not to wreck it. 'I was sure I'd seen a snake. And I am sadly averse to snakes. Greatly averse to them, actually. From my years in India.' I had never been in India in my life but he was not to know that.

'I'm with you there, madam,' the barman said. 'I can't abide the things. Not even in a glass case at the zoological

56

garden. And so you can trust me when I say there's no snakes here. I've lived here my whole life and never seen so much as a slow worm in the grasses. Isn't that right, gents?'

The few men looked up from their pint pots and all nodded. 'Nearest snake I ever seen was up Skye one summer, visiting my in-laws,' one put in. 'A right pretty wee adder. We tried to catch her in a jar and bring her home, but she was too quick for us. Never seen another. Newts now? Newts, we've got. Was it maybe a newt, madam? Where was it?'

'In the water,' Alec said. I had been going to say it was under a gorse bush but he had the right idea. It moved the conversation nearer to where we wanted it, two birds and one stone. 'We borrowed a boat to go over to the island and my friend thought she saw a snake as we were tying up again.'

'Bicycle tyre, probably,' said another of the men. 'There's more and more rubbish in the river every year. Changed days from when I was a laddie.'

One of his companions snorted. 'When you were a laddie that river was chockful of who knows what from they four mills,' he said. 'Paper pulp and grease and even sawdust, floating three inches thick on the top. You're looking back through rose-tinted spectacles, Sandy my lad.'

Sandy laughed, admitting the point, and in the general bonhomie I chipped in that I probably *had* seen a bicycle tyre or a piece of old rope gone dark with river weed.

'And it's not as if you had a close look,' Alec said. He turned to the gathered men. 'I forbade her leaning over and peering, after . . . Well, forgive me. Raking things up. But we did see it in the papers.'

He was awfully good at this, I thought. Such a delicate approach to the painful subject.

'I had no intention of leaning over and peering,' I said. Out of the corner of my eye, I thought I saw something in the shadows towards the back of the bar. A slight movement,

57

it seemed. 'A glimpse was enough. And anyway, I'm a very strong swimmer.'

'Unlike young Mr Haslett,' the barman said. 'That was a terrible thing for Cramond, right enough. Young man like that, poised on the brink of life.'

I tried not to look startled at the sudden poetical turn he had taken.

'He wasn't a swimmer, then?' Alec said. 'That makes some sense of the tragedy, I suppose.'

'And I can hardly say anything, me that's been a potman all my days, but he'd had a fair few glasses of something or other.' The barman had taken up his polishing cloth again and he gave the latest glass a rueful look before he reached up to replace it on the gantry.

'He really did drown, I suppose?' I said. 'It seemed unbelievable.' And now, from the same spot where I thought I had seen a movement, I definitely heard a sound. I turned towards it. What had appeared, out of the corner of my eye, to be a shadowy corner was revealed to be a dark doorway leading through to the lounge and from it Miss Lumley materialised, with rather a fixed look upon her face.

'Unbelievable?' she said. 'What are you suggesting?'

'Merely that all the young men I know now and all the young men I knew when I was a girl myself swam like fish, drunk and sober. They were always pushing one another into lakes and rivers. I *had* wondered if young Mr Haslett suffered from a weak heart or something. The shock of the cold water, you know? But if he couldn't swim, that explains it.'

Miss Lumley gave me a smile that barely fell within the meaning of the act. 'It was all investigated and reported at the time,' she said. 'There's nothing to be discovered by asking around.'

Unlike Alec, she was absolutely hopeless at this. In her attempts to throw us off the track she had not only made me that much more sure that there *was* something fishy about

Peter Haslett's death but also done it so clumsily that her barman and her four regulars were all now frowning and puzzled.

'Forgive me, Miss Lumley,' I said. 'You must have had your fill of questions from all those newspapermen at luncheon time.'

'Newspapermen?' said one of the worthies. 'Here at Cramond?'

'What?' said the barman.

'We saw them,' Alec said.

'Yes,' said Miss Lumley. 'You hadn't started your shift, Tom.'

'Newspapermen?' the barman said.

'Yes, what did I just tell you?' Miss Lumley snapped and with that she turned and left. In fact, she fled.

We were not long after her. We could not hope to tell Miss Speir that we had been caught up with our investigations now; not when Miss Lumley had seen us in an almost empty pub with nothing much to ask and no answers forthcoming. We took ourselves off to the indifferent delights of dinner at Cramond House.

And on the way up the hill and the along the drive we turned it over and over.

'Was she warning us off?' I asked. 'Silly woman. Nothing is more likely to make us redouble our efforts.'

'I don't know what she was doing,' Alec said, 'but she made a mess of it.'

'She was lurking in the background for ages before she showed herself,' I said. 'It was definitely us discussing Peter Haslett's death that brought her out into the light to try to steer the talk away again.'

'It's very puzzling,' Alec said. 'Vesper says she killed him but everyone agrees he drowned.'

'And talk of his death rattles one of the people who knows that Vesper claims to have killed him. *Very* puzzling.'

'Actually,' Alec said. 'She didn't claim to have killed him. She claimed to have harmed him.'

'If one harms a man until he is dead, one has killed him.'

Alec said nothing.

'So why quibble? What are you getting at?'

'Something rather horrid,' Alec said. 'If he drowned, would he float out to sea? Would he wash up at Cramond Island? Perhaps what Vesper is saying and what everyone else is saying are both true. He drowned and then . . .'

I waited for him to go on and when he did not I turned my attention to what it was he could not bring himself to say. 'No!' The word burst out of me as the thought formed in my mind.

'Well, let's check, shall we?' Alec said. 'How could we find out where they found the corpse and whether it was intact when they did so?'

'Alec, this is terrible!' I said. 'This is monstrous!'

'And it certainly would explain why everyone's being so strange and secretive and why the thought of reporters is such anathema,' Alec said. 'It wouldn't do much for the tourist trade if Cramond Island was known to have a resident cannibal.'

'How can you be so cold?' I said.

'Cold?' He was stung.

'Well, chatty then. Diverted by it all.' I took off away from him along the drive, at top speed.

'I'm sorry,' he called after me, trotting to catch up. 'Forgive me. I forgot you knew him. As a child. And know his parents. And . . . all that.'

'All what?' I threw over my shoulder. In truth, I knew: he meant maternal feelings about my own two. I usually deny any such mushiness but could hardly argue the point given that I had stormed off in umbrage.

'It's probably nonsense,' he called, although not so loud since he had almost caught me. 'I was just shuffling the available facts and, at least this way round, they fit.'

As a new thought struck me, I stopped.

'What?' said Alec, beside me again.

'This way round!' I said. 'Just like the coble! That's why the boat tied up at the wrong side was bothering me. The timing's back to front. The Rev Hogg's letter to us – the third one – said that she had gone off to live on the island in a state of collapse following the death of a young man she wrongly thinks she killed.'

'Right so far,' Alec said.

'But her alibi for the time he died is that she was on the island with the young men from the university who're using it to grow their superior potatoes.'

'Ohhhh,' said Alec. 'Yes, I see. That's all twisted up, isn't it? When did she go and why? She can't have missed the thing that caused her to run away there by being there already, can she?'

'Good,' I said. 'Someone's lying, Alec. And when someone's lying, there's a truth to be uncovered. We're on the scent at last.'

'But ring Hugh anyway,' said Alec. 'Ask him if he'd be willing to pay a visit of condolence to Newburgh. Even if it was kept out the papers, Haslett's family would know if his body was—'

'Don't say it again. Have pity.'

'I didn't say it the first time,' Alec reminded me. 'I'm not an absolute brute. And if you're talking about pity, then think of Hugh. He's going to have to find a way to ask that question of the parents. Poor old thing. This might be the time he refuses to help you, Dandy. I'm not sure I could face the commission.'

'Well, I certainly can't ask Teddy to go,' I said. 'Much less send Grant to the servants' hall on a visit. She's far too brusque. Pallister could do it.' My butler, I truly believed, could do most things. 'But he wouldn't. Perhaps we should go ourselves. A day trip up and back?'

We did not, however, need to draft anyone for the nasty task, much less take it on ourselves. One telephone call to Hugh was enough; he had the information we sought already.

'And what have you been up to?' I asked, after assuring him that our journey down was uneventful and helping him place Miss Speir in his address book. Of course he knew her. He knows everyone with a place of any size from Gretna to the Hebrides; Scotland is so tiny and the land so poor that the estates are simply enormous. It makes going for dinner with so-called neighbours a terrific expedition.

'I?' he said. 'I've been down at the Grange.' He sounded doleful and also as though he need offer no further explanation. I knew from long years of wifely duty that if I asked him to jog my memory he would take it as an affront. I applied my mind to the puzzle, letting my eyes drift over the guddle of papers and other detritus on Miss Speir's desk. (She, with remarkable lack of concern for anyone else who might pass a day or night in her house, had put the only telephone in her private sitting room and had frowned with great displeasure when I asked to use it.)

'Dandy?' said Hugh after a couple of moments. 'Are you still there?' He jiggled the cradle at his end, deafening me with the resulting series of pops and clicks. Truth to tell, I had become distracted by Miss Speir's belongings. She had a remarkable number of large coloured art books sitting in a pile on her writing desk and one of them lay open at a lurid illustration, reproduced from the side of some urn or other, of Grecian – at a guess; they might have been Roman – boys engaged in a wrestling match. Miss Speir became instantly more nuanced in my estimation. What is more, the sight helped with Hugh too. For the strapping young men reminded me of Peter Haslett and I remembered that his family place was called Grange of Something as so many places are and so I concluded that Hugh had been to see

Angus and Simone on just the visit of condolence to which Alec thought I should be urging him.

'Good of you,' I said. 'How are they both?'

'Regretting the private family funeral, I think,' Hugh said. 'It was the shock. At the time. The sudden need for a decision. They dodged the issue and now the chance is gone. The boy is in his grave.'

Once again, I was without a single clue as to what Hugh might be talking about but this time there was no handy painting of an urn to help me. 'Issue?' I said. 'Decision?'

'Local kirk or Simone's lot,' Hugh said. 'And the boy himself was an atheist, Angus told me today.'

'Ah,' I said. Simone Haslett was French and therefore Catholic and, while she had caused no ructions about her wedding, the children's christenings, their schools, or the older ones' weddings in turn, it seemed that she had not found herself equal to sending her son into the hereafter without thoughts of home intruding and taking over. 'Well, they must be feeling all sorts of dreadful things.'

'Remorse, chiefly,' said Hugh. 'They had been kicking up rough about some female apparently and it's all too easy to imagine that he wouldn't have been in and out of Edinburgh so much if he could have brought her home.'

'And couldn't he bring her home?' I said. 'Why not?'

'Unsuitable,' said Hugh. 'Makes Mallory look—' He managed to stop himself, thankfully. 'Not that they provided any details.'

'That's not what I'd be beating my breast about, if it were me,' I said. 'There are greater puzzles.'

'Such as?'

'Such as how they managed to bring up a goose of a son who falls out of a boat and promptly dies.'

'Harsh words, Dandy,' Hugh said.

'And I would cut out my tongue before I said them to the Hasletts, but don't tell me the thought didn't occur to you?'

'Of course it didn't,' Hugh said. I reached out and flipped shut the great volume of ancient art from which those wrestling boys were mocking poor Peter.

'Oh come off it,' I said. It was a nasty, slangy expression that Teddy had brought into the family, along with many others, but it had no equal for the mixture of emotions I was feeling just then. 'Don't tell me you never wondered why he couldn't swim, Hugh. Was that Simone too? Not to mention why, since he couldn't swim, he took a boat out on his own—'

'Couldn't swim?' said Hugh. 'Of course he could swim. What are you talking about? It's one thing being able to swim in the ordinary way and quite another being able to swim oneself out of a forceful sucking current pulling one down.'

'What?' I said. 'Hugh, that's nonsense. The mouth of the Almond has no tremendous sucking current. It's a tame little river, hardly bigger than a burn, and even the Forth isn't exactly white water. Why, Alec and I took a motorboat over to the island and back this afternoon. I'm very glad we didn't capsize but if we had neither of us would have drowned.'

There was a silence on the other end of the line then and it was my turn to blow into the mouthpiece and rattle the hook up and down.

'Hugh?'

'Aren't you supposed to be there solving the mystery?' he said.

'Yes.'

'And you've been there more than half a day?'

'Yes.'

'But you still think Peter Haslett drowned?'

'Oh God,' I said.

'He didn't,' Hugh told me, as if it needed to be made any clearer. 'He had the boat out. The coble. And he got into difficulty with the pole. That much is true. And he fell in. That's true too. But he wasn't at the mouth of the river, Dandy. Much less out on the open water of the Forth. He

64

was headed upstream. He was passing one of the mills and so, when he fell in he was pulled . . . Well, not to put too fine a point on it, he was pulled into the wheel. Head first.'

'Head first,' I repeated, feeling a sudden chill.

'They identified him from his watch chain and his signet ring,' Hugh said. 'Don't make me say any more, Dandy. Angus told me this afternoon and I've been trying to stop picturing it ever since. Poor Simone.'

'Poor Simone indeed,' I said. 'Hugh, I'm going to make you say just a little more, I'm afraid. It's either you or his parents.'

Hugh cleared his throat. I could picture his shoulders straightening.

'So his head was hurt, was it?' I said. 'Badly hurt? I'm not being ghoulish. It's just that everyone here is saying he drowned. Except one person and she is saying something rather unpleasant.'

'Well, she's being very unkind,' Hugh said. 'There's no point in spreading upset, is there? His head was more than badly hurt, if we really must be as blunt as all that. It was crushed. Pulverised. The force of the water and the close fit of the wheel meant that his head was absolutely devoured, Dandy.'

7

Alec and I were out in the grounds, walking in the gloaming, enjoying a cigarette in my case and a pipe in his, both of which were strictly forbidden inside the house. We had left the gravel of the sweep and the fine lawns closest to it and were approaching the ancient tower. The grass here was rough and tussocky but there was a flattened path around the base of the thing and we fell into a rhythm, side by side, and began to speak again.

'She won't hear us from here, will she?' Alec said, looking back over at the house, where the windows were open onto the warm evening.

'Not a chance,' I assured him. I had already delivered the news in a whisper behind my bedroom door but the sound of the maid arriving with hot water had sent Alec to hide behind my curtains like something from a French farce. The woman, when she had edged in with her kettles, had given me an odd look, as though she had heard voices on her approach or could see that the curtain was not hanging quite true.

'So,' Alec went on. He spoke more freely as we got around the corner of the tower and its bulk separated us from all possibility of Miss Speir's prying eyes and pricked ears. 'At least we don't need to wonder about Vesper in quite such a horrid way. She might have been there and she might have some hallucinations or . . . do I mean hallucinations?'

'Delusions, I think. And she's to be pitied. If she knows for a fact, from the evidence of her own eyes, that Peter

Haslett's death was gruesome and yet everyone else is saying he drowned, she must – in her fragile state – have started to wonder. Don't you think?'

'I do. The question is: who knows the truth and who decided to hide the truth and for what purpose? It might be that everyone is covering up the nastiness – to stop the local children from having nightmares, for instance – and only Vesper is refusing to toe the line.'

'Or it might be that no one knows the truth except whoever found him and the police and Vesper is telling the truth because she was, despite all claims to the contrary, there to see it. But I don't think that's the question. Not *the* question.'

'What's *the* question?' Alec said. We were round the tower now and back to facing the lit windows of the house.

I dropped my voice. 'Why was he taking the coble upstream? Where was he going? Is there anywhere to moor a boat up there? I'd have thought one could only ground it and make a mess of its hull.'

'He was drunk, remember,' Alec said.

'Yes, but was he?' I countered. 'Do we know that? Or is that another part of the story that we must ignore, now the facts are to hand?'

'Hm,' Alec said. 'Right then. We need to speak to these lads: what are their names? The two undergrads who can give Vesper her alibi. And we need to speak to whichever of these four millers it was whose mill killed Peter Haslett. Find out who's managed to hush it up and why they wanted to.'

'There's no foul play around the death, though,' I said. 'You're not suggesting that there is, are you?'

'Aren't I?'

'If there was even a whiff of it, Angus Haslett would be here, banging on doors and demanding justice. He is absolutely devastated, Hugh told me. And as for his wife! They wouldn't take it lying down. We are here to deal with whatever's bothering Vesper Kemp, Alec. Not to get consumed by the details of her last straw. It started long before Haslett's death and we must start there too. What was that?'

I had heard a scuffling noise behind me and wheeled round to peer into the dark. The implacable bulk of the tower was right there at my back and I found myself staring into a hole in the stone. The glass in the tower's ground floor windows was long gone, if it had ever existed at all.

'Is there someone inside?' I hissed to Alec.

'I think,' he said, 'it's an animal in the woods behind. I heard it too.' Together we crept back round the corner and sped along the side of the tower. Right enough, there was a rushing sound and a few cracks as whatever it was plunged off into the bracken at the edge of the woodland.

'You think we would really have heard a fox moving on the other side of the tower?' I said.

'Perhaps it was inside and popped back out of a hole when it heard us coming.'

I nodded. 'I think that's more like it. That noise I heard sounded close. Let's ask Miss Speir if she puts traps down.'

'It was too big to trap, whatever it was,' Alec said. 'A dog or a deer, I reckon.'

'*Are* there deer?' I said. 'One doesn't think of it somehow, so close to town.'

'A dog then. Let's go in, Dandy. It's getting chilly.'

I nodded but did not move. I was still staring up at the looming hulk of the tower. It seemed to bend towards me, making me dizzy. The sky behind it was a bruised purple with just one or two faint stars beginning to show themselves. 'This whole thing puzzles me,' I said. 'I don't feel as if I've got a firm grip on any of it yet.'

Alec gave an elaborate sigh and took my arm. 'Let's go for another trudge round then,' he said. 'It's not warm enough to stand still while we're pondering. Where's your grip on things particularly shaky?'

'Mr Hogg is our client,' I said. 'But the two ladies are

certainly concerned with Vesper. Why? Who owns the island? And who owns her cottage? Who is the girl's employer? Whoever it is, why doesn't he just sack her and put her out? I know it's brutal and I'm not recommending it, but it doesn't make sense that a girl so clearly incapable of carrying out her job is managing to scupper all the plans to turn Cramond Island into Valhalla.'

'True,' Alec said.

'And besides, it makes no sense that the local publican is so dearly concerned with a few holiday cottages cut off from her pub by a coastal causeway. Why does she care? Why does Miss Speir care if it comes to that? And then there's this place.' I laid my hands against the stones of the tower.

'What about it?'

'If Miss Speir needs money, or cares deeply about Cramond, or both, and has got this eyesore sitting in her garden, why is she merely selling off the stone?'

'Oh, I don't know,' Alec said. 'There are so many new houses going up in Edinburgh these days, nasty little things to be sure, but they'd be improved no end with a few medi-aeval stones here and there. And this is a bit close to her own house for her to be fixing the roof and getting tenants in.'

I shook my head. 'What about these mythic tourists?' I said. 'Americans, even. If there was a castle in the offing.'

'It would take a large investment to get a crumbling tower fit for Americans,' Alec said. 'But speaking of the tourists: I find it odd that an island earmarked for rich guests to lark about on has been turned over to potato trials. If we're airing puzzles.'

'We certainly need to speak to these lads who're vouching for Vesper.'

'Apart from anything else, *they* can confirm whether or not Peter Haslett was drunk.'

'He must have been,' I said. 'Why would anyone sober try

69

to take a boat up a shallow river where reason must have told him it wouldn't go?' I silently thanked providence that Teddy's punting days were over and that his tastes ran to moorland over lochs at home.

'Let's sleep on all of it,' Alec said. 'Best foot forward in the morning.'

I had not brought my darling Bunty with me on this case, but such is the force of habit that I found myself out in the morning sunshine anyway, feeling the need of a nice long tramp before settling to the tasks of the day. Anyway, my early tea and toast had been so disappointing that the possibility of missing breakfast did not trouble me. So I set off down the hill to the shore and stood, as the keen wind made my eyes water and mussed my hair, looking over to the island. The tide was in and the causeway covered and the thought of Vesper still marooned there, long hours after we had seen her, troubled me. I scrutinised every bit of the island I could see in case she was abroad, but nothing moved except the wheeling seagulls and waving grasses. The beaches where she might be fishing were out of sight, as was the 'Duck House' where she laid her head. After a few moments, I turned away and faced the village instead.

The Turning Tide was still battened, hours before opening time, but further along the shore cottage doors were thrown wide and I could just see the business end of a broom whisking out onto the pavement, as some industrious housewife set about her chores. I sauntered towards her and sang out a friendly good morning as I passed her doorway.

'Mind out for the dust,' she said. 'I didnae see you there.'

'No harm done,' I said. 'Just taking my morning constitutional. I had hoped to go over and walk the path on the Rosebery land but someone said yesterday your ferry's not running.'

She paused in the battering of her skirting boards and

came to lean on the broom handle and look over at the coble tied up at the foot of a set of steps on the opposite bank. She said nothing.

'I suppose it's good news in a way,' I said. 'That no local man is looking for work and can be prevailed upon. Why, only a few years ago there would have been a stampede for the job of ferryman, especially if such a sweet cottage came with it.'

'It's a piece of nonsense,' the woman said, twirling her broom again and using the handle end to discourage a couple of bantam hens from picking their way over her threshold. She was about thirty, I guessed, but spoke stoutly for all her youth. She was not cowed by any aspect of my appearance or demeanour, certainly. 'There's five good men a stone's throw away would leap at it. They'd do it by the day till Vesper's on her feet again, or they'd move into that cottage and do it till they were ready for their pensions. A piece of absolute blessed nonsense.'

'I agree,' I said, frowning deeply as if all of this was news. 'Who's in charge?'

'No one!' she said. 'Like I'm telling you.' One of the hens made another rush at the doorway and she darted to the side to stop its progress with the side of her foot as though she were a goalkeeper in a game of soccer football. When she had run it back out onto the pavement again she heaved a sigh. 'It's Vesper's own boat that her daddy left her, but boats are easy come by if you know who to ask. I'm guessing the Earl's happy to have a quiet life with no one dropping picnickers off at his back door. It'll suit him down to the ground. It would suit me too. Who wants a lot of apple cores and sandwich packets blowing around their back green if they don't have to?'

Lord Rosebery owned too many acres for a few apple cores to make a real difference to his comfort but, displeased as I had been at the idea of Mallory's mother-and-baby picnic, I had no room to talk.

'Well, I think it's a shame,' I said. 'Not that I can't have a lovely walk up this side of the river. You live in a pretty spot, my dear. But someone mentioned an accident, I think? An accident that wouldn't have happened if Miss Kemp had been at her post?'

'No,' the young woman said stoutly. 'Who's been saying that?' She came out and looked upriver towards, I assumed, the scene of Peter Haslett's death. Both bantams took their chance to rush into the doorway and speed along the corridor to the back where delicious things might be left unattended in the kitchen. 'He might have gone swimming just there anyway, even if Vesper had been around to take him over to the shell beds. Who's to say?'

'Gone swimming?' I said. 'You think he jumped in deliberately, for fun? I had heard he *fell* in.'

'He couldn't have,' the woman said. 'Not in the summer. The path's a good ten feet from the edge. The only time I can mind someone fell into the river off the path at that bit was back when I was a wee girl and we made a slide on the ice. Not thinking, you know? And *he* got out again quick enough, because it was that cold the mill wasn't ru—' She stopped and made a chewing motion with her lips as though trying to swallow the words she had let slip.

The half-spoken word sank into me and left me reeling. This woman not only knew about the injury caused to Peter by the mill wheel, but she knew it was a secret. 'I must have picked up the story wrong,' I said as lightly as I could manage.

'Or I did,' she said. It was vanishingly unlikely. The trouble was, she knew the story and she knew the truth and she had just mixed them up. 'Where are those blessed chickens?' she said and cocked her head. We could both hear them squawking deep in the cottage somewhere, no doubt fighting over some morsel neither of them had a claim to. Bantams are such belligerent little things. The woman gave me one last determined look and went inside, banging the door to shut me out no matter that she'd have to open it again to shoo away the hens.

'Ten feet from the edge,' I repeated to myself as I made my way upriver away from the cottages. There was a workshop of some kind at the end of the row, rather scruffy in the way of such places. As I passed it I tried to determine what its business was. There were oilcans and coils of rope stored on hooks and there were piles of sacking, too high to be incidental, whose purpose I could not fathom. It was probably something to do with boats, I decided, and walked on. Next, as the path veered away from the edge, much further than ten feet, the resulting space was filled with what looked like a bowling club, complete with flat lawn, pretty flower borders all around it, a decorative fence to prevent stumbles onto the precious green, and a clubhouse. After that the trees closed overhead and I was in a green arcade, silent and serene, smelling of moss and mushrooms.

A few yards on, the silence was broken by the sound of rushing water and I emerged from the trees in the lee of a large stone building, built unhelpfully right over the path and backed by even larger brick sheds further from the water's edge. The first of the four mills, I surmised. I stood well back, watching the wheel turn. It was as tall as a cottage roof, as tall as a double decker omnibus, and it was perhaps only the recent tales I had been hearing but it looked a wicked, monstrous kind of thing, dark wood stained even darker with creosote and then soaked to a greenish black with weed and water. It creaked and rumbled as it turned, its voice unnervingly human, although grown by some magic until it sounded like a giant groaning and cursing and, of course, relentlessly churning the endless brown water.

There was a rudimentary jetty built out into the tidal deep in the middle of the river, I noticed, and I was glad to see it for it explained Peter Haslett's fateful last journey.

If he knew a boat could be tied here then his expedition upriver was less troubling. I made my way past it, past a rather grand building with a clock set in its gable end and past a row of workers' cottages that looked to have seen much better days and appeared empty. I was looking, increasingly in vain, for the . . . I scarcely knew what to call it . . . the engine room, or factory floor or workshop or whatever it was where something was happening in this place. It had to exist, I told myself, because the water wheel was turning and all of that rushing energy would not be wasted. This place might no longer grind grain or spin wool but it was making something. I stopped. It certainly *was* making something. The jetty was not the half of it, I now saw, for here in front of me was a dock. I am no expert but it looked big enough for quite a sizeable craft. This must be Peter Haslett's destination. The only question was why.

I turned back to face the way I had come and perused the scene from this new angle. The place looked terribly down-at-heel, with weeds growing up between the cobbles of the yard and cobwebs in every window on the long, brick sheds, but there was one little patch of it that showed signs of recent use if not of life exactly. In one corner furthest from the lade and the churning wheel, there was a small cart, probably a handcart, drawn up beside a door. The cart's sides were badly in need of a fresh coat of paint and the door's paint was positively peeling in strips but it did have a shining new padlock, winking at me in the morning sun. I walked over and took a closer look. The cart was definitely not abandoned. The pole handles shone from constant accidental polishing by whoever habitually pushed it. As to whatever they pushed in it, all I could say was that it must be fragile, for it was full of hay and burlap sacking and smelled strongly of something I could not identify. I leaned in for a closer sniff.

'Great minds,' said a voice behind me, causing me to rear up and then stumble as I took a step back.

'Alec,' I said. 'What do you mean by creeping up on me like that?'

'I didn't,' Alec said. 'I hailed you three times but the noise of that wheel drowned me out. So you had the same idea as me?'

'I'm not sure I'd say it was an idea exactly,' I admitted. 'More of an urge. It beggars belief that no one knows how Peter Haslett died. I've just heard a third version from one of the cottagers down the way. She says – if you please – that he went in swimming off the riverbank, not from the boat at all. So we can add that to the official tale of drowning, the apparent truth of injury to his skull, and to Vesper's nonsense.'

'And in this third version,' Alec said, 'is he supposed to have fallen in just here?'

'I don't know that either. I simply wanted to shed some light on the thing altogether. Interviewing the millers seemed like a good start. But there's a bit of an air of the *Marie Celeste*. Apart from the wheel going round, anyway.'

'Perhaps the night shift's finished and the day shift hasn't begun,' Alec said. 'Let's press on upriver to the next one and try again on the way back.'

I agreed and we fell into step. I missed Bunty more than ever now. She would have loved the novelty of a new walk, and a new river walk at that, with countless holes to dig into in hope of voles and water rats as well as the usual mice and squirrels. On the other hand, it was restful without her barks of excitement and whines of protest whenever I called her off. As the racket of the water wheel faded behind us and the sound of the second mill wheel was still the merest tinkling whisper somewhere ahead of us, the lane was remarkably tranquil. There was a high cliff to our left side and a grassy bank to our right and the lane between appeared unused to a notable degree, given that there was a village a few hundred yards behind us and that in it there had to be courting couples and naughty schoolboys, not to mention dog owners who, unlike me, had their dogs to hand.

'It's awfully quiet, isn't it?' I said. 'Doesn't it seem peculiarly quiet to you?'

'At this moment,' Alec said. He had picked up a stick and was off at the edge of the sheer rock rise whacking at some tall thistles, for no better reason than to see their seed heads burst into puffs of white fluff. I shook my head, mother of sons that I am and familiar with the temptation a ripe thistle offers. But the very fact of them being there for Alec to vanquish only raised a further question. Where were the children of this village? Did the brambles rot unpicked in the hedgerows come August? Did the conkers lie neglected underfoot in October?

'And no wonder,' Alec went on. 'Look at this, Dandy.'

I wandered over, picking a few bits of thistledown off my tweeds as I passed through the cloud of them that was still settling. Alec was holding back a rampant head of sorrel, quite four feet high with sturdy stalks and leaves so full and juicy they squeaked against his stick. What they had been hiding was a surprising sight but unmistakable.

'Railway tracks?' I said.

'Tram perhaps,' Alec said. 'But certainly tracks of some kind.'

'Is that strange?' I said. 'Or is it just that I know nothing of mills?'

'It's a little odd,' said Alec then, as we returned to the lane and made our way upriver again, he added: 'Oh! No it's not.' He was still holding the stick and he pointed with it. Just ahead was the source of the faint noise I had taken to be another mill wheel in the distance. In fact, the river was blocked just here by a weir and the sound we had heard was the peaceful fall of water coming over its mossy edge to chuckle into the glittering shallows below it.

'Hence the tracks,' Alec said. I frowned and he explained. 'That dock back there's all very well for the first mill but this dam, while it helps the wheel go round, does nothing at all to get the whatever it is away to market.'

'Ah,' I said. 'One question answered. In fact, two questions answered, wouldn't you say? We now know that if Peter Haslett fell in off the ferry boat, he fell in at the first mill.'

'Which would have been wonderful yesterday,' Alec said. 'Before you found out that he quite possibly wasn't in the boat at all.'

'Well, we know he didn't fall in here in either case,' I said. 'It's not deep enough and the path isn't ten feet from the edge, as my cottage-dwelling informant has just told me was the case.'

'And here's the mill,' Alec said.

Perhaps I was beginning to need my breakfast, or perhaps the constant rushing sound of the water was beginning to make me giddy, but as we came upon the looming stone building, the row of neglected cottages, the crumbling brick sheds and the weedy cobbled yard, I had that sudden disquieting sense of unreality the French call déjà vu. I turned to Alec as if to reassure myself that he was there and not, as my fancy suggested, just about to come around the corner and speak to me as I bent over a handcart near a padlocked door.

Of course he was there. He grinned at me and then walked away towards the great black beast of a wheel thrashing and thrashing as if to punish the water, or even – it seemed to me in my current dizzied state – as if to haul the entire mill down the bank and out to sea.

I shivered and turned away.

8

It was a relief to get back over to the island. The tide obliged after a late breakfast, which was exactly as disappointing as I had foreseen, consisting of pale bacon, hard potato bannocks stuck together in a lump, and a dish of mushrooms introduced by Miss Speir as 'picked fresh this morning'. I let the lid of the dish fall closed again, thinking that if the same cook who had piled up bannocks without a dot of butter to keep them supple had also been in charge of selecting the mushrooms then they might be anything at all and not worth the wager. Alec took a great ladleful of them and grinned at me. If he was in bed clutching his middle before luncheon time I would grin back and relish it.

We had only a few minutes to wait at the water's edge until the causeway was uncovered completely and not even the liveliest wave obscured its shining length.

'And we've got two hours until we need to set off back again,' Alec said. 'Noon, Dandy.'

'Noon,' I said. 'I'm glad you're coming with me,' I added. 'I half expected you to leave her to me, on account of her . . . wardrobe. And I wouldn't have minded if you had bagged the boats and mills and potato scientists for yourself.'

'I'll bet,' said Alec drily. 'I admit I do hope Miss Kemp has dressed herself for society this morning but if not I shall tough it out. Doctors do it all the time, after all. And explorers. In Africa and such like.'

'I hope you're right,' I said. 'Doctors I'll give you from my own unpleasant experiences. It's excruciating but everyone pretends it's not happening. But I do hope explorers aren't beasts to the village women in Africa. And I hope these potato enthusiasts aren't beasts to Vesper.'

'She can't have been a ferrywoman all these long years without learning how to keep order among crowds of young men,' Alec said. 'When she's at her best anyway.' We were silent a moment then, enjoying the new-washed feeling of the wet sand under our feet and the pleasant prospect of blue sky, scudding cloud and wheeling gulls. 'Sorry about the unpleasant experiences. I can't say I'd happily see a lady doctor. Unless it were a toenail or a tonsil.'

'This is what makes me so angry when Hugh opines about lady doctors. As he does. It's all very well for him.'

'Indeed, indeed,' Alec said. He is terribly fond of Hugh and holds him in high esteem as a land manager. It leads him, sometimes, to forget that he is my friend and should take my part. This current failure made me cross enough to continue and give air to a theme I more often reserve for my private thoughts, the kind of private thoughts that make me wish I kept a diary.

'Not to mention politicians!' I said. 'And sovereigns. Hugh is fond of telling me I don't understand all the ins and outs of it, Alec. But as far as I can see, every time this country of ours has a queen she is absolutely magnificent and in between times we make do with a succession of barely adequate kings. I don't care if it's treasonous. Mrs Simpson is a private citizen of a foreign land. This mess cannot be laid at her door. The King is the King and should know better. Victoria *did* know better. As did Elizabeth. Meantime, that stupid little man—'

'Mr Hitler?'

'A joke and a disgrace and yet, because no one will stand up to him, a pertinent danger. And there goes our sovereign mixing cocktails and making cow eyes at a woman who'd make a perfectly fine mistress but cannot be his wife. I could box his ears. Truly.'

'I cannot disagree with you in any particular,' Alec said. 'I mean, I hadn't thought of the "queens" angle, if I'm honest, but about His Majesty and Mrs Simpson, and the mustachioed menace, of course I absolutely agree.'

I was beginning to calm down. It is well-nigh impossible to walk across a sandy causeway to an island on a warm summer's morning and stay in a bate. The sound of the ruffled water lapping at either side of the path, the fresh scent of newly uncovered mussels clinging to rocks here and there, and the cheerful sight of the island, ablaze with late gorse like a little heap of sunshine among the blue – all served to soothe me remarkably.

'Of course, if he does plight his troth to that dreadful woman,' I said, 'you see what it means.'

'It means a great many things,' said Alec.

'It means that he'll be forced to abdicate—'

'Never!'

'And so his brother will step in—'

'He couldn't! He'd never manage it.'

'And in time we shall have a queen again.'

'I hardly think so, Dandy,' Alec said. 'If such an enormity came to pass as an abdication – and you can't be serious, can you? – wouldn't they be sure to have a son as part of the general upheaval?' Then, at my look, he raised both hands in surrender.

'Yes, of course,' I said crisply. 'God forbid we submit to another like Victoria. Sixty blameless years. Heaven forfend!'

The waves and breeze and mussels and gorse were powerless against my new fit of temper. I stamped away ahead of Alec and was soon hauling myself up the shingle to the start of the path. With his tail between his legs, as I could just see from the corner of my eye, he trailed after me.

There was no sign of Vesper as we scaled the central

rise of the island and descended its far side. There were plenty of trees however. She could easily have been hidden by any of the copses we passed. In fact one planting was almost sizeable enough to be called a wood.

'Let's check her house first,' Alec said. 'Do you suppose this path leads there?'

'It makes sense,' I said. 'Is *that* it?'

In the distance ahead of us, right at the edge of the land and looking rather romantic against the sea behind it, was a tiny cottage, a lean-to really, butted up against an outcropping of rock. A door faced us and a small window looked out towards the open water. A stovepipe jutting out around a smoke-stained hole at one corner and a barrel serving as a water butt at the other corner completed the amenities. As we drew up, though, I saw that there was a pot of mint and one of parsley sitting on the doorstep and a drying rope, currently bare of washing despite the fine morning, stretched between the high gable end and a post stuck into the turf a few yards away. A fine wisp of white smoke, no more than a thread, was drifting up out of the stovepipe into the air.

I stepped close and knocked gently on the closed door.

'Vesper?' I called. 'Miss Kemp?'

There was no answer from inside the little house. Alec and I shared a look, then a nod, and I tried the handle. The door was locked. I bent down and peered into the keyhole.

'She's out,' I said.

'How do you know?'

'I can see right through to the far wall. No key in the lock.'

'Is it odd that she'd shut the place up?' said Alec.

'No,' I replied after a moment to think. 'She's so isolated over here. I'd lock up if it were me.'

'Well, she can't be far,' Alec said, casting his eyes around with his hands on his hips. 'We watched the causeway as it cleared so we know she didn't go over to the mainland. Let's search her out.'

It was such a tiny island it did not seem worth the effort to draw up plans and charts, but after a half-hour of rambling around in the sun, as it rose high into the sky and began to beat mercilessly down upon us, I was ready for a cool drink and a rest in the shade. And of Vesper we had seen not a whisker. We found the quarry one of the ladies had mentioned, flooded now, and for the first time I began to see that this might indeed make a beauty spot where moneyed Edinburgh residents could play at island life like Madame de Pompadour and her pastoral flights. A pleasant boating pond would be just the ticket for ladies and children who quailed at the thought of sailing out on the open river.

We found the rest of the cottages too, set in a row under the trees we had seen upon our arrival, but they were empty and lay open, slipped slates on their roofs and broken glass on their floors. We wandered through the rooms and called her name but there is no mistaking the sense of stillness in an empty building. Soon enough we stepped back outside again.

'They'll have to cut some trees down before these'll make a holiday camp,' Alec said. 'Dreary as they stand, aren't they?'

'Let's try over this way,' I said, heading to the south-west corner, which I was sure we had not covered. I picked my way through the remains of a cottage garden, with gnarled roses forming a thicket and a drystone wall tumbling into ruins beyond it. Then I heard something. 'Listen,' I said. 'There she is, wouldn't you say?'

But, as we passed under a stand of beech trees and back into open ground, it was not Vesper we found. Two young men, stripped to their waists and with their braces hanging down in loops, were busy with a pair of shovels, making a high mound of earth in the middle of a patch that had been cleared of grass and weeds.

For one wild moment I was convinced that they had killed and were now burying Vesper, for that mound had a distressingly familiar look about it. Then realisation and relief flooded in together. This, of course, was the potato trial. They certainly looked a lot more like scientists than farmers: their bent backs were as white as snow and one of them, the spindly one, had a curve to his spine that would have been a serious handicap behind a plough, although one assumed it was a boon over a microscope. The other one was not quite so willow-wandish; he was in fact corpulent, his flesh – white blushing to pink as he wielded the shovel with increasingly erratic strokes – wobbling most unpleasantly. I averted my eyes.

'Hallo there,' Alec said. Neither of the young men started. They were either temperamentally serene or life on the island with Vesper as a neighbour had rendered them immune to surprises.

'Hello,' said the one nearest to us, the one with a spine like a pipe cleaner. 'Oh, do forgive us. Fordyce, put your shirt on. We've got a visitor.'

The plump one went plodding over to where a few garments had been thrown against a field wall and shrugged into a rather dingy vest. It was no increase in formality but it was a distinct improvement otherwise. He tossed another vest, whiter at least, to the thin boy and, both having met their standards of decorum, it seemed, they came to meet us.

'Bill Irvine,' the thin one said. 'And that's Harry Fordyce. Beautiful day, isn't it? Have you come to see the trial or just on a stroll?'

Alec introduced us and I shook hands with both of them. The fat one, Fordyce, had a large doughy hand, pulsingly hot from his spadework, but dry at least. The thin one, Irvine, had a handshake as limp and wet as an eel. I saw Alec shudder as he gripped it.

'Neither as a matter of fact,' I said. 'We're looking for Miss Kemp. Have you seen her today?'

'Vesper?' said Mr Irvine. 'Has she been about this morning, Fordy?'

'She caught me dipping my flask into her rainwater-butt first thing,' Mr Fordyce said. 'Chased me off, as usual. It's not exactly chummy of her. We've got enough stuff to lug over here without canteens of water when she's got plenty.'

'Do you have any idea where she is now?' I said. 'She's not in the Duck House and we can't find her. We've had a good old rootle.'

'Oh, she'll turn up,' said Mr Irvine. 'She always does. She might be swimming.'

'We didn't spot her,' Alec said.

'Off the rocks at the far side of her cottage,' he explained. 'She lets herself out there and climbs down. Seems foolish if you ask me when there are a handful of beaches but I suppose it's private.'

'Swimming and patrolling her water butt,' I said. 'Am I being too hopeful in thinking that she's feeling a bit better?'

Mr Fordyce snorted. 'I should say you are. She was as bad as ever earlier. Raving about snakes and rabbits and goodness knows what. Poor thing,' he added after rather too long a pause.

I tutted and shook my head. 'Terribly upsetting for you to have her here at all,' I said. 'And we believe, that is we heard in the village, that she's been saying some pretty wild things about your friend.'

'Peter?' said Mr Irvine. 'I thought the village was managing to keep that quiet. It's nonsense, you know. Just silliness.'

'You're absolutely sure of that?' I said.

Mr Fordyce snorted again. 'Vesper was here as we saw Peter off the island. Well, that is to say we watched him go and hallooed him until he was out of earshot, telling him not to be such a goose and to come back. We had a good fire going that night, didn't we Irvine? And a decent catch to fry too. But Peter was in a temper and insisted on leaving.'

'A temper about what?' I said.

'Not to speak ill of the dead,' said Mr Irvine. 'But we'd run out of beer. He'd drunk it all, actually, and wanted more. He got quite exercised about it. Smashing bottles and roaring. As if we had let him down, failing to provide the refreshments he'd been expecting. So he went pegging off across the causeway saying he'd rather be in a civilised pub anyway than roughing it over here with us.'

'When we didn't even have the decency to stock up,' Mr Fordyce added.

'He went to the pub?' Alec said. 'We hadn't heard that.'

'My guess is that he tried both pubs,' Mr Irvine said. 'And got short shrift at them. I wouldn't have served him if I'd been a barman. So then – we assume, don't we Fordy? – he got in an even worse temper about that and set off either home to Daddy's cellar or at least to Queensferry, in hopes of a more amenable landlord.'

'He doesn't have another friend at Cramond he might have turned to?' I said, struck by a sudden thought.

'There is no "Cramond" across the river,' Mr Irvine said. 'Just Vesper's cottage and it's sitting empty. I'd be surprised if she had so much as a bottle of medicinal brandy.'

'I was thinking of a miller,' I said.

The two men looked back at me owlishly.

'Which miller?' said Mr Irvine. I was beginning to see him as the brains of the pair, while Mr Fordyce was the jester.

'Well, not a miller, I suppose,' I said. 'But whoever lives in the first mill if Mr Haslett fell off the boat. Or one of the other three if he fell off the path.'

'Other *one*,' said Mr Fordyce. 'The path only goes to one more.'

'Fordy,' said Mr Irvine with a warning note.

'What?' said Mr Fordyce, a look of innocence and injury spreading across his broad face.

'We know Peter didn't fall off any path. He fell into the

85

water off the ferry and drowned. Why cast suspicions at some miller we've never even met, just because someone comes asking about millers for no reason? No offence intended, Mrs . . . sorry. I've forgotten.'

'Gilver,' I said. 'I must have got muddled.'

I think I got away with it. Each of the young men looked at me pityingly but neither of them had a trace of interest in their eyes as to what I might have been thinking.

'And how goes the work?' said Alec, before their interest could grow again. 'Is it top secret or can you tell us what the hypothesis is?'

'We're simply running trials on new varieties,' said Mr Irvine. 'Blight. Drought. Pests.'

'All the plagues of Egypt,' I said.

'Ha ha ha!' said Mr Fordyce. 'Oh I say, that's jolly good, isn't it Irvine?'

But Mr Irvine was watching Alec and Alec was scrutinising the ground at his feet. 'And how do you keep track of them?' he said. 'They're so deeply earthed you can't actually see so much as a leaf tip.'

Now I was peering at the ground too. My lack of interest in trials on drought-resistant potatoes would be hard to under-estimate and I am not a horticulturalist of any stamp, but my years with Hugh had ensured that I knew more than I would ever have chosen to and would ever need to and Alec was right.

'Photosynthesis,' I said.

'What?' said Mr Fordyce. I stared at him, insulted that he found it so remarkable to have a woman display knowledge.

'Quite,' said Alec. 'You'll weaken the plant, old man.'

'Or,' said Mr Irvine, bristling, 'will we strengthen it? Will the vicissitudes of photosynthesis deprivation temper it as the forge the steel?'

It was on the tip of my tongue to ask him if he had swallowed a dictionary. Truly, I sometimes wonder if I brought up my sons or if they dragged me down.

'Well, you'd know better than us,' Alec said, diplomatically. 'We'll take our leave. If you do see Vesper, would you let her know we'd like a chat? No rush but if she'd be so kind.'

'Certainly,' said Mr Irvine. 'If we see her to talk to we'll pass it on. Won't we, Fordy?'

'Call us the bush telegraph!' Mr Fordyce said. 'Or the gorse telegraph, more like. Ha ha!'

With as much polite laughter as we could muster we left them. I set my course for the south-west corner and the beginning of the causeway but as soon as we were out of sight, Alec took my elbow and steered me into the trees again. 'Let's make sure,' he said. 'I don't believe Vesper is swimming off those rocks at the far side of her cottage. I think she's hiding from those two buffoons. Or one buffoon and his keeper, perhaps. And I don't believe they'll help us track her down. So let's slip a note under her door, shall we?'

The wisp of smoke had died down completely back at the Duck House and the place looked utterly forlorn. Alec picked his way around to the back and viewed the jagged rocks there.

'I'm not going to risk my neck to double check, Dan,' he said, 'but I don't think anyone in their right mind would go swimming here.'

I was writing as friendly and soothing a message as I could on a page of my little notebook. I ripped it out, folded it into a dart and crouched to slide it under the door. It was a skill developed in my childhood and I was pleased to discover that I had not lost it. I checked the gap, which was comfortable, and then with a flick of my wrist I shot the paper forward, deft and quick, and heard the faint breathy whistle of it crossing a good way over what I guessed was a stone floor.

'What did it say?' Alec asked when he was back on level ground again and kicking the stones out of his boot soles against a tuft of grass.

'"We have learned the truth about Peter's death and are eager to help you in any way we can".'

'Have we?'

'Not remotely,' I said.

'Are we?'

'That depends.'

Alec glanced at his watch and opened his eyes wide. 'Let's go,' he said. 'It's not quite warm enough to paddle. And we should just catch opening time at the Turning Tide if we hurry.'

9

Our old friend the portly potman who hated snakes, was on duty for opening time at the Turning Tide. I really did feel a genuine rush of warmth at the sight of him and that fact intrigued me. I have learned that such flashes of intuition, illicit as Alec might find them, are worth attending. For some reason, after meeting Rev Hogg, Miss Lumley the landlady, the grand Miss Speir, and the double act of Irvine and Fordyce – not to mention that most peculiar young lady Vesper Kemp – my deep subconscious mind appeared to be telling me that this chap was the only one with whom I had felt any kind of camaraderie. Or at least this chap was the only one about whom I had no misgivings.

'Morning,' he said. He had no glasses to polish as early as this when none had been used yet, so he was polishing the wooden top of the bar, wearing a large chamois leather mitten that reeked of beeswax on one of his hands and a large flannel mitten on the other. He had a methodical way of circling his arms, crisscrossing them like a Charleston dancer's ankles, so that every inch was polished and buffed. It was dizzying to watch him.

'Good morning,' Alec said. 'Tom wasn't it? No, don't stop. I can wait till you're done. I'll fill my pipe and then take a pint of your eighty shilling when you're ready. Dandy?'

I perused the row of bottles suspended upside down behind the barman's bobbing head and saw OVD rum, several different middling whiskies and a double-sized gin, all of which, at just gone eleven on a summer's morning, made me shudder. I did not want to antagonise him by asking for dry sherry, being unsure whether such a place as the Turning Tide would stock the stuff.

'Port and lemon?' Alec suggested with an impish look on his face.

'I can do you a coffee,' Tom said. 'It's only bottled but the cream's fresh off the farm. And a ginger biscuit.'

'Lovely,' I said, although another shudder had passed through me at the mention of a bottle. I would heap in brown sugar and all would be well.

'Glad we caught you quiet, actually,' Alec said. 'We wanted to ask a question and it might not be quite the thing to air it in front of a crowd.'

'What's in the pies, is it?' said the barman. 'Whether my boss dyes her hair? Best mutton and my lips are sealed.'

'It's about Peter Haslett,' I said. 'The young chap who died.'

'Ask away,' Tom said. 'But thank you for picking a quiet moment to do it.'

'You said, last time we spoke,' Alec began, 'that he was drunk.'

'That I did. That he was.' Polishing complete, he shrugged off his mittens and started running the hot tap from a tiny geyser into an equally tiny basin set under the suspended bottles. When steam started to rise he lathered his hands enthusiastically with a bar of carbolic soap, rinsed them under the scalding water and then rubbed them dry on a glass cloth that he tucked afterwards into the waist strings of his apron.

'And we were just wondering,' I said, 'if he was drinking in here.'

'I wouldn't have served him, state he was in,' Tom said.

'So you saw him?' said Alec. 'Did he try to get served? Did you turn him away?'

'To his death? I'm glad to say I did not. That would have

90

been a burden upon me. I've had the opposite happen. Back in my younger days when I didn't have the presence I've developed since.' He slapped his ample middle as he said the word 'presence' and laughed easily. Then he cleared his throat and his face grew solemn. 'I served a man till he was staggering drunk, years back, and then didn't he go and fall in the river when he pegged out at the end of the night. He didn't die. But he sobered up fast enough when he hit the water. That I can tell you. January it was.' He was laughing but he cleared his throat as he took up the matter of Peter Haslett again. 'I wasn't on that night,' he said. 'I was at the Powderhall dog track getting rid of my wages. But no, he wasn't here. Not that I heard. Did you hear different?'

'It was a possibility we considered,' I said. 'We thought if he tried to get a drink here or round at the other place and got refused, he might have mentioned – as he was sweeping out, you know? – where he was off to next.'

'Queensferry,' the barman said. 'Where else? There are five fine drinking establishments there.'

'So how did he end up where he did?' I said. 'I don't know much about currents but if someone, inexperienced and inebriated, found the coble more than he could handle wouldn't he end up out in the Forth? Not up—'

'—ended in the drink,' Alec said hastily, talking over me. 'We shall never know, I don't suppose. There weren't witnesses, were there?'

'None that I've heard about,' the barman said. He was about to say more. He had licked his lips and darted a glance behind him at the doorway to the back premises, but just then the pub door opened and a group of cyclists came tumbling in, in high spirits and with great thirst, and claimed his attention.

Alec and I withdrew to a table.

'Forgive me, Dan,' Alec said in an unnecessarily low voice. 'But that struck me as a piece of information to be kept to ourselves. The question of who thinks what might be crucial and we shouldn't muddy the waters.'

'Indeed,' I said and took a tentative sip from my cup. The sugar had not helped much. We said no more while we sat there long enough for Alec to drain every drop of his beer and for me to choke down a polite portion of my nasty coffee. When we left, I announced that a port and lemon could not conceivably be worse and I did not care if he found it amusing.

The Cramond Inn however, as I had suspected at first glance, was a rather more salubrious watering hole than the Turning Tide and the barmaid there assured me that they had both sweet and dry sherry and were willing to mix the two if anyone ordered a medium.

Alec joined me in my choice and as we sipped from our painfully dainty little glasses we began tiptoeing towards the subject once more.

'It's such a lovely spot,' I said as an opener. 'Cramond.'

'Bit out of the way,' the girl said. She looked like someone who would prefer a livelier setting. She was a pretty thing in her mid-twenties and wore her hair, even at not quite noon on a Saturday morning, in what Grant tells me is known as a 'lotus blossom'; that is, a bun formed rather low on one side of the neck. I have always thought they look more like the last slice of a swiss roll but until Grant tries to make me wear one it is not worth arguing.

'Even more so without the ferry,' Alec said.

'That was a terrible thing,' I said. 'And was it here he'd been drinking just before he took the boat out?'

'Here?' said the girl. She opened her eyes very wide, showing the white gap between her blacked lashes and her swipe of eyeliner. 'He was never in here that night. I was on the bar from teatime to closing, on my own most of the time, and the first I knew was the next day when the constable came in to use the telephone.'

'The next day?' I said. 'They kept it quiet overnight, did they?'

'They didn't know,' the girl said. 'It was after dinner on the Saturday before anyone saw him.'

I tutted and shook my head.

'He was in the water all that time?' Alec said. 'That's a pitiful thought, isn't it? I don't think that ever got into the papers.'

'Thank goodness,' I said. 'His poor mother.' I paused and took a sip of the sherry. It gave me worse shudders than the bottled coffee and I wished I had, against all my habits, asked for a sweet one.

'Who found him?' I asked. It was a question that had hitherto not occurred to either of us. I had assumed, and I expected Alec had assumed the same, that there had been a commotion at the moment of his tipping in; a rescue attempt and then a sombre acceptance that it had failed. This idea of poor Peter floating in the river all night and half the following day before anyone discovered his corpse was a new one.

'Ehhhhhhhh,' said the barmaid, apparently rattling through the index of village gossip her curly head contained. It took her a minute or two to come up with the relevant card. 'Eck Massey.'

Alec blinked. To a Dorset man it might have sounded like Latin, but I had been in Scotland long enough to decipher it. 'And where might we find Mr Massey?' I said.

'He's got the grain mill for his studio,' the barmaid said. 'The old ironworks as was.'

I was glad then that my sherry glass was such a thimble; I wanted nothing more than to knock it back and escape, to beat the second path of the day up to the mill and rouse this Alexander Massey by hook or crook. The word 'studio', spoken so innocently by the serving wench, had given me hope. A blameless miller was one thing; a doughty ironworker was much the same; but the owner of a studio was just the sort of louche individual who might well be concerned in a

93

death. Of course, I would hold any such prejudice in check when it came to gathering evidence and forming hypotheses, but it was a wisp of a sniff of an opening and I was glad of it.

Minutes later, we were out on the street again. We took the set of steps known as Sailor Street down between the cottages to the shoreside. At the bottom, Alec clutched my arm.

'Look,' he said, pointing at the river. 'The ferry.'

My eyes grew wide at the sight of the coble, tied up and bobbing on the rising tide, just as it had been the previous day, but on the far side of the river from where we stood.

'It's moved!' I said.

'Was it there this morning?' said Alec. 'Do you remember?'

I tried to cast my mind back to the early walk up the riverside to the weir. The tide had been going out, the river water sinking and the mudflats emerging and the coble had been grounded and listing to one side, almost brushing up against the reeds and ferns on the bank.

'No!' I said. 'It was still over here. You're right, Alec. Someone's used it since then.'

'Vesper?' Alec said. 'I'm sure she wasn't swimming off the rocks at the island. Could she have got across the causeway without us seeing her?'

'Not before us,' I said. 'But if she waited until we were on the island she could have made her escape. Tchah! To think we spent an hour searching. One of us should have stayed on the beach to intercept her.'

'You don't suppose, do you, that she's just suddenly come to her senses and gone back to home and work?' Alec said.

'One way to find out,' I said and gestured. He leaned out over the stone steps to the ferry bell and rang it a few good hearty clangs. We waited. Behind us, the barman put his head out of the doorway of the Turning Tide and one or two cottagers pushed aside their lace curtains to see who was

94

making the commotion but, on the far side of the river mouth, the garden gate of Coble Cottage remained shut.

'Now what?' I said.

'The miller can wait, wouldn't you say? We've got a standing offer to use Miss Speir's outboard. Let's quickly pop over and see if Vesper's come home. I'd say it's a very good sign, if so.'

It struck me as faintly ridiculous to go to all the bother of tramping up to the boat club, picking our way from deck to deck over to the dinghy and then destroying the peace with another rip of the smoky engine, all to traverse a very few feet of shallow water and tie up again. Apart from anything else we had attracted attention. Miss Lumley was out in front of the pub now, standing watching us with her hands on her hips.

'Are you leaving?' she called, with a little too much hope-fulness in her voice.

'No,' Alec called back over. 'I don't suppose you noticed who took the ferry over, did you?'

Miss Lumley stared at the boat and frowned. She shook her head.

'Ask Tom if he happened to see,' I called. 'Please,' I added as her frown deepened. When she had disappeared back inside the pub door I turned to Alec and gave him a shove in the base of his back. 'Hurry up,' I said. 'I don't want her to know we're looking for Vesper.'

'Why not?' Alec said. 'And please don't jostle me when I'm standing up in a boat, Dandy.' He was making every effort to disembark quickly but that was merely causing the boat to rock. He stood still to let it steady but then grew impatient and too soon began to move again. The motorboat, on a swell of the rising tide, bumped against the bow of the coble and then bounced away from it and began to spin. Alec leaned out, grabbed the coble by a hook and with a great groan of effort brought us close again. This time he wound the mooring rope firmly around his fist and stepped with deliberation into the ferry and then with greater deliberation onto dry land, where he secured the rope to a bollard. When we were fast I followed him.

'A hunch,' I said, when we were side by side again. 'If Vesper has left the island and managed to keep it quiet then I would like to know why and I think showing ourselves to be allies who will also keep it quiet is a good way to gain her confidence. I'm not at all sure Miss Lumley and Miss Speir have her best interests at heart.'

We let ourselves in at the garden gate to Coble Cottage and shuffled to one side so that the luxuriant hawthorn hedge hid us from view.

'Oh, Alec,' I said. I hoped he knew what I meant because I would have been hard pressed to put it into words. What lay before us was testament to Vesper as a gardener. Her cottage garden was a record of remarkable order combined with equally remarkable charm. Its rows of peas, tied with brown string to latticed canes, spoke of care and industry and its blousy profusion of dog rose and wisteria, both scrambling so enthusiastically up the walls of the cottage that they were beginning to nudge a few roof slates out of line, spoke of an easy delight in nature and her bounty. A month ago, it would have been quite entrancing. Now, after her descent and desertion to the Duck House, it was all beginning to collapse. The neat rows of peas were yellowing for lack of water and the roses were going over, their petals littering the grass of a small drying green and their hips, from neglected deadheading, beginning to swell. The wisteria blooms were as much brown as purple too and in the cabbage patch a handful of white butterflies were having a field day. Already the broad, bluish leaves were lace-edged where caterpillars had been munching.

Saddest of all, somehow, were the two linen teatowels drooping from wooden pegs on the drying line. They had hung there through several showers and downpours, I thought, because the metal springs of the pegs had rusted and the rust had spread in four long stains down the white cloth. It was a pitiful sight. And more than that, it suggested to me that wherever Vesper was she had not come home. The woman who had set out her purple cabbages in such precise rows could not, surely, have walked past those dismal glass cloths into her cottage. I am no housekeeper and it took all *my* restraint not to twitch them down and roll them up to be rewashed as I was passing.

Alec was on the doorstep with his hands cupped around his eyes, peering in through the bullseye in the front door.

'Dark,' he said. He opened the letterbox. 'And quiet. I don't think she's here, Dan.' Still, he lifted the knocker and rat-a-tat-tatted. It echoed through the house with a melancholy note that must surely have been our imagination.

I stepped forward and tried the handle. It turned easily and the door creaked open.

'Vesper?' I called, leaning into the dimness of a passageway. 'Are you here, dear?'

Only silence answered me.

'She must be here,' Alec said. 'She wouldn't lock up the Duck House at her back and leave this place lying open. Would she?'

I shrugged. 'Ves-per!' I called, louder. 'Maybe she's sleeping,' I said. 'She's been through it, after all. Yoo-hooo!'

Again we waited and again the stillness was all that came in return for our waiting.

'Shall we search?' said Alec. 'We can say we were looking for her, if someone comes. But I'd like to see if there's anything here that . . .'

'That what?'

'That anything. And "looking for her" isn't just a story. I do want to find her. I am worried for the poor girl.'

'Let's leave another note,' I said. I scrabbled in my bag

97

and ripped a second sheet from my pad. "We are staying with Miss Speir and are eager to speak to you", I wrote. "Please do not hesitate to ring up or stop in. We are here to help".

'Are we?' Alec said.

'I think so,' I said. 'It depends, of course. But if I had to place a bet, I'd say yes.'

If Vesper's garden had been pitiful to behold, with the memory of her wildness and her feverish imaginings still fresh, then there were no adequate words for the inside of her cottage. The faintest film of dust lay over everything after a week without an inhabitant to disturb it or wipe it away. It rose and fussed around us as we moved through the rooms. Under the dust though, the cottage spoke of a settled life and of competence at housewifery – for there was an empty mending basket on the floor by the kitchen chair and a fire of newspaper bows, newly split sticks and perfect foot-long logs sitting waiting in the grate for a taper that had never come. Vesper's life had not been a gay one; there was no wireless set, certainly no gramophone, and the books beside that kitchen chair and on the bedside table in the small bedroom under the eaves did not strike me as entertaining. Her tastes ran to history, natural history and religion. The Bible was the most well-thumbed of the lot.

'She never spread herself out,' came Alec's voice from across the landing. I went to join him. The big bedroom with its brass double bed was evidently still her father's even all these years after his death. A row of boots sat under the window and a pipe rack was the only decoration on the chimneypiece. Alec opened the top drawer of the chest and I could see collars and gentlemen's handkerchiefs neatly folded there.

I tutted, but from sorrow rather than disapproval. When I had first heard of this ferryboat woman I had imagined someone quite dashing, perhaps even too full of herself to invoke sympathy. This small life, still being lived in the shadow of a father long gone, was surprising. Where had she found the mettle it must have taken to stick to her guns all these years when the village and the wider world must have been pressing her back into her place?

'And much good it did her!' I said. Alec gave a sad smile and a nod. He usually does understand me.

'I agree,' he said. 'If she'd chosen a nice young man, moved into that brass bed after the wedding breakfast and filled this cottage with rosy-cheeked babies to eat all that bounty she's so good at growing, no doubt she'd be here in her kitchen this very day.'

'I wonder if any nice young men applied for the position,' I said.

Alec was looking at the coloured photograph of a much younger Vesper that sat on her late father's bedside table. 'She was a sweet thing,' he said, 'as far as one can tell past the smudges of paint – why do people do that to photographs? – and with a cottage and a job waiting for the chap, once she was busy with children . . .'

'Maybe she had a sweetheart who didn't come home,' I said, 'as well as a father.'

'She wouldn't be the only one,' said Alec, 'and yet other people manage to dust themselves down and carry on.' Abruptly, he turned and made his way back down the narrow cottage stairs. He does tend to shy away from questions of marriage and celibacy when they arise. I lingered a moment or two to let him compose himself but then, as a thought struck me, I hurried down after him.

He was in the kitchen-living room of the cottage. He had taken one of the books from beside Vesper's chair and was leafing through it.

'If you think her difficulties would have been avoided had she embarked on the usual life's journey of womankind,' I said, 'does that mean you're beginning to agree with me that her nerves have collapsed?'

'I must say I'm surprised to hear you taking that position, Dandy,' Alec said. 'I thought your time with the nuns had shown you that women with unconventional lives can do very nicely. I'm surprised to hear you bandying thoughts of "spinsters' hysteria" around.'

'But *are* you?' I insisted.

Alec did not answer. His eyes had widened and he tipped the book he was reading towards the window to get a better view of it.

'What *is* that?' I said. 'Have you found something?'

'In a sense,' said Alec. '*The Ancient and Modern State of the Parish of Cramond* by John Philip Wood. 1794! Gosh, that's an early one. Listen to this, Dan. It's in the chapter on the island. Vesper underlined it. "The Kirk Session minutes of 1690 refer to the island's use as an asylum for unfortunate females whose situation required temporary retirement".'

'You do know what that means, don't you Alec dear?' I said. 'There is only one reason that females typically require "temporary retirement". Oh!'

'*I* know,' Alec said. 'I wonder if Vesper knew. Oh, what?'

'Perhaps that's the very trouble she's in,' I said. 'Hear me out. Perhaps the boat was making her sick and that's why she took to the dog cart.'

'It would make her sick in rough weather not calm,' Alec said. 'Besides—'

I cut him off. 'Or maybe she wasn't sick but she couldn't be seen in light clothes in fine weather. She needed to be bundled into a thick jacket. And sitting hunched over in the driving seat of a cart is very different from standing up in a boat for all to see. Why are you looking at me like that?'

'Because you're talking absolute nonsense. Of all the ways ladies try to disguise their figures when they are in interesting conditions, stripping to the waist is not one of them.'

'Ah,' I said. 'Yes, I forgot about that. And what an indictment on my life these days. That I can forget that a girl is half-naked and running about an island thick with undergraduates.'

Alec once again was not listening. He had bent even closer over the book of Cramond history. 'I know it was before we had taken the case,' he said, 'but I also know you. Did you happen to jot down Vesper's ravings in that little notebook of yours?'

I gave him a serene smile, feeling my stock rising again after the recent gaffe. I fished the notebook out and opened it. 'Don't drink blood-red cinnabar,' I said. 'Don't drink slaked lime. Or you will be crushed like oyster—'

'Oyster shells!' said Alec. 'That's what I thought. Look at this. Back in the mists of time, before the island was used to incarcerate fallen women until their babies came, it was used to produce lime from crushed oyster shells.'

'Well!' I said. 'And she talked about mercury too. I've written it down here. "In the name of Mercury". She said it more than once.'

Alec shrugged and frowned at me.

'Cinnabar!' I said. 'Cinnabar is a mixture of mercury and lime, isn't it?'

'Is it?' Alec said. 'How on earth do you know that? I thought it was a spice, if I'm perfectly honest. Cinnamon's grander cousin. I stand corrected.'

I read from my notebook again. '"Don't drink blood-red cinnabar. Don't drink slaked lime." I've no idea what slaking lime is, when it's at home. "Or you will be crushed like oyster shells and fall into the warren".'

'The warren?' Alec said, his eyes very wide.

'I think so. Why?'

'Because it says that here too. Before the fallen women and even before the lime production the island was a mediaeval rabbit warren.'

'Well!' I said again. 'That makes a tiny bit more sense, doesn't it?' Then the flush of having made a connection receded and we were left looking at one another. Alec frowned harder than ever and I chewed my lip. 'Or does it?'

'Do you know,' said Alec, 'I don't think it does. I mean, yes it explains where these particular notions came from. It explains why it's mercury instead of brimstone and it explains why it's oyster shells instead of anything else that could be readily crushed, but it doesn't make it any less mad. Her smattering of historical knowledge about the island has just given her the ingredients for her ravings.'

'You really do think that too now?' I said. 'That she's mad.'

'It seems wilfully stubborn to resist the conclusion any longer,' said Alec. 'It's almost as though her reading has betrayed her. Exactly what all those stuffy old gentlemen always said would happen to bookish women.'

'Is there anything in there about snakes?' I said. 'Or people having their heads eaten?'

'Nothing about snakes that I can see,' Alec said. 'But we know that the eaten head is something she might actually have heard about. That particular element of her madness came from the real world, not from a book. Poor Vesper.'

'I think we should take the book with us,' I said. 'When we find her, if we persuade her to seek asylum somewhere, the book might help her doctor make sense of it all. Well, not sense exactly, but you know what I mean.'

'And speaking of finding her,' Alec said, 'where the devil is she?' He closed the volume and slipped it into his pocket. 'She's certainly not here. Make sure and put that note you scribbled somewhere prominent, Dandy, and let's go.'

Guessing that she would enter by the kitchen door, I put the note on the corner of the table, just under the edge of the sugar bowl in case of draughts, reading it over once again as I did so.

'We are staying with Miss Speir and are eager to speak to

you. Please do not hesitate to ring up or stop in. We are here to help.'

Despite the message we did not feel obliged to rush back to Cramond House. We had given Miss Speir notice of missing luncheon and so, after we had tied up the motorboat again, we had a decision to make between the Turning Tide and the Inn. I particularly wanted not to have Miss Lumley hover in the shadows while we ate, and more to the point while we struck up conversations with other diners, but Alec persuaded me that the Turning Tide was the place. That was where the newspapermen had roosted, that was the place with the view of the river and the ferry and that was the place with the nearest thing we had, besides the Rev Hogg, to a friend in this village.

As we pushed open the door, it was to see the Rev Hogg himself, sitting at the bar nursing a half-pint glass of dark beer and a small tumbler of whisky. I could not have been more astonished if Miss Speir had been sitting there, with a pipe and a pint, playing dominos.

'Mr Hogg?' I said. I glanced behind the bar but our friend Tom the potman was nowhere to be seen. Nor was Miss Lumley herself in evidence.

'Don't be shocked, Mrs Gilver,' he said. 'And don't tell my elders, I beg of you. That's one good thing about none of them being drinkers of ale!' He spoke rather wildly and I wondered if those two glasses were his first of the day. 'As long as they don't spot you coming in or going out they'll never know because they'll never darken the door.'

'Are you quite well, Mr Hogg?' Alec said. 'Come and sit at a table with us and have some lunch.'

'I'm *not* well,' the man said. He ran his hands through his hair until it stuck up in every direction. His hat was on the bar beside him and as he brought his arms down again he knocked it to the floor. 'And yet what do I have to complain of compared to others in this cruel world?'

A sudden flash of inspiration hit me. Had not Miss Lumley said he visited his wife every Saturday? I could forgive the poor man strong drink and self-pity after such a trip.

The new barman was a vastly inferior object. He offered bread, cheese and ham with a distinct lack of enthusiasm and brought the boards with even less. But the bread was fresh, the cheese sharp and the ham sweet. Alec made a rough sandwich of all three, slathered it with mustard, and pushed it towards the Rev Hogg. He blinked at it once or twice, then heaved a sigh and lifted it to take a bite.

'Thank you,' he said, through his first mouthful. 'I was letting myself wallow.'

'In?' I asked. The trouble with gossip is that one ends up a party to information one should not have and it makes one either a brute or a liar. I had decided Rev Hogg was too upset to withstand brutality and so I was lying to him; or misrepresenting myself anyway and asking questions whose answers I knew. 'Worry over Vesper? I'd hardly call that wallowing. And besides we might have good news in that quarter.'

Rev Hogg washed down his bite of sandwich with a draught of beer and waited expectantly to hear more.

'She's off the island,' Alec said. 'We think.'

'Home?' said Rev Hogg. His eyes misted as he said the word. 'Oh, how wonderful that would be! If all the wanderers and lost souls could be safely home again.'

'She's not at the cottage,' I said. 'But any change is a good sign, wouldn't you say?'

Rev Hogg, after another bite and another swig, nodded. 'Forgive me,' he said. 'I've had a very trying morning.'

'And I'm afraid you might have a rather trying luncheon,' I said. 'We are going to disappoint you, Mr Hogg. We've come to the reluctant conclusion, you see, that Vesper's peculiarities really do need a doctor, not a detective. Of course, if she's better then jolly good. But if not, we can't in all conscience stand by and watch her carry on the way she has been. We will try to find her for you and we're quite happy to help you get her settled somewhere.'

'No!' said Rev Hogg.

'I understand how upsetting the idea is,' Alec said. 'But it's the lesser of two evils.'

Rev Hogg stared back at him with a quizzical look on his face. 'The greater evil being what?'

'Prison,' I said. 'A trial. A sentence.'

'For Vesper?' Rev Hogg said in a voice that cracked with strain. 'Prison for Vesper? For what?'

'She knows far more than she should about Peter Haslett's death,' I said. 'Considering she's supposed to have been on the island when it happened.'

'There's no "supposed" about it,' Hogg said, quite sharply and quite loud. The lethargic barman looked over and registered what was almost interest. 'Those two biologists are ready to put their hand on the Book and swear to it.'

'Hm,' I said. 'Those two biologists were happy to say she was on the island this morning too, or rather swimming off it, but we couldn't see any sign of her. Could we, Alec?'

'And what is there to know of his death anyway?' the good reverend said. 'Why shouldn't she know? It's the talk of Cramond.'

'Is it?' I said. 'You surprise me. Why weren't we provided with the full facts then? If it's the talk of Cramond, why were we of all people kept in the dark?'

'In the dark?' said Rev Hogg. 'Why, I put it in the letter as soon as I heard the news and I told you again the day you arrived. I held nothing back. Not a thing.'

'You said Peter Haslett drowned,' I reminded him.

'Yes.' He looked from Alec to me and back again. 'Of course I did. What else would I say?'

I leaned forward to keep my next words to ourselves. 'Mr Hogg, you are not helping Vesper. You are, in fact, doing her a great disservice. Now, please.'

'Please *what*?' said Rev Hogg.

'In the course of the last day,' I told him, 'we have heard that he jumped in off the bank, that he was pulled under and crushed by a mill wheel, and – from Vesper's own lips, mind you – that she . . .' but there my courage deserted me.

'That she ate his head,' Alec said, as quietly as I had been speaking but with great determination.

'Dear God!' said Rev Hogg.

'Now, the *claim* probably has its source in the same unfortunate nerve strain that caused all her other wild stories about rabbit warrens and oyster shells,' Alec said. 'But those stories do have a grain of truth about them, or so we have learned.' Alec drew the little book out of his pocket.

Rev Hogg's eyes flared at the sight of it. 'Yes, yes,' he said. 'The history of the island.'

'And so we find it compelling,' Alec went on, 'that Vesper would make up a story, or be taken captive by a delusion, about an injured head when there is indeed an injured head.'

'I see, I see,' Rev Hogg said. 'The fact is the father of the tale, you mean.'

'Nicely put,' said Alec. 'So you'd better come clean. If you didn't tell Vesper what happened, and nor did the two young men who were his friends and are her neighbours, and I assume neither Miss Lumley nor Miss Speir has been a-tramping over the causeway, then how did she find out? If she is innocent, how does she know?'

'I can assure you, both of you,' Rev Hogg said, 'that Peter Haslett fell into the river off the ferry and drowned. I don't know what evil is afoot to make anyone in our community tell such nasty tales. His head mangled by a mill wheel? What nonsense! The mill wheels don't turn in the evenings when the day's work is done. Scurrilous tittle-tattle.'

He was wrong, of course, but he was absolutely sincere in his belief. And he was warming to his theme.

'It's a coincidence,' he said. 'People make up the nastiest

things they can, whether through illness or mischief. And plenty of Vesper's . . . imaginings are just that. Made out of whole cloth in her own troubled mind. The snakes, for one.'

'But not the sanctuary on the island,' I said.

Rev Hogg blushed.

'Or the appeals to Mercury,' said Alec.

'Mercury?' Rev Hogg's cheeks did not only fade, they paled.

'Well, cinnabar,' I said. 'Which is mercury and lime, isn't it?'

'Cinnabar is nothing to do with lime,' Rev Hogg said. 'It's a sulphide. And mercury has no place at Cramond. That's just like the snakes. Just the ravings of a poor girl who needs our help.' He was on his feet, dabbing at his lips with a napkin. 'And you say she's disappeared? Oh dear, dear.'

With that he was gone.

'My chemistry is not as good as I thought it was,' I said. Then I regarded my plate where as fine a sandwich as I could make from rough bread using a coarse knife awaited my attentions.

Alec turned the pages of the little book as he ate. I often told the boys not to read adventure stories at the nursery table, thinking that great excitement and good digestion were warring forces. And Hugh has more than once spluttered and had to be banged on the back when he combines the political pages with his bacon and eggs in the morning. But I would not have imagined a history of Cramond parish to pose any threat to the safe consumption of bread and ham. When Alec gasped, choked and began to change colour I did not, at first, think the trouble had come from within those turning pages.

'What is it?' I said, passing him a clean handkerchief to wipe his eyes. 'What have you thought of?'

Alec, still coughing and streaming, waved the book at me. 'Mercury,' he managed to say.

'What?'

'Read it,' he croaked.

I took the book from his hand. "'The first discovery, made in the grounds of Cramond House, was part of a stone altar to the Matronae goddesses. Other discoveries followed, notably a centurial stone pertaining to the emperor Augustus' second legion and a remarkably intact altar to the god *Mercury*!'" But Mr Hogg just denied all knowledge of Mercury! Why would an ancient altar upset him enough to lie? What does any of it mean?'

'And where do the snakes fit in?' said Alec, which was hardly helpful.

I I

Our earlier plan to interview the millers of the Almond had been roundly taken over by subsequent revelations, in my view, and so instead of tramping up the riverbank again, we found ourselves headed back towards Cramond House to see if Miss Speir had any light to shed on why the village's ancient history would cause Rev Hogg such consternation.

Alec continued to read out loud as we went. 'It was a fort, Dandy!' he said. 'A garrison! Home to some unknown number of cohorts of a Roman legion! Rumabo!'

'What?' I said.

'There's a sort of gazetteer from the eighth century that mentions a place called "Rumabo" somewhere around here. The history chaps think it might be an early version of "Cramond". Golly.'

'Why are you so excited?' I said. 'Weren't there Romans in Dorset?'

'Tons,' said Alec. 'Vespasian set up shop there. And then Vikings, Normans, you name it. I don't know . . . It's just the thought of this being the last frontier, I think. This is as far as they ever got. The very edge of the mighty empire. Don't you find that thrilling?'

'They probably went to up to Perth, had a look round and decided enough was enough,' I said. Of all the annoying traits of the Scots, none is more so than the pride with which they view the fact that they stopped 'the mighty empire'. Twaddle in my view. It was the emperors Hadrian and Antonine who built the walls, to keep the savages out.

Alec looked up from his book to give me a smile in appreciation of my little joke and as he lifted his head his eyes widened. 'Look, Dan,' he said.

Up the hill, Rev Hogg was just emerging from the gates of Cramond House and scuttling off towards the manse with his head down and his elbows wagging.

'What on earth?' I said and began to walk faster. Alec slipped the book back into his pocket and caught up with me.

The first thing we saw when we turned in and made our way along the drive was that Alec's motorcar was no longer alone, parked on the sweep. Beside it was a machine with the outline of a resting feline, in an unlikely and impractical shade of pale grey and with a great deal of glitter in its finishes. Despite being nearly half as long again as any motorcar I had ever seen it had only two seats, most of its sprawling excess being taken up by a ridiculous bonnet.

'What is that?' I said.

'About a thousand pounds worth of German engineering,' said Alec in awestruck tones.

'German?' I said. 'Who would—'

'Well, French really. And quite Italian in its way. It's a Bugatti.'

'Who the dickens can it belong to?' I said. 'Not Miss Speir, surely.'

'Ssh,' Alec said. 'There she is.'

Miss Speir, astonishingly enough, had just emerged from the studded door in the ground floor of the old tower followed by a gentleman in a suit exactly the same shade as the motorcar, who wore his hat on the back of his head and held a cigarette in his teeth. He was tucking some papers into an inside pocket and looked rather annoyed at the sight of us. Miss Speir, on the other hand, hallooed us with more enthusiasm than we had roused in her at any moment since our arrival. She was carrying a parasol and she twirled it on her shoulder as she greeted us.

'Mrs Gilver. Mr Osborne. How is your day proceeding? Hasn't it been fine weather?'

'Lovely,' I said. I did not intend to give a report on our case in front of this stranger. Although, as we drew towards them, something about him arrested my attention and rang a faint bell. His middle, just like his motorcar, was glittering. I looked as closely as I could without rudeness and saw that his dark waistcoat had jet buttons and they were winking and sparkling in the sunshine. This, I was sure, was one of the newspapermen we had seen in the Turning Tide the previous day.

'We don't meant to interrupt you in your . . .' Alec said, clearly as stumped as I was and fishing.

'We're finished,' said Miss Speir. 'Mr—'

'Ah-hm-hm-hm,' said the man, just as clearly trying to stop her from saying his name. 'Yes, I was just leaving.' His voice was plummy. There is no other word for it. Despite the vulgar car and the ostentatious clothes, he sounded like a gentleman. 'I'll let you attend to your guests, dear Miss Speir,' he added. On second thoughts, he did not sound like a gentleman. There was something of the London streets about him. He sounded like a common man with some theatrical training, who was playing a gentleman and almost succeeding.

Miss Speir waved him off and then turned to Alec and me with a gracious smile.

'How is Vesper?' she said.

'We couldn't find her,' said Alec. 'Mr Irvine and Mr Fordyce said she was swimming but we're not so sure.'

'Who?' said Miss Speir. 'Oh, the biologists, you mean? Swimming is surely a good sign, isn't it? Perhaps she's on the mend.'

'We were worried,' I said, as the three of us trooped up

the steps and into the hall. The maid, Christine, was hovering there to take her mistress's parasol and gloves. 'Not knowing how good a swimmer she is and after recent events, you know.'

'Oh, but she wouldn't come to any harm in the pond,' said Miss Speir. 'It's deep but it's very still. Much safer than sea bathing, with our currents and all those rocks. It was the pond – the quarry—that first started us thinking of holidays on the island, as a matter of fact. She'll be fine.'

I chose not to tell her that Vesper was supposedly swimming in the very sea Miss Speir disparaged. There was no point in worrying the woman for no reason. And besides, I was champing to find a way of asking who the strange man with the jet buttons was.

'Let's have tea,' Miss Speir said, marching across the hall towards her habitual sitting room. 'It's rather early but Christine has made a cherry cake and I'm feeling celebratory.'

'Oh yes?' said Alec.

'Mr . . . Well, he does rather prefer to keep his name out of it but that person you saw just now has agreed a very favourable price for a good lot of bits and bobs. I'm quite delighted about it.'

'Bits and bobs from the tower?' I said, guessing.

'Yes, I've got high hopes of the whole eyesore being gone before too long,' she said. She had let herself drop into her armchair and she treated us to a beaming smile. Her spirits had been more buoyed up by this sale of rubble than I could fairly account for.

'He's a builder?' said Alec. 'Surely a very prosperous one. That car!'

'He's a dealer,' said Miss Speir.

'Were they all dealers?' I said. Miss Speir hooked an eyebrow. 'We happened to glimpse that chap in the Turning Tide yesterday along with many of his fellows. We thought they were reporters.'

113

'*Reporters?*' It came out as a horrified squawk and a stain began to climb Miss Speir's neck. 'Reporting what?'

Alec and I shared a glance. Neither one of us wanted to answer, particularly. But Alec is better than me at avoiding unwelcome tasks. He took out his pouch and began filling a pipe. It was an even better ruse than usual, since Miss Speir's embargo on smoking in her house meant that, once it was filled, he could flee the room if he wanted to.

'Vesper's retreat,' I said, as gently as I could. 'The trouble with the ferry. There are always willing readers when an accomplished woman is finally humbled.' I was glad Hugh could not hear me and I did not care if Alec shook his head at me. If he had wanted to be in charge of what was said then he should have taken the trouble to say it. 'I mean, look at Dr Inglis's obituaries. They made my blood boil.'

'We've kept Vesper's difficulties out of the public eye, I'm glad to say.' Miss Speir delivered the words waspishly and her eyes glinted. 'That is until Jerry fired off that letter to you two. The ferry is not a public service, like a corporation omnibus. It's a favour bestowed on our fellow man out of civic spirit. If people choose to tramp five miles through the estate in hopes of it, then—' Feeling perhaps that her claims to civic spirit and concern for her fellow man were about to be undermined, she did not complete the sentence. Besides, Christine was just now entering with a loaded tea tray and the resultant bustle allowed the subject to drop.

'Or it could have been Peter Haslett, of course,' I said, when the tea was poured and slices of dry cake, studded with very occasional bits of cherry, had been handed round. 'The drowning.'

Miss Speir looked at me as though over a vast distance, trying to determine what I was talking about.

'But as we've now discovered,' Alec said, 'they were not reporters at all. They were "dealers". And there were quite a dozen of them. Are any more coming here today?'

Miss Speir raised a hand to her collar and fiddled with the bow of her shirt, depositing a few crumbs there. 'A dozen?' she said. 'Are you sure? They must have been . . . day trippers.'

'On a Friday?' I said. 'After the end of the trades fortnight? It doesn't seem likely. And there were no wives or children. Just a lot of men, of the same sort, all waiting in the Turning Tide for who knows what?'

'I suppose you trust all these dealers and builders, Miss Speir, do you?' Alec said suddenly.

'I only have business dealings with that one,' Miss Speir said. 'The one you just met. And I trust him. Why do you ask?'

'Because,' Alec said, with a glance at me, 'last night when we took a late turn we rather thought we heard someone in the tower.'

'Alec!' I said. 'You told me it was a deer.'

'There are no deer at Cramond,' said Miss Speir.

'Or a dog,' I added.

'I didn't want to alarm you,' Alec said. 'Since whoever or whatever it was went hightailing it off into the bushes, there didn't seem any point in making a fuss and ruining your night's rest.'

I said nothing but I gave him one of my better glares. I dislike being treated as though I am too delicate to be trusted with the harsh facts of life and when it gets as far as withholding useful information – such as 'intruders lurking just outside my bedroom window' – chivalry becomes an actual menace.

'But then I suppose there's not much in the way of building supplies one can purloin under cover of darkness, place in a pocket and then slip out of a window.'

'Building supplies,' said Miss Speir vaguely. She was fussing at her neck again. At least she dislodged the cake crumbs this time. 'Perhaps I misled you. The . . . The builder is going to take stones and slates once the . . . the sales are all completed. But I assure you, I own the place and if I want to sell any of my possessions, I am quite within my rights to do so.'

'Oh my!' Alec said. 'Are you sure of that, Miss Speir?'

I had no idea what had caused the exclamation, nor the question, but Alec had a fixed look upon his face and he was rummaging in his pocket. I wondered if he had forgotten that his baccy pouch and pipe were already out and sitting on the table at his elbow. Then he laid his hands on the object he sought, pulled it out, waved it at Miss Speir and slapped it down with a sharp smack on the tea table, making the cups and teaspoons rattle.

I frowned at it, wondering what aspect of the history of Cramond could—

'Oh!' I said, as the penny dropped. 'Artefacts, Miss Speir? Ancient Roman artefacts? Are you absolutely sure they're yours to sell? Have you spoken to anyone at the museum or the university?'

Miss Speir tutted and patted and shook her head, evidently annoyed, but she said nothing.

'And did you know that someone's been in there in the night, rootling around for whatever he could find?' Alec said. 'Shouldn't you secure it? At least board up the windows. The place is lying absolutely unprotected.'

'It's locked,' said Miss Speir. 'The keys are safe in the kitchen.'

'And what is it that's in there?' I said. 'We read about the altar stones.'

'That altar stone was my father's!' she said. 'It was on his land and therefore it was rightfully his.'

'I don't think the Crown would agree with you,' Alec said.

'Well I know it!' she cried. 'It was snatched away to the museum and my father saw not a ha'penny.'

'How annoying,' I said.

'And so when it comes to smaller items,' Miss Speir said. 'Trinkets, really.'

'I'm not so sure,' I chipped in. 'Hugh knows all about this and therefore, as is the way of marriage, so do I. Treasure trove, in Scots common law, Miss Speir, applies to *all* antiquities, altar stones to arrow heads.'

'Vacant goods!' Alec said, dredging the term up from heaven knows where. He has, I suppose, known Hugh for fourteen years; perhaps it is beginning to rub off on him too.

'But the man we met is English,' I said. 'Is that the idea? He takes the . . . coins? pots? . . . over the border where matters are handled rather differently?'

'And does Mr Hogg know about it?' Alec said. 'Is that why he was upset to discover we had stumbled upon Cramond's Roman past?'

'Mr Hogg?' said Miss Speir. 'Jerry? He knows nothing. Not that there's anything to know. This is all nonsense and even if it weren't, it's nothing to do with your commission here. How could Vesper's nervous collapse or even Peter Haslett's untimely death have any connection to my affairs? If my affairs were even close to what you're suggesting. Which they're not.'

Having thus tied herself into tight knots, she finally stopped talking.

'Mr Hogg was distressed when we mentioned Mercury,' I said.

Miss Speir sat back in her chair and let her shoulders slump as though in profound relief.

'Oh!' she said. 'Well, yes. The altar stone. Jerry was shocked when it was discovered.'

'Is it shocking?' I asked. 'Some of these carvings can be pretty fruity. But I'd have thought Venus was the principal cause of all that.'

'No, no,' said Miss Speir. 'Jerry was shocked because some of the villagers found it, years before my father ever discovered he owned such a thing. And they, for reasons best known to themselves you understand, being simple folk, worshipped at it.'

'Good God,' said Alec, which threatened to make me giggle, being so pertinent to the current discussion. 'What is Mercury the god of anyway?'

'Commerce,' said Miss Speir. 'Business in general. And luck. So who can blame them? It's all very well for Jerry sitting in his comfortable house with his stipend, but you've seen the cottages on Sailor Street.'

'And is it more altar stones you've uncovered now?' I said. 'Is that what your pet dealer is planning to take to auction?'

'No,' said Miss Speir. 'Not stones. Not that I'm admitting— confirming that it's anything at all.'

'Armour?' said Alec. 'Helmets? It was a fort, after all.'

'There was a fort,' said Miss Speir, jesuitically. 'But there was also a villa and of course we've known since the altar stone was found that there was a temple.'

'A bona fide temple?' I said. 'I thought the Romans tended to knock up a shrine wherever they spent a few nights.'

'As far as the goddesses of battle go, perhaps,' said Miss Speir. 'That was more than likely the work of the soldiers. But the altar stone to Mercury must have been part of a true temple. If there was such a place. And as I say, I can't confirm it. But it would have been well hidden.'

Alec's eyes were dancing. 'Under a mediaeval tower, for instance?' he said. 'How much of it has survived intact?'

'Enough for us to be sure what we were looking at,' said Miss Speir, giving up her unconvincing pretence that this was merely conjecture. 'The village folk did me a great favour, when they dragged the altar stone away and set it up again. If it had been found in situ there would have been all sorts of awkward questions. But it was discovered in the kirkyard—'

'Truly?' I said. 'On hallowed ground? Oh poor Mr Hogg!'

'And so no one has ever seen the temple except me.'

'And the nameless dealer with the jet buttons,' I said. 'And once you've cleaned it out a local builder's going to fill in the site with rubble and be paid in salvaged stone?'

Miss Speir frowned at my baldness. 'That altar stone isn't even on display,' she said. 'It's not in a glass case with my father's name on the card. It's in a dusty basement where only scholars ever see it. Can you blame me?'

12

'But it's got nothing to do with why Mr Hogg – our client, let me remind you – asked us to come here!' I said. 'In fact, we know that our client particularly abhors the whole subject.'

We were in Alec's room, which was just as dismal as mine but had a view of the newly thrilling tower from its ill-fitting and draughty window. Alec was leaning on the windowsill with both hands, his forehead against the pane.

'We don't know that, Dandy,' he said. 'It might be connected. Vesper did, after all, have a history of the village, so she had an interest in it.'

'What connection?' I demanded. 'Go on. If you can suggest one single possible connection between Miss Speir ransacking ancient treasures for her own personal gain and poor Vesper's nervous complaints then I shall gladly go rummaging around the tower dungeons for . . .'

'Exactly,' Alec said. 'You don't even know what's under there.'

'Cooking pots and hairpins,' I said. 'Very interesting, I'm sure. Were you never dragged to the British Museum when you were a boy, Alec? Did it never rain when you were in town?'

'Of course it did and of course I was,' Alec said. 'Nanny knew all the omnibuses that went to Bloomsbury off by heart.'

'And did you stand breathlessly gazing at the cases of Roman cooking pots and hairpins?' I said. 'Of course you didn't. You raced past them to get to the mummies. But that's besides the point. You were about to tell me how any of this is pertinent to the question of Vesper and Peter Haslett.'

'She might have gone off her rocker,' Alec said, 'because she meddled with dark forces.'

I stared at the back of his head for a moment or two until he turned away from the window and winked at me.

'Was that supposed to be a joke?' I said. 'It was in very poor taste if so.'

'Oh come on, Dandy!' Alec said. 'Or perhaps her nervous collapse is a punishment because she has displeased the gods.'

'Is that a joke too?' I said. 'You're being awfully unkind.'

'She is a ferrywoman after all. And Peter Haslett did try to cross the river without giving her any silver.'

'Isn't that Greek?' I said, desperately trying to dredge up lost morsels. 'Hades and Charon?'

'I'm pretty sure Virgil talks about the River Styx,' said Alec, just as doubtfully, probably doing some dredging of his own. 'But you're right. I should be serious.'

He came away from the window and threw himself down sideways on his single bed as though it were a divan. It let out a series of rusty squeaks from its springs. 'It's odd; that's all. Miss Speir's cache of Roman antiquities and her decision about what to do with them are odd. And Mr Hogg's reaction to the question of Roman Cramond is odd. And Vesper invoking the name of Mercury is odd. And Peter Haslett's death is odd and Vesper's state of knowledge regarding it is odd and, in any other case we've ever investigated, we would sniff out all these oddities and follow them to their sources, hoping that it would turn out to be only one source and, having connected them all, we would thereby have solved the case.' He took an overdue breath and held up a hand to stop me interrupting while he did so. 'The fact that one of our chores – to wit: going on an honest-to-goodness treasure hunt – happens to be a boyhood dream of mine cannot be helped. There.'

I nodded. 'You're right. Of course, you're right. I just . . . I wish we didn't have to. Stop!' Now it was my turn to hold a hand up against his interruption. 'I'm not being a bore. But if Vesper really is coming back to herself again and if Peter's death was an accident – as it must be, mustn't it? Despite the rumours and counter rumours – then I would rather we could just leave Cramond be. But if we see evidence of a crime with our own eyes, then we'll have to report it. Won't we? And then Vesper will have her settled life disrupted all over again. And what good will it do? The cooking pots and hairpins will go into boxes in the bowels of the National Museum never to be seen.'

'You keep saying that, Dandy,' said Alec. 'Cooking pots and hairpins. Do you really think that oily chap could have got himself a Bugatti by dealing in hairpins?'

'What else would be likely to fetch up in a villa and a temple?' I said. 'Statues?'

'Vessels for oil?' Alec said, screwing up his face with the effort of remembering history lessons from his boyhood.

'Not that different from cooking pots,' I said. 'Does Miss Speir have a library?'

'Even if she does, we can't sit in it and pore over books of Roman antiquities.'

'Urns!' I said. 'When I was using her telephone yesterday she had a big book open at a picture of a carved urn.'

'A cooking pot by another name,' Alec said, in revenge. 'If it wasn't Saturday teatime we could take a jaunt to the National Library and look it all up there.'

I nodded, smiling. Alec does love a library visit. Few are the cases we tackle in which he does not manage to fit one in. 'Or,' I said, 'we could consult the fount of all knowledge.'

Alec laughed. 'He'll be cock-a-hoop,' he said. 'Day two of a case? That's a record.'

We did not, however, manage to finagle a telephone call to Hugh that evening. After dinner, Miss Speir sat in her sitting room, as why would she not, and when I airily asked if I could use the machine, she simply gestured towards it with an open hand and inclined her head. She was not, her expression seemed to say, going to take herself off and let me speak in private. I could not blame her. I smacked my head and pretended to have remembered that the friend I wanted to ring was away. I had no idea if she believed me.

I could not bring to mind a public telephone kiosk anywhere in the village that we could stroll to in the course of an evening airing either. Besides, it was chilly and black outside, great rolling clouds just beginning to release large drops of cold rain to fall onto the dusty ground. It smelled delightful, as summer rain always does, but it was not enticing to walk out into.

The next morning, therefore, Alec and I begged off church. Miss Speir and Christine, both in straw hats and pale gloves, stood at the bottom of the stairs and gaped at us.

'Not go to church?' Miss Speir said. 'What will I say to Jerry?'

'Should he ask,' Alec said, 'which I doubt, assure him that we are hard at work on the task for which he employed us. I'm sure he'd rather we did that than swelled his flock.'

Christine looked unconvinced but she held the door open for her mistress and the pair of them stalked out, jabbing the points of their rolled umbrellas unnecessarily hard into the gravel with every stride as though they were picking up litter in a park.

'Is there anyone else in the house?' Alec said.

'I think Christine's it,' I said. 'Which explains the cooking. And the dust, I suppose.' But Alec was already halfway to the sitting room, Miss Speir's desk and the telephone that waited there.

I was sure Hugh came to the telephone quicker for Alec than he ever had for me. On the other hand, Alec was obliged to chat about the weather, the hay, the grouse chicks and the European news for five minutes. When I am on the telephone to Hugh he is deeply concerned to work out what I want as quickly as possible so that he can provide it, or explain why he is withholding it, and get away again.

When I had smoked a forbidden cigarette, stubbed it out and emptied the ashtray into the fireplace, I heaved an ostentatious sigh and at last Alec cut in to Hugh's flow. 'Actually old man,' he said, 'we're in need of your scholarship this morning.'

Hugh was instantly silent, unable to resist such flattery. Alec grinned at me.

'The god Mercury,' he said. 'No, you heard me. The god Mercury. God of commerce, isn't that right? So we were just wondering if you knew what sort of thing a temple dedicated to Mercury would be likely to contain?' He waited. 'No, of course I haven't been drinking.' He waited again and gradually his eyebrows rose up his forehead until his brow was rippled like a ploughed field and I could see the whites of his eyes all around.

'What?' I whispered. 'What's he saying?'

'Are you sure?' Alec said. Then he listened further. At length, the muffled sound of Hugh's voice stopped and Alec let out a long, low whistle. 'And – it's almost a waste of time to ask after all that but – what about a villa? Yes, at Cramond. If there was a villa as well as the fort and the temple, what sort of thing . . .?' He fell silent and again his eyebrows began their upward journey. The whistle that came this time lasted until his breath gave out. 'Well, stone the crows,' he said. 'You'll keep all this under your hat, won't you? Much obliged. Thank you. Dandy sends her—' But Hugh was gone.

'Well?' I said.

'Give me a chance,' Alec said. 'I'm gathering my thoughts.'

'Gather them faster!' I said. 'What did he tell you?'

'Mercury,' he began, and once again I had to shake myself at the sound of it. These were uncharted waters we were navigating, Alec and me. 'Mercury is indeed the god of commerce, but that's pretty much a sideline. Or rather it goes along inevitably with his central concern, which is money. He's the god of filthy lucre. The god of financial establishments and practices, was how Hugh just put it. And so, apparently, a temple to Mercury would be more or less . . . a bank.'

'Did Romans *have* banks?' I said.

'No,' said Alec. 'So when I say a bank, I don't mean an office kept afloat by notes and guarantees of credit. I mean – Hugh meant, rather – a great big stockpile of gold.'

'Gold,' I repeated.

'And anything else that's small, easily portable and worth a great deal.'

'The sort of thing that would keep a dealer in Bugattis and jet buttons.'

We stared at one another.

'At Cramond?' I said when the staring had not produced answers, but only more questions.

'Ha,' said Alec. 'Yes, absolutely at Cramond. Especially at Cramond. Or so Hugh thinks anyway. As with the villa too.'

'Yes, what did he have to say about the villa?' I asked. 'It sounded noteworthy.'

'It's because of where we are,' said Alec. 'The Antonine Wall, Dandy!'

'It's miles away,' I said. My knowledge was far from sturdy but to the best of my recollection the wall started well up the Forth from this estuary, crossing Scotland at its nipped waist, which must have saved those poor Roman soldiers, or their slaves, no end of shovelling.

'Exactly,' Alec said. 'The Cramond branch of the Bank of Mercury would be where all the money to pay all the soldiers at all the forts along the wall was gathered and guarded. It would have been brought up the North Sea – much safer than travelling over land in those days – and amassed here. And the villa, Hugh reckons, would have been the most palatial and sumptuous digs imaginable. Much posher than anything else because this was where visiting bigwigs would be billeted when they came on tours of inspection and also where soldiers of high rank would be rewarded for acts of valour with little holidays.'

I was shaking my head in wonder. 'And Hugh had all of that at his fingertips?'

'All of that and more,' said Alec. 'He said there's been a long-rumbling argument among classicists and historians about where the eastern outpost was.'

'But wasn't the—' I said, when I was interrupted by the ringing of the telephone. I lifted the earpiece. 'Cramond House,' I said.

'Dandy?' came Hugh's voice. I could not ever get used to these automatic exchanges and the abrupt way they pitched one into conversations but just this once I was glad of it.

'Hugh?' I said. 'Wasn't the discovery of an altar stone to Mercury a bit of a clue to these warring scholars that the "eastern outpost" had been found?'

'That's why I was ringing back,' Hugh said. 'Don't let yourself be duped, Dandy. I've been thinking and doing a bit of reading to refresh my memory and I'm sorry to be a cold spoon but there's nothing in it.'

'Oh?' I said.

It was Alec's turn to whisper 'What? What?' at me. I shushed him.

'It all springs from an over-zealous local author by the name of Wood.'

'John Philip Wood,' I said. 'Yes, I'm looking at his history right now.'

'*One* of his histories,' Hugh said. 'He wrote a few. And he made a great many leaps of conjecture. That's the kindest way to describe his scholarship. If one were being brutal one would say he made it all up. No one else thinks that altar stone was dedicated to Mercury, for instance. The university boys came down on the side of Jupiter, actually.'

'Jupiter?' I said. 'What's he god of? I've forgotten, if I ever knew.'

'Bad weather,' said Hugh. 'Which makes sense at a port, if one's about to set off to Italy. That and the rest of it – the centurial stone and the altar stone to those goddesses of the army and what have you – soberer heads concluded that it all got knocked up at the harbourside for use before embarkation. There's no independent evidence of a fort or villa, much less a temple. Sorry to disappoint you. Osborne threw me off with his questions out of the blue. So I thought I'd better ring back and set you straight.'

'How kind of you,' I said drily. I knew nothing gave Hugh greater delight than to know better, especially if what he knew was disappointing. 'Very well then, dear. I'll tell Alec. Thank you. Give my love to—'

Before I could name either son, my daughter-in-law or a grandchild, or even Bunty, which was what I had been about to say, he was gone. I put my tongue between my lips and blew out hard. It is not an elegant noise but it is tremendously satisfying.

'Well?' said Alec.

'Hugh reckons John Philip Wood isn't a trustworthy source,' I said. 'His exact words were "no independent evidence of a fort or villa, much less a temple". What do you say to that?'

Alec's eyes were dancing. 'I say yah boo sucks to Hugh. And don't give me that look. You just blew a raspberry into Miss Speir's phone. You should wipe it with your hanky, by the way. I say too bad for the poor old chap, stuck in his library pooh-poohing our discovery when we are here, on the ground, with the independent evidence just a stroll away across the garden. Shall we?'

'Shall we break into the tower while our hostess is at church?' I said. 'I should say so.'

Alec was kind enough not to mention my volte-face. I had been sceptical of the notion that the ancient treasures of

Cramond were part of our business here; but with Hugh pouring cold water I was seized with an urgent desire to find something that would prove him wrong. 'We wouldn't be breaking in, anyway,' I said. 'The windows are agape to the elements. One can't break into a building that's lying open.'

We stopped off at the motorcar to pick up our tungsten torches and the length of stout rope Alec keeps there in case of mishap. Then we scuttled off round the corner of the tower to the quiet side. No matter what we had said about our not breaking in I did not want to be discovered with one leg over a windowsill, torch in hand.

'They're much higher when one's looking at them with a view to climbing in,' I said, standing with my hands on my hips and regarding the lower edge of the lowest window hole, which was level with my shoulder.

'I'll give you a leg up and then clamber in after you,' Alec said, bending and making a cup out of his interlaced fingers. I had not stepped up into someone's hands and pushed off again since I was a girl climbing trees, but it is the sort of thing that never deserts one. I put one hand on the stone sill, one on Alec's shoulder, bent both knees and with an ungainly puff of breath and a bit of scrabbling I found myself bent over the edge of the window as though over Nanny's knee for a spanking, my head dangling in the darkness of the tower and my feet dangling down the outside, while Alec tried not to laugh.

'Don't shove me!' I said. 'I don't want to go head first.'

I rolled and wriggled my way to the corner of the window and then hooked one leg up. Alec gave up the effort and started giggling.

'That's a very stout petticoat,' he said. 'For July.'

'Shut up,' I said. 'You shouldn't be looking.' Now astride the windowsill, I sat upright and smoothed my hair back. 'I'm going to drop down inside,' I said. 'The floor's higher than the ground, thank goodness.' Then I swung my other leg in and slithered off the sill. I dusted my hands and turned to ask Alec if he wanted to throw in the rope to help me haul him but he was already up, swinging his legs easily over the sill and jumping down to stand beside me.

'Right then,' he said. 'Let's get away from the window and let our eyes adjust to the darkness.' It was indeed quite remarkably dark for a sunny summer's morning, but then the window was narrow and faced a stand of trees and the walls were thick enough to swallow what little light there was.

I stepped tentatively, feeling the scrape of grit under my feet, and this shuffling saved me from tripping over the edge of a soft object on the floor. 'Switch your torch on, Alec,' I said, fumbling with mine. 'There's something in here.'

But it was only a sack, ripped open along its seams and spread on the floor. I clicked my torch off again. I agreed with Alec that using the dim light throughout the whole room was better than following a thin beam. Once or twice before we had relied on torchlight and missed useful clues in the dark corners beyond its reach.

'So where do we start?' I said.

Alec bounced up and down on the spot a few times. 'The floor feels solid enough,' he said.

'It would. It's earth,' I replied. 'The whole place smells like an open grave.'

'Don't be such a ghoul,' Alec said. 'You could just as easily have said "potato trial". Let's just see what there is to see.'

What there was to see was a large square room with two open fireplace holes, mantels and carvings long gone; a dent that was probably a bread oven or a salt cupboard once upon a time; and the first seven steps of a spiral staircase leading up to an upper floor so rickety I could see thin beams of dusty light between the boards. Even if there had been an eighth stair and more besides to reach up there I would not have dared to put my weight on those floorboards. And I could *not* have said 'potato trial'. There was no fresh earthiness about the air in here. As we moved and disturbed the dust, what arose was foetid and cloying, thick with mould and mouse dirt.

We made a thorough job of it anyway. We poked in and out of those myriad side chambers with which every ancient tower is always well provided and found nothing more, apart from bird droppings, the twigs of yesteryear's nests, many little piles of woodworm dust below some even more rickety-looking floorboards overhead and, under one of the front windows, a smashed lemonade bottle, probably shied through the hole in a bet or a dare.

'Well, at least Hugh's not here to gloat,' Alec said as we made our way back to the window where we had entered. I gave the sheet of sacking a wide berth. Alec, in contrast, stopped at its edge and stared at it. I turned to see what aspect of a humble split sack could possibly be arresting his attention.

'Odd, isn't it?' he said. 'Why is this here?'

I opened my mouth to scoff at such straw-clutching, but stopped myself. An intact sack, left behind from some period when the tower was used to store oats, would not have been notable. And a heap of sacking in a corner might have borne witness to a tramp's bolt hole. But one single sack, split open and lying flat in the middle of an otherwise bare floor, was indeed an oddity. I bent and grasped it at one corner, whisking it aside with a puff of mouse-perfumed dust.

'Well, well, well,' Alec said.

Under the sack, flat against the earthen floor, was a trap door, crossed by broad iron bands and secured with a sturdy brass padlock on a hasp as thick as my wrist.

13

'If we only knew how long Rev Hogg's sermons were,' Alec said, as he landed back on the grass by my side a minute or two later, 'but it's not worth it.'

Getting out of the tower had been easier than going in, with only an ungainly dangle to regret, and the impetus was greater. We could not let Miss Speir discover us here when she returned from church. We needed to affect a state of perfect innocence about what lay underneath the tower, with a view to returning, picklock at the ready. Alec had purchased a set of the things – heaven knew where and he would not tell me – and I had mocked him.

'Treasure!' he said, as we brushed ourselves down.

'Something worth securing under a pretty stout lock anyway,' I said. 'Treasure, for short. And I shall take great pleasure in telling Hugh he was wrong, if we ever get a look at it. But, not to be a killjoy, it's probably nothing to do with Vesper and Peter.'

'We need to speak to these four millers,' said Alec. 'Or two millers, I suppose. Or just one. We need to find out where and how Peter Haslett died.'

'Four,' I said. 'It's just occurred to me that it *is* all four. Because it doesn't matter where Peter's body was found, in the end, does it? If he died upstream of the first mill wheel his body could have floated all the way down, over the weir, all the way to the river mouth. And unless someone saw him go in off the ferryboat, there's nothing to say he actually did.'

'Four millers it is,' Alec said. 'Did we ever hear their names?'

I cast my mind back to Miss Lumley's breathless gossiping on our first day. 'I'm not sure we did. We know the mill names, or the middle two anyway: Peggie's and Fair-a-Far. But I've no idea about the ones on either end or the men themselves.'

'"My dear fellow" and "my good man" it is, then,' Alec said.

'And while we're pestering strangers,' I said, 'you should come and talk to the cottager I spoke to yesterday morning. She's *sure* Peter was on the path.'

I peeped around the corner of the tower. There was no sign of Miss Speir and Christine on the drive. Of course, if they had returned already and one of them was looking out of a window we were sunk, but no matter how short Rev Hogg's sermon, there was still the matter of a couple of hymns, a couple of prayers and the weekly intimations and I did not see how the congregation could possibly have dispersed so soon. We marched at haste straight over the lawn and in at the front door, only breathing out fully when we had got there.

'I just need to change my shoes,' I said. 'I don't know how I'll explain these scuffs to Grant when I get home. And your coat and trousers could do with a brushing.'

'Where are we off to?' Alec said.

'The four millers,' I said. 'I thought we had just agreed. There's no time like Sunday lunch to go bothering people, wouldn't you say? We'll find them at home and they won't be able to claim they're too busy to give us an interview.'

Alec went bounding off up the stairs to his room and was back down, pacing the entrance hall, when I returned with hair brushed and in fresh shoes and gloves minutes later.

'To the mills!' he said, holding the door open for me, 'although they're not actually milling anymore, are they? Do we know what they do?'

'Beyond the fact that one of them is a studio, no,' I said. 'Ah! We do know that *one* name Mr Eck Massey.'

132

'Tscht,' Alec said, a sound I could not immediately interpret, but as I looked along the drive I saw Miss Speir and Christine advancing. The lady was leaning on her maid's arm and had a handkerchief pressed to her mouth.

I surged forward. 'My dear Miss Speir, are you ill?'

'She's needing her bed,' Christine said, warding us off with a raised arm as she ushered her mistress past us. 'Never mind them, madam.'

'But what's wrong?' I said. 'Has something happened?'

'You'll see soon enough if you're away a walk,' Christine said over her shoulder. Miss Speir had not uttered a word.

Alec looked at me and I looked at him and then, as one, we were along the drive and down the hill to the top of the Sailor Street steps as fast as our legs would take us.

We began to hear the hubbub before we were halfway down the steps, and as we emerged at the bottom we saw a large crowd, most of the village I should have said, clustered on the path by the water's edge just opposite the last row of cottages before the trees closed in. Most of them were dressed in Sunday best and most of that was dark and sober despite the sunshine. Black and grey cloth coats predominated for the women, with black straw hats or at least black ribbons on the straw-coloured ones. Naturally the men were in dark suits too. And even the children were in navy blue and gunmetal grey. Overall the effect was of a funeral gathering. And as we neared them, the impression grew stronger, because some of them were crying and all of them were shaking their heads and muttering in low voices.

We pushed through the crowd, filling the gap left by a white-faced young woman who was shooing two little boys ahead of her.

'What was wrong with that lady, Mammy?' said the larger boy.

'Was that lady no' well?' said the smaller one.

'Wheesht now, never mind,' their mother said. 'She's just

133

playing a game. Never bother your wee heads. Let's get home and see if Granny's got the dinner ready.'

I think I knew before we had reached the front what we would see there. There were three men down on the foreshore, up to their knees in the river, with no regard for their Sunday trousers and what was probably their only pair of good shoes each. One of them held the end of a coiled rope and another was just that moment trying very gently to slip the other end, which was tied in a loop, from around the foot of a figure floating in the shallows, her long skirts sodden and dark and the white cotton shift I had given her plastered against her torso. Her hair, lately so wild and windswept, now lay in a wet hank over her face as the third man lifted her shoulders. Her head flopped to the side and a horrified murmur rose up from the watching crowd. Another young mother came to her senses and pulled a crying toddler away from the sight.

'Why is she tied to a rope?' I said to the elderly man standing beside me. He had tears in his eyes.

'Billy there flang it,' he said, pointing to the man who held the coil. It was dripping water. 'Cowman. He lassoed her to get her into shore. The tide's rising.'

'Is she alive?' Alec shouted. He jumped down from the path onto the pebbles and made his unsteady way towards the little group, just as the men let Vesper drop onto the ground.

'She's not breathing,' one of them said. He had given up trying to untie the rope and simply stood gazing down at the form on the stones by his feet. She was streaming water, soaking the pale rock and sending rivulets back into the edge of the tide.

'Turn her,' Alec said. 'Turn her onto her side and I'll squeeze her. She might only have choked.' He looked up. 'Dandy?' he said. 'Help!'

Despite a lot of muttering from the women around me about letting the men take care of it and about leaving her to people who knew her, I slithered down onto the rocks, feeling the scrape of another pair of shoes being ruined, and went staggering and clambering towards Vesper.

Alec was on his knees behind her with his arms wrapped around her ribs. He grunted as he made sharp jerks again and again, trying to dislodge the water he seemed to be sure was choking her. With every squeeze, a flood was pressed out of her hair and her sopping clothes but nothing emerged from her mouth.

'Should we lie her on her front and thump her back?' Alec said. I came up beside him and pushed the wet hank of Vesper's hair back from her face. She was a pale greyish blue, her lips the same colour as her cheeks and, when I took up one of her hands, it was icy and lifeless.

'Oh Alec,' I said. 'She's cold.'

'Of course she's cold,' said Alec. 'Floating in this water. I'm cold just from touching her and look at *him*.'

The man who had lifted her shoulders was shivering, standing in the sunshine hugging himself as he streamed. I turned Vesper's hand over and tried to find a pulse. 'Has someone sent for a doctor?'

'First thing when we spied her,' said the man who was holding the rope. Billy, they had called him. 'Miss Lumley went to ring up fae the pub as soon as we saw her floating.'

'And where's he coming from?' I said. Time often seems to slow to an unbearable crawl when shocking things happen, but if Miss Speir and Christine had had time to climb the hill and walk along the drive and we had had time to talk to them briefly and then hurry down here I thought the doctor was overdue.

'Just the west avenue there,' Billy said, as if I would know where that was. He too frowned and looked up over the heads of the crowd towards the road, as if hoping to see a motorcar approaching.

Alec had been watching me search for a pulse at Vesper's wrist. 'Well?' he said, as I let it drop again.

135

I gazed at him, standing there clasping her against himself. He could not see her face. I grimaced and shook my head. 'I'm sorry, darling,' I said. 'She's gone. There's nothing for it, I'm afraid. She's long gone.'

Alec heaved in a huge breath and then walked backwards, laying Vesper down on the rocks. He slipped his jacket off and laid it over her face and the clammy shift that was clinging to her breast without preserving any of her modesty. As he did, a wail rose up from the watching crowd and the sound of it made the hair on my neck crackle. A dozen and more women were keening, making a high, thin sound that filled the stillness like the cry of a wild animal. A few of the smaller children took fright at it and began sobbing. I cannot remember a time before or since when I have felt more wretched than I did at that moment, standing there damp and chilled on the foreshore, listening to wails and sobs and looking at the body of the girl we had been brought here to protect leaching river water in a wider and wider stain onto the pale rocks, while the men who had tried to save her took their hats off and bowed their heads in helpless defeat.

Just when I thought it could not get any worse, there was a bustle at the back of the gathered villagers and Mr Hogg, still in his cassock and pulpit robe, emerged.

'No, no, no, no!' he said. 'That isn't Vesper under there, is it?'

'It is,' I said. I cast my eyes over the crowd. 'Did anyone see anything? Did anyone see her go in?'

'She came downstream,' a voice called back. 'I saw her floating down from the weir. I didn't know what it was.'

'She was face down,' another voice called out. 'If she'd been face up we'd have kent. But it looked like a rag. We watched her float.'

'When did you realise it was a person?' said Alec. He was not shouting but his voice carried.

The villagers turned this way and that to look at one another but no one spoke.

'Are you sure it's too late?' said Mr Hogg. He had put one hand on the ground as if to scramble down onto the foreshore. 'Has anyone tried lifting and lowering her arms?'

'Mr Hogg,' I said, stumbling back over towards him. 'Please come away. It's far too late for Vesper.'

'But has anyone rung for the doctor?' he said.

'The doctor is on his way. We need to telephone to the police too. Come with me and help me.'

I raised my hands for him to pull me up and his natural chivalry made him respond. He hauled me up to stand beside him and then tucked my hand under his arm, tutting about how cold I was.

'I took Vesper's pulse,' I said. 'She's cold and I got cold touching her. But don't worry about me. I'm fine.' I patted his arm and then turned to the crowd. 'Who was it who realised this was a drowning?' I said.

'It was Miss Lumley that started shouting,' someone said. 'She came out the pub door and started up shouting.'

'That's what I heard,' said a young man, who looked abashed to be speaking up in front of so many witnesses. 'I heard a to-do and came to see what was up. I thought it was maybe a . . . well, I didn't know what it was, but it was Freedy Lumley shouting, for sure.'

I looked over at the pub doorway and wondered why she had not returned after ringing for the doctor.

There was one way to find out.

Rev Hogg held the door open for me and we entered together, into the dimness and silence of the public bar, such a stark contrast with the crowded scene out there in the sunshine. Miss Lumley was sitting alone on one of the high stools drawn up at the customer's side of the bar.

'What did the doctor say?' she asked, when she had seen who it was in the mirror.

'He's not there yet,' I said. 'But it's too late anyway. Vesper is dead. I think she's been dead for hours.'

'Poor soul,' said Miss Lumley. 'That it should have come to this.'

'You saw her first, I believe?' Miss Lumley did not respond I tried again. 'You were the one who raised the alarm, they're saying?' This time Miss Lumley nodded and turned to share a wan smile with me.

'I was looking out my top window,' she said. 'I thought it was a bundle of rags at first. Then it hit me.'

'Dreadful thing to see,' said Rev Hogg. 'What a shock it must have been.'

He patted Miss Lumley's hand and she grabbed his fingers and squeezed them.

Since the two old friends looked to be comforting one another, I thought I could safely leave them to it. 'Might I—'

'We don't open on Sundays,' she said. 'I keep the Sabbath. I'm a Highlander on my mother's side and—'

'No, I don't want a drink,' I said. 'Although Mr Hogg is in need of something. I only want to use your telephone, please? We need the police.'

'Oh dear, dear,' said Mr Hogg.

'The police again,' said Miss Lumley. 'What's happening to us?'

I bit my tongue on the remark that sprang to my lips: that nothing was happening to her except that the village where her pub plied its trade was once again going to receive a measure of notoriety. Apart from anything else, I knew she did not share this view. She had been very concerned to keep Vesper's trouble quiet and had been annoyed with Rev Hogg for writing to Alec and me. I was glad to see them cleaving to one another over this fresh upset.

'Miss Lumley,' I said. 'The telephone?'

She waved a hand at the back room and I slipped behind the bar. The back room was a marked contrast to the polished wood, brass and glasses out in the front. I surmised that Tom the potman spent no time in here and that the dirt and disorder did not trouble Miss Lumley. The telephone sat on an untidy desk where it appeared she did her accounting and paid her bills. I took it up and lifted the earpiece, but I heard neither the strange breathy buzzing of an open automatic line, nor the chatter of the girls at the exchange as in the old days. I heard nothing. I rattled the little lever but the deathly silence continued. I had got as far as peering under the desk to check the wire that joined the apparatus to the wall when I heard distant klaxons and realised I had been pipped. The police were here.

I left Rev Hogg slumped on the next stool along from Miss Lumley as I hurried out. The police motorcar and the doctor's motorcar had arrived neck and neck, it seemed, and had dispersed the knot of villagers as only two large motorcars driving with some insistence towards them can. Those mothers who had not already withdrawn their little ones from the pitiful sight down on the foreshore withdrew them now and even the men stepped back to a respectful distance. I, in contrast, pushed forward.

The doctor was already crouched beside Vesper's body. He had pushed Alec's coat away and was bent over her, with a stethoscope on her chest. A plume of hope rose in me, but as I drew near, he sat back on his heels and shook his head.

'Did she drown, Doc?' said one of the policemen. There were three of them, all in uniform and all hatless. They stood in a line with hands clasped behind their backs.

The kneeling doctor put his hands on either side of Vesper's head and tilted it back sharply, making her mouth drop open. I winced but managed not to gasp so loud that he could hear me.

'No doubt of it,' the doctor said. 'Bloody froth in the back of her throat and in both nostrils. Absolutely no doubt at all.' He stood up and brushed his knees where cobbles of grit were clinging to his tweeds. 'But let's make doubly sure, shall we? For the Fiscal. Turn her over, lads.'

The three policemen and Alec rolled Vesper onto her front and then the doctor threw one leg over her waist so that he straddled her. He pushed her hair out of the way and placed both hands on her back. Then he looked up at me. 'Avert your gaze, madam,' he said. 'This is not a sight for ladies' eyes.'

'I was a nurse in the war,' I told him. It was almost true. I was a volunteer nurse's aide, but we got the filthiest jobs and I was sure that nothing I was about to see could shock me.

The doctor shrugged, then turned his face away and began kneading Vesper's back in long rhythmic strokes, as if he was making bread. After half a dozen of these movements, an unspeakable noise emerged from under his hands and a great rush of pink-tinged liquid came foaming out from under Vesper's head. The doctor stood and brushed his knees again.

'No doubt at all,' he said. 'Ingested and aspirated water. She drowned. Accident, was it?'

'Possibly suicide,' I said. 'She has been terribly unwell with a nervous complaint. Worse and worse, actually.'

The doctor tutted and shook his head. 'Selfish to do it here and upset everyone.'

I said nothing, but I glanced at Alec to see if he thought the same as I did about this heartless remark. Alec was not listening. He was pale and rather glassy, wringing his hands. 'I've never seen that before,' he said. 'If I had done that, might she have survived? I was squeezing her under her ribs, you see, when I should have been doing what you did. Could I have saved her?'

The doctor tutted and waved the handkerchief he was using to dry his hands. 'She's been dead for hours,' he said. 'You have nothing to berate yourself over.' His hands dried, he put the handkerchief away and glanced at the policemen again, all of whom were pasty-looking after what they had witnessed. 'Over to you chaps,' he said. 'Can I write you a cert, or do you need the police surgeon?'

140

The three policemen gazed glumly at one another, each as unwilling as the others to take charge.

'We'll get an undertaker to come,' one of them said at last. 'There's no need to bother the sarge on a Sunday.'

'Right,' said another of them. 'You ring up the Co-op at Barnton and we'll take the statements.' He waved at the crowd of villagers, thinning now but still a dozen strong.

'No one saw her go in,' I offered. 'She floated downriver, they say.'

The doctor frowned at that. 'But the tide's still coming in,' he said. 'She shouldn't have floated downstream at all.' Then he shook his head as if to dislodge an annoyance.

'In any case, can we turn her over again?' I said. 'Can I close her eyes and fold her hands?'

The three policemen shrugged. None of them was willing to get any closer to the unpleasantness of a drowned woman and the pink froth that the doctor had forced out of her. I knelt down and, as a first step, I tried to gather Vesper's sodden hair together and twist it into a knot at the back of her neck. I lifted it, squeezing out as much water as I could and then froze. Unmistakably, on one side of her neck, there were four small round bruises. I bent over her. The smell of the water mixed with blood that had come out of her was indescribable. I felt my gorge rise but I was determined not to give up until I was sure. And there it was! On the other side of her neck high up under the bend in her jaw was a single fifth small bruise. I let her hair drop and stood, turning to face the policemen and spreading my arms to make a barrier.

'She was killed,' I said. 'This was murder.'

14

The sergeant arrived, bothered on a Sunday afternoon after all, then an inspector and finally the police surgeon himself all the way from the middle of town. He took a cursory glance at the death certificate written by the local man, then shook his hand and turned from him. His air of dismissal could not have been more marked if he had rung a bell for someone to clear the poor chap away. I felt for him; he had carried out an unpleasant task with competence if not flair and deserved better.

As the police surgeon's examination got underway, on the other hand, the actions of the first doctor were cast into a different light. This one was rather dashing and made the most of it with a full-skirted coat and a silver-topped cane. Once he had swished the coat aside and given his cane – with something of a flourish – to a constable to look after, he threw a mackintoshed mat down beside Vesper's body, knelt upon it and swept away Alec's jacket with far too much of the matador about the action. Then he pulled a monocle from his top pocket, polished it, screwed it in to his eye and bent over.

'This woman didn't drown,' he said. He had one of his long elegant fingers on Vesper's chin holding her mouth open.

'Really?' I said.

'There is none of the characteristic—' the surgeon began. I wondered if he was associated with the university. Perhaps he trained younger doctors there. For not only was his volume set at a suitable level for a lecture hall but his every utterance was declamatory too.

'Ah, well now,' Alec said. Surely the great man was never interrupted in those imagined lecture halls. He did not take kindly to it happening here on this foreshore. His face twisted as though someone had waved smelling salts under his nose. Alec ploughed on regardless. 'She did have the characteristic foam, you see. And lungs full of water too. Only the doctor did a sort of massage on her upper back and it all came out. Look. There, and there. Do you see?' He pointed at the drying residue on the rocks. It was only a pinkish wash. It could have been anything at all and yet as I looked my gorge rose again. To spare myself the sight, I looked back at Vesper. Of course, she was no easier to behold. Her mouth had stayed open and was drying out. Her tongue was pale and crusted and her lips were cracked. I was almost glad the surgeon started up with his scolding again, simply because it distracted me.

'And what were you all doing when the local sawbones was tampering with my victim?' he said. He raised his eyebrow to let his monocle drop and glared at the policemen.

'I wasn't here,' said the inspector.

'Me neither,' said the sergeant. 'I mean, nor I.'

'We didn't know it was murder,' I chipped in. 'Not then. It wasn't until I went to tidy her hair—'

'You did what?' the surgeon said. 'Hairdressing?' Now that his glare was turned on me I understood why the two senior policemen had rushed to explain themselves.

'We thought she had had an accident,' I said. 'A suicide at worst. And so I tried, out of pity, to tidy her up a bit. That was when I saw the finger marks. On the back of her neck.'

He did not like that at all. With a roughness I winced to see, he turned Vesper's shoulders over. Her hips were now twisted like a corkscrew and her feet scraped on the rocks as they settled. The surgeon shoved her hair aside and re-screwed his monocle.

'These are finger marks,' he said, exactly as though I had

not just told him that. 'This woman was held underwater until she drowned. This is a murder.'

Alec caught my eye and shook his head in wonderment. I stepped back as quietly as I could, while the surgeon was busy measuring and studying the five little bruises. He paid no attention. When we were out of earshot, Alec began muttering.

'Right,' he said, his lips barely moving. 'Where do we start, Dan? She wasn't held under here right in front of everyone's noses, was she? And the boat's still on the other side. So where did she go in? And when? We need to find out exactly when Irvine and Fordyce last saw her—'

'No we don't,' I said. 'We know when she came over from the island. The only time it can have happened is after we walked the causeway in the other direction and before the tide turned.'

'Sunday morning,' Alec said. We had reached the top of the beach and he handed me up onto the path, with a grunt. 'A very good time to drown a woman in broad daylight. When everyone's at church.'

'Not these days surely,' I said, rearranging my skirts after the step up. 'Not even a majority these godless days.'

Alec clambered up beside me and nodded rather absently.

'But you're right that we need to find out where she went in,' I said. 'So we need to speak to anyone who wasn't at church. Starting with the local *artist*. Eck Massey.'

'The owner of the grain mill?' said Alec. 'Why?'

'Because he found Peter Haslett's body,' I said. 'Or at least he claimed to. He raised the alarm at any rate. And didn't someone say none of the millers are church-minded? Besides . . .?'

Alec waited. It is one of his most appealing characteristics. Hugh, long years after he resigned his commission, still regularly treats me like a junior officer who must account for myself and not waste his time with my pondering.

'There's something amiss,' I said in the end. It was hardly worth the wait but Alec simply nodded. It is another of his better features; he knows what I am talking about without my ever actually having to say anything.

'I agree,' he said. 'Why did Vesper float downstream with the tide coming in? And why does no one know whether Peter Haslett went in off the boat or the edge?'

'That's not it,' I said. 'What does it matter where the river meets the tidal waters and which way they send whatever's floating in them? Vesper was murdered and even Peter didn't drown. Whatever this is about, Alec, the water is neither here nor there.'

'As we go to interview a miller,' was all Alec said, and he said it mildly.

Perhaps if he had said it less mildly I would have been chastened into defending my claim with more vigour. And perhaps then I would have realised how wrong I was and how much we were missing.

Cockle Mill, the old grain mill and ironworks as the barmaid had told us, and the studio in its current incarnation, looked less shuttered and abandoned this Sunday morning, which was rather odd. The padlocked door was standing open now for one thing and although the handcart was gone and the wheel was not turning, something about the place was welcoming. Alec homed in on the salient fact, unsurprisingly.

'Someone's cooking,' he said, with his nose in the air. 'Roasting pork.'

'Are you sure?' I had taken a deep sniff too. 'Rendering bones, I'd have said. And not pork. Beef, I'd say.'

'Perhaps Mrs Massey has gone down to see what the fuss is about,' Alec said. 'The klaxons and what have you. And left her Sunday lunch to spoil. Should we try to track it down and save it for her?'

'We can't go poking in someone's kitchen,' I said. The smell that struck Alec as a delicious luncheon of roast meat going to waste really had seemed to me to belong in the back room of a butcher's shop, but I did cast my eye around the buildings, wondering which one was the miller's cottage. There was nothing that looked more domestic than the engine room, mill house and sheds, except for the row of workers' cottages, and they were definitely abandoned. Alec had taken the sensible first step, however, by walking over to the open door and knocking.

'In you come,' a voice called. 'There's two of us beat you!'

Alec turned to me, gave me the look I am sure is the twin of the one he must have worn as a small boy when putting frogs in his nanny's spectacle case, and walked in.

I knew that whoever had called was expecting someone in particular and that we were not that person, but nevertheless I followed him.

The smell was even stronger inside, and much more clearly unconnected to the creation of luncheon. I briefly wondered if rendered fat had a place in some artistic pursuit, but then I was distracted by the sight that met our eyes as they adjusted to the dimness.

We were in some sort of storage room, or warehouse. There were stout shelves four high and as deep as double beds all around the walls. Most of them were empty, with only a few boxes gathering dust here and there. In the middle of the floor a couple of packing cases had been pushed together to form a makeshift table and two men in Sunday suits, collars and ties and shiny shoes sat at it, whisky glasses in hand. A bottle of the stuff – the worst sort of blended filth – sat on one of the packing cases. The men stared at us in silence, for a moment.

'Mr Massey?' I said, dividing a smile between the two of them.

'Who's askin'?' said one of the men. He had a ratty look about him, his hair rather too long and oily at the parting. His eyes, close together anyway, squinted as he peered at me.

146

Of the pair, he did look the most at home, since he was sitting at the head of the table, if two tea chests can be said to have a head, and his tie had been pulled down and his collar stud undone. He could pass for an artist.

'Mr Massey,' I said again. 'I'm Mrs Gilver.' I advanced with hand outstretched. 'And this is Alec Osborne. We're acquaintances of Mr Hogg, here at his bidding to—'

'What's the minister sending you here for?' said the other man. He was a colourless little shrimp, so round-shouldered that I could not decide whether he was hunchbacked or merely slouching.

'Not here,' Alec said. 'Cramond, we mean. We're detectives. We were engaged to look into the problem of Vesper.' He paused. Neither man said a word or even breathed. Both were apparently turned to stone. But then hearing that we are detectives had had that effect many times before.

'And so, as you can imagine,' Alec continued, 'we are rather set back on our heels this morning.' He paused again. Again the two men sat silent and immobile.

'You have heard, haven't you?' I said. 'Have you?' I glanced at the whisky bottle. 'I assumed you were toasting her memory.'

'Memory?' said the round-shouldered man. 'Vesper Kemp?'

'We've been sitting here, keeping out of the wives' way since the kirk chucked out,' the ratty man said. 'It's our wee Sunday indulgence. No one knows nor needs to. Did you say the lass's *memory*?'

'She drowned,' said Alec. 'Well, she died by drowning. This morning. In the river. The police surgeon is down there outside the Turning Tide right now and five policemen too.'

'Five policemen?' said the shrimp.

'How d'you mean "died by drowning" and not "drowned"?' said the ratty man, squinting even more. 'What's the difference?'

Before either of us could answer, the half-open door

147

swung wide and a third member of their drinking club appeared, another working man in his Sunday best. He did not strike me as an artist. He had work-thickened fingers and a complexion of brick red. I would have guessed at farming or even fishing if I had passed him on the street. 'You're here,' he said. His breath was ragged and he staggered as he stood there, as though he had been running and could not quite find his balance now he had stopped. 'You'll not have heard, if you're just sitting here same as ever.' He flicked a look at Alec and me but carried on regardless. 'Someone's been put to death. There's been a murder, down the shore front there. Place is crawling with coppers and half the village is standing gawping, like they've brought back hangings. I don't know who it is and I didn't ask.'

'It's Vesper Kemp,' I said. 'She was held underwater by her neck until she drowned.'

The man groped his way to the table, using the edge of a shelf to steady himself. He dropped into a chair and took the tumbler of whisky one of his friends had slopped out for him.

'Vesper?' he said. 'Wee Vesper from the ferry? God almighty. Who'd ever want to be doing that?' He searched our faces as if we might truly have an answer, his cheeks pale from the shock.

'Killed?' said his rat-faced friend. 'Murdered?'

'We came here to ask if you had seen or heard anything,' I said.

'Us?' said the slouching man, with a frown.

'Mr Massey,' I said, gesturing towards the man I had assumed to be the mill owner.

'Why me?' said the new arrival, surprising me. His eyes glittered in his beefy face as he glared.

'Well, we're here to ask you because this is your . . . studio,' I said. 'And then we'll go on upriver to ask the others in turn. Did you?'

'Studio?' said Massey. When he drew his brows down and pulled his chin back he really was quite ferocious-looking.

'Someone said so,' I told him. The notion clearly troubled him. 'One of the serving girls at the pub.'

'The Brig was this?' Massey said. 'Or the Inn?'

'The Tide, wasn't it?' I said to Alec. I remembered clearly otherwise but there was something so threatening in Eck Massey's face and voice that a protective instinct had sprung up in me when I thought of that curly-haired child with her rosy cheeks and careless chatter.

'Well, this is no studio,' Massey said. 'And I'm no waster mucking about daubing messes and calling it a day's work. I'm a working man, Mrs Gilver. I make goods I'm proud of here in my factory and I don't take kindly to any barmaids having fun with my good name.'

I could hardly blame him; I had gone truffling after the scent of an 'artist' exactly because I thought he might be the loose-living sort. But he did not know that and so I was not about to apologise. I gave the man a tight smile and said nothing.

'Serving girl at the Tide,' he went on in a musing sort of voice, forcing me out of my silence after all.

'I'm sure nothing was further from her mind,' I said. 'We had asked her a question and she was simply explaining who you were.'

'Oh aye?' he said. He really was the most unpleasantly belligerent individual. 'What question was this?'

'We wondered who found the first body,' Alec said. 'And we discovered it was you.'

'Well, I didn't find this one,' Massey said.

'I take it you didn't see Miss Kemp this morning?' Alec asked. 'On the way to church or on the way back?'

The three men looked at one another and shook their heads.

'Wee Vesper,' said Massey again. 'Wee soul. After all her troubles, this is the end she's come to.'

The round-shouldered man lifted the whisky bottle and refilled each glass with a grim look on his face. 'God rest her,' he said.

'None of us saw a thing,' said the ratty man, when they had all drunk and lowered their glasses again. 'If we saw a rough stranger hanging round we'd not go letting him pass. We'd not go letting him get his hands round the throat of one of our own, would we lads?'

They shook their heads and each of them took another swig, in self-congratulation. Or so it appeared to me. Alec and I muttered our goodbyes and left.

'I suppose,' I said, when we were a good distance away, 'putting one's hands round someone's neck is the most obvious way to cause drowning.'

'Oh, you spotted that too, did you?' said Alec. 'Yes, I did wonder. You definitely said "held under". And *he* definitely said "hands round the throat". And that's not all.'

'Indeed not,' I said. 'Do you really believe that anyone would see police and neighbours all standing around and not ask who had died?'

'I do not,' said Alec. 'Mr Massey might be a good actor but he did not convince me. Think about it, Dandy. Think about his arrival.'

I cast my mind back and the truth of it struck me. 'Oh!' I said. 'He was listening at the door.'

'He was listening at the door,' Alec said, nodding. 'If he'd come running as he pretended we would have heard him approach. But the first we knew was when the door opened. He probably tailed us all the way up from the village. He called you by name too but he hadn't arrived when you introduced us.'

'Why?' I said. 'What was the point of the pretence?'

'I don't know,' Alec said.

We paced in silence the rest of the way back down the riverside, until we were out from under the trees. The police surgeon was gone and so was the ambulance, although the five policemen were standing in conference on the shore. Almost all of the villagers had dispersed now. The only creatures unconcerned with this fresh tragedy were the few little black bantam hens stalking around the weedy edge of the path, lunging at grubs and scratching up dust.

'Shall we keep asking around? Alec said. He waved at the row of cottages all with their windows facing the river. 'Someone must have seen something.'

'I know just where to start,' I said, catching a woman's eye. The owner of the bantams, the sweeper of her doorstep, the cottage woman who had let that tantalising snippet about Peter Haslett escape her was one of the few still at her post, watching the policemen.

Holding her gaze, I made my way towards her. She shifted a few uncertain steps in one direction then in another and she glanced around as though looking for supporters. But no one stood anywhere near her. Presently, she stopped shuffling. She even lifted her chin in a show of defiance.

'Well?' I said, as Alec and I drew near. 'What did you see this time?'

'I'm sure I don't know what you mean,' the woman said. She did not lift a fluttery hand to her neck like Miss Speir. She folded her arms and spread her feet until she stood like a bulwark, forcing us to step to the side.

'Alec,' I said. 'This good woman— what's your name, dear?'

'Mrs Cullen,' she said, causing me to blink. I had not expected to be put in my place with such a show of formality.

'Well, young Mrs Cullen told me yesterday, Alec, that Peter Haslett wasn't on Vesper's boat at all. That, on the contrary, he was swimming at a point where the path along the river is quite ten feet from the edge.'

'Not me,' the woman said. 'You were asking, if you recall, madam. And I said there's plenty good swimming ponds here and there up the river, and the path meanders. But I never

151

said poor Mr Haslett was in any of them. He poled the boat when he'd been drinking and fell in. I thought everyone knew that. It was in the report. It was in the papers.'

It was all I could do to stop my jaw from falling open.

'Twenty-four hours ago,' I said, 'you stood in your doorway and looked me in the eye and said he went in off the river-bank. And now you stand there and look me in the eye and deny it?'

The woman's expression had been getting more and more fixed as I spoke and her jaw was now clenched hard. It was not until I saw her shoot a quick darting glance over my shoulder that I realised the problem. I turned and then took a faltering step away. A man had come up behind us, stealthy on the grassy edge of the lane, despite his height and bulk and the fact that he wore working boots instead of Sunday shoes. His hat brim was broad and threw the top half of his face into deep shadow. The bottom half was covered with a thick and rather oily-looking beard.

'All right there, my girl?' he said. His voice was deep and surly.

'Aye aye aye fine,' the woman said, with a tremor in her voice. I found myself hoping this was not her husband, for there was something deeply unsettling about his silent approach and his neglect of even the slightest nod towards social niceties. That was clearly troubling Alec too.

'Osborne,' he said, offering his hand. 'I don't believe we've met.'

The man simply looked at Alec's outstretched hand, gave a gruff laugh that was halfway to a snort and lumbered away again off up the riverside.

'What a delightful chap,' I said, relief making me frivolous. 'Who is he?'

'No one,' the woman said; back to her habitual style of quite pointless untruths. 'No one at all. He's not anyone. I need to go. I need to get on. Sunday dinnertime.'

'Might we come with you?' I said. 'We still have questions. You can cook and we can talk. Can't we?'

'No, no indeed,' the woman said. 'Leave me be.' She took a deep breath with a sob at its back. 'In the name of Mercury, leave me alone. Please. Forget what I said and, snakes upon me, let me go.'

15

By mutual agreement we made our way up the Sailor Street steps to the Cramond Inn to warn the little barmaid, if she was working the midday shift, that we might have been indiscreet and caused her some trouble. Then, by further mutual agreement, we were headed back to Miss Speir to check that she had recovered from her shock. Lastly, we were determined to find a quiet spot to sort through not only the alarming events of the morning but also the hints and clues and various tiny false notes that were beginning to make me feel that nothing in this village was at all what it seemed and that everyone was lying and that we were the butt of what would seem an elaborate joke, were it not for a young man in his grave and a young woman now in a police hearse on her way to the mortuary.

'I know one thing,' Alec said, as we toiled up the steep steps.

I shushed him. The garden walls to either side were high and anyone might be standing on the other side, listening.

'I know one thing,' he whispered. 'There were four seats round that tea chest and four glasses set on top of it. And I know exactly who I think the fourth man was. Rather late but headed that way now. Don't you think?'

'That looming bear?' I said. 'Rather a leap, darling.' We had emerged at the head of the steps now and stood to catch our breath before crossing to the inn. 'But you are dead right about the table for four. That chap called out "two of us are here already". If only three were expected he'd have said "both of us", wouldn't he?'

'Exactly,' Alec said. 'Snakes upon me, those stairs are tough.'

'Don't!' I said. 'Don't joke about it. I found that utterly chilling, even if you didn't.'

'I did!' said Alec. 'I'm doing the equivalent of whistling past the graveyard. That's all.'

With that, he held the inn door and ushered me, for the first time in my life as far as I could recall, into a pub for Sunday opening.

The pretty little barmaid was indeed at her post, and hard-pressed to keep up with the orders, it appeared, for a great many people had gathered here to rake over the morning's happenings. She greeted us cheerfully. Alec bought me a sherry – sweet this time; I had learned my lesson – and we settled down to wait until she came clearing glasses and we could have a quiet word. The talk was, naturally, of Vesper but although the police surgeon's words had seemed loud enough to me, no one else in the bar seemed to know it was murder. Drowning was the word on everyone's lips. The barmaid's main theme was that things went in threes and something had to be done before another soul was claimed by the river.

'Soul claimed by the river indeed,' Alec muttered to me. 'Never heard such nonsense.'

'We need to keep the wee ones off the beach,' said a woman who looked old enough to be a grandmother.

'And no walking on the causeway,' said a stout man with a red face. I would have been astonished to hear that he had embarked on much of a walk, on the causeway or anywhere else, in the last twenty years.

'We should put a sign up,' said a young woman, over-dressed and nervous-looking. 'On the board where they post the tides. Urging extra caution.'

'On what grounds?' muttered Alec. 'Really!'

'And when's the funeral going to be?' said another woman. 'She's no one to bury her. If it's on the parish it'll not be quick.'

I could not for the life of me think what was troubling her about a long wait before Vesper could be laid to rest, but I was in the minority. The rest of the Sabbath clientele of the Cramond Inn started to mutter.

'Now just you hold on there.'

'Not cold yet.'

'Have some respect.'

'And don't be thinking you've got it in the bag, for there's more and better than your lad.'

Alec frowned at me. I shrugged back.

'For *my* boy has a wife and three weans,' the last contributor added. 'And he was in the navy.'

'Aye, on a stone frigate counting envelopes,' said the first woman. 'And there's my Tom a lifeboatman these last seven years.'

Alec's face cleared and I think mine must have too; suddenly he was nodding. These villagers, like ghouls – and cold-hearted ghouls at that – had their eye on the ferryman's job.

'We were led to believe,' Alec piped up, causing an instant hush to descend, 'that the boat was Vesper's own. Her father's before her. That's a shame, isn't it? To think of the new ferryman having to buy a boat when the coble's sitting there.'

'Wouldn't catch me on board that thing now,' said the cautious young woman who had urged the sign. 'It's claimed two lives. And, like Maudie said, things go in threes.'

I am sure that Alec only knocked back the entirety of his whisky to help him hold his tongue but banging his empty glass down had the additional result that Maudie came out from her station to clear away the empty. She was rather grim-faced, but then it must be difficult to combine hospitality and cheer with respect for the recent dead and fellow-feeling for the crowd who had gathered to enjoy the tragedy.

'I'm glad you came over,' I said in a low voice that invited her to draw near and bend down. 'We have something to tell you.'

156

'About Vesper?' she said. 'What do you know?'

'No,' said Alec. 'About Peter Haslett. Well, about Eck Massey.'

Her eyes opened very wide, wide enough so that I could tell she wore her lash black even today.

'I'm afraid we referred to Mr Massey's finding of the body,' I said. 'Although we didn't reveal the source of the information. He seemed most displeased.'

'He seemed enraged,' said Alec. 'Of course, you know the man and we don't. Perhaps his bark is worse than his bite but you might want to keep your distance for a day or two.'

The girl was gaping at us now.

'Although,' I said, 'odd as it is, it wasn't *that* he took such exception to. It was the accusation of his being an artist.'

'Artist?' squeaked Maudie, so quietly and at such a high pitch that the both vowels sounded exactly the same as one another. 'I never said that.'

'You said he used the place as a studio,' I reminded her. I wondered what was wrong with the child.

'Aye, he does,' she said. 'Paint. He makes paint. Mixes colours. Makes up orders. That's what I meant. He's not a painter. He's just a . . . he makes paint.'

Alec was gazing at her with an expression it was no trouble to decipher. One might assume that a maker of paints had enough dealings with artists to render him contemptuous of them as a class and to cause him grievance to be thought among their number, but take it any way one might, the greater slur was surely that he was mixed up in the death of a young man whose fatal injury was inflicted by Massey's water wheel.

'A simple misunderstanding.' I said. 'No harm done.'

She swiped up my sherry glass, despite the fact that I was not quite finished with it, and with a drilling glare at both of us she flounced off back behind the bar. The exchange, which had started so discreetly, had inevitably attracted attention

157

as it wore on and I was more than happy to slip out of my seat and bolt for the door.

My egress was prevented by walking straight into Rev Hogg on his way in. We both breathed out hard and then clutched one another by the forearms to steady ourselves.

'I'm not on a pub crawl, I assure you, Mrs Gilver,' he said. 'I've been fortified adequately down at the hotel. I'm only stopping in here to see if Christine has left yet. I don't mind climbing the hill to share the news but I'm just as happy to relay it.'

'Christine?' I said, racking my brain. 'You mean Miss Speir's maid?'

'She quite often comes down for a stiffener once the meal's served at Cramond House,' said Rev Hogg.

It sounded most irregular to me, but I suppose it went some way towards explaining her cooking.

'I don't think she'll be here today of all days,' I said. 'After all the upset. She'll surely be tending to Miss Speir. She *was* doing in fact – wasn't she, Alec? We met them coming in as we came out, just after the terrible discovery, and she was being most solicitous. I'd be very surprised if she leaves her mistress's side this afternoon.'

'But we can save you a trip anyway,' Alec said. 'Miss Speir already knows. She knew before us. She told— Well, no. She didn't exactly tell us. But she told us trouble was afoot.'

'Really?' said Rev Hogg. 'Are you sure?'

'Quite positive,' I said. 'We met them coming along the drive. She was rocked on her heels by it all. She was tottering.'

The minister stood with his chin drawn in and his mouth drawn down. After a long pause and deep breath, he shook his head. 'I'm sorry to be obstreperous, dear lady,' he said, 'but that is quite simply not true. I watched them from the church gate. I don't stand at the door and then bang it shut on the heels of my flock. I always walk to the gate and wave them off on their way. And Miss Speir and her good Christine turned in at their own drive. I saw it with these two eyes. Then, as I was just about to turn away myself, back through the kirkyard to the manse, I heard the first voices down on the shore.'

I opened my mouth to argue, then thought the better of it. The man was upset and he had been drinking; more than one small sweet sherry whisked away half-finished, I was willing to wager. I simply smiled and patted his hand. Then we both bade him good day. Alec held the door open for him and he disappeared inside. Whatever he said about only being there to track down Christine, he had decided not to waste his trip. I hoped he would raise the tone of the bar room conversation above base gossip.

'Poor old man,' Alec said, once the door had swung shut again.

'She definitely knew, didn't she?' I said. 'I'm casting my mind back and she didn't tell us. But it beggars belief that there was some other enormity taking place on the same spot at the same time.'

'Perhaps Miss—' Alec began, then shook his head.

'What?' I said.

'I'm getting muddled,' Alec said. 'I was going to say perhaps Miss Lumley telephoned to her when she went to ring the doctor but that was afterwards. What? What is it, Dandy?'

I had stopped walking. The street was steep enough that it made my ankles ache to stand facing uphill, but I have never been able to suffer revelations without breaking my stride and it is astonishing how often revelations break when Alec and I are on the move.

'Who telephoned the police?' I said.

'You did, you goose,' Alec said. 'And they came jolly quickly too.'

'No,' I told him. 'I didn't. I couldn't. I was still trying to get the dratted thing to work when I heard the klaxons. But that's only half of it. Alec, who rang for the doctor?'

'Miss Lumley,' Alec said.

'I don't think so. I know that's what she said, but I really don't think so. When I got there, the telephone was unplugged and the wire was coiled in a neat loop and tucked away. For the Sabbath. I'm sure of it. Miss Lumley said she doesn't open on Sundays. She prides herself on it, because of her Highland forebears and we know what they're like well enough. But she was slumped at the bar. If she had plugged that contraption in to summon the doctor I do not believe she would have unplugged it again and tidied it all up before she went to sit at the bar plunged in gloom. She is not a tidy-minded woman. The office was in a state of settled chaos, for instance. Unplugging the telephone again would have been the work of a habitually orderly one.'

'Perhaps one of the cottagers has a telephone,' Alec said. But as we both thought over the row of little houses, so modest even though they were snug and trim, it did not seem at all likely.

'It must have been Miss Speir,' I said. 'Once Christine had got her up the steps and into the house. The Rev Hogg is mistaken. She must have bobbed down the Sailor Street steps and back up again to see what all the fuss was about, then telephoned once she was home.'

'Let's see,' Alec said. We had started walking again and had just turned in at the drive. I gave the tower a glance as we passed, thinking that few were the mornings when the discovery of a trap door to a treasure trove could be shoved out of my mind by more notable happenings.

Inside the house, all was quiet. The dining room lay bare and in the drawing room the fire was unlit and the windows still open for the daily airing. Even Miss Speir's sitting room had an abandoned look. The enormous art history books had been closed and re-shelved. The desk top was bare.

We stood back out in the hall again and pondered, waiting

for one of us to have a brainwave. I had never been a guest in such an ill-run place before. Even taking into consideration the time my hostess was murdered at her own birthday party, Cramond House was in a separate class for poor management.

'She must be lying down,' Alec said, at last. 'Let's beard Christine. Where's the kitchen?'

We found it easily enough. Even a house as jumbled and added to as this was easily navigated so long as one did not mind barging.

'You're back on your feet then,' Christine said as we pushed open the door and let ourselves in to a large airy room tiled in blue and redolent with that same smell of roasting pork bones. Perhaps the local pig farmer had just been killing and every house in the village had taken a share.

'It's us,' I said, baldly. I wished I knew the woman's surname to address her politely. As matters stood, I simply called her nothing and it made me feel brutish.

'Mrs is lying down, after her turn,' Christine said. 'I didn't know where you two had got yourselves to so I'm afraid I've put the chicken in the larder for tomorrow and I've hashed the potatoes for supper. I didn't do any veg. Didn't want to waste them since Mrs is off her pegs and you were who knows where. Again.'

It was a fair point. We had let more than one meal spoil in the chafing dishes since we had got here and had only ourselves to blame.

'I'm sorry to hear she's had to take to her bed over it all,' I said. 'And I'm afraid we have nothing but bad news to add to what she knew already. Where exactly had things got to when you left the shore? What do you know?'

Christine had been oiling iron pans ready to stow them away in her cupboard again – and Alec looked quite bereft to see this evidence that a meal he had missed was so completely done with – but she straightened up and let the twist of greasy paper fall from her fingers.

161

'Shore?' she said. 'I never went back down the shore. I never left Mrs's side. Like I just told you. She was that upset.'

'Did she ring for the doctor?' I said.

'She wasn't able!' said Christine. 'If anyone had got the doctor to her it would be me. But she said she just needed some tea and sleep and I agreed. I'll have him out tonight if she's not better.'

'Not for Miss Speir,' I said. 'For Vesper.'

Was the woman a fool?

'Vesper Kemp?' Christine said. I was beginning to feel dizzy. Perhaps we were wrong. Perhaps two calamities really *had* occurred today. Perhaps we were going to have to break the news of the murder to Miss Speir and steel ourselves for whatever she had in store for us too. Christine's next words set me straight. 'She's beyond doctors,' she said, and there was not a trace of grief or even common sympathy for one of her fellow men. 'It's the undertaker she needs.'

'So you do know,' I said. 'But the doctor wasn't summoned by Cramond House? Nor the police?'

'Police?' said Christine.

'It was murder,' Alec said. 'Vesper was put to death. There's no doubt, I'm afraid.'

At that moment I became aware of breathing behind me and turned to see Miss Speir standing in the doorway. She had recovered, thankfully given the new shock just delivered. She had a shawl around her shoulders and had removed the combs from her hair, which hung down her back in a thin plait, but her cheeks were a healthy colour and when she spoke, her voice was quite steady.

'Murder?' she said. 'Vesper? Truly?'

'I'm afraid so.' Alec spoke gently. 'Miss Speir, this might seem an odd question at an odd time but how many telephones are there in the village?'

'Beyond odd,' she said, frowning.

'Only, we can't work out who rang the police,' I said. 'Or the doctor. And we can't work out how the word got around.'

'Oh this village!' Miss Speir said. 'By nightfall, I assure you . . .'

'No, but you see, forgive the impertinence,' I said. Then I took a breath and tried to speak with less wittering: 'How did you find out, Miss Speir? Mr Hogg thought you came straight home from church, you see. And Miss Lumley didn't ring up for a doctor yet a doctor arrived. And then police arrived and no one seems to have rung for them either.'

Miss Speir was suddenly not so rosy-cheeked. She stood quite still as her face drained.

'Jerry,' she said.

'Yes, Mr Hogg,' Alec agreed. 'He was on his way here to tell you the news when we met him and told him you knew already. He couldn't work out how.'

'What? No, no, no,' said Miss Speir. 'Heavens, there's no mystery there. Gert, the oldest Hamilton girl, was at the top of the Sailor Street steps telling all and sundry at the top of her voice. That's the Cramond way. I meant it was probably Jerry who telephoned.'

'No,' said Alec. 'He didn't. He was there on the shore.'

'Miss Lumley?'

'Not the police,' I said. 'And I don't think she rang the doctor either. So, as we asked, are there other telephones?'

Miss Speir looked at her maid and appeared to be thinking. 'There's a public kiosk up at the Brig,' she said. 'And of course the box in the Brig Hotel itself.'

'But no one would scamper through those winding lanes to get to either of them,' I said.

Miss Speir fished in a pocket and drew out a handkerchief. She pressed it to her mouth. 'Oh! Oh!' she said. 'You see what this means, don't you? Well, of course you do. You're detectives. You do see?'

'Tell us,' I said.

163

'You really mean it when you say murder?' she said. 'Did the police say so?'

'I saw the marks on her neck with my own eyes,' I said. 'I'm sorry to be so brutal but there's no doubt. Can I just bring you back to what you said though, Miss Speir? What is it that you're thinking, that upset you so?'

She looked at me and then at Alec, as though we were idiots. 'If Miss Lumley didn't ring and nor did Jerry and nor did I,' she said, 'and there was no time to get to another telephone after the body was discovered and before the doctor and police came . . . then it must have been the murderer. He's the only one who doesn't need to wait for discovery. He's the only one who already knows that murder has been done.'

164

16

As though she had exhausted herself with that display of cool logic, Miss Speir went tottering back off to her room assuring the maid that she was not hungry, but would welcome a little something light at teatime. Alec was getting fidgety about his missed luncheon and as I cast my mind around the possibilities, I did not foresee much joy. A Scottish village on a Sunday afternoon, once the hammer of the licensing laws has come down again, is not a cornucopia.

'Poor Mrs,' Christine said, when her mistress had gone. 'Her that was such a good friend to Miss Kemp down the years. She stuck out for her when the menfolk wanted to rip that job away from her, you know. Miss Lumley and Miss Speir were her staunchest allies.'

'It's terribly sad,' I agreed.

'Are you staying in?' Christine said. 'Because usually when I'm done with Sunday dinner I get out for a walk and I did just want to go down the shore and see if there's anything I can do to help. I used to be the midwife in Cramond in my young days and I still do the laying out for folks that don't want a big bill from that undertaker on the top road in his fancy wee shop. Maybe I can help them with Vesper.'

Alec swallowed hard. 'Vesper is gone, Miss . . . Christine,' he said. 'She's been taken to the mortuary for a post-mortem. The police are combing the beach. Unless they're finished. But in any case it's all in the hands of the law now.'

She nodded, looking just as avid as she ever could. It was clear to me if not to Alec that her offers of help were

165

poppycock. She desperately wanted to get down to the village to find out what she had missed and tell what she knew.

'If the police come here when you're out, where shall we say they can find you?' I said.

'Police?' said Christine. 'Here at Cramond House?'

'At every house, I'd have thought,' I told her, as she scuttled off.

'But Miss Speir's will no doubt be high on the list,' Alec said, once she was gone. 'If you're thinking what I'm thinking,' he added.

'That we put notes through the door of Vesper's principal residence and her summer cottage and signed them?' I said. 'What are we going to tell the police about *that*?'

'We'll get to it all in good time,' Alec said. 'First things first.' He opened two other doors first before he found the larder, but then he piled the stone pot where the chicken was cooling, a butter dish, a loaf of stale bread from the crock and a jar of virulent-looking piccalilli into his arms and brought them back to the kitchen table. 'See if you can scare up a pint of milk from somewhere, Dandy,' he said, then proceeded to make himself a sandwich that constituted the best meal of the entire case. I could not join him in the consumption of the piccalilli, for even the smell of it was enough to make me wince and the colour of the bread as it seeped in was revolting; and we had to make do with a cup of coffee, since the milk was the usual bluish last gasp of a Sunday afternoon; but as we looked at the wreckage of the chicken, at least for once we were not still actually hungry. Alec pulled off a wing, sprinkled it with salt straight from the pig and took a bite.

'Don't stick your fingers in the salt pig,' I said. 'Isn't there a spoon?'

He peered and shook his head. 'Christine's fingers must be in and out of it four times a day,' he said. He wiped most of the crusted salt off on the remains of the chicken wing and licked the last of it.

'How can you?' I said. 'Doesn't your tongue hurt?'

'From the piccalilli,' said Alec. 'Not from the salt.'

'She wasn't in the river,' I said, suddenly. I was not aware of choosing to speak. It was almost as though I was as surprised to hear the words coming out of my mouth as Alec was. 'She was drowned in the sea.'

'What?' said Alec. He paused in his chewing, eyes wide and one cheek bulging.

'Her mouth was crusted with salt,' I said. 'Her tongue was coated with salt. I looked right at her and I saw it, only I didn't realise, at the time, what I was seeing.'

'Well, the mouth of the river is brackish at best, Dandy. And when the tide's coming in it must be very salty indeed.'

'But the local doctor pushed all that water out of her lungs,' I said. 'If it was fresh water it would have rinsed out her mouth and washed the salt away. But it didn't.'

Alec took one last look at the scraps of skin and tendon he was nibbling off the chicken wing and put it down.

'You don't need to take my word for it,' I said. 'When the police post-mortem is done, they'll say the same. Or – I tell you what – let's go and take a sample, from the foreshore. We could analyse it ourselves, since we don't trust the police to do a proper job.'

'Don't we?' said Alec.

'After what happened with Peter Haslett?' I said. 'Do you? He didn't drown and no one knows why he was where he was. No one even seems to *know* where he was, come to that.'

'How are we supposed to have a sample of regurgitated water analysed?' said Alec. 'Do Donald and Teddy have chemistry sets left over from their boyhoods? Do you know what you're looking for?'

'No,' I said, 'but there are two scientists not a mile away who could help us. And we'd be killing two birds with one stone. I want to speak to them again. Now we know Vesper more than likely didn't leave the island we need to ask them if anyone else was there this morning. They might have heard the murderer arrive. They might have heard the murder. Come on, if you've finished gorging. Let's take Miss Speir's boat again and get over there.'

I took the time to put the chicken back in the larder, with a twinge of guilt about what Christine would think when she saw how much of it was gone. The loaf of bread was rather ragged on the cut end too, neither Alec nor I being all that adept with a breadknife, and the jar of piccalilli was a ghost of itself.

'That's another thing,' I said, as we were leaving the house minutes later, armed with a hastily assembled kit that made me feel like Sherlock Holmes. 'I don't know if the local force is corrupt or just incompetent but if Miss Speir is busy selling Roman treasure that should be in the museum and barely bothering to hide it then they're one or the other, wouldn't you say?'

It shames me to say it but I am afraid that when we got down to the spot where Vesper had died, I pretended to be standing with my head bent in prayer while I scoured the dents and dimples in the rocks to see if any of the water – I found it preferable to call it 'water' no matter how inaccurate that was – had survived the policemen's attentions. When I saw a hopeful-looking puddle, Alec bent and, while putting down the fistful of poppies and wallflowers he had swiped up from Miss Speir's herbaceous border, he scooped some of the water into the little jar we had found in Christine's dresser drawer and pushed the stopper in hard. Then he stood beside me, head bent like mine, and showed it to me. It looked clear enough against the palm of his hand. It wasn't until he held it up with his shirt cuff as a background that the deep rose-coloured swirls in the cloudy liquid really sprang into sharp relief.

'Oh God,' I said.

'Oh God, yourself,' said Alec. 'I've got it all over my hands. Look, let's get going. I don't think those two boobies are in any danger but you never know.'

Miss Lumley's telephone aside, a southern village like Cramond was not the hotbed of Sabbath observance that we have come across in more northerly parts on earlier cases, but I felt horridly conspicuous as we picked our way over the boat decks to the Seagull and then even more so as the outboard motor roared into throaty readiness again. No one appeared at a cottage door – not so much as a curtain twitched – but once again I itched under the certainty of myriad eyes marking our progress. And the thought troubled me. Was it possible that anything nefarious had been done under so many watchful eyes?

At least the engine announced our arrival. Irvine and Fordyce would not be caught without so much as a vest on again. I half expected them to appear on the beach as we drew near but Alec switched the engine off, hopped out and pulled the boat up the shingle without either of them showing his face, so we made our way back to the middle of the island and the trial plots, hoping that we were not about to stumble on a delegation of policemen engaged on the same task as were we.

'Although, of course the police aren't here,' Alec said as we toiled past the gorse towards the top of the rise. 'There would be a boat, if they were.'

'Unless they got dropped off and left here,' I said. 'While they collect evidence. I do hope not because we are bound to be scolded for trampling all over the place leaving irrelevant footprints. We might even be accused of bringing our feet back deliberately to cover the clue of our footprints from earlier. Oof!'

We topped the hill and the potato trial plots lay before us with no sign of either biologist.

'Maybe the coppers have come and gone and taken the lads with them already,' Alec said.

'Maybe,' I said. 'Or maybe they're simply typical youngsters who're loath to work on a sunny Sunday. Especially with no supervision around. Let's try to find them.'

'Are you worried?' Alec said.

'They certainly need to be told that Vesper is dead and that they need to keep their wits about them.'

'Unless they already know Vesper is dead,' said Alec. 'Unless they know only too well she is. Or at least one of them does.'

I screwed my face up, trying to see if that theory made any sense. 'Why would two undergraduates who happened to cross paths with a peculiar young woman up and kill her?' I said. 'She wasn't interfering with their experiment.'

'Even if she was,' said Alec. 'Is anyone so passionate about potatoes as all that?'

I was walking around the nearest of the trial patches as we spoke. 'I think the police might have come and taken the boys away, you know.' I pointed. 'They've left this row half-lifted.'

Indeed, there at my feet was a high ridge that halfway along became a deep trench. At the side of the trench was a pile of very spindly plants with paltry handfuls of extremely small potatoes clinging to each.

'I hope this is the . . . what is it you call it?' Alec said.

'I don't know,' I told him. 'You see what the problem is, don't you?'

Alec shrugged and looked at the plants.

'They went in upside down,' I said. 'Look, the roots are bent back and so are the shoots. They were planted the wrong way up. Now why would that be helpful, I wonder? I must ask Hugh.'

'Did you ever think, when you were a girl doing the Season,' said Alec, 'that you would come to know which end of a potato was the top? Come on, Dan. Let's see if Irvine and Fordyce are still on the island.'

When we had exhausted every other inch of the place we

found ourselves outside the Duck House again. The day, which had started so bright, was turning more typical of a Scottish summer now. Grey clouds had stolen across the sun and the wind had begun to whip the branches of the gorse bushes and the stand of beech trees behind us. The Duck House, without the help of sunshine and perhaps with the knowledge that its resident was gone never to return, no longer seemed romantic. It was a hovel.

Still, it was the only hovel around and it was possible that the two young men had taken shelter here ahead of the coming rain. I knocked on the door and waited.

'It was always an outside chance,' Alec said. 'Let's go.'

More from habit than hope, I think, he tried the handle as he turned away. It is difficult not to try the handle of a door to any room where one has hoped to gain entry; as a detective, it is beyond one's capacity altogether. Likewise it is impossible not to read the address on any envelope left lying where one can see it, and to peek at any letter inside if the envelope has been slit. Of course, as a lady and gentleman, such deeds are beyond the pale and Hugh has been disgusted with me many a time when I do not make a sharp enough distinction between my professional life and the habits dinned into me by Nanny Palmer. One of the comfortable aspects of spending time with Alec is that he does not scowl at me and feign shock at any amount of snooping. In the current moment, as the door fell open under his touch, he raised his eyebrows and pushed it wide.

'Hello?' he said. 'Is anyone in?'

Only silence came in reply. I leaned in and looked around the single room. It was neat and sound, with swept floor, crisp cotton curtains at its tiny window and a crisp cotton cover on its small table. The bed was pushed to the side on castors and a candle, trimmed and clean, waited in a brass holder for sunset. Still, set against the Coble Cottage, it was spartan in the extreme and new questions arose in me about what had disrupted Vesper's settled life and why on earth she had traded one house for the other.

'Now here's an ethical teaser,' said Alec. He was pointing to the truckle bed against the far wall. 'The police might have picked up Irvine and Fordyce but they haven't been here. Look, Dandy.'

I bent and peered at where he was pointing. There on the floor was the letter I had shot under the door the previous day.

'What do you mean?' I said. 'You mean take it back before they see it?'

'We know we didn't kill her,' Alec said, striding over and reaching under the bed frame. 'No harm done. Best not to tax the brains of the average bobby.'

'Don't let Inspector Hutcheson hear you,' I said, unfolding the paper absently. Alec smiled. We had met Inspector Hutcheson, of the Perthshire Constabulary, over a decade previously and, despite his scolding, mocking and chivvying us relentlessly throughout the weeks of our acquaintance until we felt like something between raw recruits with a zealous sergeant-major and grubby kittens with a zealous mother, we still thought of him as the detective of final authority, and with real affection.

'Inspector Hutcheson is far from average,' said Alec. But I was barely listening. I was reading the note in my hands. 'We are staying with Miss Speir and are eager to speak to you. Please do not hesitate to ring up or stop in. We are here to help.'

'It's the wrong one, Alec,' I said. I held up the piece of paper. 'This is the note I wrote in the Coble Cottage and left on the kitchen table. Not the one I wrote here and put under the door.'

'Are you sure?' Alec said, reading it. 'What did the other one say?'

'Much the same—'

'Well then.'

'No, but I mentioned Peter in the note I left here. I know I did. Don't you remember me saying so?'

'I can't honestly say I do,' Alec said. 'Far too much has happened too quickly. Are you absolutely sure, Dandy?'

'Absolutely. I was worried about her reading his name and thinking we were threatening her. It seemed reckless to put his name in writing at all, if I'm being quite honest about how uncourageous I am.'

'It's the wrong way round then, isn't it?' Alec said. 'I mean why would someone take the more incriminating note and leave the innocuous one?'

'The police would take the note,' I said. 'But they wouldn't leave one in its place. So it wasn't the police.' I turned the thing over and over in my hands, thinking deeply.

'Unless,' Alec said, 'someone took both of them. One from here and one from Coble Cottage, to show someone, perhaps. To ask advice. And the advice was to put the notes back and then . . .'

'They forgot which one came from where?'

'We can check the first bit of it anyway,' Alec said. 'To Coble Cottage, to the kitchen table. And if the other note's there we shall snaffle it too. I try to be law-abiding, as you know, but if someone else is making mischief here, I feel no compunction about preventing them.'

We saw it as soon as we entered the cottage kitchen. It lay on the table, moored by the sugar bowl where we had left its mate. It was flat, but the lines from where I had folded it into a dart were plain to see. And even Alec was convinced now.

'Whoever this is,' he said, 'who purloined them and then switched them, he is not the brightest star in heaven. Why would anyone make a paper aeroplane to leave on a table?'

'Unless whoever it is meant us to know,' I said. 'Is that a sensible notion?'

'Surely not,' Alec said. 'Why would "whoever it was" think we'd revisit the Duck House? No, Dandy. That's a twist too far. I think this was a mistake and knowing it was made is valuable.'

'How?' I began.

'In some way I can't quite put my finger on right now,' Alec said. 'But it must be.' He wandered into the sitting room and let himself flop down into Vesper's chair. I followed him and took her father's, feeling callous as I did so.

'Should we put the volume of history back?' I said. 'John Philip Wood? Even if it's not evidence and so of any interest to the police, it's part of her estate.'

Alec cast a glance at the pile of books on the table beside him and his eyes widened.

'What?' I said.

'It *is* evidence! Look, Dandy. *High Wages* by Dorothy Whipple, *The Film Review Annual*, and *Easy Recipes for One*. Only the Bible is still here. Someone has been in and swapped everything else.'

'It's as though someone's trying to paint her as quite a different person from the girl she was,' I said. 'How rotten. I wonder if there's anything else.' I leapt to my feet and trotted upstairs to look in Vesper's bedroom.

'Oh Alec! No!' The room was in disarray. All of her father's clothes were heaped on her single bed and his shaving equipment and pipes were stacked carelessly on the dressing table top. Alec arrived beside me. 'Oh, the beast! Whoever it was. Trying to make it look as if she shoved her poor father's clothes in a heap all anyhow and left them there? I would have been shocked to see such a thing. Why—?' Our eyes met and we surged as one towards the other, bigger, bedroom.

'This is unconscionable,' Alec said. The double bed was

174

tumbled, both pillows dented and all the blankets untucked. There were two glasses, one at each side of the bed, and an empty brandy bottle sitting on the floor. A chocolate box lay upended beside the bottle and wrappers were all around it on the bedside mat as well as caught here and there in the sheets.

'If it weren't for the books,' Alec said, 'I could just about believe someone had a tryst here. Nothing more. But the books.'

'And her father's clothes,' I said. 'No, this is definitely an attempt to smear Vesper's reputation.'

'Or her memory,' Alec said. 'And if it's her memory they must have been quick about it. She's only been dead . . . Well, we don't know. I wish we had found those two youngsters and checked when it was they last saw her.'

'But who would do that?' I said. 'And why? Film annuals? Chocolates and brandy?'

'To make the police think she's a silly girl and a floozy who had a quarrel with a lover,' Alec said. 'It doesn't mean they won't investigate, though. Nothing so extreme.'

'But it'll send them off on the wrong tack,' I said. 'Good grief, Alec, if we'd seen all this yesterday instead of what we did see, we'd think very differently of Vesper.'

'I wonder if this rotter knows we snaffled old John Philip's history of Cramond parish,' Alec said. 'It must be driving him demented, if so.'

'Where is it?' I said. 'In your room at Cramond House?'

I did not have to say any more. Alec was halfway down the stairs before the words were spoken, the possibility of someone breaking into his room and purloining John Philip Wood not at all lessened by the fact that he had himself broken in and purloined it only a day ago.

His expression was one of outrage and his tread was thunderous as he made for the front door. He stopped on a sixpence, however, as it swung open to reveal the inspector, the sergeant and one of the constables, standing shoulder to shoulder on the doorstep forming a solid blockade and looking very keen to see who was on the rampage.

17

If they had insisted on searching us, and had found the two notes tucked into my bag, I would have come clean about everything. They did not insist; I expect the thought of summoning a police matron to the village on a Sunday afternoon was daunting and they knew that to rummage in Alec's pockets without taking the trouble for me would render the whole exercise a travesty.

Likewise, if they had asked outright what we were doing in Coble Cottage, even separating us and asking us individually, to play one off against the other, I would have answered the question fair and square. They did not ask and they did not separate us. They lost forever the chance of Alec's and my help, through sheer incompetence.

The inspector, once he had finished staring, simply announced his understanding of what met his eyes and let us agree. 'Oho!' he said. 'So you thought you'd see if you could smooth it all over, did you? Yes, the minister told us he engaged you to hush up her state of mind. And so you thought you'd hush up her suicide too, I see!'

'Suicide?' I said. 'What about the marks on her neck?'

'The surgeon thinks they could just as easy have come from someone trying to pluck her out of the water as from someone holding her under,' the sergeant put in.

Alec boggled at him. 'No one would try to lift a woman out of the water by her neck!' he said. 'Like a kitten!'

'The minister told us all about her,' the inspector said, with a glare at his sergeant for grabbing the chance to expound

177

the new theory. 'Nervous troubles, left her post, wild talk. Sounds much more like a suicide than a murder victim to me. And anyway, someone saw her go in.'

'Who did?' I asked. 'Was it one of those lads?'

'They'll not thank you for that,' said the constable. 'Men in their forties.'

'Who?' I said. 'I didn't mean any man in his forties. I meant—' But I managed to stop talking before I said either student's name, thinking it too unfair to drop them into this silly man's cooking pot.

'And did whoever it was – forties or otherwise – also see someone try to pluck her back out again by the scruff of her neck?' Alec said.

'I'm not here to answer your questions,' the inspector said. 'Sit down and wait while we— I'm not here to explain what I'm doing to you.' He was the silliest man I had run across in quite some time. Having declared that we were not to know the details of the operation he could hardly give orders about it to his underlings in our hearing; but being therefore forced to turn his back and mutter in their ears seemed to annoy him. When he turned back his face was set in even more of a scowl.

'Well?' he barked.

Alec and I had subsided into the two armchairs again and we looked up at him with expressions of innocence that were quite sincere but which annoyed him yet more.

'Well what?' said Alec. It sounded like insolence and the inspector began to change colour, but in all fairness there is no other way to ask that question, except by circumlocutions that would likely annoy him even more.

'Upstairs—' I began.

I was interrupted by a shout from above. 'Sir? You need to see this.'

'Inspector,' I said to his already retreating back, 'if it's Vesper's bedroom—' but he was already gone.

'Are we admitting we saw it then?' said Alec once we were

178

alone. The ceiling creaked in protest at three large men in boots standing close together in the room above our heads. I looked up at it and shrugged.

'Let's see,' I said. 'See what they make of it. If anything.'

When the inspector returned, he had recovered his good humour. In fact, he had become lordly and, with it, insufferable. 'Did you enter Miss Kemp's bedroom?' he said, giving us a pitying look.

'No,' I said. If he was such a hopeless listener that he had not registered me trying to speak of Vesper's bedroom two minutes ago, then he deserved to be lied to. 'We were on our way upstairs when we heard you arriving. Why?'

'I'm not here to answer questions,' he said. But it was beyond him to resist showing off and with barely a pause he sailed on. 'We're trained, you see, to interpret a scene even when the players are missing. And Miss Kemp's bedroom suggests suicide more strongly than ever.'

'How?' I said. 'Was there a note?'

'Not a note but evidence of a life worth leaving behind.'

I stared at him, aghast. 'The marks,' I said. 'On her neck.'

'Probably nothing to do with her death at all,' said the inspector. 'Probably the marks left after a passionate embrace. They do it on the pictures. Not so much an embrace as a wrestling match sometimes.'

'Hang on,' Alec said. 'You're suggesting that those finger marks – those dark bruises on Vesper's neck – came from a lover?'

'So you've stopped pretending there is no such person,' the inspector said. 'Hogg the minister thinks butter wouldn't melt. Maybe suicide will change his mind. It's still against the laws of the church after all, no matter what else has gone by the wayside.'

'She was murdered!' I said. I was beginning to feel quite giddy from the effort of challenging such a bloom of nonsense, coming up so exuberantly, like mushrooms.

'Or if she was,' said the inspector, with a fresh efflorescence, 'then we can hardly be surprised. A girl like that. Did you know the name of this ne'er-do-well she got herself mixed up with? We could have him behind bars tonight and all the paperwork done by this time tomorrow.'

'He's an idiot,' I said to Alec, minutes later as he wound the starting rope tightly on the spindle, ready to pull the engine into life and take us away from the inspector's outpourings and the sergeant's sheepish looks and bitten lips. 'And the other two know it. I hope there's an even-higher-up whose ear they can whisper into. Without losing their jobs for insubordination.'

'He is a bit of a fool,' Alec said. 'Still, it was the constable who made the biggest error. At least if discretion is the watchword.'

'What do you mean?'

'I bet you the next unpleasant task that you can work it out before we get across this river and tie up again.'

He tugged the rope and grinned at me as the engine roared. I took tight hold of the seat underneath me, expecting the boat to move, but Alec, although his hand was on the clutch, did not let it in, but only sat staring at me, still with that annoying grin on his face. He is nothing if not honourable and would not begin until I took his wager. At my nod, he depressed the clutch so sharply that the boat gave a bounce as it got going.

I studied him as I cast my mind back. The constable had said precious little. 'Sir, you need to see this' and 'They'll not thank you for that.'

'Oh!' I said. Alec could not hear me over the racket but he saw my lips move and saw the truth break over me. 'Men in their forties!' I shouted. He grinned even wider. We were already at our destination and he turned the key to switch the engine off again.

'A group of men, all in their forties, any of whom might have seen Vesper go into the water, if they were just going about their daily business at their places of work,' I said. 'You win the bet.'

'Those four millers do keep coming up, don't they?' Alec said. 'And their workshops might have telephones, you know. More and more factories are getting them, in case customers want to ring instead of writing.'

'Shall we go and see?' I said.

But Alec was shaking his head. 'I shall never malign your little book again,' he said. 'I badly need to sit and work all of this through until it begins to fall into some kind of order. At the moment it's swimming around me like a barrelful of apples.'

Our long sojourn in Miss Speir's sitting room only tipped more apples in and swirled the water more thoroughly. Some of the difficulty was that we kept having to stop talking as Christine brought tea, more scones, more hot water and finally a fresh siphon of soda in case we were ready for a drink. I did not blame her for her intense interest in whatever we were doing, but if she had admitted it and joined in to help it would have been less disruptive.

Still, by the time we parted to rest before dinner we had at least seen all that there was to see and looked at it square on. The view was not comforting.

'If Vesper had a hand in Peter Haslett's death we are never going to find it out now,' I said. 'We don't know why the story of his death being a drowning got started or how many people believe it. We don't know why that cottager woman, Mrs Cullen, let the truth slip and why she changed her tune today. We certainly don't know why she suddenly started echoing some of Vesper's most disturbing slogans.'

'In the name of Mercury,' Alec said, as if I could have forgotten. 'Snakes upon me.'

'I suppose, given that there was a shrine to Mercury here,

a temple even, the local people might have kept the habit of calling on him by name.'

'For two thousand years?' Alec said.

'Why not? Mother to daughter, father to son. That's how people live and their words live with them.' Alec looked askance, as well he might at such a philosophy, and I hurried on. 'Whether it's a whole temple, or just a shrine, Miss Speir should not be chipping away at it and selling it off to the highest bidder, via that sharp-suited chap or any of the rest of them. And Miss Lumley is in that up to her neck, isn't she? Because she knew all those dealers were there in her pub the first day and she did not like it when we ran into them.'

'But this is nothing to do with Peter and Vesper,' Alec said.

'Peter and Vesper?' I said, struck by the way he had said their two names. I had not heard them put together just like that before.

'No!' said Alec. 'She was thirty-five and he was twenty-four.'

'I suppose you're right,' I said. 'Although there's something whisking around the back of my brain. But I merely meant that the two deaths must be connected. They *must* be.'

'I agree. If Vesper had committed suicide, the connection might be no more than that the death of a young man was the last straw. But as it stands—'

'Stop distracting me. The deaths. The Roman temple. Those two young men on the island with their potatoes. The plans for the island as a watering hole. I'm overlooking something.'

'What are you getting at?' Alec said. 'None of that goes together.'

'That might be exactly what's bothering me,' I said. 'None of it *does* go together. If there's a Roman temple, why not throw it open? People would come in droves. And even if a few cottages and a boating pond are as far as your ambitions reach, a muddy potato patch plonked in the middle isn't helpful, nor is a madwoman in the only cottage currently habitable. Why was she not just sacked, Alec? Why wasn't she turned out? The Rev Hogg wanted to help her and had high hopes, but what of the rest of them?'

'The rest of whom?'

'Well Miss Speir and Miss Lumley, of course. The champions of a prosperous new Cramond. And there are the four millers. Except they're not millers, and God help us if we said they were, since the one who makes paint was so mortally offended by the suggestion that he might use it to paint with. I've never met such a touchy individual. They are in this somehow, Alec. If one of them claims to have seen Vesper fall in the river, why did he not jump in after her?'

'She didn't drown in the river.'

'No. She drowned in salt water. I am sure of it. But when he told the police, I mean. Think about it, Alec. "Oh yes, indeed, Constable. I saw the girl slip on the river path and fall to her death and yes I did happen to notice a shadowy figure holding her under until she stopped struggling. But I was wearing my Sunday best and had my grandfather's watch in my pocket." Nonsense. And Peter Haslett died from being pulled into a water wheel. Besides, could anything be more suspicious than the way they gathered for a toast immediately after Vesper's body was found?'

'Not much,' Alec said. 'If they wanted to raise an innocent glass they'd be in the pub with all their friends and neighbours. Then there's the question of the switched notes and the attempt to traduce Vesper's reputation with the chocolate wrappers and tousled blankets. It's so nasty and yet so pointless.'

'It bamboozled that idiot of an inspector,' I said, but I was thinking about what he had just said. 'With all their friends and neighbours,' I said.

'What of it?'

'Remember what Miss Speir – or was it Miss Lumley?

183

– said at luncheon on the first day. That Cramond was a friendly place but there was no love lost between "the up mills and the down mills". I remember because those are not phrases I had heard before. Have you?'

'You're mistaken,' said Alec. 'It was Rev Hogg who said it and the Misses were none too pleased. You're right; there's something very, very odd about those four. I think they hold the key to two murders. I have no idea how but I am sure of it.'

We set off bright and early after breakfast the next day. The foul weather that had threatened the previous afternoon had arrived, as though the very sky was mourning Vesper. It was chilly enough for October and the rain was unrelenting, except when a gust of wind whipped it into a brief squall now and then.

'I'm in no mood to see Mr Massey again,' I said, as I climbed into Alec's motorcar and slammed the door shut. 'I vote that we start at the top and work our way back down.' I rifled through my sheaf of notes and found the makeshift map I had sketched. 'Dowie's Mill,' I said. 'Almost all the way back up to the bridge. Do you think you can find your way round the lanes again?'

Alec had set his windscreen wiper going and now rubbed a patch of the inner condensation with his coat sleeve. 'If anyone can see anything. What a day.'

It took a mere ten minutes and very soon we were parking in the most sheltered spot of another cobbled yard. In every respect, Dowie's Mill was a much more extensive operation. The waterfall looked to be an eight-foot drop and two wheels were hammering round at the end of an impressive lade. The water in the sluice was brown with the mud washed into the river from all the rain and I shuddered to look at it. It is always dizzying to look down into churning water and I could not help but imagine Peter Haslett and how helpless he must have felt as he tried to thrash his way clear of the sucking current pulling him towards those blades.

'It might not have been this one, old thing,' Alec said, with a friendly nudge. He had read my mind. I gave him as much of a smile as I could muster and turned away.

'There are no telegraph poles,' I said, nodding at the ugly lines of the electricity wires that stretched from the only pole in sight to the outside of the factory wall. 'So the telephone call to the doctor and police didn't come from here. I don't suppose we could attack it from the other end, could we?'

'Ask the girl on the switchboard at the police station?' Alec said. 'I shouldn't have thought so. She must need to exercise great discretion.'

'I never thought I would miss those minxes on the exchange,' I said. 'Right then. Which one of the four do you suppose we're just about to meet again?'

I squared my shoulders, got an approving look from Alec and marched up to a door lying ajar beside a lighted window. One good thing about the foul weather was that it made it easier to tell which rooms were in use. The yellow light blared out into the grey day like a beacon.

'I never thought I'd miss gaslight either,' I said. 'What do you suppose he does in there that needs it so blinding?'

Alec knocked on the open door and then ushered me in ahead of him.

'Hallo! Hallo!' he shouted as we pulled the door closed behind us. 'Forgive the barging but it's a filthy day. Hallo? Anyone there?'

When we looked around, it was to see a large workshop of mystifying intent, at least to my eyes. There was a lathe, much festooned with sawdust, and a forge and bellows the like of which I had not seen since my childhood visits to the village smith, unequalled for entertainment in those simpler days. I wandered over to the anvil that lay just in front of

185

the forge in hopes of warming my hands, but the fire was not yet lit and that corner of the room was colder than any.

Alec was still hallooing, no answer having yet come. I inspected a large collection of what looked like broom handles, only thicker, lying stacked like firewood in a frame, and then found myself intrigued by a handcart that sat beside them. It was well used but not well maintained. Although its handles shone with use its paint was peeling. I was almost sure. I bent into it and took a deep sniff. There was no mistaking it now. This was the same little cart, with the same unfamiliar pungent odour that had been lying, quite miles away by the lanes outside Mr Massey's 'down mill' two days ago.

Finally Alec had raised someone. There was a rush of cold air as a door opened somewhere and our host appeared. It was the ratty man. He wore a pair of goggles pushed up on his head and a leather apron over his Monday work clothes.

'And what can I do for you today?' he asked, genially enough. 'No more trouble down in the village is there?'

He had given me such a swift darting look as he saw me standing there with my hand on the peeling side of the handcart that I knew I must hide my interest in the article or raise all manner of suspicions.

'We weren't introduced yesterday,' I said.

'Joe Georgeson,' he said. 'I won't shake. My hands aren't fit for a lady and gent.'

He was right; his fingers were something worse than just dirty. They were singed and blackened as though he reached into his oven and pulled out molten metal with his bare hands.

'What is it that you do, Mr Georgeson?' I asked him.

'Me? I'm a spade maker,' he said. 'Georgeson's Spades. I'm sure if you looked in your garden shed at home – or interrupted your gardener at his toils, more like – it would be a Georgeson spade he'd lean on. Snow shovels, ashpans, and all manner of spades.'

186

'Ah,' I said, walking back over to the rack of wooden poles. 'They're spade handles.'

'In waiting,' Georgeson said. 'My grandfather was a hoop maker back when the fashions were very different from today. His father had been a wheelwright, making carriage wheels. If they ever come up with a way to grow a garden without digging, it'll be all change again. But for now I'm a spade maker.'

'I think you're safe enough,' I said. 'Unless those lads over on the island are looking into such a thing.'

He seemed to go very still at that and his rat-like eyes glinted. I felt a bit of a heel. A precarious existence running a small factory workshop does not get any sweeter for strangers making quips about it.

'Well then, Mr Georgeson,' Alec said. 'You must be wondering why we're here.'

The man said nothing.

'It's about poor Vesper,' I said. 'I know you feel her death very deeply. Why, didn't we intrude on your toast to her memory only yesterday? The thing is, you see, that Rev Hogg employed my colleague and me to look into her troubles. He hoped she could be persuaded to take up her duties again. At least, he hoped we could find out what it was that had set her off on her downward trajectory and perhaps make a change to it. So you can imagine what we think of ourselves today. The poor girl is dead. Far from helping her, we can't help but wonder if we made matters worse. Would she have been killed if Mr Osborne and I hadn't come? We don't know and I am not cold-hearted enough to dismiss the worry.'

'Nice speech,' said Georgeson. I managed not to gasp at his rudeness.

'Very well,' Alec said, 'if that's how things stand. We know that one of you four millers told the police you saw Vesper go in. We want to know which one and why you said it. Of course, in the unlikely event that it's true, evidence would be

187

very nice too. But we shan't be holding our breath on that score.'

'Out!' he said. 'Get out. Get off my property. Cheek of you, thinking you can come trespassing in here, throwing your weight around, dropping your sleekit wee hints and pretending it's Vesper Kemp that's bothering you.'

'There's no such thing as trespass in Scotl—'

'Not now, Alec,' I said, taking his arm. For the ratty man had lifted a steel hammer from beside the anvil and was advancing.

18

Outside it was raining harder than ever. We splashed through deep puddles making our hasty way back to the motorcar and then sat dripping and panting as Alec started up the engine. Thankfully Mr Georgeson did not follow us. I had not liked the way he grasped that hammer handle.

'Well, that was not entirely successful, was it?' Alec said, blowing upwards to dislodge the raindrop forming on the end of his nose. I was pressing my handkerchief over the portions of my head not covered by my hat, hoping to salvage something. My hair, when left to its own devices after a soaking, quickly turns me into a sight that cannot knock on doors and try to conduct dignified business.

'I beg to differ,' I said, laying my handkerchief flat on the dashboard where it would catch some warm air from the heater. 'I think we learned much more than Mr Georgeson knows he taught us. Think of what he said, Alec.'

Alec thought for a minute. 'That he was a spade maker. From a family of ironworkers. That we were trespassers and cheeky and were throwing our weight around.'

'You have managed to miss out the only bits of any import,' I said.

'I'm leaving them for you,' Alec said, as he started up the engine. 'Not stealing your thunder.'

I smiled. 'Well, yes. He said we were dropping "sleekit hints" and were only pretending to care about Vesper. He thinks, or at least fears, that our business at Cramond is about something else.'

'The Romans,' Alec said. 'The temple. The ransacking of the tower treasure.'

'You make it sound like something from Rider Haggard,' I said. 'And anyway, no. Not the tower. The island. The two lads on the island. You probably didn't notice, Alec, but when I made that little joke – well, little sally really – about the biologists discovering that we should all stop digging, he gave me a very strange look. I thought I had been crass about the man's business but now I think otherwise. That is the only remark either of us made in the time we were in there that could be construed as a hint. Whatever Georgeson is up to, or hiding, or worried about, it's got something to do with the trials on the island.'

'Do you have any idea what it might be?' said Alec.

'Not an inkling,' I said. 'Peter, Vesper, the island, the trials, the holiday venture . . . No, not a clue.' I craned round to help as Alec reversed to drive away. He was very close to a sturdy brick wall and the windows were so fogged that the mirrors were no help at all. 'Let's do things differently at the next mill, shall we? Let's tread a bit more lightly and try not to get run off with a poker.'

'Peggie's Mill,' Alec said. 'Which of the three shall we find there, I wonder.'

It took only a very few minutes to reach the place, along the riverside. Alec's driving made me grip the door handle with both hands at one point. He is not usually nerve-wracking behind the wheel but he was more interested in what we were passing on my side than in what might lie ahead on the road and he leaned over in front of me and peered out of my window without slowing down.

'Those weirs are a mess,' he said.

I glanced to the side. I could see a waterfall, partially hidden by the trees and almost entirely hidden by the dreadful weather.

'What do you mean?' I said. 'Alec, do watch the road! What if someone comes the other way?'

Alec shook his head at my fussing but he relented, sat up straight and faced forward. 'Four mills on this little stretch of pretty tame water,' he said. 'So one miller builds a weir and gets some gravity to help the wheel go round but that makes life even worse for his neighbour so the neighbour builds a weir too, and a lade and a sluice, then miller number three finds his lights beginning to dim and sets to. Whatever brought those four together over the brandy bottle yesterday, I believe Rev Hogg that there's years of bad blood.'

'I don't,' I said. 'I think they are on *very* friendly terms. I know this is going to sound silly but did you notice that handcart in the workshop just now?'

'Cart?' said Alec. 'No. Why?'

'Because I'm convinced that it was parked outside the Cockle Mill – Eck Massey's place – on Saturday. I'm sure it was the same cart. It had the same polished handles, the same colour of the same peeling paint and the same smell.'

'Smell?'

'Smell. It was most particular. It made me think of Fife. And Edinburgh tenements.'

'Fife?' Alec said. It was the county between us up in Perthshire and the Lothians, where Edinburgh lay with Cramond snuggled in at its bosom.

'Coastal Fife,' I said. 'I leaned into that cart, took a deep sniff and was transported back to the Luckenlaw road. Another sniff and I was climbing the stairs to visit Mrs Tilling's sister in her top flat.'

'Odd,' said Alec. 'I believe you. Your powers of observation are trustworthy. And your deductions are correct too. No one lends a cart to an enemy.'

The conversation petered out as we arrived at Peggie's Mill. This place did not have quite the elaborate system of lades and sluices we had seen at Dowie's and so it was very close to the river. We came at it from behind as a result, past a clutch of workers' cottages, empty now and with metal over the windows as though to stop tramps breaking in and sleeping there. It would have to be a very desperate kind of a tramp that forced a window in one of these cottages, I thought as we passed. Tucked under the hill that billowed out over the water and cut the up mills off from the down mills, they were damp, dark and cheerless, with only a very few chimneys on the long stretch of their roofs, hinting at rooms without warmth; living conditions I was glad to see begin to end across this land of ours.

'Right then,' I said as we pulled through a cart arch into the work yard. 'I'll do the talking this time. Since you're in such a hot-headed mood this morning.'

We did not have to decide between knocking and waiting in the rain or risking more wrath by strolling in uninvited, for the miller came out as we parked, his shoulders even rounder as the rain battered down on him and his face even more colourless in the cold.

He stood aside as we scurried over. The wind had dropped and left the stage clear for sustained vertical hammering.

'Filthy day!' the round-shouldered man said, as we shook ourselves. It is inevitable that bad weather leads to some level of camaraderie. The weather of our island nation, and especially its northern shores, is the common enemy in peacetime and it draws us close to one another.

'Absolutely vile,' I said.

'And what brings you out in it?' he said. 'Come away in and get warm at least. I've got the wee stove going.'

He led us along a short passage towards the river side of the building where the workshop lay. Once again I looked around with interest to see what manner of business was going on here. There were deep drawers around the edges of the room and large tables set in the middle and there was something that might have been another forge, or perhaps a kiln, in the farthest corner. But the owner of the premises was leading us towards the opposite corner and a tiny paraffin stove that had clearly just been lit, filling the room with an oily scent along with its growing blast of heat. I sniffed. Was that the smell I had smelled in the cart? Was it used to deliver paraffin? If one of the four had a paraffin-delivering business on the side then the movement of the cart they used, from one mill to another, was hardly suspicious after all.

All that said though, I did not think the smell in the cart *was* paraffin. If I were the suspicious sort I would even have said that the paraffin stove had been lit, and recently, to mask another smell underneath. If the round-shouldered man had known we were coming I would have said so, anyway.

While I was sniffing and musing, Alec had begun the pleasantries, no matter that we had agreed I would take charge this time. He spoke up to be heard over the racket of the water wheel, so close to where we sat, and so loud that it all but drowned out the sound of the hammering rain on the tin roof overhead.

'A paper mill?' he was saying. 'Yes, I think we heard there had been one here somewhere.'

'Before my day,' the miller said. 'There was a decent ten-foot fall back then before all the nonsense started.'

'Those weirs,' Alec said. 'I marked them as we drove past.'

'And when my father bought the place it was a going concern. Rag shed, presses, finishing house full of equipment, drying house with a modern heater so good every rat for ten miles around moved in every winter. It took three ratting cats to keep them down. Nothing in this world comes free. The only good thing about the paper mill shutting down was getting to put those three mangy cats in a bag and throw them in the river.'

He shared this reminiscence as though we might be

charmed by it and, despite the paraffin stove, I felt myself shiver.

'When that went toes up we took to spade-making,' he continued, 'but you know how that went.'

Alec arched an interested eyebrow.

'Up the road,' the man said. 'When the hoop business lost its lustre they took over spades and drove us out of it. Then we took to furniture-making, and that's what I do to this day. John Weller at your service. Manufacturing upholsterer since 1919. Only, if they're right what they're saying about another war, that'll go the same way as the spades and paper. But I don't think it'll come to that. Not again. Do you?'

'I do not,' I said stoutly. 'I have two sons of fighting age. And I cannot let myself believe it will come to that again.'

'Mind you,' said Weller, 'if a war starts up, I daresay any factory building will be in clover. If I can turn back to iron-works and get a contract I could be laughing. Even if it's girls on the shop floor with all the men away.'

Alec gave me a look and I gave a look back. This was an odious man. He had been mourning the fact that a war might not go well for him but hearing that I had sons appeared to cheer him up. Added to the cats, I was ready to declare him a monster. A quiet sort of monster, but sometimes those are the worst of all.

'The reason we're here this morning keeping you from your upholstery, Mr Weller,' I said, hoping to have the business over and done with promptly, 'is that one of the policemen investigating the death yesterday said something intriguing.'

'Oh aye?' Mr Weller said.

'He suggested that one of you four millers saw Vesper Kemp go into the water.'

'Did he?' said Weller. 'Did he now? He just started gossiping with outsiders, did he?' Of course, no one could have been happy to hear what I had just said and it was true that the policeman should not have been doing any such thing, but I had such a cold feeling about this little shrimp of a man that I hastened to alleviate the damage I had just done.

'Not the local bobby,' I said. 'I'm sure his village loyalties are strong. And actually he didn't tell us so much as we overheard him. We were eavesdropping. The sergeant is blameless. But to the matter itself. Is it true?'

'Why would you want to know even if it was?' said Weller.

'In hopes – slim enough – that I might be able to tell something to Rev Hogg that would comfort him,' I said.

'Oh aye, right, right,' said Weller. 'You're worried you might not get your envelope at the end of all this, aren't you? You didn't solve any of the problems. You just made more. You didn't help. You made it worse. She's dead and so you're thinking of your pay packet. Well, I don't know what the sergeant was on about. I never saw the woman jump in the river and I never heard that anyone else saw it either. If I'd seen her, would I not have been in after her? Or are you saying you think I'd stand on the bank and watch a woman drown? Is that what you think of me?'

'Heaven forfend,' Alec said. 'Cats only, I'm sure.' I had wondered how that nasty little nugget struck him; now I knew. He loathed the man as I did.

'Must be nice to keep a cat in meat that you don't need,' Weller said. 'Must be nice never to have to think where the next meal's coming from.'

Alec said nothing. But, as he stood up from where he had been leaning against one of the chests of deep drawers, he brushed dust off his trousers and apparently his meaning was clear to Mr Weller.

'Oh aye, right,' he said. 'It's all so easy when you don't have to do it. You think you're the first toff I've had round here telling me I'm wasting the place and I could just doll it up and turn it to use? Them two women are never away from me. Snipe, snipe sniping about tearooms and whitewash and a boarding house. Oh it's all very easy when it's not your pocket being scraped out to get it up and running.'

'You're probably right, Mr Weller,' I said. 'What would we know about running a manufacturing business? Why, in our detective agency a typical Monday morning sees us sitting at our ease by a fire going through correspondence. It's another world.' I cast one last look at the paraffin stove, the armchair he was curled into and the empty dusty tables that filled the rest of the so-called workshop and flounced off.

Alec caught up with me halfway along the passage.

'You were supposed to be the cool-headed one,' he said. 'What happened?'

'Vile little man!' I said. 'Looking forward to war if he thinks it'll help him. Only bemoaning it if his damned upholstery business might suffer. And the cats!'

'I'm glad we offended him, though,' Alec said. 'The rain's gone off a bit and I wanted to have a squint about without him watching.'

'What for?'

'Telegraph poles,' Alec said. 'Because I think Mr Georgeson from Dowie's Mill warned him we were coming. Think about it, Dan. Weller said just then that we knew what happened to the spade-making business. Did you remark it?'

'Yes, you're right,' I said. 'But that might just be . . . what's the word . . . solipsism. He did strike me as a remarkably self-regarding sort. Perhaps he can't imagine that the world at large doesn't take an interest in all his doings.'

'I don't think so,' Alec said. 'He said "up the road" with a jerk of his head. I think he knew we'd just been there.'

'It was a silly mistake, if so,' I said.

'It wasn't the only one. When he was scoffing at us for our interest in Vesper he got jolly close to quoting what we'd just said to Georgeson, word for word.'

Even though it was still drizzling, I stopped walking and stood in the middle of the yard, thinking back. 'You're right,'

I said. 'He sneered that we had made the problem worse and felt guilty about it, which are our words. Of course he put his own cynical topspin on them, accusing us of caring about money and money alone. It never struck me that he shouldn't know that. Because it's true.'

'That's exactly the same mistake he made!' Alec said. 'It didn't strike him that he shouldn't know we'd come from Dowie's Mill because we had. Because it was true.' He turned round and cast his gaze over the rooftops of the buildings. They were quite a jumble, what with all these rag sheds, finishing houses and drying lofts he had described. There were wind bonnets and chimneys, skylights and foul pipes but there were no telegraph connections. There was another electricity wire running down into the factory and a rope on a pulley connecting several of the lesser buildings, but if Alec was right that Georgeson had found a way to warn Weller of our approach it was certainly not by telephone.

'Let's go,' he said. 'Mill number three awaits.'

I nodded and turned to go, but as I did a movement caught my eye. One of the other doors in the large workshop building had opened and there in the doorway stood none other than . . .

'Georgeson?' Alec said.

There was no mistaking the turtle-like stoop and the pinched eyes of the Dowie's Mill spade maker, even though he pulled himself back into the shadows sharply when he caught sight of us still standing there.

'Ha!' I said. 'Those water wheels thrashing round make it pretty hard to tell when visitors are arriving and leaving, I suppose.'

'Well, that clears that up,' Alec said. 'We suspected he'd forewarned Weller, because of the slips Weller made, and then hey presto! There he is.'

'Hey presto there he is *afterwards*,' I said. 'Too late for any forewarning. He can't have pipped us, Alec. Even in a

197

motorcar – does he own a motorcar? – he'd have driven us into the hedge or the river when he overtook. No, I reckon he arrived as we were leaving and poked his nose out the door to double-check that we were gone.'

'No doubt you're right,' Alec said. He made one last slow turn in the middle of the yard, scanning the rooftops and the sky above.

'Double-checking for telegraph poles?' I said.

'I was thinking of pigeons,' said Alec.

I laughed, then turned it into a cough when I realised that he was serious. 'Let's go to Fair-a-Far,' I said. 'If the miller there seems to know more than he should about what just passed here, I promise to check the skies for pigeons with you.'

'It would be even more odd if word gets down to Fair-a-Far,' Alec said. 'Because there's no path at all. Do you remember? Mr Hogg told us at luncheon on that very first day.'

'I remember getting lost and feeling stupid for not being able to follow the course of the river,' I admitted.

Alec paused with his hand on the motorcar door. 'You don't suppose, Dandy. . .?'

'What?' I was waiting on my side of the motorcar, trying to be patient, but although the weather had improved it was still far from comfortable, in my damp clothes and with my hair dripping on my neck.

'Don't laugh,' Alec said.

'Nothing could be further from my mind,' I assured him. 'I am cold. My feet are wet. My last meal was dreadful and my next will likely be worse. Miss Speir's bed springs have put knots in my back and this case is becoming a source of shame and despair. Laughter is a long way off. What are you thinking?'

'Secret tunnels,' said Alec.

My lips may have curled. At any rate, he scowled and

wrenched open the door, flinging himself into the driving seat.

'I'm sorry, darling,' I said, climbing in beside him. 'But really. We've got a secret dungeon full of treasure. I think that might have to do.'

19

Fair-a-Far is such a charming name. One thinks of the illustrations from nursery books, of rabbits in jackets and pixies with acorns for hats. But coming at it from the back lanes presented us with an even more dismal prospect than our first approach along the river by the disused dock and the overgrown railway. Such rows of brick cottages are well known to me from the nastier parts of the county where housing for miners was thrown up, without thought for where the children would play, where the washing would dry or how families of nine and ten would keep themselves decent without so much as a pump in the scullery. Millworkers' houses were evidently planned with the same carelessness and botched together with the same penny-pinching view to the balance sheet rather than the fellow man.

At least these hovels appeared to be empty; no young wife was trying to get a soup cauldron to boil while rain dripped down an ill-placed chimney and no young husband was trying to sleep off a nightshift with his children in the same room sheltering from the rain.

'Godforsaken sort of spot,' Alec said as we passed the last of the cottages. 'Look at that window, Dandy. Sill's four inches deep at most. A single course of bricks and a spot of lath and plaster.' Alec is much taken up with housing improvements on his estate and easily shocked by shoddy building elsewhere. 'I wouldn't store deckchairs in a shed that flimsy,' he concluded.

'Let's hope they've all gone off to Corporation bungalows,'

I said. 'And don't tell Hugh I said so.' Hugh, until his recent flirtation with double windows, had always tended towards a belief that cold houses and even colder water temper the populace and turn out manly men and capable women. He based this view on the fact of Gilverton's having been glacial when he was a boy and his having grown up never to ail a day. I tried once or twice to point out that he had plentiful food and warm clothing to fall back on and that if he did get seriously chilled he had hot bottles and a doting nanny, but he dislikes being disagreed with and dislikes being scorned for softness even more. He harrumphed a good deal and said that his nanny exhorted him, scolded him, upbraided him and occasionally spanked him with a slipper but never doted on anything in her life. I said nothing. I found the knitted leggings of Hugh's infancy and childhood while clearing attics for Donald and Teddy's things to be stored as they went up to Oxford. Lambswool on the outside with angora linings and doubly thick knees for when he knelt down on the curling pond. His jackets had rabbit fur in the hood too. He spent his tender years positively cocooned against the cruel elements of Perthshire and had a cheek to mention the coughs and chilblains of cottagers.

'Now then,' Alec said, stepping down and rubbing his hands together. It was from cold rather than anticipatory glee but it did have a marvellous stirring edge to it nonetheless. 'Are you willing to make a wager, Dan? Shall we find the glowering stranger who cowed that young woman or shan't we? I say yes. What say you?'

But before I could take the bet or let it pass, he was upon us. He came round the corner from the river side of the main building with a large umbrella held over his head and his shoulders hunched as though he was battling a deluge. His feet, in oilskin boots like a fisherman, were streaming with water.

'Hallo there,' Alec shouted.

The man raised his umbrella and peered out from under a cap pulled low on his head. It was indeed the chap we had met on the foreshore the previous morning but he was in different spirits today. He waved as he saw us and his bushy beard split to show large grey teeth as he grinned at us.

'Good morning,' he called back. 'What can I do for you?'

'A quick word if you're not too busy,' I said. 'It's about this business yesterday.'

'Funny you should mention it,' he said and his tone struck me as badly out of kilter with the subject matter. 'Perhaps *you* can help *me*. I was just away to the police station to tell them something they need to know about that very matter. Maybe I could trouble you for a lift. I've no motor of my own and it's no weather for cycling. If it wouldn't put you out of your way, that is. It's only Barnton.'

'We'd very happily deliver you to the police station,' I said. 'Lucky you turned back and saw us.'

'Turned back?' the man said. Then he looked up at his umbrella and down at his boots. 'Oh, no. This is not me dressed for the polis. I was just tending my lade there before I left it.'

I nodded, as if I had the faintest clue what kind of tending a mill lade took, given that it was no more than a channel for the water of the race to rush along. Alec gave a similar nod.

'Look,' said the man, 'maybe you'd step in a minute and advise me. I think I'm right in thinking on the polis but if I could just chew it over with you I'd feel a sight happier.'

Alec and I practically fell over our feet in eagerness. We crowded into the building after him and waited while he shook out his umbrella and shrugged off the heavy coat he was wearing, then we followed him towards a lit doorway at the end of a short passage.

I slipped on the wet floor halfway there and grabbed at Alec to stop myself falling down.

The man turned and gave a shout when he saw the pair of us teetering.

'Here here,' he said. 'I forget what it is to wear street shoes these days, me always in my oilies or my steelies like I am. Here, away out of the puddle I've left there like a fool.' He ushered us – practically shoved us, actually – into the room ahead of him and then went bustling off and started rummaging, banging cupboard doors. At length he returned to the passageway with a pile of sacks in his arms and spread them on the floor of the hall. It seemed like a sledgehammer for a walnut to me. I had only skidded on a few droplets from an umbrella and now the chap was carpeting the entire flagged floor with sacking.

Alec was not paying attention to what was happening out in the hallway. He had wandered over to a forge chimney and was warming his hands. It was similar to the forge at Dowie's Mill and the kiln at Peggie's Mill but this man, for all he was setting off to the police station when the working week had hardly begun, was otherwise more industrious than either of the first two individuals with whom we had spent time that Monday morning. This fire was glowing red at the edges and white in the middle and there were mystifying tools lying all around and soldering rods of varied types gleaming and glinting. Alec, a boy at heart like most men, was instantly fascinated by them.

'Lead,' he said, 'and silver. And pewter and what on earth is this one?'

Then the large man was with us, drawing up chairs and offering tea. I took one look at the squat brown teapot, and the quarter-pound bag of black tea standing open with a teaspoon dug into it, and declined.

'What is it you'd like to tell us?' I said.

But Alec spoke over me. 'What is it you make here, Mr . . .?'

'Hamilton,' the man said. 'Jackie Hamilton. I'm still an

ironworker. Although, it's fancy goods mostly as you've seen from my solders there. If a lady's got to have a shovel sitting on her parlour hearth it helps to have few blobs of brass stuck to it and a stamp with a fleur-de-lis. Don't ask me why but then I'm a plain man.'

'And *what* is it you'd like to tell us?' I asked him again. I had just about had it with ironworkers and spade makers for the day.

'Well now,' Hamilton said, 'it's about Vesper Kemp. I think – or at least, I thought – I saw her murdered yesterday.'

Alec and I both sat as though turned to stone. My breath was knocked out of me. Of course, we had heard the sergeant hint that one of some band of 'men in their forties' had witnessed the crime and we had deduced that the four millers were the men in question, so I do not know why it struck me quite so much like a smith's steel hammer to have it confirmed.

After a short pause and a licking of his lips, Hamilton went on. 'And that's what was amiss with me when I ran into you yesterday, madam, sir. I'm sorry I was so short with you both. Hardly a neighbourly welcome to you, new to Cramond as you are.'

'We're only visiting,' I said. I could not have said why it mattered. Perhaps the thought of living in this strange place with its secrets was so inimical that I needed to quash the suggestion wherever I met it.

'Well, all the more reason to set out the welcome mat,' he said. 'But like I was saying. I thought I saw her jump to her death.'

'Jump?' Alec said.

'Or fall,' said the man. 'What I saw was a man and a woman standing up in a boat. I thought they were having a wee cuddle. I wondered why they didn't sit down and be more comfy. Then she just sort of slipped out of his arms and went down into the water with no more splash than a trout leaping.

I blinked and rubbed my eyes, sir, I'm not ashamed to say it. I couldn't believe what I was seeing, if you catch my drift.'

'She fell in?' I said. 'Where was this exactly? When?'

'Just out there,' said Hamilton. 'Where my sluice empties again down from the weir. Just at the broad of the river before it nips in again. And it would be . . . oh ten o'clock? Round about ten o'clock anyway.'

'What did you do?'

'I watched to see what *he* would do,' Hamilton said. 'If his sweetheart had somehow fallen in the water, I thought he'd either shout and jump in after to save her or he'd laugh and reach a hand down to pull her out, but he did neither. He sat down and lifted his oars and started to pull away. So naturally . . . I mean, I hope you understand anyway, because saying it now seems a wee bit off colour if you catch my drift, but what I did was think to myself my eyes were playing tricks. I told myself it wasn't a woman I saw. It made no sense to think they were lovers anyway. I told myself the lad was dropping a log overboard or something. Maybe he'd pulled it out of the weir and rowed it clear and now he was tipping it in the water to let it drift out, you know?'

I tried to look encouraging but the tale did not strike me as plausible. Alec's face was rather twisted up too.

'Then when I heard that Vesper had died I thought I knew exactly what I'd seen,' Hamilton went on. 'I thought I saw her murder and I said as much.'

I glanced at Alec. If we were right about the salt water in Vesper's lungs there was no way she was killed up above the tidal estuary of the river.

'But of course, I didn't see her murdered at all,' Hamilton went on. 'I saw her body, her lifeless body, being put over the side of the boat to be found. Wherever she was killed and however she was killed what I saw was just the disposal. I'm sure of it. And I need to tell the polis because they'll have the time all wrong and they'll be looking in the wrong place for clues after what I said to them.'

'I see,' I said. 'Well then yes I agree, Mr Hamilton. You do need to get this straightened out. One thing before we set off, though.'

He looked up at me and some of his genial mask slipped just a little, or so I thought. His eyes glinted under his lowering brow. 'What would that be?' he said.

'Just this: what made you say they likely weren't lovers after all? When you had time to think about it? Did you know who the chap was? Is he not someone Vesper would entertain?'

'Oh,' Hamilton said, sitting back. 'I see what you're getting at. No indeed, madam. I didn't know who either of them were. All I saw was a girl with her hair down her back and a slim young lad with his arms around her. No, what made me think they weren't lovers was that there was somebody else there too. Another laddie, sitting in the prow of the boat. Couldn't say who *he* was either. Just that he was a big fellow, plenty meat on him. It's been many a year since I went courting but some things don't change and that struck me as not right, you know?'

'At ten o'clock, you say?' said Alec. He was making a better fist of remaining calm than me. I could no longer pretend to be interested in anything Hamilton had to tell us, because I knew exactly who it was he had seen. Two young men, one slim and one portly, hurriedly getting rid of a corpse far from where they had presumably found it, or possibly far from where they had committed the murder that made it.

'Round about then yes,' said Hamilton.

'And no one else was on the river? Or walking?'

'Not a soul,' said Hamilton, with a frown.

'I don't suppose you recognised the boat, did you?' Alec said.

Hamilton stopped with his mouth open and appeared to consider the idea for the first time.

'No, now you mention it, I didn't,' he said.

'A rowing boat, you said?' said Alec. 'With a sail? Or just a dinghy? A motor?'

Hamilton screwed up his eyes even tighter. 'Just a— Just the two sets of oars, I think. I was looking at the people standing up, if you get my— wait no. There was a sail but it was furled and there might have been a motor but I wouldn't have seen it. Not from where I was standing.'

'You didn't wait until they left again then?' I said. 'Or did you?'

'Ocht, no,' said Hamilton. 'I get that fed up with folk telling me what I can put in the river and what I can't. I decided to turn a blind eye. This was when I thought it was a log, or maybe . . . Well, at worst the likes of a dead dog or a . . . Well, the truth is I didn't know. I keep myself to my own self. So I came in and I made myself a toddy and I took me to my bed.'

'Oh!' said Alec and I in unison.

'You mean ten o'clock at night!' Alec went on.

'Aye, that's right,' Hamilton said. 'Didn't I say that? Ten o'clock in the morning the foreshore and the path would be full with children too wee to be at the kirk and some old men that have served their years in the pews and got a bit of respite. Well, you saw yourselves the crowd that was there by dinnertime. Ten o'clock at night, to be sure. Or I wouldn't have made such a daft mistake. I'd have seen who it was and what was afoot.'

'Seen who it was,' I echoed. 'Do you know who it was then?'

'I mean the girl,' said Hamilton. 'By day I'd have recognised Vesper. I've known her all her life since she was a wee tot sitting in the floor of the coble with her daddy.'

He shook his head in sorrow, then with a great gathering breath he clapped his hands on his knees and stood up. 'I'm obliged to you for this offer,' he said. 'If you're still willing.'

* * *

There was tense silence as we trundled him up out of the village to the police station sitting in a row of shops just off the high Edinburgh road. Hamilton was no doubt gearing himself to tell his tale to the police. For my part, I was thinking over all that we had learned. Alec, as he revealed as soon as Hamilton had left us, splashing through puddles in his oilskin boots with his jacket collar turned up and his cap pulled down low, had been stewing with a bitter rage that came pouring out the minute we were alone.

'Fool! Idiot! Blasted cretin!'

'Who are you angry with?' I said.

'Me, of course,' Alec said. 'Ugh. I helped the man get his story straight before delivering him to the coppers. I could kick myself, Dandy. I could bang my head on the wall.'

'What are you talking about?'

'All that stuff about not knowing whether it was a girl going for a swim or a log being tossed overboard like a caber. Tommy rot! And then saying he melted discreetly away? More tommy rot. The man lives on that river. Of course he'd want to know what was being shied into it under cover of darkness. What miller would be sanguine about a dead dog going downstream to get into his neighbour's wheel workings? Rot, I tell you. But that's not the thing that's bothering me most of all.'

'I agree with what's bothering you most of all,' I said.

'How do you know what it is?'

'I guessed just then when you were talking about him living on the river.'

'And I'm right, aren't I?' Alec said. 'There's no way he wouldn't instantly have noticed whether a boat had a sail or not. And there's no way he wouldn't instantly have noticed if it was a local boat that he sees every day or a strange boat that had no business here.'

'So he's lying.'

'Through his teeth. The one thing I do believe is that he

208

didn't recognise Irvine and Fordyce. He would have no reason to know them, would he? But he identified them just the same.'

'And do you think they killed her?' I asked. 'One of them or the other? Or did they find her, panic, and try to get rid of the body?'

'I don't know. The fact that they've disappeared from the island doesn't help. They'd do that in either case.'

'Hmm,' I said. 'I'm not so sure. If one of them killed her wouldn't it make more sense for them to stay put and carry on? Not raise suspicions by running off?'

'Neither of them struck me as having nerves of steel,' Alec said. 'And this is the second death they've been mixed up in: their friend Peter and then their neighbour, of sorts.'

I looked at him speculatively.

'What?' he asked.

'Something you just said.' I kept staring, hoping it would come back. 'Their friend Peter.'

'Yes,' said Alec. 'What about it?'

But it had gone. I shook my head to chase away its shadow and asked the question that was near enough to the front of my mind that I could form it into words. 'Is that boating pond on the island salt water or fresh?'

'Upon my word, Dandy,' Alec said. 'That's a thought.'

'Because all of the beaches on the island are in plain view of the shore. Either from the village or from the path through the Dalmeny Estate, anyone with a spyglass, or even sharp eyes, could see a man in the shallows holding a woman under by the back of her neck. But that pond is absolutely isolated.'

'It must be salt water,' Alec said. 'It would be folly to risk drying a well to flood it, with so much water all around. When you're thinking of trying to set up holidays anyway.'

'Let's ask,' I said. 'Or if we can't get the conversation round to it, let's go and see. I'm trying to think what was growing at the edges of it. Pond weed? Does anything grow in salt water? I'm not sure I've ever thought about it before.'

'Plenty of vegetation in the tidal bit of the river mouth,' Alec said.

'And on the path and in the yards and up the lanes,' I said. I lifted my foot and laid it across my other knee. A great clod of rather slimy weed was caught in my instep. 'Do you have a pipe cleaner to spare?' I asked.

'Not if you're going to flick mud onto my floor,' said Alec. 'Or drop it out of the window right outside the police station either. Wait till we're back at the house and wipe your feet on Miss Speir's scraper.'

'We're not going to the fourth miller then?' I said.

Alec stared at me.

'What?' I asked him.

'Something about that bothers me,' he replied.

'The number four? The millers themselves?'

But it too was gone.

20

This case had quickly become the knottiest, slipperiest, most bamboozling and frustrating of our career and somehow, amidst the deaths and twists and revelations, we had lost sight of our client there in the manse; the man who had employed us to help with a problem only to see that problem blossom and darken like a bloodstain. It was long past time for us to face Rev Hogg and hear if he was done with us.

'Could you bring yourself to charge him a fee?' I said, as we turned in at his gate ten minutes later.

'It's four days' work we've put in,' said Alec. 'We usually charge for our time rather than by results. And after four days of Miss Speir's hospitality and Christine's cooking I rather think I deserve some pay.'

The maid who answered Rev Hogg's door told us he was in his library and if we would see ourselves through she would bring coffee.

He was indeed in his library but not writing sermons or reading his newspaper. He was sitting behind a bare desk with his hands splayed on its wooden surface. As he heard us enter, he looked up and his face wore an expression of such abject misery that I felt myself spring forward to offer comfort.

'My dear Mr Hogg,' I said, lifting one of those hands and chafing it in mine. It was cold and yet had left a damp print on the polished surface of the desk. 'Are you ill?'

'I am . . . sick at heart,' he said.

'Has something happened?' said Alec. He did not take

Rev Hogg's other hand, but rather stood on the far side of the desk, shifting from foot to foot. It is difficult for menfolk when other menfolk are in distress. I have seen it before. Once a chap moves beyond the curative reach of a hearty back slap and a shared hip flask, the job falls to us women.

'Something happened,' Rev Hogg echoed in a small voice, then he shook his head and let his chin drop onto his chest. I shared a look with Alec. Surely if it were bad news about his wife the maid would have warned us. 'I think,' Rev Hogg went on, lifting his face to look at me, 'that yesterday I was in a state of shock. Initially. And then, after an hour in the Turning Tide with Miss Lumley, I was well buffered against anything. It wasn't until today that the fact of it truly began to steal across me. I killed her.' The breath stilled in my throat and I let his hand fall. He did not appear to notice it drop with a thump onto the desk top. 'As surely as if I'd throttled her myself, I killed her with my foolishness.'

Suddenly light-headed, I groped my way to the edge of his desk and leaned against it. Alec dropped into a chair on its far side.

'You gave us a bit of a fright just then, sir,' he said. 'We thought you were confessing, didn't we Dandy?'

Mr Hogg was too sunk in his gloom to pay much attention. He nodded vaguely and kept talking. 'Miss Lumley and Miss Speir had the right idea all along. As soon as Vesper started up with her . . . well, I hardly know what to call it but when she wouldn't cross the river unless it was bad weather and then when she wouldn't cross the river at all, I wanted to let her go. They stopped me. And when the poor girl started talking so wildly and it became obvious she was unwell, they wanted to send her somewhere to let her rest and get better. I stopped them. I put my foot down. And now look at where we all are. You must think me a heel. A monster.'

I gave what I hoped was a non-committal smile, unsure

212

whether we were officially supposed to know about Mrs Hogg. Thankfully, Rev Hogg took it out of our hands.

'It's my wife, you see,' he said. 'She went into a sanatorium for a short rest ten years ago and she's still there. I hardly recognise her. She's a wisp. She'll be there all her days now. I just couldn't bear to see Vesper going the same way.'

'My dear Mr Hogg,' I said. 'I'm sorry to hear that. Poor lady. Is it quite hopeless? Is she getting some sort of treatment? Perhaps a change of scene? There are plenty of new ideas about how to treat . . . nervous complaints.'

'Absolutely,' said Alec in a stout voice. 'There's not much to be thankful for about that ghastly war, but it forced the medics to get inventive about helping people no longer themselves.'

Rev Hogg was shaking his head. 'The war,' he said. 'She wanted to go home, you know.' He took a deep breath and fixed us with a defiant look. 'She's German.' He waited to see how that snippet took us and then: 'Those four years were very hard on her. Ten years ago when she started being so troubled again she wanted nothing more than to go home. To the valley where she was born. To eat *dampfnudel* and pick wildflowers. I told her a few months in a nice calm nursing home would be so much better for her than all the upheaval of travel. And now she'll never be home again.'

'Is she too frail for the journey?' I asked. 'If not, perhaps it would be worth trying.'

Finally, Rev Hogg lifted his gaze and met my eye. He frowned at me. 'Germany?' he said. 'Cologne? Aren't you reading the papers, Mrs Gilver? They're in the Rhineland now. All over it. That dreadful man. People laugh at him. They think he's a joke with his silly little moustache and all the marching. *I* don't laugh. My poor wife doesn't even smile anymore.'

There was a long silence after this speech, as can well be imagined. Rev Hogg was attempting to gather himself. I could not begin to imagine what Alec was thinking. For myself, I was seized with a vision of smoke, perhaps fog, rolling out and out, on and on, and never clearing. If we had thought Armistice Day was the end of it, we were wrong. That war, so ill-named for there was nothing 'great' about any of it, was still ruining lives. Mourning daughters, broken men, and the wives of country vicars. Where would it ever end? And if there really was to be another one, what would be left of us?

I shook the thoughts away. The silence continued. Eventually, when it became clear that Alec was never going to open his lips, I cleared my throat and made an attempt.

'Mr Hogg, when you say "you wanted to let her go" and "they stopped you" and then when you say "they wanted to send her away" and "you stopped them", I do ask myself over and over again . . . who employed Vesper? Who had the casting vote in what happened?'

'But you've got that first bit the wrong way round, surely,' said Alec. 'They wanted to let her go and you wanted her to stay. Surely?'

'No,' said Rev Hogg. 'Miss Lumley and Miss Speir were absolutely adamant on the point. Vesper was not to get her freedom. She was to stay in her post and do her job, no matter that she was doing it so badly and so intermittently.'

'Why?' Alec said.

Rev Hogg opened his mouth to answer, but no sound came out. Presently he shut it again and a frown pulled his brows together. 'I don't know,' he said. 'I'm so used to those ladies arguing with me about every dratted thing that I didn't stop to wonder on that occasion. But you're right. It makes no sense.' He shook his head and gave me a sharper look. 'As to who employed her, Mrs Gilver, she was her own boss about the ferrying. Miss Lumley employed her to take delivery of supplies from boats on the Forth and land them and Miss Speir employed her to cart goods out to waiting boats from time to time.'

'What supplies would these be?' I said.

'For the pub,' said Rev Hogg. 'Barrels of ale. Bottles of spirit. Jars of pickled eggs, I daresay. Miss Lumley has a taste for the old ways of water traffic, from before these high roads were carving up our countryside willy-nilly.'

'But delivery of ale and spirits off a boat,' Alec said, 'did no one ever wonder if perhaps . . .?'

Rev Hogg waited, blinking, for a suggestion about the subject of this wondering.

'If perhaps,' I took up, 'the point of it wasn't tradition at all but rather avoidance of the exciseman. Where did the stuff come from, Mr Hogg? I mean unless a brewery somewhere has a delivery boat – and I've never heard of such a thing. Have you?'

'I've seen carts and I've seen vans,' Alec said. 'I've never heard of a brewer's *boat*.'

'Much less a bonded distiller's boat,' I put in. 'Don't be shocked, Mr Hogg, but have you ever had an inkling that Miss Lumley's business practices are in any way . . . slippery?'

'But what of Miss Speir?' said Rev Hogg.

'Well, what *of* Miss Speir?' said Alec. 'What goods are these that she has ferried out to waiting boats?'

We knew, of course. But we wanted to find out if Rev Hogg knew too. And from the guilty look he shot out from under his hair as he hung his head forward, I rather thought he did.

'I don't want to tell tales out of school,' he said. 'She is an old and dear friend of mine and, besides, we're all in it together.'

'In what?' I said, my disbelief shading my voice.

'Hard times,' said Rev Hogg. 'Shrinking incomes. I have my stipend and my wife has a little family money, I am glad to say, which just about covers the cost of her remaining where she is, but things have been very hard for Miss Speir.'

Hugh considers me a true-dyed Bolshevist these days, a

point of view I find frivolous, but I admit that I felt a stirring just then, as Rev Hogg described a woman with a large comfortable house and a maid enduring hard times. The house was mere yards from those Sailor Street cottages where much harder lives were being lived and if anyone should be on the side of the meek it was surely a priest.

'And so you see,' Rev Hogg was saying when I applied my attention to him again, 'she has been selling things off. I don't know what, exactly, and I don't ask. Paintings, perhaps. China. Jewellery. Someone said they saw a fireplace being removed once. That didn't seem likely. It was probably a bedhead, don't you think?' It was probably an altar stone, I thought, but I said nothing. 'Anyway, whatever heirlooms Miss Speir is shedding to keep the wolf from the door,' Rev Hogg went on, 'Vesper had the job of taking them from the dock out to the waiting carrier.'

'In that coble?' I said. 'With a pole?'

'In Miss Speir's own motorboat,' Rev Hogg said. 'She hasn't had to sell that yet.'

Nor would she, I thought to myself, given that she used it to shift antiquities into the hands of waiting buyers away from the scrutiny of the Crown.

'From the dock, you say,' Alec put in. 'So that miller is in on it, is he?'

'Who?' said Rev Hogg, round-eyed.

'Massey,' I supplied. 'They use the dock at his paint workshop to land the barrels and load the . . . paintings, as you say.'

'There's no need to be using phrases like "in on it", surely?' Rev Hogg said. 'Might I remind you that it is your own conjecture and nothing more that Miss Lumley is cheating the taxman and Miss Speir has a perfect right to sell any of her possessions. I'm sorry to speak so brusquely to you. I plead my current distress and beg your forgiveness.'

'Of course,' said Alec rather distractedly.

'I meant the lady,' said Rev Hogg.

'But answer me this,' Alec said, sweeping on as though the interruption had not happened. 'Did she still do it?'

'Hm?' said Rev Hogg.

He is not as used to Alec as I am, not as adept at filling in the unspoken details of his cryptic questions. I understood.

'Did Vesper still do the collections of antiques and deliveries of barrels even after the ferry work began to trouble her?' I said.

Once again Rev Hogg opened his mouth to answer and was arrested by the thing he found himself about to say. 'Yes,' he breathed, after a short pause. 'Why yes, she did. Upon my word. How extraordinary. It never struck me before how very peculiar that was, but it is *most* peculiar. Isn't it?'

'Most,' Alec said.

'It suggests they were right to encourage her to stay,' I said, seizing on the chance to comfort him. 'And that you don't need to berate yourself.'

'But when she became ill,' said Rev Hogg, 'I should have let her go somewhere to get better. Instead of keeping her here until she was so desperate that she . . .'

'Mr Hogg,' I said, thinking back over the tumultuous events of the past two days and asking myself if it was possible, 'you do know, don't you, that Vesper did not take her own life?'

'What?' he said in a small voice, almost a croak.

'Did no one tell you?' said Alec. 'She was murdered. She was deliberately held underwater until she drowned. That's why when you said you had killed her, we were so set back on our heels.'

Rev Hogg stood up. 'You thought I . . .?' he said. '*I*? A murderer?'

'We were surprised,' I pointed out. 'We didn't see it coming.'

'I have never killed a living thing in my life,' he said, becoming quite flustered. 'I was a disappointment to my father because I wouldn't go shooting. I only went fishing

217

once, as a boy, and the first trout I caught looked so abject, lying there gasping in my net, that I put it back and never went again. I catch bees in cups and let them out. I leave spiders undisturbed over my bed. I have a cat for the rats in my carriage house, but that's *her* nature. Not mine. I? Kill Vesper? Oh my, oh my.'

He was pacing now, wringing his hands. Or perhaps he was rubbing his hands. Certainly when he spoke again it was with great vigour and resolve.

'I had been going to settle your bill and ask you to go,' he said. 'Now that Vesper is beyond help. But I've just this minute changed my mind. I want you to stay and solve this monstrous crime. I have no expectations of the police. None at all. They showed me their true colours in 1914, coming and making pests of themselves because of my poor dear wife's family background. I have no hopes of justice from that quarter. But you two? Have at it. Let me give you my blessing to rain down blazing coals and burning sulphur on the wicked. In the name of—' He stopped himself. I felt my mouth drop open and my eyes grow wide.

'In the name of . . .?' I said. *Mercury*. The word hung unspoken in the air between us.

'I was going to say in the name of God, but then it struck me as blasphemous. After all it is God himself who rains coals and sulphur.'

'Is it?' I said.

'Exodus,' said Alec.

'Psalms,' said Mr Hogg, who should know.

'Well, we should get started then,' I said. 'There's not a moment to waste. Two young people have died and I want to get to the bottom of both mysteries. If there are two, that is. Of *the* mystery, if it is just one. Do you know, Mr Hogg, that an attempt was made to mislead the police about Vesper's character? A scene was set in her cottage that hinted at debauchery. I very much look forward to confronting the scoundrel who not only killed her but soiled her reputation too.'

Rev Hogg sent us on our way with no more fire and brimstone but with a steely glint in his eye and a cheque for a week's fees tucked into Alec's inside pocket. He would not take no for an answer and I thought to myself that either Mrs Hogg's family money was more than 'a little' or that her upkeep in the nursing home was a bargain, because he wrote the figure with more ease than one might expect to see in a country minister signing away such a sum these days.

'But are Miss Speir's antiquities racket and Miss Lumley's tax racket anything to do with why Vesper died?' Alec said as we drove away again.

'Probably not,' I said. 'If Fordyce and Irvine – or one of the two – killed her, definitely not. If they only found her body, panicked and moved it, then possibly, although I don't see how. Or why.'

'It's odd that she would set out to the open sea in a motorboat but not pole across a quiet river, isn't it?' Alec said.

'Very,' I agreed. As we passed the entry to Cramond House, I asked him: 'Where are we going?'

'To find that cottager who took fright when Jackie Hamilton hove into view,' Alec said. 'I plan to ask her why she changed her story and why she started on about snakes and gods. I shall press her until she squeaks if need be. I'm sick of the feeling that no one is being entirely honest, aren't you?'

'Mr Hogg was honest,' I said. 'And Miss Speir was honest too, actually. Remarkably so if you think about it. Recklessly so. I'm willing to believe that those two biologists are honest as well. We've only got Hamilton's word otherwise and whom would you rather trust?'

'Recklessly honest,' Alec echoed as we took the turn onto the shore road and I prepared to scrutinise the cottage doorways to be sure of knocking on the right one.

219

It was easy in the end, because the door once again stood open and the bantams once again were scratching around the weedy step. Alec rapped smartly on the jamb and young Mrs Cullen appeared with a cloth in her hands and an apron tied over her dress.

'For heaven's sake!' she said. 'Come in before somebody sees you.'

We jostled our way into the narrow passage and followed her along it to the kitchen, where she was busy whacking a Swedish turnip into lumps for boiling. Alec leaned against the dresser and let me take the only chair.

'What is it now?' the woman asked us with some irritation.

'Jackie Hamilton,' I said and was rewarded by her looking over her shoulder with eyes grown large from fear. I felt a small tremor of remorse along with the vindication. 'That's who you don't want to see us, isn't it?' I said.

'What do you *want*?' she asked again, even more irascibly.

'We want to know why you changed your story about how Peter Haslett died.'

'And I want to know why you invoked Mercury and invited snakes to visit you,' I said, even though it made me feel foolish to do so.

'It worked,' she said. 'I wanted you to go and you went.' She was right. We had scuttled off like scolded children, as I remember. I looked at her back as she spooned salt into the turnip pot and fitted the lid on. Her shoulders were rising and falling rapidly. For one wild moment I thought she was laughing at us for running off at a few strange words, then she took a breath and I realised she was crying. She wiped her eyes with the cloth she had used to touch the hot pot lid and then turned to face us. 'Vesper was my friend,' she said. 'She was a wee bit older than me but we walked to the school together every day. And she was my bridesmaid. I had no sister and she had no one either so we were friends. She let me read her books when my mammy hadn't a penny to spare for the circulating library and she let me grow vegetables in her garden over there, for I've no room for more'n a coal bunker out that back door. None of these houses have, all along the row.'

'That's *your* garden over there?' I said. 'We thought it was Vesper's, because it's beginning to look a bit . . . neglected.'

'Sure and it is,' the woman said. 'I had time here and there – ten minutes when the baby was asleep or half an hour when they were at the Sunday school – and I'd nip over and see to it, but then she stopped the ferry and it was a case of all the way up to the Brig and all the way back. I've not got that kind of time, with the three of them and him.'

'Why did she stop the ferry?' Alec said. 'That's the question that's got us both racking our brains. If you were her friend, did she tell you?'

'That she didn't,' the woman said. She was unwrapping a brown paper packet of fat bacon. It was really just a wedge of white lard with the thinnest streak of pink along its middle. She pulled a frying pan onto the front of her range and set the lump of fat in it. I suppressed a shudder.

'I don't know what it was about,' she said. 'But Vesper was determined, whenever she got an idea in her head. Well, I don't need to be telling you that. She took over that ferry and never cared what anyone said about it. I could no more have stood up to them all than I could fly. But she never wavered.'

'So as she became more and more . . . troubled over the course of the last few months . . .' I began carefully.

Mrs Cullen cut me off. 'I'd have said she was happier at first, this year, in the springtime. I was over at the garden one light night and she came back from a run over the river and said to me "You know what? Life is full of surprises." And I asked her what she meant and she just laughed and wouldn't tell me.'

'So she didn't share her joys *or* her troubles with you?' I said. 'Her dearest friend?'

The woman was stretching up to a high shelf to lift down a sack of oatmeal.

'Let me,' said Alec, leaping to his feet. He set it on the table and carefully the woman dipped a cup and lifted out a heaped measure.

'She did.' The words were unexpected. 'She shared just about everything. She told me things I wished I didn't know, if I'm honest. That was what made it so funny that she wouldn't talk about the ferry to me. I knew she wanted away. I knew she tried to get away. I thought she had done it. I can't believe she's been killed for trying.'

'Away from what?' I said. 'Peter Haslett's death? Something else? Or is it from whom? Is it a person she longed to escape from?'

'I shouldn't say any more.' The woman looked up at the clock on her mantelpiece. '*He'll* be in any minute. You need to go.'

'We know about Vesper's other job besides the ferry,' I said. 'The pub deliveries and the collections.'

'Pub deliveries?' Mrs Cullen frowned and it struck me as genuine, so I answered.

'Vesper took barrels of beer and cases of spirit for delivery to Miss Lumley,' I said.

'What?' the woman said. 'Miss Lumley has her ale and bottles off the van from Fountainbridge. I see them every Thursday.'

'But you knew about the collections for Miss Speir,' Alec said.

This hit home. The woman nodded. 'Yes,' she said. 'That's right. At night. On a boat, out to a bigger boat. That's right enough. She told me.'

'And she kept on with that job even after she gave up the ferry?'

222

'Of course,' said the woman. 'How could she stop? How could she ever get out unless it was because she was too ill to carry on?'

'So it's a "what",' I said. 'It's a "what" she wanted to get away from. Not a "whom".'

'Yes,' said Mrs Cullen.

'The sale of treasure that shouldn't be sold,' said Alec.

'Well, if you knew why did you go asking!' She sounded angry now. 'How could Vesper walk away when she'd committed crime after crime? It is a crime, isn't it? I don't know what it would be called in a court or a polis station, but they'd have found something to lock her up for.'

'Handling stolen goods,' I said. 'Fencing, in common parlance.'

'No,' said Alec. 'Fencing is selling them, not just handling them.'

'It's not a parlour game!' the young woman burst out in anguish. 'She died. She *died*.'

'And we mean to avenge her,' I said. 'We shall find out who did it and he shall be brought to justice. We have a strong lead to be going on with. Those two biologists on the island.'

'They're not,' she said. 'On the island. They've packed their traps and gone. I wish *you'd* go, before *he* gets in.'

'Even more suspicious,' I said. 'We shall find them, don't you worry. I thought we'd only have a stroll to find them but we can just as easily go to the university.'

'There's one other thing,' Alec said. 'Since we're not heading over the causeway to find Irvine and Fordyce, perhaps you could tell us whether the boating pond is salt water or fresh?'

'The *what*?' Mrs Cullen took a couple of blinks to catch up. 'Oh, the flooded quarry on the island? Why are you asking about that? Oh! Oh no! Is that where she drowned? Is that where it was done? Is that why those two have gone running away? Oh no! Oh Vesper!' And she put her face in her hands and began weeping in earnest, great ragged sobs tearing at her, tears and worse leaking until her hands shone with them. Alec shushed and patted, while I took over at the frying pan where that monstrous lump of fat bacon was beginning to melt.

That is how *he* found us and perhaps it is just as well. For a young man coming upon his wife crying as though her heart would break, another man very close to embracing her in an effort to give comfort and a strange lady in hat and gloves tipping oatmeal into bacon fat and trying to stir it without spattering is all the more likely to believe that it is a scene of grief and succour, not a scene of successful interrogation.

'Vesper, is it?' he said.

He put down his canvas satchel and water bottle on the table, shrugged out of his coat and took his cap off, then took over from Alec, putting his work-soiled hands on his wife's shoulder and letting her sob helplessly against his chest.

'Vesper,' said Alec. 'We were passing and we heard such sobs.'

'Aye, aye,' said the man. Then: 'Come on now. The bairns are a minute away and they can't see this. Go out to the scullery and splash your cheeks, eh? Let this lady and gent get away. Come on now.'

He saw us to the door as she went towards the scullery pump and nothing in his words or demeanour suggested that he had questions.

'Dark days in Cramond,' was all he said. 'Thank you for helping her.'

Alec and he shook hands and we went on our way.

21

'Is it too late for today?' I asked Alec as we stepped outside. 'It's almost five and even if Fordyce and Irvine are still in their laboratory – would potato specialists work in a laboratory? – no doubt the porter has gone home and the college is closed for the night.'

'We could lurk at the gate and catch them on their way back to their lodgings,' Alec said.

'If there's only one gate,' I said. 'Or two if we take one each.'

Alec shrugged. 'Let's leave it until morning,' he said. 'Let's finish today's task instead, in an orderly fashion.'

'Eck Massey, you mean?' I had little appetite for it. 'Why? Hamilton was the one who saw the incident on the boat.'

'You believe that, do you?' Alec said. 'I rather think they might have drawn straws. And that's the point. I don't want them, at their next confab, to start comparing notes and discover that we pestered three of them, then went to see Mrs Cullen then didn't bother with the fourth. She was genuinely terrified of Hamilton, Dandy. Let's not give any of them a reason to trouble her again.'

'Very well,' I said. 'But let's leave the motorcar here and walk, shall we? I need to shake off the taint of bacon and turnip. Ugh, can you imagine what it's going to taste like when she's done? The turnip boiling before the oatmeal's started.'

'Let's see what Christine wheels out tonight before we go disparaging a plate of oats and bacon,' Alec said. 'And I've

225

got an ulterior motive for the visit. I want to look at this dock again and ask Massey about it. There's something very fishy about the whole thing, wouldn't you say?'

'I would.'

'But we're beginning to get to the heart of it. Vesper wanted to stop doing what the Misses Speir and Lumley were having her do. The strain sent her off her rocker. Mr Hogg didn't and doesn't know what they're up to and that's why he was all for her being let go. That's also why he was all for keeping her around when she was clearly unfit. They weren't his barrels and altar stones that were in danger of ending up in the soup if she suddenly blew her gasket mid-trip.'

'But why weren't the Misses all for sacking her early on and getting someone else?'

'I don't know,' Alec said. 'Because it's illegal and the new chap would have to be persuaded?'

We were passing the row of empty workers' cottages at the Cockle Mill as he spoke. I could not believe it would take much in the way of persuasion to get a new man into such an easy, pleasant job, with tips.

'And how did the women come to be in such an unholy alliance in the first place?' I said. 'The Misses I mean, not Vesper.'

'What makes you think they are?' said Alec. He dropped his voice as we walked through the mill yard towards the dock and the buffers at the end of the railway track. 'Miss Speir's sacking of her treasure trove and even Miss Lumley's dodging of the taxman – if we're right about that – are nothing to do with one another. They both used Eck Massey's dock and Vesper's boating skills as a matter of convenience, I daresay.'

'But they presented a united front to us that first day at Mr Hogg's,' I reminded him. 'And besides, it's Miss Speir's boat. Why does she let Miss Lumley use it? What do you suppose the relative penalties are for failing to pay tax on strong drink and for the selling of treasures that should belong to the Crown? I can't imagine.'

'And we can hardly ask,' Alec said, then he grinned. 'We could telephone to Inspector Hutcheson this evening if we get the chance and ask *him*. He trusts us enough not to come swinging in like . . . what's that chap's name?'

'Tarzan,' I said. 'Don't make the noise!'

I was too late. Alec, like Donald and Teddy, and every male person I had ever encountered who had been inside a picture house in the last few years, counted among his life's ambitions to perfect that horrible blood-curdling yell. I had even heard Hugh at it, through the many corridors between his part of the house and mine. Heaven knows what his dogs made of the racket.

'And now I suppose we need to go and make our presence known officially,' Alec said. 'I've rather uncovered us with my jungle cries.'

Indeed, Eck Massey was at the door of the workshop already. He had evidently finished his day's toil. His collarless shirt was unbuttoned, showing a grubby vest and a thicket of black hair that would not have been out of place in one of Mr Weissmuller's adventures. His braces hung down on either side of his hips like swags and his boots were untied, as though his feet might have swollen over the long day. He was, despite all of that, remarkably unspattered by any paint.

'How do,' he said, companionably enough, as we walked over. 'I've been expecting you two all afternoon.'

'You were forewarned then?' Alec said. 'Yes, we thought we'd take a tour of the mills of Cramond. One of the policemen let slip that one of you four saw Vesper's death. Well, that was a red rag to Mrs Gilver and me, as you can imagine. We were brought here to help with Vesper, you see. And we want to salvage something from the mess it's all turned into.'

'That Hogg is a sentimental old fool,' said Massey, with

227

such cold indifference in his voice that I was shocked. 'The police will see to all of it. No need for you to worry.'

He was clearly not going to let us into his workshop again. He stood just by the doorway with one hand resting on a pile of sacks, or rather on a mysterious object covered with sacking. With a leap of recognition that I hoped did not show on my face, I realised what it was and, bending to tie my shoelace, I took a quick peek from near ground level and confirmed it.

'There is one thing you could help with,' I said. 'Have the police asked you about the night Peter died?'

'Peter?' said Massey.

'Sorry,' I said. 'I had known him since he was a baby. Mr Haslett.' Alec, at my side, flinched. Massey flicked a glance in his direction, then returned his attention to me.

'Asked me what?' he said, grimly.

'Well, his head was crushed in a mill wheel, wasn't it?' I appeared to be doing what my sons called 'going for broke'. I continued: 'And his friends claim that he was on his way here when he died.' Alec flinched again. 'Or rather they didn't deny it when we made the suggestion.'

'Head crushed in a wheel?' said Massey. 'In a mill wheel? *My* wheel? Where did that story come from? Who's said that? The boy drowned.'

'Well, one of the villagers reckons that he fell not out of the boat at all but off the path. So it needn't have been your mill. But one of the four. So you see that's the other reason we were so keen to talk to you all.'

Massey was reeling. He was physically stumbling backwards through his doorway, staring aghast at me. 'No,' he said. 'No way. You don't pin this on me. This isn't my doing.'

'That's what I just said,' I reminded him. But he slammed the door in our faces and we heard the bolts being shot home. 'Good,' I said. 'Now that he's gone, guess what's under all this tarpaulin and sacking, Alec.' I grasped a corner of it and with a flourish worthy of any music hall magician I whipped the sack aside to show that same handcart back again from Dowie's Mill. Alec's eyes rounded and his mouth dropped open.

'Fools,' he said.

'Idiots,' I agreed. 'They'd have a hard job claiming there's nothing to hide when something is literally draped in sacks to be hidden. Something was delivered here in that cart. Sometime today.'

'Spades,' said Alec. 'Georgeson of Dowie's Mill is, after all, a spade maker.'

'Secret spades?' I said. 'Contraband spades?'

'Let's go,' Alec said. Then, as we crossed the yard, he added: 'But let's come back. Under cover of darkness tonight, let's come and see if this load of spades or whatever it is gets picked up on a boat and taken away.'

'Why tonight?' I said.

'It must be tonight,' said Alec. 'Why else would they move the cart from Dowie's back down here when they know we're sniffing around? If there was no rush they'd leave the cargo where it was, not move it and then cover the cart with sacks. Why didn't they put it in one of the unused sheds? The place is pared to the bone, after all. There must be half a dozen empty corners to hide a cart.'

'One would think,' I said. 'And yet there it sits. Maybe the sheds are not empty after all.'

As we drew near to the motorcar again, I found myself looking over the river to Vesper's cottage and then over the broad stretch of water to the island, thinking that both cottage and island were deserted now. Even the neat garden was bound to run to weeds and rabbits now that Mrs Cullen had been forced to let it go. 'What was it you suddenly thought of?' I said as we climbed in. 'I heard you squeak.'

'I don't squeak,' said Alec. 'I may have snorted as an idea formed, but I didn't squeak.'

I waited.

'Just this,' he said eventually. 'Irvine and Fordyce and Peter.'

'What about them?'

'Irvine and Fordyce spoke to you and me about "Peter".'

'I'm sorry, darling,' I said, 'but for once you're being too cryptic.'

'They are friends,' Alec said. 'And they call one another Irvine and Fordyce.'

'You and Hugh call one another Osborne and Gilver,' I said. 'I always want to laugh. And I'm waiting for the day when Teddy starts up with it. Donald began when he got married. Oh!'

'Exactly.'

'They both call Peter "Peter". Do you think it's significant?'

'I truly do,' Alec said. 'We have taken them at their own word about a great deal. They vouched for Vesper's whereabouts at the time of Haslett's death. And then they vouched for her presence on the island the morning after we now think she died.'

'Unless Hamilton is lying about ten o'clock on Saturday night.'

'And we certainly took their word for it that Peter was a friend of theirs, didn't we? But they didn't speak of him the way they speak of friends. They got it wrong.'

'I am very much looking forward to a trip to the university tomorrow,' I said. 'To put all of this to them. I promise not to be so bald as I was just then with Eck Massey.'

'Tush,' Alec said. 'I think it was the right thing to rattle him. And besides, we've got our cover story all set to tell to the lads.'

I blinked at him. We had pulled up on the sweep at Cramond House and he turned off the engine and pulled his hat down. The afternoon had turned terribly gusty.

'We're taking the vial of water to have it tested,' he said. 'To see if it's salt, fresh or brackish.'

'They'll wonder why we don't just taste it,' I said. 'Unless we admit that it's regurgitated.'

'Please,' Alec said. 'It's hard enough looking forward to dinner in this house.'

As matters transpired, though, that evening's meal happened to be one of Christine's small pockets of accidental competence. Even the most dismal cook has usually hit upon some recipe over the years that is impossible to spoil, or that requires exactly the heavy hand or neglect that she uses to render most other dishes inedible. Tonight, we were served with a stew comprising some cut of beef that had done a great deal of hard work during the cow's life and was now joined by vegetables tossed in whole and enough wine to turn the dish a deep red as though it were laced with beetroots. Christine had then left the cooking pot for hours on end and done nothing more than to throw potatoes, not even peeled, into the oven alongside it.

The result was an unctuous, rich, melting broth and potatoes that burst open into creamy clouds at the touch of a fork. Alec applied quite an ounce of butter to his share of the feast and then ate steadily until his plate was scraped clean.

Miss Speir was displeased. 'Hmph,' she sniffed. 'Forgive me, Mrs Gilver. Christine sometimes forgets herself and reverts to the cottage kitchen of her childhood. When she is very busy you understand. But she shouldn't have taken this way out of her difficulties when I have guests.'

'Is she spring cleaning still?' I said. 'Jam-making?' I meant nothing in particular by it, only just that in this house of dust and disorder where the bed linens were barely pressed and not at all aired, it was hard to see where the busyness might lie.

Miss Speir froze as if I had levelled a shotgun at her. 'I . . . I . . .' she said eventually. 'Yes. Jam.'

'Yummy,' said Alec. 'Will it be set by suppertime?' I am sure that he meant nothing more by it than I had but Miss Speir licked her lips and put a hand to her collar.

'Well, that's the worst of it,' she said. 'It didn't work. It didn't set at all. After all her efforts.'

'What was it?' Alec said. 'Strawberry? Blackberry? Do you have any crab apples? A few crab apples in there for a second boiling will put it to rights. Pectin, you see.'

'Alec is quite the chemist,' I said.

'We have no crab apples anywhere near here,' said Miss Speir.

'Or lemons or even rosehips,' Alec persisted.

The poor woman was just about breaking out in a sweat. I took pity on her.

'I for one will not be in the market for supper this evening anyway,' I said. 'After this robust dinner.'

'Yes, I do apologise,' said Miss Speir, hearing an insult in the word 'robust', I imagine.

Alec was unrepentant afterwards in her sitting room. Although his pipe was forbidden he stretched his legs out with more contentment than I had seen since we left Perthshire. 'I put the wind up her,' he said, rather too smugly. She was an elderly lady and we were her guests, after all. 'I think you're right, Dan. There's something afoot tonight and Christine has been helping with the preparation.'

'I think you're making rather a leap,' I said. 'How could Christine and Miss Speir be mixed up in whatever that cart's being used for? Look, never mind that. Quick, while she's out of the room. Shall you telephone to Inspector Hutcheson or should I?'

'You,' said Alec. 'I'll keep watch at the door. Where is it she's supposed to have gone?'

'I don't know. Lots of ladies withdraw after dinner. Lots of men do too. Don't be vulgar.' I was already dialling the number of Inspector Hutcheson's villa in Dunkeld. I imagined the bell ringing out and the doughty Mrs Hutcheson tutting and glaring at him over her spectacles.

'Dunkeld 39,' came his deep rumble of a voice after a minute. I was bathed in comfort at the sound of it.

'It's Mrs Gilver, Inspector Hutcheson,' I said.

'Home from Cramond?'

'Now how did you know I was at Cramond? I am still here by the way, but how did you learn of it?'

'Mr Gilver mentioned it when I was over there earlier,' he said. 'Shush, shush. They're all fine. Small matter of a stolen pony. Perhaps not stolen, exactly. The child leapt on its back and then didn't know how to stop it. It put its head in at the Post Office door in passing and the postmistress's son grabbed its bridle. Good thing or it might be in Glasgow by now. Why are there twenty-five wild bairns running amok over your estate, Mrs G? If it's not too nosy of me to be asking?'

'My daughter-in-law,' I said. 'You'll see soon enough. How are your two boys?'

'Walking out the pair of them but with sensible lasses both,' said the inspector. 'Now what can I do for you?'

'Fingers slightly crossed,' I said, 'I want to pick your brains on a point of law. Penalties for various crimes, actually. What sort of punishment would a publican face if he found a way around paying the excise on a barrel of beer?'

'A barrel?' said the inspector. 'A single barrel? Tap on the wrist at most. Too many bobbies like their pint at the end of a shift.'

'Not a barrel,' I said. 'Spirits too. And on a regular basis.'

The line whistled as Inspector Hutcheson sucked his breath in over his teeth. 'Different story then,' he said. 'Lost licence and a very hefty fine at least. Maybe even a stretch at His Majesty's pleasure.'

'Oh,' I said.

'What?' Alec hissed from the door. 'What's he saying?'

'And this is why you're asking *me*, is it?' Inspector

233

Hutcheson said. 'Because I won't come all the way down there and start slapping handcuffs on the landlord? I remember when you two would call the constable over a scrumped apple. Changed days.'

'And another question,' I went on. I did not address his last point. What prigs we were back then, Alec and I. 'What about breaking the laws of treasure trove?'

'Treasure?' said Hutcheson. 'You're telling me you and Mr Osborne have found treasure? On Cramond Island? No, you're pulling my leg.'

'We haven't found anything,' I said. 'Life rarely offers up such plums as a treasure island. Would that it did. How jolly it would be. But antiquities. Roman coins and that sort of thing. If one were to have found a cache and kept it, would one be in much trouble?'

'Less trouble than from smuggling booze,' Hutcheson said. 'If you're thinking of a sideline these difficult days, I'd fence the Roman coins, Mrs Gilver, and stop running the whisky.'

'You are a terrible man,' I said. 'But thank you.'

'Dandy!' Alec hissed. I flapped a hand to shush him. It is irritating in the extreme the way he believes I can have a conversation on the telephone line and relay the gist of it to him at the same time. 'Dan!' He sounded frantic and, just too late, I realised that Miss Speir was approaching, was at the door, was in the room.

'Well, then dearest,' I said into the mouthpiece. Inspector Hutcheson shouted with laughter. 'I'm glad you got it sorted out. Give my love to the boys and Mallory and the babies of course.'

'Ah, you've been caught out, have you?' Hutcheson said. 'Yes, goodbye, *dearest*. I shall dream of you.'

'Silly man,' I said fondly and replaced the earpiece before he could make me blush any more. 'Do forgive me, Miss Speir,' I said. 'I was seized with the desire to speak to my family. And I'm glad I did. Great ructions at Gilverton today.

A young friend of my daughter-in-law got carried off on a runaway pony.'

'I've warned you about that pony,' Alec said. 'He's fine in harness but he's a demon with a saddle on his back. You need to sell him before Edward and Lavinia get old enough to clamber onto him.'

Miss Speir was far from interested in the minutiae of my domestic life but she seemed convinced by the exchange and the penetrating look she had shot me as she entered softened into a smile.

'Well, I'm glad you got a chance to speak to your loved ones,' she said. 'Mr Osborne, you should feel free.' She gestured to the telephone still in my hands.

'Oh, no one loves me,' Alec said. 'I'm a bachelor, Miss Speir. A few years more and I shall be a confirmed bachelor.'

I had a pang as I always do but Miss Speir was not discomfited. 'A game of cards then?' she said. 'Or will you read? I'm afraid I need to leave you to your own devices this evening. Monday is my evening for the sewing bee. We are making flannel bags for babies down at Miss Lumley's.'

'Bags?' said Alec.

'Nightgowns with buttons along the bottom so they can't kick them up into scarves,' I said. 'I have two grandchildren, Miss Speir, and they are can-can dancers, both of them. Are they for a sale of work or for sending out in charity? If the former, put me down for a couple. Pink and blue if you go that far or plain white by all means.'

'I . . . I . . .' said Miss Speir. I had done it again. 'They're for sending to China,' she blurted out. 'Charity, as you say.'

'Is China chilly overnight?' said Alec cruelly.

Then with a hasty goodbye and a lot of fluttering about supper and more coal, Miss Speir was gone.

'She's not going to any sewing bee,' Alec said, as her footsteps receded. 'But I do believe she's going to do whatever it is with Miss Lumley. I have no difficulty believing that much.'

'And do we think Christine has gone with her?' I said.
'Give her a five-minute head start and then let's see.'

Once the minutes had ticked past, I pulled the bell by the fireplace and we waited. When no one answered, I tried again. After waiting long enough so that Christine would have appeared even if we had disturbed her in the lavatory or if she had popped up to her own room and rolled her stockings down, we went on the prowl.

Stopped in her kitchen doorway, we both sniffed deeply.

'No one made jam in here today,' Alec said. 'Shall we go down to the Turning Tide and smash that story too?'

'Or . . .' I said, pointing at the far wall where, upon a nail banged into the high wooden mantel over the range, there hung an iron ring big enough to serve as a bangle if one's wrist were slender. Dangling from it, among many other smaller examples, were two enormous keys, one elderly and slightly rusted, one brand new and shining.

A beam spread over Alec's face. He trotted over, lifted the ring and slipped it into his coat pocket. Then we crossed the room to the scullery passage and, taking a lantern from the shelf by the back door, stole out into the dark garden.

It was no kind of night for spying. The sky had cleared, but for a few scudding clouds, and the moon was at three-quarters and bright enough to throw shadows. But all was silent and still. We were alone in the blue moonlight, and we struck out boldly towards the tower, which stared sightlessly back at us out of its hollow black eyes.

22

We are bold, but not reckless, and as we drew close enough to feel the chill of the stone we slowed until we were inching forward. Alec even fumbled a little as he inserted the rusty old key into the lock. I winced at the scraping sounds it made and cringed at the creak and groan as the door swung inwards. I took a step but Alec put out a hand and laid it gently on my arm, cocking his head to one side, sending me the message 'listen'.

I stopped moving and stilled my breath but could hear nothing except the wind in the trees and the faintest shush of the tide in the distance. I could see nothing either, despite straining to pick out any outline beyond the doorway or movement across it.

'Hello-o?' called Alec suddenly. 'Miss Speir? Is anyone there?'

'Sssh,' I hissed at him, darting away to the side. I suddenly felt like a sitting duck, standing out there on the lawn in the stark moonlight. My heart was still hammering as I tucked myself into the shadow of a little tree growing nearby.

'What's wrong?' Alec said softly, coming to stand beside me. 'There's no one there. And even if there is . . . We came out for a smoke – light a fag Dan, keep the story straight – and . . . let's say we saw the door standing open and the keys hanging from the lock. We were concerned about burglars.'

'Robbers,' I said. 'Not burglars. But yes, you're right.' Once I had my cigarette lit, I raised my voice too. 'Miss Speir? Is there anyone there, Alec? There's no one round this side.'

'I think we should take a quick peek,' Alec said, in a loud hearty voice that would not have got him a part in a play if he employed it for an audition. 'Make sure there's nothing nefarious going on,' he added. Then he clutched my arm and whispered, 'Look, Dandy!'

'What?' I breathed back. I had seen nothing and when I glanced at him he had his head back and was gazing straight up. '*What*?' I repeated, feeling a chill.

Alec reached into the tree we were crouched under and tugged. 'Crab apples,' he said, holding his hand out with a little orb in his palm. 'Is there nothing they haven't lied about?'

Together we stepped with steady tread, if unsteady heart in my case, back to the front of the tower and the open door.

'Miss Spe-ir!' I sang out. 'Chris-tine!'

'They're not in there,' Alec said. 'It's as black as coal. Let's light the lantern and go in.'

The interior of the tower had been no picnic in the plain light of an afternoon when we thought the trouble was nothing more than a trespasser. Now, in the darkness, with the lantern sending wild, swooping shadows up around the walls at every step we took, it gave me the most severe willies. It didn't help that the moon just at that moment disappeared behind a cloud and we were plunged from stark blocks of navy blue and white to an enveloping, soft, inky blackness.

'They're not here,' I said, as though Alec had not just said it to me. 'But let's go. I want to go upstairs to my room and put a chair under the door handle; I don't know about you.'

Alec did not answer. He was standing in the middle of the floor. At least the lantern light had stopped swirling.

'Alec?' I said. 'Can we please go? I'm sorry to be such a ninny. If you like, we can try to find this sewing bee. Yes, let's do that. Let's ask in the Tide and at the Inn and see if anyone has anything to say. Alec? Are you listening? What's wrong?'

'Hold the lantern,' he said. 'While I . . .'

238

'While you what?'

'Look,' he said. I could tell even from behind him that he was staring down at the floor, and my pulse began to quicken. Was something, or someone, lying there? Would I not have noticed a shape on the floor as we entered the room? I certainly had not. The skirl of the lantern light had shown me nothing but bare walls and window holes. Then I frowned and stepped to Alec's side.

'Oh my goodness,' I breathed.

The sacking was gone from over the trap door.

'What if they're down there?' I said. 'What if we open the trap door and surprise them – one or both of them – at whatever they're at?'

'They can't be down there,' Alec said. 'The keys were in the kitchen.'

'There might be two bunches. Miss Speir must have keys of her own as well as that gaoler's ring.'

Alec knows me well. Too well for my comfort. He mounted no further argument and did not try to persuade me. He simply waited, giving me a steady look, until I came round all on my own.

'Listen first, at least,' I said. 'I'll hold the lantern. Go on.'

Alec grinned, handed the lantern over and then got down onto his hands and knees on the trap door and, sticking his bottom up in the air, applied his ear to the join at the hinge side. I waited.

'Nothing,' he said, presently. 'Complete silence. Not even any creaks or drips or draughts. It sounds absolutely dead down there.'

'Oh heavens, don't say that!' I told him with a shaky laugh.

Alec sat back on his heels and held his hand out. 'Keys, Dan,' he said.

I set the lantern down on the floor and Alec's face instantly leapt into ghoulishness as the orange light cast shadows upward from below him. I suppose mine did the same. Then

239

I picked over the bristling ring of keys for that second enormous iron one as shining new as the padlock it opened and handed them over by it. Alec applied it and I heard the padlock spring open and fall against the floor with a dull clunk.

There was no shout or scuffle from below us and when Alec let out the unsteady breath he had been holding, I did the same.

'Right then,' he said. 'Place your bets. A strong room? A set of steps leading down to a ruined temple? An ordinary dungeon, but filled with riches?'

He stood as I lifted the lantern again, then he grabbed the hasp and threw the trap door open. It fell against the stone flags behind it with an almighty clang like the largest steel hammer ever swung hitting the largest anvil ever forged. It reverberated through my feet and up my legs. It rattled my teeth. I drew in a sharp breath and looked downwards.

'Huh,' Alec said.

'Hmph,' I said.

'Well, that's disappointing,' Alec added.

'How very odd,' I put in.

For below the trap door was not a hole, nor a tunnel, nor a set of steps, but a shallow rectangle of pressed earth with an old wormhole in one corner and a thin thread of root crossing its middle. The floor had been gouged out to the thickness of the wood so that it sat flush when closed, but below that the ground lay undisturbed.

'It's fake,' Alec said.

'It certainly seems that way.' I knelt beside him. 'I don't suppose it's a tray sort of an affair by any chance? Is there an edge that might lift up at all?' I set the lantern down again and wiggled first my fingers then my spare hat pin into the dirt at the edge of the opening and could no longer doubt it. This trap door covered nothing and led nowhere.

'What's the point?' Alec said, as he hauled the door back

over and re-applied the padlock. 'Let's get out of here. Christine might only have gone to post a letter. She might be looking for us as we speak.'

When we were back outside, trap door locked and front door locked, and were quick-marching over the lawn to the house again, I asked: 'Shall we still go and try to rouse this sewing bee? Once we've put the keys back?'

'I've lost my appetite for it,' Alec said. 'I'm more unsettled than I can tell you by that, Dandy. What is going *on* here?'

I shrugged and shook my head. The clouds had passed over and the cold blue light was showing us the way again. Neither of us gave the lantern a thought, so keen were we to put the keys back on their hook before anyone missed them.

After a night of troubled sleep, visited by dreams of footsteps outside my room and whispered conversations of which I was the subject, it was a relief to be awake again. I bathed as lavishly as was possible in the spartan bathroom, with not a care as to the portion of the household's hot water I might be using up. I brushed my hair with the kind of strokes Nanny Palmer used to recommend, dealing blows to my head more than anything, and I buckled my belt and tied my shoelaces more tightly than usual too. When I met Alec on the landing he gave me a startled look.

'You look as if you are going into battle,' he said. 'Although I can't work out what you've done that's different.'

'I'm very glad we're getting away from here this morning, Alec,' I said. 'I want to walk on city streets and look into shop windows. I do not want to hear another mill wheel gushing, nor another gull crying. I'd rather like to ride on a bus, in fact. On the top deck.'

'Well, well,' Alec said. 'We can certainly take a bus, if you prefer.' He is the kindest of men. I smiled at him.

'A cup of coffee in a shop and a turn around a municipal park will do,' I said. 'I spoke generally.'

Was it my imagination that Miss Speir was reserved at the breakfast table? She greeted us by flapping a napkin at the chafing dishes but had a watchful look in her eye.

'How was your sewing bee?' Alec said, eyeing the toast rack. 'Did you pick up any news about the case?'

'News?' said Miss Speir. 'Case?'

'Forgive him,' I said. 'Gentlemen always do think any collection of women is a gossip factory. But it would be entirely understandable if poor Vesper was the talk of the evening.' I gave her an expectant look, as I stirred my tea. It was not hot and I had had to choose between inadequate milk and a temperature that was barely warm. I chose to eschew the milk, but I was even more determined to get into a teashop at some moment during this day.

'Well, Mrs McTearnie was there and she did say – her husband is Sergeant McTearnie – she did say that quite a few details of Vesper's life had come to light when they went through the cottage. It might be—' she craned over her shoulder as though to spare Christine's elderly innocence, 'a *crime passionnel*. Or even, such wickedness, a suicide.'

'Oh, that's got round, has it?' I said. 'I see.'

'*Such* wickedness,' said Miss Speir. 'When you think of all those poor soldiers giving their lives to protect us and then for some lucky girl like Vesper to throw her own life away. It is no more than spitting on the graves of heroes. If it does come to it again,' she went on, 'we should think carefully before giving the girls their head in factories and the like. What has come of it, after all?'

I had lost my appetite. I put my napkin down beside my place and stood. 'I shall wait for you outside, Alec. Please don't be too long.' Even as I stalked off, I knew I was being ridiculous. My boys were no nearer conscription because Miss Speir was talking nonsense about Vesper Kemp's sad end. And I am sure that she didn't count me among those women who had been given their head and then cut up rough

242

when it came to knuckling back down to feminine pursuits again. As I stepped out into the freshness of the morning sunshine, I tried to put it all out of my mind.

The University of Edinburgh is a venerable institution of many hundreds of years standing and is beginning to sprawl all over the south side of the city as disciplines become ever more varied. The original college, a proper quad just like Oxford, was outgrown many years ago. The new college, tucked under the castle rock and looming above the art galleries of Princes Street, came next but only the Department of Divinity fitted in there now. The arts had taken over a pretty Georgian square and were spreading year by year along the drab Victorian street behind it. The School of Veterinary Medicine was, understandably, set out on its own where its noise and smells would not disturb more delicate scholars, and the rest of the sciences were miles off, deep in the suburbs at the southern edge of the city in a park-like campus known as The King's Buildings. It was to these King's Buildings, and to the School of Agriculture within the boundary wall, that we were headed today.

'How on earth do you *know* all this?' Alec said.

'Years of dinner parties,' I said. 'Decades of doctors and solicitors. I'm as surprised as you. In my girlhood I never dreamed I'd be able to serve as a tour guide to a provincial university in my middle years.'

Alec whistled. 'Don't let them hear you,' he said.

I sighed. It is one of the more tiresome conceits of the Scots ever to be vigilant on the question of their standing and England's standing and the precise nature of the relationship between the two. Hugh is insufferable. It is one of the many reasons I value my time with Alec so dearly. 'Oh for heavens' sake,' I said. 'Don't *you* start. England is twice the size and has three times the population and all the money.

If Scotland floated off into the North Sea, no one would notice until the grouse season opened.'

'I'm not holding a brief,' Alec said. 'But don't get so cross so early in the day, darling. You'll give yourself a headache.'

We were climbing one of the main arterial routes out of the city to the south. There are three running parallel and I was not entirely sure we had picked the one that led straight to the gates of the King's Buildings. I was paying close attention in case we shot past and were out in the Borders countryside before we noticed. I let myself have a very brief daydream of what would happen in such a case: we would drive and drive and then would be in England again. On the other hand, the bit of England that lies just across the border is Northumberland and it outstrips Perthshire for bleakness by a mile. Northamptonshire, golden and gentle, was two long days' driving away and the daydream was no more than a distracting indulgence.

'There it is!' I said, as a startlingly modern gateway appeared at one corner of the crossroads we were bearing down upon. Alec swung across and drove in.

'Golly,' I said. Something between a temple and a new cinema rose up importantly before us.

'Is that it?' Alec said. 'The Agriculture School. It's got some sheep and sheaves on that marble frieze, I think. Look, Dandy.'

'Let me down and I shall enquire,' I said.

As soon as I entered the grand picture-palace, I suspected it was not our destination. There was an unmistakable whiff of mice in the air and I could not think what aspect of agriculture mice might play a part in. The porter, sitting behind his desk with his chin on his chest – how dull summers in colleges must be! – confirmed my hunch.

'Chemistry, madam,' he said. 'You'll need to follow the road all the way round and then turn before you hit the hedge. The Agrics are down there with a view of the fields. Well, they wouldn't be complaining about that, would they?'

I laughed dutifully at his little joke and tried to fix the directions in my mind before rejoining Alec.

'Stick to the edge and go round anti-clockwise,' I told him. 'We're looking for six o'clock if this is twelve, apparently. The good news is I wasn't asked to account for myself or questioned about my business here. If there's another friendly porter down there we should have Irvine and Fordyce in our sights within minutes.'

It was a different story at the School of Agriculture, unfortunately. Perhaps lady chemists are more common than academic lady farmers, or perhaps it can be put down to the natural variation in temperament between one porter and another, but we got very short shrift when we presented ourselves at the cubby hole in the foyer of the right building.

He took great umbrage at being called a porter, for one thing.

'I'm a servitor,' he informed us with a level of pomposity more suited to someone telling us he was a duke. 'And what is your purpose in entering us today exactly?'

'We're looking for two of your students,' Alec said.

'Undergraduates or postgraduates,' the man said.

'Not sure,' said Alec. 'Post, probably.'

'No, I mean we do not call our gentlemen "students",' the man intoned. 'We call them undergraduates, postgraduates, and postdoctoral fellows.'

'Post*doctoral*?' I made the mistake of saying. 'Can one really take a PhD in farming?'

With a sniff that must have pulled the floorboards tight to the soles of his boots the man fixed me with a frigid stare.

'Their names are Irvine and Fordyce,' Alec said, sensing that we only had a short time left before this chap drove us off with a broom.

He shook his head and pushed his lips out. 'No one by those names in our School, sir,' he said, his politeness perhaps intended to send the message that I was the problem and

245

that Alec and he might deal with the matter better if I would go away.

'Mr Irvine and Mr Fordyce,' Alec insisted. 'Dandy, can you remember their Christian names? Did we ever hear them?' The porter was still shaking his head. 'They are part of – well, perhaps they are all of – but they are working on the potato project out at Cramond.'

'The trial of new varieties,' I said, hoping to raise my stock.

'Potatoes?' the man said. 'It's Dr McMann who does most of the study of potatoes. *Solanum tuberosum*,' he added for no reason at all. 'But he has no fellows by those names, as I'm telling you.'

'Perhaps they're only here for the summer,' Alec suggested. 'Do you have visiting scholars over the summer?'

'Is Dr McMann here today?' I asked. 'Could we speak to him?'

'He's very busy,' the porter said. 'He's writing. He'll be here all day, but he's writing a paper. He doesn't even stop for his dinner when he's writing a paper. I slip over to the refec and get him a sandwich. He's a very, very busy man. What is it about?'

'Well, young Haslett,' Alec said. If he thought that would open the door to the inner sanctum of Dr McMann's office, he was much mistaken.

'Peter Haslett brought our School into disrepute,' the porter said. 'Brought the whole of these Buildings into disrepute. That sort of nonsense, drinking and messing about on boats? That's the sort of carrying on you get down at George Square or, worse, at *Oxbridge*. Not here. Never here.'

'I understand,' I lied. 'But if we could just have five minutes with Dr McMann. Five short minutes would do.'

'He's *writing*,' the porter said with great deliberation as though I were an imbecile.

Just then the glass door beside his cubby hole swung open

and an untidy middle-aged man with wispy hair and some of the baggiest tweeds I had ever seen, excepting on tramps who sleep in them, came out.

'Just slipping over for a cuppa, Billy,' he said. 'I'll bring you back a piece of shortbread if it's on the counter already.'

We would never have guessed who it was if 'Billy' had not turned a deep brick red from collar to hairline and narrowed his eyes in fury. Without a word, Alec and I turned and hurried out of the building and down the steps, only catching up with Dr McMann when he had just about disappeared into the mouth of a shrub-lined path that reminded me greatly of the gorse maze on Cramond Island.

'Dr McMann?' I called and he stopped and wheeled back, with a ready grin on his face.

'Guilty!' he said. 'What can I do for you?'

'Alec Osborne,' Alec said. 'Perthshire. You're a potato man, the servitor just said.' It sounded rather a rude way to describe him to my ears but McMann did not blink. 'This is Mrs Gilver,' Alec went on. 'Her husband—'

'Hugh Gilver,' said Dr McMann. 'Of course. A fine farmer and an inquisitive scholar, madam.'

I simply stared. It never occurred to me that the cripplingly dull off-prints that Hugh seized on in his correspondence and then devoured would connect him to a seat of learning by sturdy enough threads that the academics there would get to know his name.

'We're trying to track down a pair of your students,' I said. 'Or employees, perhaps. From the potato trials.'

'Oh yes,' said Dr McMann. 'Nothing wrong, I hope?'

I did not know how to answer him. If the death of Peter Haslett had been passed by already, so that there must be something newly wrong to explain an enquiry, then this world of science was a cold one indeed.

'We're not at liberty to say,' Alec plumped for, which was true and also piqued McMann's interest. He was now avid to hear more. 'But they have left the island and we urgently need to be in touch with them.'

'Which island is this?' McMann said. I had no idea that potatoes were being studied so extensively that we would have to specify.

'Cramond,' I said.

'Cramond Island?' said McMann. 'Across the causeway? Halfway to Queensferry? I'm afraid you're mistaken. I've no potato trial there. No one has a potato trial there.'

'Irvine and Fordyce?' I said, still unwilling to believe what appeared to be unfolding.

'Those are not the names of potato varieties,' he said. 'It might be a private trial but then the strains wouldn't yet be named.'

'Those are the students,' Alec said.

'I assure you, they are not,' McMann said. He was not yet annoyed but he was no longer smiling.

'But we met them,' I said. 'They are there, or were there, with trial plots all laid out. We saw them planting potatoes. With our own eyes.'

'When was this?' McMann said. Annoyance was whisking around his features now.

'Two days ago!' I said as though I were helping my case. Alec was already wincing; he had seen – finally – what we should have seen at the outset.

'No one plants potatoes in July,' McMann said. 'Now if you don't mind, I'm rather busy.' He gave a tight smile and short bow and then took off after his tea and shortbread, leaving us standing there.

'And even if they did,' Alec said. 'They'd know which end of the spud was the top. We've been had, Dandy. I don't know why but we've been absolutely taken for a trot round the paddock, haven't we?'

248

23

I tried to mount an argument that Fordyce and Irvine were undercover and not using their own names but my heart was not in it.

'So who are they?' Alec said as we sat, stunned, side by side in his motorcar minutes later. 'Who *are* they?'

'Murderer one and murderer two,' I said. 'If they were up to no good it stiffens the motive for their bumping off Vesper. Even if it removes the connection between them and Peter Haslett.'

'Dandy, your language!' Alec said. '"Bumping off" indeed. *Stiffens*?'

'I am weakened from lack of tea,' I said. 'Please take me back down into town to a nice teashop, Alec. Upstairs in Patrick Thomson's would do in a pinch.'

'You must think I was born yesterday,' Alec said, as he let in the clutch and we moved away, 'if you expect me to enter a department store with you. What is it: gloves? Hairpins? I shall find a nearby teashop with no haberdashery and then it's back to Cramond with us.'

I said nothing. I find it irksome when he disparages me as one of the monstrous regiment. Besides, he was right about the gloves counter.

'And you've got the whole thing upside down about Peter Haslett, you know,' he was telling me when I recovered. 'The removed connection, as you put it, is the whole point.'

'How so?' I asked him.

'Picture it,' he said. 'Peter Haslett is on a jaunt to Cramond—'

249

'Why?'

'Fishing? Old friends? It doesn't matter, Dandy. He arrives and hears in the pub – or the hotel, or somewhere; it doesn't matter – that two students from the School of Agriculture are on the island doing a potato trial. What a stroke of luck! So he waits for the tide and off he goes to say hello. But when he gets there . . .'

'Hm,' I said. 'I'd say he hears somewhere in town that there are two of his fellows doing the trial and that's what brings him to Cramond, but otherwise yes. He knows right away they're not who they say they are . . .'

'But who are they?' said Alec again. 'Why would Peter Haslett finding out that Irvine and Fordyce are not experts on potatoes put his life in danger?'

'I don't know,' I said. 'Ask me again after I've had some tea.'

He chose another of the three parallel streets for the trip back to the city centre. Newington Road, which becomes Clerk Street, then South Bridge and eventually North Bridge before it tips out at the railway station, was a bustling thoroughfare of market stalls and dairy carts and brewer's vans and general seething humanity. I thought once again upon the matter of the delivery boat, in place of ordinary motorvans, and upon the matter of the handcart popping up at spots miles apart by road and now being hidden when it did so. Then Alec was slowing, just beyond the university's Surgeons' Hall and the Festival Theatre. He pulled in to the side of the road and stopped. I craned around. There was a fish and chip shop ahead of us on one corner and a bookshop on the other.

'Are you peckish?' I said. 'I'm sure we can find a place that'll serve me China tea and make you a sandwich but please don't make me sit in the fug of frying fish.'

But he was not listening. He was sitting forward in his seat and squinting hard. 'Look, Dandy,' he said. 'And tell me I'm wrong.'

I looked where he was nodding and gasped, for there crossing the street ahead of us, from the university's old college building towards the bookshop, was none other than the svelte Mr Irvine. I was sure of it. The last time I had seen him he had been dirty and rumpled and without his shirt but there was no mistaking his willowy frame, even draped in a soft collar and a tweed jacket. As though to remove all doubts, when he hopped up onto the pavement on the other side of the road, Fordyce was waiting for him. I should not have recognised him if I had seen him first, for he had a cap pulled low on his head and his large figure was swathed in a black mackintosh clearly tailored once upon a time for someone even larger. He held the door for Irvine and the pair disappeared inside.

'What is that place?' said Alec, reading the name in gold above one of the doors. 'James Thin?'

'It's the university bookseller,' I said. 'At least for some of it. Not, I would imagine, for agriculture. Oh I wish Grant were here.'

'Why?' said Alec. He put a hand out of his window and waved at a removing van whose driver was squeezing his horn with some gusto, displeased at Alec's stopping. 'Go round, can't you?' Alec said into his wing mirror and then turned back to me. 'What can Grant do that we can't?'

'She can start up a conversation with every person ever born,' I said. 'And they don't know her.'

'If Grant had been at Cramond since last Wednesday they would,' Alec countered. 'Let's slip in unobtrusively and see if we can eavesdrop on them. Or why don't we just go and say hello? Say we were passing and saw them. Even if they did drown Vesper in that boating pond they're not likely to do us harm in a busy shop in broad daylight.'

'You're right,' I said. 'Can we leave the motorcar sitting here?'

'I'll pull round the corner into Chambers Street,' Alec said.

'And give some urchin a tuppenny bit to keep an eye on things for me.'

Sad to say there was a selection of urchins willing to compete for the job, for Chambers Street has a museum on it and on wet summer days when they are not at school, a museum is a great draw for children of every stripe. Alec managed to bargain the boldest one down to a penny and I slipped him an extra sixpence, then we made our way back to the main road, even stopping to look around the corner like veritable spies before we made ourselves visible.

And what a good thing that we did.

'Is that . . .?' I said, pointing my umbrella at a departing back. She might have come out of James Thin's; certainly she was now walking away down South Bridge. We could not see her face but there was something in her gait and the cluster of curls under her hat that seemed familiar.

'Miss Lumley,' Alec said. 'As I live and breathe. Now that is very interesting, wouldn't you say?'

The inside of the bookshop was heaven sent for anyone trying to do a bit of subtle snooping. The windows were backed by wooden display shelves so that only a smudge of daylight came in through the fan at the top of the door. And the electric lamps were sparse and dim. Add to that bookshelves jutting out at every angle, soaking up what little light the bulbs did throw off, and the place was mostly corners and shadows.

'May I help you?' said an excruciatingly genteel young man with a pencil behind each ear and a pair of spectacles on his forehead, the three giving him the look of a horned sea creature.

'Just browsing,' Alec said in a near whisper and we drifted past.

They were nowhere to be seen on the ground floor. The latest marvellous novel was laid out on a draped table looking fat and dull and I pretended to look at a copy of it while Alec skirted around the edges of the room, and then whistled softly to me from the stairs.

'Travel, modern fiction, poetry and essays,' Alec said. 'Whatever they're after it's not a guidebook to Cramond Island. I thought you said this was the university bookseller, Dan.'

'Upstairs, sir,' said the genteel young man who, unbeknownst to either of us, had been following Alec in his peregrinations.

'Do I look undesirable?' he muttered as we climbed the twisting staircase to the first floor.

'I think he's being conscientious, not overbearing,' I said. 'It's only because we know we're up to no . . . Sssh.'

We had arrived on the first floor, which was even darker, even dustier, even more beset with protruding shelves and without a table of novels to add cheer. We parted at the stair head and went around in opposite directions. I plucked a book at random from a shelf and carried it with me to lend an air of legitimacy, then I moved at a steady studious pace past English literature, philosophy, European history, French language, French literature, theology, comparative religion – which struck me as blasphemous – and onto such mystifying narrow shelves as social anthropology, physical anthropology and ancient archaeology – as though there were another kind – before finally meeting Alec again.

'Law, psychology and economics round that way,' he said. 'You?'

I filled him in on what I had seen and we looked up the narrower, steeper stairs to the second floor.

'But what's left?' Alec said.

I shrugged, for it seemed to me that all of life had been generously covered already, then I grasped the handrail and pulled myself up the first step.

We heard them before we were round the bend in the

landing. Fordyce was breathing heavily, perhaps still out of breath from the climb, and Irvine was muttering softly to himself. They were sharing a small desk in the middle of the room, hunched over from either side. Neither of them looked up as we set foot on the strip of thin carpet that ran along the shelved corridors of this attic room with its awkward ceiling and waist-height windows.

We took another tour around, but side by side this time. My heart was hammering, waiting for one of them, at any minute, to look up and recognise us. But they were concentrating quite fiercely on the book that lay open on the table between them, bent so closely over it their heads were almost touching. And so we paced the shelves as we had on the floor below, looking at the labels marking the subjects stored up here in this garret and wondering, for my part at least, why we had not known what was missing. Classics, fine art, ancient art, art history, and modern archaeology. That was why there was a table up here, one supposed. Those enormous art books were too heavy and cumbersome to leaf through standing up.

As we walked past them, so close that my pulse raced, I glanced down to see what had enthralled them and then looked away so sharply that I felt my neck snap. I hurried to the stairs and began to trot down, with Alec on my heels.

'Did you see?' I said. 'Did you see what they were looking at?'

'Ssshhhh,' Alec said. 'Keep moving.'

I slowed down by the till on the ground floor where the genteel young man was stationed and dropped the volume I had been clutching.

'Shall I wrap it for you, madam?' he said. 'Or would you like it posted to your . . .?' His voice faded as we fell out of the shop onto the blessed ordinary rough and tumble of the city street.

'Did you see?' I said again when we were halfway back to

the motorcar. The urchin had taken a seat inside and filled the other seats with a collection of his friends. They were hanging out of the windows and making full use of both the town and country horns. They would be very lucky not to be clipped round the ear if a bobby on his beat heard them. Alec barely noticed.

'Mercury,' he said. 'Wingèd Mercury.'

'They were sketching him!' I said. 'Why would two scientists be sketching pictures of Mercury?'

'They're not scientists,' Alec said. 'Now, Dandy, I don't suppose your expertise on the university extends to the location of the . . . What would you call it? The records office?'

'Matriculation,' I said. 'I've no idea. It might be department by department or it might be one central filing room. But since Fordyce came out of the quad let's try there first, shall we?'

'Before your cup of tea?' said Alec.

'Bother my cup of tea!' I told him. 'The chase is on. My heart was in my mouth up there. Thank heavens they were concentrating so hard.'

They didn't even glance up to see who it was!' Alec said.

'Quite,' I said. 'It might have been the bookseller, and he would surely have had plenty to say about them using the place as a public library.'

'Unless they're regulars,' Alec said. He stopped walking. 'We are idiots, aren't we Dan?'

I had stopped too. 'Utter fools,' I said, turning round and heading back the way we had come.

'Changed your mind, madam?' said the shop assistant when we re-entered his premises. 'You're lucky I hadn't already re-shelved it.' He reached behind him to a wheeled trolley groaning with discarded books. At a guess, I should have said he had not shelved anything for a fortnight.

'No, I think – on reflection – that I've already got it at

home,' I said, 'but I wonder if you can help me with something else?'

'You've already got *Sex and Repression in Savage Society*?' he said, looking at the book in his hands. Alec turned away and cleared his throat. 'Bronislaw Malinowski has visited us here in Edinburgh, you know. Well, I'm sure you do know. What an interesting man! What a unique mind! What a retort to Freud!'

That last sounded to my ears like a inarguable point in this Malinowski's favour but I shuddered to think of Hugh's response should I slip this volume into his library. I smiled and turned the conversation, as only women of a certain age can do.

'Very nice, I'm sure. What a treat for you. But what I did want to ask and I hope it's not too compromising . . .'. The genteel young man swallowed hard. His Adam's apple disappeared into his collar and rose again like a bobbin. 'Was that young Mr Irvine I saw upstairs? I'm a friend of his mother, you see, and she worries that he does no work at all. She worries aloud to me because my own son was something of a dilettante and she knows I won't look down my nose at her because of it. But if I can report back to dear Fanny that the boy is laying in new books even in the long vac, she will be most relieved. So. Do you happen to know?'

'Oh my,' the young man said, the bobbin sinking and rising again. 'Oh my, oh my. She doesn't know? Your friend? Do you mean to say she doesn't know?'

We drew closer, trying to look agog but still deserving of confidences. We need not have bothered. This chap was a gossip through and through. He folded his arms, threw a glance up the stairs and told us all.

'They've both been thrown out,' he said. 'Fordyce, and Irvine along with him. They were sent down at the end of last term. For cheating. On an examination paper. I only know because Mr Fordyce came in trying to re-sell his textbooks back to us, but he had taken no care with them and we had to decline. Water spots on the boards, cracked spines.' He lowered his voice even further. 'Folded pages, madam.'

'Dear God,' Alec said, and I am not sure he was entirely acting, for he is very fussy about his own library and his man, Barrow, is forever re-covering the volumes with dust papers and moving them around to save the sun from fading one more than another.

'Poor Fanny!' I said. 'But if they're still studying, does that mean they're trying to be reinstated?'

'I don't think so,' the young man said. 'Some sort of summer job, I believe.'

'A summer job in . . .' Alec said, trying to sound incredulous rather than merely uninformed.

'Roman art!' said the assistant. 'Yes, it is surprising, isn't it? I wondered if it was theatrical. Perhaps props or sets for something in the Festival but I heard them discussing "the customer" one night as they were leaving. I'm sure I can't think what it might be. Can you?'

'Not a clue,' I said. 'But it's something. To be working. I say, it's not anything to do with . . . Oh, I've forgotten her name, but I heard all about her from poor Fanny. Do you remember me telling you, Alec?'

Alec is quick-witted to begin with and, besides, can follow the train of my thoughts without any trouble after all these years. 'Ugh no,' he said. 'I can't remember her name but I remember her high heels and her curly hair, not to mention all the baubles and bangles. Poor Fanny, as you say.'

'And she's miles older than him,' I added, wondering if the assistant would take the bait.

'I think I might have bad news for your friend,' he said. 'Because there was a lady here just a while ago, this very day. Well, I say a lady.'

'That's her,' Alec said. I felt a pang for poor Miss Lumley.

'She came with a carpet bag and she went upstairs, right to the top – I can tell from the creaks – and when she came down she didn't have it with her. I called out to her that she had left it and she glared at me something evil. This was just minutes before they came in. You must have passed her on the street, practically.'

'Oh dear,' I said. 'That does sound rather suspicious.' Then Alec tapped my arm and I realised that there were movements above. I could hear chairs scraping and feet moving. I made a dart for the door without so much as a word of goodbye. Glancing back, I saw that Alec had at least managed to doff his hat as he fled behind me. Outside we hurried up halfway to the Surgeons' Hall and hid behind a protruding column at one of the sentry boxes that guard its entrance for some reason I have never fathomed. After a minute, Irvine and Fordyce came out of the bookshop and, thankfully, turned the other way, towards the station and the river. Irvine loped along with his hair bouncing and glinting in the sunshine and Fordyce waddled along behind him in his enveloping mackintosh, looking less comfortable than ever in the warmth of the day. Neither of them carried any kind of receptacle at all; carpet bag or otherwise.

We gave them enough of a head start so that, even if they turned, they would not recognise the lady and gentleman in the street behind them, and then we trotted back to the corner and in at the bookshop door.

The genteel young man had been quick. He was already back behind his counter. On it was a garish bag made up of an offcut from the worst sort of modern stuff ever to spoil upholstered furniture, with a large shiny buckle lying open on top.

'It's empty,' he said.

'Can I have a look?' said Alec. He seized the bag and peered inside it. Then he clicked his tongue as though encouraging a pony and reached inside.

'What's that?' I said. He was holding up a folded strip of blue paper, such as those my sons used to make chains out of to decorate their nursery at Christmastime. I had never seen one on its own and could not imagine what it was. But then I had never worked in a shop.

'Oh!' said the young man. 'It's a banker's band. From a roll of money! That bag was full of money!'

'I thought he looked uncomfortable,' said Alec, 'in such a voluminous mac on a hot summer's day.'

24

'Right,' Alec said, as we began the long westward journey out of the city towards Cramond again. 'Two disgraced classicists, helping with the theft and dispersal of Roman treasure from a hidden temple at Cramond, have just been paid by a pub landlady in hard cash.'

'Because their work is done?' I said. 'Or because after two deaths it's got too hot for them all and they've abandoned the scheme? Careful!'

We were descending a steep if short hill on our way to the sharp corner onto the Dean Bridge and, evidently, the broad stretch of smooth pavement at our side was much in demand for rolling hoops. A very small child had let hers get rather close to the edge just when Alec had let the motorcar get rather close to the kerb. He gave a blast on his horn. She put her thumb to her nose and waggled her fingers while sticking her tongue out. Alec laughed and turned away.

'No idea,' he said, taking it up again. 'But that is definitely what they were hiding and what was worth killing Peter Haslett to *keep* hidden.'

I nodded but it was troubling me.

'What?' Alec said. He was watching the road, since an omnibus had pulled out right in front of him and he wanted to get past it rather than apply his brakes. I have noticed that both Hugh and Alec view braking as a last resort.

'Just this,' I said. 'Irvine and Fordyce pretended to be scientists as a pretext for their sojourn at Cramond. And Miss Lumley had a litter of kittens every time we got close to the Turning Tide. But Miss Speir didn't make the slightest attempt to keep the secret. It's very odd to be vigilant enough to kill someone – two someones perhaps – and yet be lax enough to blab the secret to two other someones. It doesn't make sense.'

'It doesn't have to be decision by committee,' Alec said. 'Miss Speir was loose-lipped. As you say, Miss Lumley wasn't. Those two lads certainly weren't.'

'The four millers are a committee,' I said. 'A united front. And if Peter really did die from being pulled – or perhaps pushed – into the path of one of the wheels then one of the four is deeply concerned in it.'

'But if he didn't,' said Alec, 'if either Irvine or Fordyce killed him with a blow to the head, would they put his body near one of the mills? If the four millers are part of the scheme?'

I sat back. We were beyond the last grand terrace of the New Town now and the road opened out on either side. New bungalows set on curving streets had formed an instant suburb that threatened to join the city to the village of Blackhall and then to the village of Barnton and finally to the village of Cramond itself, and suddenly the dark thoughts that had been creeping in and out of my mind in these last few days struck me as foolish. Vesper's wild words and the abandoned island, the tower and the ancient cottages, the four dark wheels creaking wetly round and round . . . all of it suddenly seemed so at odds with this broad road and all these neat little dwellings that I could not believe any of it. Even though I could not quite say what this belief meant or where it led.

'Something is wrong,' Alec said. 'Don't interrupt. I know two murders are always wrong. That's not what I mean. Hear me out, Dandy.'

'I didn't interrupt,' I told him. 'I know what you mean and I agree. How could four millers be part of a scheme to

261

sell Roman treasure? They can't be. It must be merely that Irvine and Fordyce stuck poor Peter's body in the river and it looked as though he had been killed by a water wheel, so they closed ranks. Well, we know they close ranks, don't we? They closed them with a bang when you and I started interfering and they almost literally held a meeting the morning Vesper died.'

'Or at least the morning her body was found,' Alec said. 'Yes. And yes to the fact that they can't be part of Miss Speir and Miss Lumley's scheme. Although, you know, while we keep calling them millers, they're not millers at all, are they? They're a paint maker, an upholsterer, a fancy ironworker and a rather less fancy spade maker.'

'They live and work in mills,' I said. 'Don't be pedantic. The point is that they are in close contact with one another, despite putting about that they are rivals, enemies even. Very close contact, considering they're effectively cut off from one another halfway up that riverbank.'

'If they had telephones,' Alec said, 'it would explain the efficiency of their jungle drums and it would also mean one of them might have rung up the police about Vesper. You do remember we still don't know who did that.'

'But we checked,' I said. 'We were assiduous detectives and tramped around in the pouring rain, checking. Those poles are electricity poles. Most definitely. Not telegraph poles. So there's an end to it; they have electricity but they do not have telephones. Whatever part they played, if they played a part at all, it wasn't ringing up policemen.'

Alec was slowing down, but when I glanced over at him I did not think he was choosing to stop exactly. It was more that he had become so engrossed in his thoughts that he was forgetting to drive. Even a loud horn blast from behind did not penetrate whatever brainstorm he was undergoing.

'Pull to the side,' I whispered, hoping to infiltrate his thoughts without interrupting them and, in addition, hoping not to be smashed into by a motorvan as we drifted ever more slowly through a crossroads.

'They're not millers,' Alec said, as the motorcar came to rest with its front wheels against a high kerbstone. The horn blower from behind us passed, waving a fist out of his window. I gave him a sickly smile, for the chap had a point and was driving a dairy van, besides. We might have caused a flood of milk and a landslide of eggs if he had not had his wits about him and slowed without crashing. Alec did not notice the waving fist. He was staring straight ahead.

'They're not millers,' I agreed.

'They don't use the mill machinery,' he added. I began to see a glimmer of light.

'No,' I said. 'Not to make paint anyway.'

'And they have electricity to power whatever they *do* use,' Alec said. He twisted right round in his seat and stared at me solemnly. 'So why, Dandy, are the wheels still going round?'

'Don't they have to?' I said. 'I mean, isn't it because of gravity? Or physics?'

'Gravity is physics,' Alec said. 'And no, of course not. The weirs and lades and sluices control where the water goes and when. They have to be able to stop the wheels at night and for repair and on holidays and Sundays.'

'Perhaps they just like the sound,' I said. 'Like a fountain.'

'Those four men didn't strike me as being concerned with the restful effects of having running water in one's surroundings.' Alec was beginning to sound grim, but I knew his biting tone was not for me, nor even for my stupidity. 'The yards are falling to rack and ruin,' he said. 'The cottages are empty. All in all, Dowie's, Peggie's, Fair-a-Far and Cockle Mill are pretty much shuttered and yet there are four enormous water wheels going round, even after one of them has killed a man.'

'And actually,' I said, 'those empty cottages are suspicious too. They aren't palatial but neither are the inhabited hovels

263

off the Sailor Street steps. I'm sure tenants could be found, if sought. And who doesn't want tenants paying rent and keeping the rats out?'

'Only a man with something to hide,' Alec said. I felt thankful, hearing his voice, that I was not the target of such cold disdain.

'What shall we do?' I asked.

'We'll wait until the dead of night and go snooping. I imagine the water will be stopped then. If not we'll get wet.'

I assumed he was joking and gave a small smile.

'Of course, I don't mean "we",' he added, starting up again and pulling back out into the trickle of motorcars now leaving the city, as the end of banker's hours approached. 'I wouldn't ask it of you, Dandy. But you can keep watch.'

'While you . . .?' I said. 'Have you forgotten what happened to the last young man who got too close to one of those water wheels, Alec? I can't allow it.'

'I don't think that's what happened,' Alec said. 'I think that was the story the police accepted and the story they kept out of the papers, to spare his family's feelings. I think the truth is even worse, I'm afraid to say. And I think Vesper knew it and the knowledge got her killed too.'

'I don't care what you think,' I said. 'Look, Alec, what is it you suspect about the water wheels? Can't we check at the land registry or ask someone? Mr Hogg! Let's ask Mr Hogg if . . . what is it we'd be asking?'

'I don't know,' Alec admitted, after a long pause during which, I imagine, he searched for a preferable answer.

'Because sometimes,' I added, 'a suspicious-looking thing turns out to be nothing at all. A trap door shut up tight with a huge brass padlock, for instance. Not a Roman temple, not a strong room full of treasure.'

'But the trap door over nothing is most suspicious of all!' Alec said. 'So I can't agree with you, Dan. Not one bit. But, if you prefer to keep out of it then you toddle off to bed tonight, by all means, and I'll investigate the water wheels on my own.'

He knew I would never agree to leave him in the lurch. I knew he would never agree to abandon his plan. It seemed that we were to spend the late evening skulking about the riverside byways of Cramond then. 'Let's at least tell someone where we're going,' I said, at last.

'Hugh?' said Alec. 'Grant? Barrow?'

'I was thinking of Inspector Hutcheson. But Grant isn't a bad thought either. She won't go running to Hugh to stop us and she might have something to add to what we've got between the two us already.'

'Right,' Alec said. We had travelled as far as Barnton and he swung off onto the Cramond Road. 'If we get a chance, we'll ring up Grant before we go out tonight. Nothing like a moonlight dip, Dandy!'

'You're not seriously expecting to end up in the water?' I said. 'It's dangerous.'

'Put it this way,' he said. 'I wish I had brought my Fernez goggles.'

'Your ferny goggles?' I said. 'What are you talking about?'

'Maurice Fernez,' Alec said. 'French chap, as you might have guessed. He invented the gas mask, more or less, and thereby earned my undying gratitude. But his first love was diving. You forget what I gave up when I moved to Perthshire, Dandy. The balmy waters of the Channel, for one thing. I brought all my equipment with me, but I hadn't quite come to terms with how cold Scottish lakes were going to be. And as for the North Sea. Brrrr. Are you listening?'

'Yes,' I lied. 'There's a warm front down in Galloway.'

'Not warm when one grew up in Dorset. *Are* you listening?'

'No,' I admitted, turning to him. 'What did you say?'

'Never mind. What were you thinking?'

'Goggles,' I said. 'Joe Georgeson the spade maker had a pair of goggles on his head when we spoke to him.'

'Those weren't water goggles,' Alec said, screwing up his face with the effort of remembering.

'No,' I said, as though I would know water goggles if I found them in my porridge. 'But they weren't goggles to protect an ironworker's eyes from heat either, were they? Or a woodworker's eyes from dust, if he was busy with the other end of the spades that morning.'

'He wasn't,' Alec said. 'We were in the room with the forge and it was cold. We were in the room with the lathe and it was sitting there unused. He came from somewhere else wearing the goggles of a . . .?'

'Clock maker?' I said.

'Restorer, I was going to say. Chap who touches up valuable paintings that have got a bit tatty over the years.'

My heartbeat began to pick up. Finally, it seemed all the various parts of this most hydra-headed case were starting to come together. The two lads on the island were classicists who authenticated or otherwise shored up Roman artefacts; Vesper sailed the boat that delivered the stolen Roman treasure to its buyers; at least one of the so-called millers was a restorer who probably worked on the treasures before they were sold. Peter Haslett had stumbled into the middle of it all and lost his life for his troubles.

'The only bit that doesn't fit is Miss Lumley,' Alec said. I smiled to realise how closely his thoughts had shadowed my own. 'She got to use Vesper's seagoing expertise to get some cheap beer and whisky, but why would that little scheme see her in charge of paying off the historians?'

'Perhaps Grant will have a moment of illumination about that when we put the rest of it before her,' I said. Alec was smiling too now. And, as we swung into the gates of Cramond House, I daresay we both felt rather more buoyant than at any previous moment since we arrived.

★ ★ ★

It did not last. Miss Speir was waiting for us, like a cat at a mousehole. That is, she was sitting in an armchair in her morning room, but the door was open to the hall and she hailed us as we entered.

'Shocking news,' she called. 'Dreadful news.'

We hurried towards her.

'My dear Miss Speir,' I said, 'you look pale. Shall I ring for Christine? Perhaps tea or even brandy.'

'I'm fine,' she snapped. 'But I need to tell you both something. That police sergeant came to tell Jerry and then Jerry came straight round to tell me. Vesper really did kill herself. Wicked, wicked child.'

'No,' I said.

'There's no doubt about it, I'm afraid,' said Miss Speir. 'The police surgeon was very clear.'

'We saw the marks on her neck where she was held underwater and drowned!' said Alec. 'We saw them with our own eyes, Miss Speir.'

'Wicked child!' she repeated. 'She did that to herself.'

'I'm sorry to be rude,' Alec said, 'but such a thing is not possible. I have done some sea diving in my youth, Miss Speir. Mrs Gilver and I were talking about it only today. And it is not possible to hold oneself underwater. The body is stronger than the will in such matters.'

'Oh, she didn't put those marks on her neck when she was dying,' said Miss Speir. 'She did it beforehand. She did it to make it look as though she was murdered. To cause trouble for someone left behind. To make the police suspect someone.'

'Who?' I said. The woman was speaking with such venom I suspected I knew.

'Anyone!' she cried, but I thought I saw her eyes flash with a spark of recognition. And I thought what she had recognised was that she should, as my sons would say, 'watch it'. 'She did it to make even more trouble than she made with all her nonsense about the ferry and then her wildness on the island.

267

She put her own hand to her own neck and made those bruises. That's what the police surgeon found. He thought they were oddly placed right from the start. Thank the Lord he had the brainwave to fit her hand to her neck and see the match. An exact match! And there were scratches on her neck and still some traces of skin under her own fingernails. So there!'

Those details were indeed damning.

'How did she die?' Alec said.

'Threw herself into the river with stones in her pockets!' said Miss Speir, apparently just as angry about this piteous part of the tale as any other.

'The river?' I said. 'Fresh water? Not salt?'

'The estuary,' Miss Speir spat.

'Stones in her pockets?' I said. 'Alec, you lifted her. Did you feel anything that might have been a rock or a pebble?'

'You lifted her?' said Miss Speir. She glared at Alec as if he were an insect.

'I tried to get the water out of her lungs,' said Alec. 'Certainly she was very heavy but then her skirts were water-logged. There was nothing banging about that I can remember.'

'The stones are at the police station,' Miss Speir said. 'They will be evidence at the inquiry. Unless you think all those police and their surgeon are lying.'

'Of course not,' I said. 'It just seems so unlikely. Why would she do such a thing?'

'Wicked, wicked child,' said Miss Speir again. 'To take the life that God has given her was bad enough but then to try to put our village under a cloud as she left is worse.'

'Not worse,' I said. 'Mischief. And suicide is a sin.'

Miss Speir heaved a sigh and patted her hair. 'No, not worse,' she said, with a great effort. 'You are right. Just more shocking. Vesper was terribly ill, as we all knew. Except Jerry. So the suicide is hardly a surprise. But the nastiness of trying to make some innocent person pay the price for murder?'

'That strikes me as rather sane,' I said. 'Evil, but sane. Not at all the act of a madwoman.'

But Miss Speir had reached her limit of discussing the matter with individuals who argued and corrected, rather than clucking and agreeing. She drew herself up with a mighty sniff, then rose from her chair and stalked out of the room.

'Good,' Alec said. 'Ring Grant, Dan. Before she comes back.'

I had been startled several times recently to ring home and find out that Grant was in my sitting room at my desk and perfectly happy to reach out a hand and answer my telephone. The one time it would have been very handy, of course, she was nowhere near the thing. Pallister padded off to fetch her to the telephone in the hall, awash with disapproval, and when I heard them returning he was scolding her about the impropriety of it almost until she lifted the earpiece.

'Poor Mr Pallister's all of a flutter, madam,' she said. 'I've told him I've got two jobs till I'm blue in the face but he doesn't understand. Now, what can I do for you? Do you want me to come? I've got time to catch a good train and be there by ten tonight, so long as you don't keep me chatting.'

I rolled my eyes and shook my head for Alec's benefit. He grinned at me.

'I don't need you to come, Grant,' I said. Alec laughed and took out his baccy. 'I just need you to listen while we set some facts before you and then I need you to be by the telephone again at . . . What shall we say, Alec? Midnight? . . . Midnight, Grant, and wait for a call. We are going to do something moderately reckless. If you don't hear from me, telephone to Inspector Hutcheson, please? Do you understand?'

'How thrilling,' Grant said. She did not foresee being prostrate with grief if I failed to survive the evening. 'What are the facts you'd like me to consider?'

We told her everything. We told her about Vesper's strange

269

behaviour and her flight to the island, about the classicists masquerading as biologists, about the four millers who were not millers, and the four water wheels that were turning pointlessly all day every day. We told her about the handcart that came and went and smelled so redolent. And while we told her about *that* smell we mentioned the stink of rendering too. We told her about the goggles whose purpose we could not see, and about the cottage woman who echoed Vesper's strangest ramblings and about the man with the jet buttons with whom Miss Speir seemed to be in cahoots. We told her about the trap door in the tower and the tousled bed in the cottage, about the mystery of the missing telephone call and the horror of Vesper's last act. We told her about the vial of pinkish water we had lifted from the rock on the foreshore and the pair of notes switched from where we had left them. We told her about Rev Hogg's wife and Peter Haslett's wounds and Miss Speir's unaccountable belief that she was free to sell ancient artefacts to the highest bidder.

'You could heat a teaspoon of the water over a flame until it all boils off,' was the first thing she said. 'If there's salt left behind then it was seawater.'

'Thank you,' I said. 'Mr Osborne might well do that later this evening.'

'When you get back from your investigation,' Grant said. 'Midnight, as agreed.'

'Don't you want to know where we're going?' I asked. It was not like her.

'I assumed you were planning to wait at one of the mills and see if they are the sort that run all night or if the miller – ironworker or paint maker – diverts the race to get some sleep. Then you can perhaps poke about and see why they're running all day. That's what I would do if I were there, madam. If you'd like me to catch that train, I'd be very happy to.'

'You are a marvel, Grant,' I said. 'That is indeed what we

270

– Mr Osborne, with me on look-out duty – are going to do. No need for you to come rushing over here. But jolly well done for getting to it so quickly. If you've had any more brainwaves by midnight I look forward to hearing about them.'

'Why would a landlady risk losing her licence by selling contraband drinks?' Grant said. 'That's the one thing that puzzles me.'

'That's the one thing that puzzles us too,' I said. 'And while I'm glad to have you confirm that it's genuinely puzzling, I'd far rather have you laugh and explain to us.'

'I'll try,' Grant said. 'I'll iron and see what comes to mind. Ironing is wonderful for the brain, madam. You should—'

'Grant.' I was sure she had been about to say I should try it some time.

'You should hear the ideas that pop into my mind some-times when I'm pressing complicated lace edges,' she said, unconvincingly.

'Until midnight,' I said and put the earpiece down.

'It sounds very dramatic when you put it that way,' Alec said. 'What's puzzling her?'

'Why Vesper delivered beer barrels from a boat to the Turning Tide,' I told him.

He nodded but looked rather disappointed. 'Why Vesper killed herself is on my mind,' he said.

'After tonight, perhaps all will be clear,' I replied.

'By midnight,' said Alec. 'As you say.'

25

Cramond, being further south than Gilverton, does not have quite the excess of evening sunlight in high summer that I have had to become used to, but still it was after ten before Alec and I vouchsafed to leave Miss Speir's house and take a stroll towards the river. We did not have to come up with an excuse to offer our hostess, for she was nowhere to be seen. She had disappeared after a dinner of cold poached salmon, oily dressed potatoes and bullet-like peas; gone even before Christine brought in an apple charlotte and jug of cold custard with a layer of skin on top as thick as the sponge over the apples. Alec held the jug upside down over his plate and waited until the whole gelatinous disc plopped out. Then he ate it.

'It was delicious,' he was still telling me as we turned out onto the brae. 'Properly vanilla-ed and very creamy. As you'd have known if you'd tried some.'

'I might never eat again after seeing you saw up that slice of congealed muck,' I said and shuddered.

'I bet you don't eat the skin on rice pudding either,' said Alec.

'I am almost fifty,' I told him. 'I haven't eaten rice pudding for thirty-five years and I don't expect that to change.'

We spoke freely, having decided in advance that we would portray ourselves as engaged in an innocent evening walk until we were beyond the cottages. Only then would we pull our hats down and our collars up and make attempts at stealth. Of course, if anyone were watching from a cottage window he might see us pass and then remark that we had not passed back again, but that was a chance we had agreed to take.

Just beyond the boat club we fell silent and withdrew to the edge of the lane so that the weeds and leaf litter might dampen our footfalls.

'How do we know which one to watch?' I had asked Alec as we were whiling away the earlier part of the evening.

'Let's start at HQ,' he said. 'Meaning Eck Massey's place. And then we shall just take the evening as it comes.'

It had felt sensible enough and even somewhat clever when we devised the plan. Now however, crouched in the shade of a rhododendron bush just across from the churning water wheel of Cockle Mill, I could not have defended our scheme should anyone have come along and questioned it.

'How long do we wait?' I said. I felt Alec shrug at my side. 'Well, then let's move on to Fair-a-Far,' I suggested. 'Let's quickly get round them all and then settle in at one spot or another.'

Alec did not answer but he moved out from the shadows far enough to let him walk again. I hurried after him. My heart was in my mouth as we passed the open gate to Eck Massey's yard. If he came out of his door, with a torch in his hand, and happened to shine it our way, we would be undone. Of course, we could claim that evening stroll, but he would be a fool to believe it and whatever he was the man was no fool.

A few minutes at a steady pace brought us to Fair-a-Far, and the dark courtyard ringed around with brick sheds and stone buildings. The squat block of the miller's house was perched at the river's edge and across the yard, in the shadow of the hill, the mill house and the wheel itself loomed and groaned. We found shelter from the moonlight in the overhang of a shed roof and stood watching the glint on the rushing water and listening to the creak and thrash of the paddles as they lifted endless scoops of it and let them fall. That noise drowned out every other sound, as though there were no owls or mice or even moths in this summer night.

'Shall we go?' I said a moment later, close to Alec's ear. 'If we're taking the lanes to Peggie's, we should get started soon.'

Alec nodded, but then put a hand on my arm. 'Listen,' he said.

'Is it stopping?' I could not hear any lessening in the rush and chop of the water. If anything, I would have said the roar was growing.

'Listen!' Alec said again.

And now I was sure that the noise was getting louder, although I could not understand how. There was a throatiness to the roar now as if something was approaching.

'What's going on?' I asked.

'I think something's moving on that train track,' Alec replied, pointing to a break in the buildings, across from our hiding place.

'We need to go!' I said. 'We might be hidden from the windows of the Fair-a-Far workshop but the lights of an approaching rail cart would shine right in under this overhang and expose us.'

'No time,' Alec said, as the thundering grew even louder. 'What shall we do?'

'A tryst?' I said. It was the only thing I could think of that might explain a man and a woman huddled in shadows at night. I had seen them in Perth and even Dunkeld, clutching at one another in doorways.

'Too late,' Alec said. 'Here it comes.'

I pressed myself against the cold bricks of the wall behind me and only pride stopped me from squeezing shut my eyes as though that would render me invisible as I waited to be bathed in light. But just as I thought the sound could not grow any more deafening unless the rail cart were to plough

274

into us and drive through the shed wall, it stopped. Only the rushing sound of the water wheel at our side continued and it was like a whisper after the din.

'What on earth?' I said softly. 'No lights?'

'Why would it need lights?' Alec said. 'There is one track and one engine upon it. Sssshhhhh!' he added suddenly, clutching at my arm in that spot just above my elbow where he has a habit of reaching for me.

I held my breath and heard the tramp of footsteps. They sounded close and were getting closer. I froze as a figure passed within three feet of our hiding place and kept walking. I could not have guessed at who it was, although the engine's approach and the general outline suggested Eck Massey. We could no longer hear his footsteps as he got closer to the wheel, but we heard a door open.

'Hoi,' came a voice from the open doorway.

'Here,' said the new arrival. It was indeed Massey.

Alec and I waited for him to join Jackie Hamilton and step inside the mill building, after which I was sure Alec would be as keen as I to scurry to a better hiding place, if not all the way back to Cramond House.

'Listen,' Alec breathed again. But this time there was no new noise to hear. Rather, the sound of the rushing water was quietening. I did not dare to look in case the moonlight showed my pale face to the two men but I was sure the water wheel was slowing. The churning sound became a pouring sound and then a dripping sound. After a moment came silence, except for the banging of my heart and the rush of my careful breaths.

More footsteps, these even closer. Hamilton was coming to join Massey, so close to us now that I wondered they could not smell the pipe smoke from Alec's tweeds or my setting lotion. We could certainly hear the man's breath as well as his steps. I put my gloveless hands in my pockets, lest they show as two pale forms in the dark doorway. Alec was looking straight down at his feet, the top of his hat shielding his face from view. Then at last Hamilton was past us!

We both breathed out, slowly and carefully, and Alec groped for my hand, squeezing my fingers tightly in his.

'What are they doing?' I said. There were sounds of wood and metal, a heavy thump and a scrape, then their voices came floating back to us as if distant even though they were mere yards away.

'There must be a . . .' Alec said. Then: 'Wait and see.'

When he stepped out from our shelter I grasped at his coat to pull him back but there was no shout, no startled shuffle. He walked away and I had no choice but to follow him.

It was peculiar to look at the mill race and the wheel itself, glinting in the moonlight, still wet but yawning empty. The sight of the dark chasm hard against the rockface where the wheel sat made me think of open graves for the second time this week and, for the first time, of the trenches I had never seen but yet had dreamed of most nights for all those long years.

'Where did they go?' I asked Alec. I was speaking softly still, but I knew the two men were no longer nearby.

'Only one way to find out,' Alec said. He rummaged in his pocket, struck a match and held it before him. All I saw was the green-tinged slime on the walls of the deep race, the puddled bottom where a shrinking stream of water still drained, catching the moon's reflection and looking like a silver ribbon. But Alec whistled.

'What?' I said.

He struck another match. 'Look at the near wall.' I bent over, too close to the edge for my comfort, and peered at what he had seen. There were steps cut into the stone of the lade wall below us.

'For maintenance?' I said.

'Originally, perhaps,' said Alec. 'But not tonight.'

'But why would they clamber down to walk in the bed of the mill race?' I said. 'It only tips out into the river again.'

'They've gone the other way,' Alec said. 'I'd bet my pipe on it.'

'What do you mean "the other way"?' I peered into the darkness behind the wheel. 'It's a lump of rock that outwitted even road makers. What are you talking about?'

But Alec was already edging down the first of the steps, clinging to the wet stones at his side and placing his feet with great deliberation.

'Stop!' I said. 'Alec, for God's sake. Let's go and ring up the police. If someone re-opens the sluice gate you'll be washed away.'

'Or bashed to bits, like Peter Haslett,' Alec said. 'But no one will open the sluice gates while those two are down here. Don't tell me you don't want to see what's going on, Dandy.'

He overestimated my zeal, but I certainly did not want to be left here alone and helpless wondering what was happening out of my view. I took a deep breath and edged forward, then set my foot on the top step leading down. It slid an inch to the outside in the green slime and I gasped.

'Put your hands on my shoulders,' Alec said.

'Don't be silly,' I replied, through gritted teeth. 'If one of us goes we don't want to take the other one down too. Besides, I'm not gasping in fright. I've just thought of something. Remember how I skidded here yesterday. He covered his whole floor in sacks because of it. I thought it was chivalry at the time but now I'm remembering that clump of muddy weed I picked off my shoe, I think perhaps those sacks were camouflage.'

Alec whistled. 'Let's keep going,' he said. 'Be careful.'

I put one hand against the wall, and tried to place my feet with confidence, thinking that shaking and shivering would bring a fall more surely than some boldness. I tried to tell myself it was no different from clambering down the stone steps of a harbour wall into a waiting boat, and that this green slime was no worse than seaweed but, in truth, such adventures at a harbourside tend to take place in sunshine and for pleasure. This furtive slithering down in the dark towards who knew what was something else entirely.

It felt as though it took ten minutes to reach the muddy bottom of the race, but I was counting and there were only fourteen steps. I felt reassured to hear Alec breathing as unsteadily as me as we stood there.

'Now what?' I said.

'One more match,' said Alec. 'I can't see a thing down here. Tonight's when we should have taken a lantern with us, Dandy. Now, you stand with your back to mine and one of us is bound to see something.'

There was a rip and a burst of sulphur and then the bead of yellow light flared around us. I caught my breath and nudged Alec, for the lade was just a little wider than the wheel that sat in it and glancing into the shadows, I could see that behind the wheel was another set of steps, these leading up, and at the top, hidden all day every day by the flashing paddles, was a doorway.

Alec did not give me the chance to decline. He left me standing in the draining puddles of the race and set off at a trot.

I caught up with him as he laid his hand on the rusted iron ring that served as both lock and handle. He twisted it, it gave, and the door fell open before us.

'This is how Peter died,' I said, with a firm grip on his coat sleeve. 'We can't go in there to be trapped when the only way out could kill us. Look!' I twisted round in the cramped space and put my hand out to the nearest paddle. It was inches away from us.

'One quick look,' Alec said. 'As long as we're out before them, we'll be fine.' He pushed the door wide and slipped through.

278

I was still steeling myself when his head appeared again. 'They're nowhere near,' he said. 'There's a light quite far off. At the end.'

'The end?' I said. 'Are you saying what I think you're saying?'

Alec's teeth gleamed as he grinned at me. 'I am indeed,' he said. 'It's a secret passageway. Now, tell me you don't want to go along it, if you've got the bare-faced cheek for such a whopper.'

Yet again, he had failed to understand anything about me. As we made our way along that dark, dank, dripping passageway, deeper into the hillside, I felt nothing but dread. A grave that was open would have been a relief instead of this deadening weight of rock and soil I was sure I could feel pressing down upon me. And yet again time slowed until it felt as though it stood still and I, as in dreams, was clawing my way through it, thick and close all around me.

In fact, it cannot have been more than a very few minutes until we came upon the source of the light. There was a bend in the passageway and, as we stood against the dark wall just before it, we heard murmurs and even the unpleasant whicker of soft laughter.

Then a voice spoke up clear and strong. It did not ring out, for the walls of this underground warren were too low and damp, but it reached our ears easily.

'She couldn't stop us when she was living and she shall not stop us after her death.' It was Miss Speir.

'We should have listened to Jerry,' said Miss Lumley, 'and let her go months back.'

'That doctor knows his onions.' I could not have said who spoke now. It was not Eck Massey or Jackie Hamilton, but whether it was colourless John Weller or the ratty Joe Georgeson I could not say. 'Her nasty wee scheme is foiled.'

Alec gave me one short look, which I could not have deciphered if my life depended on it, and then slewed to the side to peek around the corner. There was no shout, no scuffle. He took a long lingering look and then straightened up and leaned against the wall beside me once more. He turned so that his lips were close to my ear and spoke on the lightest breath that could carry a whisper of sound.

'Shall we go right now, or do you want to see it too?'

I considered it for a second, if that. Then I squirmed behind him and kept on until I was at his other side. I took a deep breath and bent so that my head was out in the light. Then I was looking at the secret of Cramond, the truth that had taken Vesper Kemp's wits, the reason two people lay dead, the key to it all.

26

The room was low, its timbered ceiling held up with stout wooden props here and there. There were packing cases around the outside and large objects, most of which were swathed in sacking. The only uncovered article was a statue made of white stone, softened as though by years of immersion in water. Its limbs were worn down to nubbins but on one side of its helmet a single wing still proudly spread out its worn feathers. Mercury.

And the reason I could take such a long and leisurely perusal of him was that all of the people in the room – the four millers, Miss Speir and Miss Lumley – were standing far beyond him, clustered around a table under a swinging lantern looking down at something with great concentration.

'Well done, Joe,' Miss Speir said at last. 'Nicely done.' She took a step to one side and revealed what their close-pressed bodies had been hiding. On the table top was a glittering spill of gold, studded with a dazzle of ruby red, emerald green, sapphire blue and the pure keen white of diamonds. 'Those pearl headdresses have him panting for more.'

'We've done it,' Miss Lumley said.

'Against all odds,' said Miss Speir. 'And in spite of that pair of interfering fools.'

'Not complete fools,' said Miss Lumley. 'You know they went back into Coble Cottage and lifted that note?'

'Where are they tonight?' That was Eck Massey.

'Christine's watching them for me,' Miss Speir said. 'But I expect they'll be at the tower. They've been in there once

281

already. The idiots left a lantern lying in the middle of the floor.'

I could not help myself. At her words, I started and, even though I drew my head in as quickly as a lizard's tongue, I knew from the silence that all six of them had heard me.

'Christine?' said Miss Speir. She was walking towards our corner.

Alec seized my hand and together we ran. We ran faster than I had ever moved since I was a girl. We pelted along the passageway back to the door and were almost there when Alec slowed and looked over his shoulder.

'Why aren't they chasing us?' he said, just as I pulled the door sharply open and heard the creak and groan of the wheel beginning to turn. Above our heads, I heard the first splash. Alec hesitated. I shall never be able to say why I did not. I launched myself down the steps into the race, ankle deep as I landed and knee deep as I pulled myself up the far side, all worry of skidding on weed forgotten as I scrambled to the top and turned.

The water was rising, roiling and rushing against itself and the wheel was picking up speed. Alec was nowhere. I picked my way back down three steps and tried, despite the foaming water and the thick shadows, to see anything at all in the rising dark.

'Alec,' I whispered. I went down another step. The water was lapping at my boots again. 'Alec?'

And with a huge walloping surge he broke the surface, spluttering and retching, and I put out both hands to grab him.

'No! Get away!' he shrieked at me. 'Run!'

'Take my hand,' I said, teetering as I lost my footing under the wash of water.

'Dandy, you are in the way,' Alec said. 'Get off the steps so I can get out.'

I turned and pulled myself up on all fours. By the time I

was back on the dry ground he was with me. He coughed once and spat, then he took me round one wrist and sprinted into the darkness of the lane as though the hounds of hell were after him.

'The lantern!' I managed to say as we were passing the Cockle Mill. 'We really *are* fools.'

'I don't care!' Alec said. 'At last, we've got the answer. It wasn't beer in barrels.' He was still guttural from choking on water, but I was sure that was what he said.

'What?' I said. The words were clear but the meaning was anything but. 'Look, never mind. We need to stop running before we get to the cottages. In case anyone sees us.'

'We're past that now,' Alec said. 'We're running to Cramond House and my motorcar and we're getting out of here tonight.' But he did slow his pace a little as a cottage door opened beside us. There was no point. We were soaking wet and panting like mastiffs. Nothing we could do would persuade any cottager that this was an innocent stroll.

Besides, from the open door a voice hissed: 'This way. Quick!'

We did not need to be persuaded. Alec ducked inside and I was less than a step behind. It was the Cullens' place, the neat hall softly lamplit and the kitchen bright at the end of the passageway, but the woman who slammed shut the door and threw the bolt once we were safe inside was not Mrs Cullen.

'Grant?' I said. 'What the dickens are you doing here?'

'You told me Effie was Vesper's best friend,' Grant said. 'This seemed like the obvious place to begin.'

'Effie?' I said, although I should be used to Grant by now.

'Effie Cullen.' Grant led us through to the kitchen where young Mr and Mrs Cullen were sitting with looks upon their faces familiar to me from having witnessed others meet Grant for the first time at moments of high drama. Heaven knows what she had been saying to them. 'I rang first, madam,' she went on. 'But then it came to a choice between getting the train and missing it and that seemed no choice at all.'

I was not sure she spoke the truth, for Alec and I had heard no telephone bell, but it was hardly worth arguing now.

'It wasn't beer and whisky,' she said, 'that Vesper was bringing off the boats.'

'You really *are* a marvel, Grant,' Alec said. And it is a testament to how engrossed in the current happenings she was that she did not take a second to simper her thanks at him.

'It was supplies,' she said instead. 'Raw materials. I guessed it and Effie has confirmed it.' Young Mrs Cullen nodded dumbly. 'There are no Roman treasures. They're making them and selling them. Counterfeits. The upholsterer and the paint maker and the so-called fancy ironworker. And whatever the other one does that needs goggles. Not spades, anyway.'

'Jewels,' Alec said. 'We've just seen them.'

'Jewels,' breathed Grant. 'Oh my.' Then she sniffed. 'And vials of "ancient" sacred oil, of course.'

'Why "of course"?' said Alec, although light was dawning on me.

'It was the rendered fat and linseed oil that first got me thinking along these lines,' Grant said.

'Linseed oil!' I cried. 'That's right. The smell of Kirkcaldy linoleum factories and smart Edinburgh tenements where the stairs are kept shiny.'

'And the rendered tallow?' Alec said.

'Oh yes,' said Grant. 'The Romans used a mixture of the two to stopper vials of oil in their temples.'

'Now how on earth do you know that?' I asked.

'Mr Pallister told me,' Grant said. 'I made Mrs Tilling render some beef bones just after she'd oiled the larder tiles – I was just trying to see if I could get the smells to talk to me the way they talked to you, madam – and Becky complained about it. So Mr Pallister took the chance to show off his learning. Well, you know what he's like.'

'But how on earth did *he* know?'

'Long journeys in the motorcar,' Grant said. 'I hardly need to tell you that if Mr Gilver knows something, everyone learns it for miles around. If they listen.'

It was a fair point, even if it was her most insubordinate yet.

'And then it hit me,' Grant said. 'The trap door to the supposed Roman temple is fake because everything's fake. You see, madam?'

'No,' I said. 'To be frank.'

'It was there to be shown to dealers. To help convince them,' Grant said. 'A little bit of set-dressing, you could say.'

'Ah!' Light broke over me. 'And this explains why Miss Speir was so very indiscreet. She wanted gossip. She wanted the word to seep out about her "ancient artefacts" that were nothing of the sort. Good work, Grant. Not that it helps the Hasletts any.'

'Give me a chance!' Grant said. 'That was troubling me too. Why was Mr Haslett here? Why did he come to Cramond to find out that those two scoundrels were masquerading as scientists?' She paused. 'Effie, do you have a towel to spare? Madam, your hair is quite out of this world.'

'Grant, I shall pinch you,' I said. 'Never mind me, Mrs Cullen. Mr Osborne has been immersed in the mill race and is first in line for any towel. Or cocoa.'

'The mill race?' said Mrs Cullen, putting her hand to her mouth.

'Lucky escape,' said her husband, speaking for the first time.

'Unlike Mr Haslett,' Grant said. 'I rang up Newburgh. The dairymaid there is the sister of one of the housemaids that used to be at Benachally in the time of the Wilsons. I could have laid it all out in front of Mr Gilver but I thought time was of the essence. I hope that's all right.'

I nodded.

'Well, they didn't have any details in the servants' hall, but added to what we know at this end it all dove-tailed quite nicely. Young Mr Haslett had formed an unsuitable alliance, you see. A working woman, older than him, and not acceptable to his family.'

'Oh!' I said. 'Older than him. Goodness.' The memory came back to me of Hugh saying 'Makes Mallory look—' Mallory was thirty to Donald's twenty-five; not as bad as Vesper and Peter, but the same kind of disquiet for Simone and Angus. I should have paid attention to that niggle when it first starting tickling me.

'Vesper?' Alec was saying. 'I can't believe it.'

'Vesper,' Grant affirmed. 'Effie will back me up. He came and went on the ferry and they got talking, didn't they?'

'And I thought she was going to have what I have,' said Mrs Cullen. 'A good man and a family, at last. I thought he would move into Coble with her and do whatever job it was he did. I had no inkling he was a gentleman and would try to take Vesper away.'

I thought of Simone and Angus and again of the wild-haired Vesper with her bare breast and her mad talk of snakes and gods. On the other hand, the talk was less mad after what we had seen this evening.

'She had to finish the job,' Mr Cullen said. 'She couldn't get away until the thing was done. First she tried to drive Peter off, didn't she Eff?' It was astonishing to hear Peter's Christian name in the mouth of this working man, but nothing could better confirm the truth of what he was saying.

'Her madness was a ruse to make him go away?' I said.

'She was faking,' said Mrs Cullen, with a nod. 'She got it all out of a book! She even laughed about it. "If they think they're the only fakers in Cramond!" she said. But it didn't work. He wouldn't go. He followed her to the island and he saw those two scientists and for some reason or other she told him the truth then.'

We knew the reason. He heard them claim to be students from his very own college and he knew they were lying.

'So Vesper told him the truth,' I said. 'That there was a scheme of fraud and counterfeit just about to come to fruition and that she was mixed up in it and couldn't escape.'

'And he went plunging off to demand they let her go,' said Alec. 'Well, he would, I suppose. If he loved her as much as all that.'

'So he was where we've just been,' I said to Alec. 'Only he didn't get away.'

'And Vesper lost her mind,' Mrs Cullen said. 'She had been pretending – mysterious talk and calling on old gods – but then she lost her wits for real and true. She ran away and she ripped her clothes from her own back. She was like a wild woman the last time I saw her.'

'But why?' I said. 'What put her beyond her wits' end?'

'She thought she'd killed him,' said Mrs Cullen. 'As good as. She'd killed her love and she was still stuck with them all and their greedy rotten trick. She lost her mind for real and she killed herself and tried to make it look like murder, thinking someone would poke around and out it would all come. Oh, Vesper! Oh I miss her so.'

'So that's why she stopped the ferry in good weather and carried on in bad?' I said. 'Because it sounds so senseless and people would believe she was mad?'

Mrs Cullen mopped her tears and, after blowing her nose, looked up at me. 'No,' she said. 'At least, I don't think so. I never understood that part of it all. And now I never will.' This time she dissolved in earnest and her husband pulled her head to his shoulder. Cocoa seemed unlikely.

'Do you think we can go?' I said. 'They can't murder all three of us in the village street, surely.'

'I should have said—' Grant began, but before she could continue there came a hammering at the door. Upstairs in the cottage a child began to wail.

'Open up!' Eck Massey was bellowing at the top of his lungs. 'I know you're in there. I saw your wet footprints leading right to this door and I see that kitchen light. Open up and show yourself. Trespassers! Thieves! I'll get the polis to you!'

'Oh! Oh!' said Mrs Cullen. 'The baby. The bairns.' For at least two older children had added their cries to the piercing screams of the infant now. I thought I could hear commotion through the wall from the neighbours too.

'Wonderful,' Alec said. 'The village is awake. And the police are exactly the chaps we need. Let's not take up any more of the Cullens' time, Dandy. Let's go.'

'I meant to say—' Grant put in, trying again. But Alec was not listening.

He strode towards the door and, even though he had bolts to draw and a key to turn, Eck Massey was still banging on it when Alec pulled it open. The man was left with his hand in mid-air and his snarling face frozen in surprise.

'We know you killed Peter Haslett,' Alec said.

'What? What are you on about?'

'And why do you shout "trespassers" and "thieves" in the plural when you know there's only one of us in here?'

'What?' said Massey.

'Is there another way out? If you shut the sluice gate again and came through that door behind the wheel, you must have seen Mrs Gilver's body? And yet you still want to have the police come and start to rake through everything.'

Massey was now stumbling backwards away from the door.

'Body?' he said. 'That woman?'

'And if one looks like misfortune and two like carelessness,' Alec said, 'three is definitely going to look like murder.'

Massey had backed almost as far as the edge of the river

now. 'I don't believe you,' he said. 'She's in that house and you're trying to trick me.'

'Are you too blinded by greed to see you are incriminating yourself with every word?' Alec said. 'How many people do you think are listening?'

'Trespass,' Massey said, but it had no force behind it.

'On your neighbour's property,' Alec said. 'What's it to you?'

'What's going on?' A window two houses down had been flung up and a man in a nightshirt and holding a candlestick put his head out. 'What's the row?'

'Madam,' Grant said at my side. 'I keep trying to tell you there's no need for this.'

'You're right,' I said and I strode forward into the lit hall and out onto the street.

'Mr Osborne is teasing you, Mr Massey. I escaped unharmed. The fatalities remain at two.'

Perhaps it was at that moment that Eck Massey finally saw his hopes in ruins. All his scheming, the alliance with the two Misses, the preparation, the investment and tonight's premature celebration of expected success; it all began to fade for him then. Instead, the prison wall cast its shadow and he broke under the strain. I did not know it at first. I thought he was ill as he stumbled forward. I even put out my hands to steady him. It was not until he laid his hands on my shoulders and, with a roar that might have come from the depths of hell, lifted me bodily and threw me, that I knew he was in the grip of a rage beyond all reason. I tensed myself to hit the ground and then felt all breath leave me as, instead, I fell into the tide-swollen river.

Waterlogged already and dressed in tweeds with heavy walking boots tied firmly to my feet, I went down and down through the dark water, sinking like a dead weight, so shocked that my limbs refused to move. I felt the scrape of rock under me, and let a stream of bubbles go from my bursting chest.

289

The water was black below me, murky all around me, and spangled above, blinding me as the moonlight broke on its surface and danced in crazy patterns. I tried to put my feet underneath me to push off, but then, for the second time, I stilled. I stopped struggling. I blinked my stinging eyes. It could not be real. I was losing my mind. Is this what drowning felt like? Like madness?

Then I felt a tug and I was rising through the water and my face was out in the air with screams and shouts all around and Alec had his hand about my ribs and was pulling me into the shore.

'His head,' I said. 'She ate his head. Snakes upon her.'

'Shush now,' Alec said. 'Don't fret about any of it. I know. I know.'

On the bank, reaching down to grab me, was a figure I could not believe was real. I shook the water out of my eyes but he was still there, holding out two large hands and smiling at me.

'Inspector Hutcheson?' I said.

'I kept trying to say,' Grant shouted down to me. 'I didn't actually come on the train in the end. I rang up the inspector and he brought me.' Alec hoisted me up and the inspector grabbed me by the arms and hauled. As I left the icy water and felt the hard thump of the riverbank under my back I shut my eyes as if to sleep and fainted dead away.

Postscript

'Can you see it?' I asked.

Alec and I were sitting on the half-built jetty that now protruded from the bank below the Coble Cottage garden gate.

'I think so,' he said. 'Yes, I see something. I couldn't have told you what it was if I hadn't caught a glimpse that night.'

'It's a man,' I said. 'With his head in a cat's mouth. A lioness perhaps. Or a tiger. And snakes writhing up and down her sides. Its sides.'

'Poor Vesper,' Alec said. 'She must have thought she was going mad when she saw it first.'

'A vision in clear water on sunny days,' I added. 'Hidden in rough water on cloudy days.'

We had not been brave enough to ask a historian about it, for the case of the Cramond Ferry had garnered a great deal of attention in the press and our names had been prominent in plenty of the stories and, were we suddenly to start asking about a stone sculpture, larger than life size, and heavy with symbols of the ancient world, Cramond would have been inundated all over again. From our independent study in the top floor of James Thin's Booksellers, however, we had concluded that it was a burial stone, and for the grave of a high-ranking and prominent official of Rome. The poor man, bound and naked, was learning that no one outwits nature, that death devours us all in the end. At the same time the serpents twined around the beast's flanks told us that life, twisting and coiling, goes on and on.

And so we had decided to let it rest there in the river. Mr Cullen, who took over the ferry run when his wife inherited Vesper's cottage, had agreed to build a jetty over it and forget it was there. For the grave of a dignitary would not be placed in a wild and forgotten corner. There must indeed be a temple, or a fort, with villas and cooking pots and hairpins and painted tiles, and statues and altars, and if word got out all the cottages would be ripped apart and the villagers scattered to the four winds.

Instead, life would go calmly on and Alec and I would let our memories of the whole affair fade. Still, I baulked at the prospect. For some odd reason, the little bit of the escapade that bothered me most of all was the swapping of Vesper's books for those silly magazines and the staging of her blameless home as a sordid trysting spot. We never did find out who was responsible: Miss Speir who owned the boat and could take it across to Coble Cottage without causing comment; or Miss Lumley who, one suspected, might have the weekly papers and brandy close to hand. It was one or the other of them. And so what counted for most with me, in deciding to keep the secret, was that I felt sure Miss Speir would come to be credited with some foresight or intuition, instead of being reviled for her greed, and Miss Lumley would have her bar and lounge full of sightseers and scholars. No one would believe them to be the venal, grasping creatures they really were. No one *had* believed it. Not with kindly, saddened Rev Hogg vouching for them as his dear friends and valued neighbours. Poor man, distracted by his own troubles.

So Miss Lumley had sold up and handed the licence over to the friendly potman. And as for the millers? If they had found themselves in the thick of a real Roman find, they would have started it all up again. I am quite sure of it. A chip of paint here, a bit of iron there. A few gemstones and a drop of oil. They had escaped all punishment, save Eck Massey's thirty days for throwing me in the river, for it is not against any law to make statues of Mercury or golden neckpieces splendid enough for a goddess.

Peter Haslett had been foolish enough to go exploring a mill lade and had died for it. Vesper Kemp had killed herself. The man with the jet buttons would have had a case if the sale had gone through, but we had stopped it.

'I know they've winkled all those stones out of the gold and split the gems to repay the investments they all made,' Alec said, leaning back on his elbows and letting his legs dangle over the jetty, 'but what's going to happen to the statue of Mercury? Did anyone say?'

'Mrs Cullen told me,' I said. 'Miss Speir has kept it. It's in the garden up at Cramond House. She can look out of her sitting room window and see it. Remind herself of her folly.'

'And she's just shut in there now?' Alec said. 'With Christine?'

'Retired from the world,' Mrs Cullen reported. No one but Christine to care for her and Mercury to mock her. The god of money. Poetic justice, wouldn't you say?'

'He's the god of trickery too,' said Alec. 'I read that in one of the books at Thin's. So yes. They deserve one another.'

'Hell mend them,' I said.

Alec stood and offered a hand to pull me up beside him.

'There are babies to dandle,' he said. 'Let's go home.'

Facts and Fictions

The Craigie Halkett family owned Cramond House between 1849 and the death of Miss Dorothy Craigie Halkett in 1959, after which it came into the hands of the Church of Scotland. For the purposes of my story, I'm imagining that Miss Craigie Halkett sold the house in the late thirties and went off on extensive adventures.

Coble Cottage and Cramond Island are owned by the Dalmeny Estate, but I've pinched them, to avoid tangling with the history of the Earls of Rosebery (which is too well-documented to allow for fictional shoe-horns). The Turning Tide stands on the spot where the Royal Oak used to be.

John Philip Wood, who wrote *The Ancient and Modern State of the Parish of Cramond*, was a very interesting man. Deaf and mute at birth, he was a pupil at Braidwood's Academy, the UK's first school for the deaf, where he learned to speak. He had a successful career with the excise besides his writing and was a friend of Walter Scott. Hugh is wrong about the quality of Wood's research.

The second altar discovered in the grounds of Cramond House honoured Jupiter, not Mercury, and the lioness lay in the mud of the Almond mouth for many years after Dandy glimpsed her. She was unearthed in 1997, after being spotted by the ferryman, and is now on display at the National Museum of Scotland, at Chambers Street in Edinburgh.

Acknowledgements

I would like to thank: Francine Toon, Jasmine Marsh, Hazel Orme, Joe Hall, Jacqui Lewis and all at Hodder and Stoughton; Lisa Moylett, Zoë Apostolides, Elena Langtry and all at CMM Agency; the many booksellers who have supported Dandy Gilver all these years, especially David, Dan and Pavla at Goldsboro and Sue and Chris at Atkinson Pryce; the many librarians who have put Dandy Gilver novels into readers' hands; all the reviewers, bloggers and crime-fiction enthusiasts who help me celebrate each title as if it's the first, especially Dru Ann Love, Kristopher Zgorski, Deborah Lacy, Kerry Hammond and Kathy Reel; my co-bloggers at Criminal Minds and Femmes Fatales, for their patience and camaraderie; my ever-expanding family of blood relations, in-laws and friends. And Neil, always.

Catriona McPherson

A STEP SO GRAVE

Wedding bells are set to ring as Dandy Gilver, family in tow, arrives in windswept Wester Ross on Valentine's Day. They've come to celebrate Lady Lavinia's fiftieth birthday and to meet her daughter Mallory, a less-than-suitable bride-to-be for Dandy's son Donald.

But soon love is the last thing on Dandy's mind when the news breaks that Lady Lavinia has been found dead, brutally murdered in the middle of her famous knot garden. Strange superstitions and folklore abound among the Gaelic-speaking locals. But, Dandy suspects that the tangled boughs and branches around Applecross House hide something much more earthly at work . . .

'A deliriously fun tale, flawlessly written.'
Saga

'An absolute must.' *Crime Review*

HODDER